Thomas and Beal
in the Midi

Thomas and Beal
in the Midi

CHRISTOPHER
TILGHMAN

Farrar, Straus and Giroux
New York

Farrar, Straus and Giroux
175 Varick Street, New York 10014

Printed in the United States of America
First edition, 2019

Library of Congress Cataloging-in-Publication Data
Names: Tilghman, Christopher, author.
Title: Thomas and Beal in the Midi / Christopher Tilghman.
Description: First edition. | New York : Farrar, Straus and Giroux, 2019.
Identifiers: LCCN 2018041576 | ISBN 9780374276522 (hardcover)
Subjects: LCSH: Man-woman relationships—Fiction. | GSAFD:
    Love stories.
Classification: LCC PS3570.I348 T48 2019 | DDC 813/.54—dc23
LC record available at https://lccn.loc.gov/2018041576

Designed by Jonathan D. Lippincott

Our books may be purchased in bulk for promotional, educational, or business
use. Please contact your local bookseller or the Macmillan Corporate and
Premium Sales Department at 1-800-221-7945, extension 5442,
or by e-mail at MacmillanSpecialMarkets@macmillan.com.

www.fsgbooks.com
www.twitter.com/fsgbooks • www.facebook.com/fsgbooks

1   3   5   7   9   10   8   6   4   2

I

Paris

1

Madame Lucy Bernault, RSCJ, sat on a small pile of freshly sawn lumber, gazing idly but expectantly down the narrow slip off Le Havre's grand basin, into which, however unlikely it seemed, a large steamer was soon to insert itself. There were more luxurious spaces for visitors to await the arrival of steam packets of *grand luxe*, but Madame Bernault was a simple person and she was more comfortable here among the stevedores and mariners. She had grown up in Canada and had taught girls for many years in the wilds of Louisiana and Brazil before being called to the Mother House in Paris more than a decade earlier. She liked being around men, seeing them work, listening to their badinage, finding the mother's son within them. "Excuse us, Sister," one said daintily, taking off his cap and holding it squashed in his scarred hands as they wrested an immense crate of hams past her; "Mind your hem, Sister," they said as a stream of runoff peppered with horse manure, rotting fish entrails, and spoiled vegetables flowed from the market square behind her and into the harbor.

She had arrived in Le Havre the evening before and had spent the night as a guest in the convent of another order, but the conversation there was much the same as at home in Paris, in the boarding school that the Sisters of the Sacred Heart had long operated in the once-aristocratic Hôtel Biron. When she'd gathered for dinner with a dispirited band of nuns and lay sisters, the talk turned to the government. The Third Republic was *tightening the screws of persecution around them*. The Catholic schools had long provided *the most progressive, most scientific education for boys and girls available anywhere in the world!* Yet now, *nuns lacked the necessary training and qualification to instruct young minds?* Imagine. *Sister, I would like another small piece of bread, if you don't mind*. Madame Bernault passed the basket. *What was the Trente-Trois*—the famous Mother House of the Sacred Heart at 33 Boulevard des Invalides—*doing to protect them, to protect all the religious in France at this dark time? What was the counsel from la Mère Générale, from le Pape?*

They were disappointed when they discovered that Madame Bernault was not the plenipotentiary they had assumed; they turned somewhat surly, it seemed to her, and ignored her for the rest of the meal. Which was fine, because otherwise she would have had to explain that in fact, this very morning, she had indeed been called—for only the second time in her life—to the *Trente-Trois*, had met with *la Mère Générale* herself, and had been dispatched on an unusual mission that filled her soul with the longing and ache of romance, which she had no desire to share with anyone. Even to herself she could hardly describe the emotions she felt upon discovering that she had been requested by name to perform this duty, a request that came from America, from a girl—now a woman of course, but they remained girls to Madame Bernault—whom she had taught and cared for years ago.

Thus she sat among the stores at the edge of the harbor, waiting for the tip of the bow of a *paquebot* to pierce her view, which was, except for the massive spire of the lighthouse off to the side, a jumble of boats and rigging and sheds and commercial activity of every possible sort. M. Victor Hugo had described this lighthouse as *le chandelier de Dieu*—so Madame Bernault had been told the evening before—and yes, for her it had appeared as "the candlestick of God" when she first saw it from the deck of a ship these years ago. The lighthouse had seemed a beacon guiding her home. She wondered if the young people she was there to meet were seeing it now from the deck of their steamer. Madame Bernault had made the passage on a ship of no account compared with this liner of the highest style, called . . . called—she searched the pockets of her tunic for the much-consulted letter she'd been given of the particulars of her mission—*La Touraine*. Yes, *La Touraine* it was called, and ocean travel had progressed to such a degree of exactitude since her own crossing that the arrival, so claimed the letter of instruction, could be expected within a minute or two of ten o'clock, the hour specified in the schedule. After the ship arrived, it would take an hour or so for it to be nudged alongside the pier and made fast, and for the gangplanks to be readied for the debarking of the passengers. Still, she had been sitting on her pile of lumber since a little before seven.

She sensed someone approaching from the side and turned to see that it was a gendarme getting ready to speak to her. "Sister," he said, "we'll have to ask you to draw back while we load prisoners." He cocked his head toward the small rusted and rotten schooner directly in front of her. She had not noticed this sad little ship, but now that she looked at it, she could see that the hatches were open but were latticed with iron bars, that much of the fetid odor she had been smelling emanated from it, and that a small and motley detachment of soldiers was lounging on the main deck.

She moved to one side, where a small crowd of onlookers—men who might have once been or might soon be among the prisoners—had gathered. She heard the clank of leg irons from the alley behind her and then saw the bayonets and the kepis of the soldiers bobbing above the crates of cargo, and when the first ragged prisoner came into view, hollowed eyes glowing from his coal-black face, Madame Bernault's breath left her and she stepped back into the side of one of the men behind her. "Don't fear, Sister. Those chains could hold a gorilla," came the voice from the arms that were propping her up, but that wasn't the problem. The prisoners kept coming, a string of ten or so men attached neck to neck by chains and collars, and though only the first one was African, the sight had drawn her back to Louisiana and the many times she had seen lines of black men and women and children chained in this way. In all her years in America, the horror of American slavery had never left her, even as she taught the daughters of families who had become rich on slave labor. The Civil War had ended all that, she thought, but now, if she understood correctly—if her mission on this very day could be seen as a piece of evidence—the Americans were at it again, driving the Negro back into servitude with a whole new set of laws and restrictions. Would they never desist in this? Madame Bernault had never imagined herself as part of any community other than her family and her church, but still, Americans had seemed a reasonable, even admirable people to her on every account but this one.

The line of prisoners was now tripping its way along the edge of the pier, toward the gangplank to nowhere. Most of them simply stared ahead, but one or two seemed to be darting their glances everywhere, as if saying goodbye to civilization. The last person in the line was, to Madame Bernault's dismay, a woman—a girl—and then, following along after this procession, a young man, his eyes fixed on the girl. She was not beautiful, and really, he was not especially handsome, but these two people were young and wounded, which stirred Madame Bernault's heart.

Once the prisoners were aboard the vessel they were immediately led belowdecks, and the last view Madame Bernault had of them, like the first, was a pair of hopeless eyes in a ravaged face. The young man was now standing directly in front of Madame Bernault, and she wanted to say something to him, but she couldn't think exactly what. She supposed the girl had done something awful, but love was at the foundation of everything the Society of the Sacred Heart believed in: it was the pathway of God's will. This morning it seemed that love was hard to do, hard to have. The young couple she was here to meet—in order to proclaim and live their love, they had to escape to France.

"Oh, you'll forget her soon enough," one of the men in the crowd said to the young man. The others laughed. "Before midnight," said another. The man turned to face them; the birdshot of his gaze fell on Madame Bernault, and it was clear that the last thing on earth he wanted was some consoling phrase from an old nun. The Word, finally, has its own place and occasion. The man said nothing, defended neither himself nor the girl being loaded on the schooner. She had done wrong, or had been wronged, it didn't really matter which. Finally he thumbed his nose at the men, a gesture of silent, selfless, and innocent loyalty, and not an invitation to fight about it, as if whatever could be said about either of them had long ago been accepted or contested. At that, Madame Bernault concluded that he was not the girl's lover, but her brother, the last member of their family who still cared enough to see her off to Devil's Island.

The loyalty of a brother for a sister, or a sister for a brother. Another of the themes of this morning's mission. Madame Bernault had known the sister, a student at the Hôtel Biron in perhaps the winter of 1881 or 1882, an American girl named Mary Bayly, an extraordinarily accomplished but driven child, an austere person. She was the issue of an old Maryland Catholic family, the Masons, who owned a vast farm on the Chesapeake Bay called Mason's Retreat. Mary Bayly had kept in contact with the Society, and they had followed her progress through continued academic achievement in Baltimore, followed by a failed engagement and thence—duty, loyalty—back as the oldest child to pick up the burden of her family's farm, which by then, so her letters had informed them, was suffering a spectacular collapse owing to blight in their peach orchards. And then, months ago, came the first letter from her saying that her younger brother, who under normal circumstances would be taking over the farm on their mother's death, might one day soon need their protection and their help.

Madame Bernault carried no watch of any sort, and from where she stood she could see no clock tower, but she figured it must be close to ten o'clock, if not a minute or two past. It was going to be a hot day, unusually hot and humid, as if the Americans she was meeting had brought a little of their mid-Atlantic climate with them. And then, just when she began to doubt that a steamer could travel across the sea and arrive on the dot of the hour, she was shocked by the sudden but stately appearance of the bow of a ship, as sharp as a scalpel, in exactly the way she had imagined it, almost as in a dream. "Oh," she said, surprised by this huge manifestation of her own thoughts; she trembled a bit in the knees, but this time there was no rough hand to keep her upright, and she backed into her pile of lumber. No harm done, she thought as she reclaimed her cloak and her wits, settling again in her familiar seat, but this light-headedness was becoming a problem, something she had not mentioned in her last visit with the Society's physician. She was no longer the mistress of a dormitory, as she had been when Mary Bayly was at the school, but her room was a snug garret, and she did not want to be moved to the wing off the kitchen on the first floor, as happened to ladies and sisters who could no longer manage the stairs.

About half of the ship had now come into view, and the tug-boats were turning it in place in order to come straight into the harbor and alongside the pier. Madame Bernault had no knowledge of boats and no interest in shipping, but this stylish vessel did seem to be rather, well, racy—*osé* was the word she used. Not so much a steamer as a very large yacht, with two raked funnels and masts and a gay, flowery gathering of passengers along the rails of the upper decks. Thomas Bayly—she didn't need to refer to her letter to recall his name—was in there somewhere. The letter contained no instructions on how she was to identify him; in context, it seemed obvious to everyone how she was to do that. She scanned her eye along the ship, but of the people she could make out only smudges and blots of brilliant blue, purple, red, and an occasional stripe of white.

It was time to move over to the arrival lounge, to the customs desks and luggage terminal. There had been some discussion about the luggage, as it was assumed there would be a good deal of it. This was, after all, not a vacation tour, but a relocation, and if Thomas Bayly and his young bride had not made any arrangements for it to be shipped to Paris, Madame Bernault would have to do that herself. This was the only part of the mission that caused her real anxiety. What did she—a nun who had in her life traveled on three continents never carrying anything more than a small carpetbag—know about shipping luggage?

The tugs had now brought the ship alongside with a deep but grateful thump on the thick wooden pilings, and the men on the ship were pulling the stout hawsers aboard. The whole thing seemed slightly miraculous to Madame Bernault, this great ship that had departed New York only days ago and was arriving now in France as if it had traveled in a cocoon of its own time and space, but she supposed no one else gave it much of a thought, the crews and the stevedores did this all the time, the passengers were probably mostly veterans of this event, used to traveling aboard these floating hotels. All but one, that is. All but the young Mrs. Bayly. She was described in the letter of particulars in a single sentence, but that sentence had led Madame Bernault to understand that this was a girl who had lived a life probably simpler even than her own youth in Quebec—a farm girl like herself, an innocent, a savage, one might say. How was she to manage this new life, so far removed from her home? Madame Bernault herself had traveled very far, but from the instant of her first vows she had stepped into the care of the Society, and of its founder, Madeleine Sophie Barat, and into the care of the Virgin herself. And all that had been hard enough for little Lucy Bernault. This child, not much older than the students at the school, had been ripped away from everything she had ever known and understood. Madame Bernault could not imagine her feelings right now, only that she must be terrified, that the reassurances from Thomas Bayly, her husband, could do almost nothing to quell the rank dread in that taut young stomach, or to still the trembling of her hands, the tingling in her blameless fingertips. Madame Bernault took a moment to say a small prayer of protection for this girl. She remembered her odd, quite American-sounding name, but she had yet to use it in her thoughts. She was just the girl, the child, the bride, the reason for all this, but whether cause or beneficiary, Madame Bernault could not pretend to discern.

With the securing of the ship, the gangplanks went up and the derricks swung over the deck to begin to unload the mounds of luggage—the luggage! This was all happening rather quickly. Madame Bernault had been told that Thomas Bayly and his bride were traveling in the first-class cabins and would therefore be among the very first to disembark. Her heart was pounding. She had found a place behind a customs barrier not ten feet from where the gangplank met the pier. A professed sister like herself was supposed to be humble and take up a place at the end of every line, but Madame Bernault had never minded so much that crowds tended to part for her. *This way, Sister, you'll have a much better view.* Passengers were coming down the gangplank, gentlemen in stylish suits and top hats, and the ladies! Such carriage, such fabrics, such milli-nery! Madame Bernault didn't need to know anything about fash-ion to perceive the perfection of the ensembles, down to the most trivial of features: the men's collars, their watch chains, their boots; the women's veils, their red and green capes, moleskin and feathers, satin and velvet, and those waists.

She was enjoying this pass in review but the line at the top had thinned out, and she began to worry. *La Touraine.* Ten o'clock. All quite correct. And then there they were, Thomas and Beal—yes, that was her name, *Beal Terrell*—and she was giving her hand to her husband to help her onto the gangplank, which clearly, from the uncertainness of her first steps, she did not trust. Oh, so young, such babies in this strange land! The girl walked stiffly, a sort of exotic doll in a traveling suit, the brown porcelain of her face spar-kling in the sun. Madame Bernault identified her, as they all as-sumed she would, by her dark skin, but in years to come, Madame Bernault would reject this, or at least argue that even if she had not had this convenient racial identifier, she would have recognized Beal anyway, so precious, so beloved, so innocent and unformed. She would have known that this was the girl that Thomas Bayly, lately of Mason's Retreat in the State of Maryland, had given up every-thing to love.

And Thomas Bayly, yes, she believed she would have recognized him too. Tall, like his sister—Mary's height was something Madame Rolondo and other teachers had proposed as part of her discom-fort, as she was very, very tall for a girl—but he wore his height heedlessly, a head above everyone else around him, and so what? Men did that. Even as a teenager Mary had had a sharp face, not terribly feminine, but handsome, well boned, the kind of woman who has beautiful children of either sex. Such a shame that she had none. Thomas Bayly had the same thin face and strong jaw, but his nose and cheekbones were more delicate than Mary's, less mascu-line. He had the face of a man who needed a sister's guidance and protection. He was descending the gangplank now, his dark eyes searching the crowd for a nun. He was carrying his hat, and in the sun his soft brown hair had a reddish tint. No doubt he was ex-pecting to see coifs and wimples of greater eccentricity—the Sisters of the Sacred Heart eschewed anything that would draw attention to themselves. With less familiarity, he might not be able to spot her as the mariners and stevedores had done, as the man following the prisoner, as the people in the crowd greeting the arrival had done. But it didn't matter: she had him in her sights; she had not failed in her mission.

He landed on the pier, his first step on French concrete, and he turned to give his hand again to Beal. The girl reached out to him. Even through the gloves Madame Bernault could see the length and delicacy of her hands and fingers; these were not the hands of a farm girl—Madame Bernault looked down at her own stubby farm-girl hands—but of a pianist, she thought, a ballerina. Her suit was woolen, of coarser cloth than the mesdames around her, skillfully made, but not chic—in other words, American—yet it was already clear to Madame Bernault that high ruffs and outlandish sleeves and brocade, silk, and lace were not necessary on a body of such lithe but solid beauty. Madame Bernault remembered the days—oh, there was something about Beal that was forcing her to recall sensations and memories from many years ago—when her own body was muscled and firm and youthful, but she had never been a girl that got a second look.

She was musing a bit on this when she noticed that the couple following Thomas and Beal had held back far more than necessary to give them room; indeed, men and women above them were craning their necks around the line to get a look at the young couple, and it was not difficult for Madame Bernault to figure out why. The same was true of the passengers who had preceded them onto the pier and now turned to gape. At best they were surprised, but one man, red-faced, with white whiskers, was mouthing his contempt to his own proper, plump wife: *Outrageous! Immoral!* Americans, certainly, or perhaps British, it hardly mattered which. Neither Thomas nor Beal seemed to notice. They prepared to march toward the customs desk, but right then Thomas's eyes caught Madame Bernault's and there was the double take of recognition. He approached the barrier. "Madame Bernault?" he said with some relief in his voice. "I'm Thomas Bayly."

Whether he would have any French was one of the unknowns

that Madame Bernault had discussed with the Mother General. Mary was still remembered by all as an American with extraordinary, even musical fluency in the language, but her elegant letters had warned the ladies that Thomas was not, well, the student she had been, and that his Greek and Latin might be passable, but he would have very little French. Of Beal, it went unsaid that she would have none. This was one of the reasons that Madame Bernault had been requested and sent; when Mary knew her, her English was still very good. But ten years had passed.

"Thank you," said Madame Bernault, these first words of English feeling like a fish bone in her throat. "I give you welcome." She said this first to Thomas, but then turned on the last syllable to Beal. Oh yes, the fear Madame Bernault had anticipated was there, but she—well, both of them—appeared undaunted. Beal seemed strangely vacant, almost as if she had floated down the gangplank and onto the pier, but she was darting her glances around with birdlike curiosity—these strange sights, sounds. Her strikingly pale eyes were like opals; her dark skin was absolutely flawless, without freckle or pock or scar, as fine-grained as silk. Her features were flatter than Thomas's, and she was almost as tall as he and perhaps even more broad shouldered, but there was no mélange of gender here: this was a beautiful young woman. Thus, the sentence about her in the letter, quoted from Mary Bayly herself, was now fully confirmed: "Please tell Madame Bernault that my brother's wife is a Negro, 19 years old, well raised on our farm by accomplished and reasonably educated parents, of extraordinary appearance and grace." Mary had also added, as a postscript for Madame Bernault, "She and my brother fell in love as children amid great danger to themselves and their families, and nothing any of us could do could break their commitment to each other."

"Welcome to you, Mrs. Bayly," said Madame Bernault, and with that the opal eyes winced. What Madame Bernault did not know was that during the passage, even to the moment of her taking his arm at the top of the gangplank, they had maintained the fiction that got them boarded in New York without controversy, which was that she was his maid. Not that a single man under any normal circumstance would travel with a maid, but it was the best they could do, and besides, when he took meals in the main salon, he dined alone, and he slept alone, and this "maid" was almost invisible, dining in the lower decks presumably, even if her tiny inboard servant's cabin was just down the corridor from Thomas's stateroom. Thomas and Beal had been married by a priest in a Catholic place of worship in Virginia just a few days before the ship departed, but it was, at last—in the eyes of everyone, perhaps even including God—on the gangplank that they finally became husband and wife.

The girl did not meet Madame Bernault's eyes, but thanked her with a very respectable pronunciation of her name.

Madame Bernault was getting ready to ask her how the voyage had been—her own, fifteen years earlier, had been terrifyingly stormy—but a customs official was coming over to break this up, and Thomas himself, clutching his papers, was pulling Beal toward the desks. Madame watched them go, noting that he sat Beal down in a chair in front of the desk but remained standing himself, and she observed finally that the *douanier* paid the girl not the slightest notice, neither her race nor her beauty, stamped their passports, ruffled through their papers, passed the packet back to Thomas without looking up—nothing to see—which must have been the best welcome of all.

A religious in Louisiana in the years Madame Bernault had been there had to get used to the idea that sexual relations between the races—between white men and women of almost any ancestry: African, Indian, mulattoes, Creoles, even Orientals!—was occurring and would continue to occur all the time. Each year a few of the girls under her instruction in the *pensionnat* were of mixed blood, some of whose tuition was quietly paid by prominent families. Perhaps this tolerance was never as rooted in the states settled by the English, and Madame Bernault gathered that it was no longer the case even in Louisiana. But here in France . . . Well, she understood that there was no law against marrying outside your race, and that there were those who argued that such *métissage* refreshed the blood of all those who professed themselves citizens. But who could say what trials awaited Thomas and Beal? Who could say they would not encounter scorn—even, Madame Bernault feared, within the Society that had taken this couple under its wing, beginning with the Mother General herself. Mother Digby, so newly installed as superior, was an English convert, after all. Yesterday, as she read Mary's letter to Madame Bernault, her lip had curled inside out with distaste when she was forced to speak the word *Negro*.

When Thomas and Beal were allowed to pass through the final cordon, Madame Bernault came forward. She went straight to the matter of their *bagage*, lapsing into French.

"I'm sorry," said Thomas. "Are you asking about our luggage?"

"Excuse me. Yes, luggage."

"We have arranged to have it shipped to our hotel in Paris while we get settled. We understood we would be heading straight there tonight."

"Oh yes," answered Madame Bernault almost giddily. "The train to Rouen and then to Paris," she informed them. Following the Seine. Napoleon had said that Paris, Rouen, and Le Havre were all one city, of which the main street was the Seine. Perhaps they didn't know that. They would be at the station in Paris by six o'clock. Remarkable, wasn't it, how fast one traveled these days! Their hotel was a lovely establishment not far from the Hôtel Biron. Mother Digby would send a carriage tomorrow if it would be convenient to meet with her then. Yes? I'll tell her you will come by at ten. They would enjoy the train ride. There were many charming vistas on the trip. They would pass by Caillouville, where the water of a fountain was said to have miraculous powers. The tunnel at Rolleboise was more than two thousand meters long. Too bad they could not stop in Rouen to visit the cathedral. "I've never seen it," said Madame Bernault, and then she realized that she had been carrying on. She was relieved to discern, from the way they had been reacting, that at least she had stayed in English.

"It all sounds very nice," said Thomas. "Don't you think, Beal?"

The girl nodded; Madame Bernault could hardly imagine what she would think of any of this. They were standing a few feet from where Madame Bernault had waited for them, just under the iron lattice of the vast pier shed. The first-class passengers had long departed in their waiting carriages, leaving the porters and their servants to claim and load their steamer trunks, hatboxes, gun cases, and escritoires; the last second-class passengers were filing in by now, preparing to locate their own more modest baggage. Madame Bernault noticed that Beal had been looking at them with some interest, counting them off as if she knew them, and then suddenly, at the top of the gangplank, appeared an extremely tall African man. Was everyone in this story a giant? wondered short, squat Madame Bernault. He stepped with the assurance of one who had done this all before, and about halfway down, he scanned the crowd in a confident manner and found what or whom he had been looking for, displaying no emotion when he found her, simply settled his eyes upon her. Beal turned away in a sudden jolt, took her husband's arm. "Yes," she said, the trip on the train sounded "right nice."

"Do you have the necessities for the trip?" asked Madame Bernault, feeling that she should keep her engaged in the conversation, because the man was now on the pier just paces behind her, and behind Thomas. Beal said she did, holding up her handbag, but Madame Bernault wasn't listening. It was odd: from the way this man stared openly at Beal, it seemed that he had no idea that anyone else, Madame Bernault herself most probably, would notice, or that he didn't care if they did. In his suit and clean white collar and his rather bizarre embroidered hat, he was far better dressed than any of the other passengers in steerage, an imposing-looking man. To Madame Bernault's eye, he was of pure African heritage—which would account for the hat—undiluted by life, willing or unwilling, in the New World. West African, if Madame Bernault was right. She wondered what his business might have been in America.

Now it was her turn to have lost the drift of the conversation. She heard Thomas invoking the name of his sister, and she snapped back to attention.

"In your dormitory? In the Hôtel Biron?" he was saying.

"Oh yes. We all remember her very well. Mary and her cousins."

"Mary wouldn't want to be remembered in the same breath as Cecile and Dolly," said Thomas with a laugh. He turned to Beal. "Our cousins. Neither of us ever liked them."

"Poor girls," said Madame Bernault. "They were not, how would you say, at the same level as your sister."

"No one ever was," said Thomas. "Except for Beal's brother, Randall."

"Ah," said Madame Bernault. She took this opportunity once more to search out the African man. He was at the customs desk, showing, if Madame Bernault could tell from this distance, none of the anxiety most people of lesser means displayed when confronting authority, certainly none of the fear any American Negro might suffer in this situation. He was now engaged with the customs official, and at this moment Beal turned slightly to look at him over her husband's shoulder. His hat was a head taller than the top hats in the crowd. Beal's full lips parted slightly, and she released a breath, as if she had been holding it since he appeared on the gangplank, but Madame Bernault had no idea what emotion she might be expressing with this: A desire to speak to him? Fear that he might find her? When she looked up the last time, the hat was gliding toward the street, and in a moment it was gone. Relief or regret?

Enough of this. Madame Bernault returned to her mission, which was now only half discharged. "We should make our way to the station. We'll be able to catch the twelve o'clock train. The sisters have sent their porter in the carriage to take us."

Out on the street, she steered the couple through the tangle of men, carriages, horses, cargo, and luggage to the alley where M. Marain had been waiting for them. M. Marain was a tiny, perhaps mentally compromised man who had a habit of spitting at the end of every brief sentence. The sisters had warned Madame Bernault about it, one of several deep and long-standing complaints, but this was typical: convents always had porters they longed to be free of but couldn't function without.

"Thank you for waiting, Monsieur," said Madame Bernault. "Here are the new arrivals."

M. Marain pulled the brim of his cap to them and spat. He spat again after he had helped the couple into the carriage, and Madame Bernault realized that this spitting was not just about speaking, but was a concluding punctuation mark for any gesture. A demon forced him to do this, she thought. She kept this little point on her mind as M. Marain helped her into the carriage, spat, and set off for the station, and it suddenly occurred to her that this marriage of Thomas and Beal could itself be the work of one of these demons. This couple sitting across from her, such lovely young people, she with her gloved hand on his, he with his interested face and gaze, they had been put here in this time and place by a demon bent on putting God's favorite creations through their paces. They had been given no choice in this. Perhaps they would fail the test. Perhaps this child would be abandoned by her husband in favor of a more suitable *femme du monde*. Perhaps she would return to her homeland in Africa. Yet what great works were being offered to them, to make a life together in such unusual circumstances. Madame Bernault tried again to catch Beal's eye, this country girl here in the *métropole*, and would have offered an encouraging smile, but Beal did not give Madame the favor of her attention; instead, she kept behind that innocent face the secrets of this moment.

Some years later, in one of Madame Bernault's last hours, when she was too frail to be moved even to nearby Conflans from the Hôtel Biron after it was seized by the government, too much lost in her own thoughts to notice the turmoil around her, she thought of this day, the first time she met Thomas and Beal, the beginning of her last vocation, the girl and the boy whose lives and trials on earth grew to matter more to her than almost any other mortal events. In the years to come, after the couple had left Paris, they returned only once, and it happened to be a difficult period for them, but as much as Madame Bernault could, she followed their lives closely, and whenever she learned something of interest, she passed it along to Thomas's sister, Mary Bayly, back in Maryland raising cows. Madame Bernault and Mary Bayly were not the only people watching Thomas and Beal. Sometimes it seemed that the whole world had these blameless young people in its sights.

2

B eal felt the nun trying to catch her eye, and she did not know exactly why, but she refused to give it to her. *Beal*, she was thinking over and over, as if calling out to herself. What is a Beal? Am I Beal? Am I still, was I ever, will I ever be again? Why am I riding in this carriage with Thomas and this nun through these streets of France, where everything is made of stone, where the sun doesn't shine on the streets? She heard the chatter from the people walking single file between the carts and carriages and the building fronts, and she knew it was a ridiculous thought, but still, she wondered if she was the only one who realized they were just mouthing made-up sounds that didn't mean anything, that they were just pretending to understand one another. She tried to calm herself: I am riding in this carriage with my hand on my husband's hand, and this is the same hand I used to take at home on our bench by the stable, this same white hand that seemed so pale in mine. She looked down at her gray gloves: these soft gloves were crazy. Why were they ever invented? Why did every inch of her skin have to be covered? She was heading into some kind of panic. She focused on the picture of the two of them on that bench, passing the time under the honey locusts and pecans, looking down the creek and into the broad mouth of the Chester River. She tried to recall what they might have talked about all those hours, in those years when they were still children on the Retreat, when they were just friends, and suddenly the thought she had been suppressing all morning came out in a desperate *Why?* Why did I marry Thomas when I knew what was going to happen to us, even though, of all that I dreamed, I never thought what would happen is this—me, Beal, in France? Couldn't she just go back, back to the Retreat, or better still back to Hampton, Virginia, where she had a good job as a maid in Colonel Murphy's house? Why did she have to pretend she was a lady in a carriage, with grown men on the streets tipping their hats before they really looked at who was in it, and then letting their jaws drop. Why not just be a colored girl in a farm wagon that no one paid no notice of at all, that people just looked *through*? Now weren't that a kind of *freedom*! Why not still be that girl? Beal.

The carriage broke into a large square around a fountain, and though the sun finally found its way to them, it was just another acre of stone, the iron-rimmed carriage wheels scraping and clattering on the uneven pavers. She looked up at the driver as he hunched over the reins, and she couldn't help wishing that if she blinked three times, she'd open her eyes the last time to see her father's strong back and massive bald head up there, not this little weasel. Her Daddy driving a team of mules back on the Retreat, and if she blinked again, she'd see her Mama and maybe her sisters Ruth and Ruthie on their porch at Tuckertown, waving to her as if at a homecoming. She'd have to stop loving Thomas, or he would have to stop loving her, for this dream to come true, but right now she wasn't sure she wouldn't make that choice. She had been told that if she and Thomas went forward in this, if neither of them would call it off for the good of the other, they would have to leave, and she would never see her mother and father and sisters again. The whole thing had been spelled out to her by older and wiser people, and she had ignored them. Now that this thought was in her mind, she knew why she wouldn't meet this nun's eyes; if she did, she would burst into tears and the nun would throw the look back upon her, saying, *Well, what did you think was going to happen?*

"*Encore plus vite, s'il vous plaît, M. Marain,*" said the nun when a clock tower suddenly broke into view, and in any language Beal could understand, she was asking the driver to speed up. He gave a slight jiggle to the reins and leaned over the side to spit.

On that boat, in that windowless closet she slept in, she'd cried and cried. In the middle of this lie they were living for the voyage, neither of them could think of intimacies—those would come, she supposed, soon—but Thomas came in one night in his pajamas and lay down beside her on that tiny bunk and held her. "Shush now, Baby," he said, and he knew her mother used to say that, *Shush now*, which meant there wasn't anything that could be done now, but things would work out in the end. It was the kindest thing Thomas had ever done, to try to give her back a piece of her mother when he was the reason Beal would never see her again. "I know," he said. "I feel it too." Beal asked what it was that he felt, and he answered, "Homesick." And when he said it, she remembered that he had given up his whole life too, that even if his own father was dead and neither his father nor his mother had ever shown him an ounce of real love, and even if now he had nothing to do with his mother, which Beal would never understand for a second, and the best friend he had ever had, her brother Randall, was dead, still, for her he had given up what had sustained him through all that unhappiness—the farm, the land, the Retreat, which would have been his and his alone when his mother died. What Beal had given up—the love of a family—Thomas had never had; what Thomas had given up—family wealth—Beal couldn't imagine. So there they were, huddled like lost children, Beal against the bulkhead in her white nightgown and Thomas curled up behind her in his blue pajamas while the vibrating engines of the ship powered them, mile after mile, ever farther from home.

"Look," Thomas said now, pointing between the buildings at the end of the square. "The Seine," he said, the river Madame Bernault had been talking about earlier.

Beal didn't know why it was so special, but she and Thomas were both children of the Chesapeake and of its rivers, and she smiled back at him. Both smiles were forced—Beal knew that in his own way, Thomas was working as hard as she was just to get through these hours—but smiling felt good.

"We're just a few blocks from the station," said Madame Bernault. "We'll have to hurry when we get there."

Beal still hadn't looked at her. A nice person, she believed. Beal was trying to feel better, as if feeling better were a costume she could put on, and she calmed herself by looking around with more interest at the churches that seemed to pop up on every block, at the soldiers and police in their brilliant red trousers, at the children playing tag, laughing. Women in black and gray were heading home from market with bread and the long stalks of some sort of late-season greens sticking out of their baskets; protruding through the end of one basket, the tail of a large fish flapped up and down comically as the woman strode along. All that was reassuring to Beal, timeless and placeless. She looked ahead at what must be the train station coming into view, and among all the muted tones of the buildings and the clothing, she spied a sudden dot of color above it. Her chest tightened when she realized what it was, that dot of color, the hat worn by M. Touré. Yes, she knew he was going to be on a train to Paris, and she feared it would be the same one, and there was nothing she wanted less than to see him or to be seen by him. Before she could think, she let out a small, troubled breath, and it was loud enough and expressive enough for Madame Bernault to notice, to turn and glance ahead and see the same dot of color and then look back at Beal and finally their eyes met, and it was in a sort of shock and confusion, but also in full acknowledgment of the cause of the problem, if not of the true nature of the problem. How quickly the nun seemed to figure out that at the very least, Beal did not want to be arriving on the platform at the same time, and Madame Bernault cried, "*M. Marain, un moment, s'il vous plaît*," which must have meant for him to stop, because he did stop, and she fumbled about her feet as if she had forgotten something, her bag or her cloak. Thomas noticed none of the drama, but he leaned forward as if to help her find whatever it was that she had lost.

"How silly of me," she said, still not offering a reason for all this. "Such an old fool."

"Hardly," said Thomas, and he glanced at Beal in a lighthearted way.

This time, when Madame Bernault looked up from her searching, Beal was ready to meet the care of her gaze, to thank her with high eyebrows, but also to promise her that she had not done wrong, that she was hiding nothing from her husband, that this man would disappear into the station and that would be that.

The first night after leaving New York, Beal had descended four ship ladders to the lower dining salon on the *Touraine*. She was so homesick and frightened that she wanted to die, and she was also hungry and worried about how she was to get her supper in this place. As she dropped deeper into the ship, farther and farther from real light and real air, she was thinking as well of those horror stories of the slave ships and of being chained in the bowels of a vessel. She had heard these tales time and time again from an old woman at home—Aunt Zoe Gale—who had been driven crazy by the history of her people in America. *Why, oh why, did God let them bring us here?* That was Zoe's refrain, that was her question, and she kept asking it to the very end, when she could no longer dress or feed herself or keep herself clean. She kept asking, as if an answer that made sense to her would suddenly wipe away the visions of bondage and mutilation that clouded her eyes and thus would silence the screaming of the lost and damned she heard in her ears. Beal suffered no hallucinations, heard no voices as she entered the dining salon, but it seemed to her, with Thomas and their escape and the lie about being his maid all muddled in her head, that she understood what it meant to be utterly and completely powerless to influence her fate. Whether she wanted it or not, whether she'd had second thoughts or just wasn't quite ready, this ship was taking her to a new world.

She stood at the doorway to the salon swallowing terrible, hollow gulps of air, trying to steady herself with a hand on the railing that ran on almost every wall throughout the ship, but nothing about the scene in front of her calmed her fears. She gazed down the long tables, the lines of chairs bolted to the deck on swivels, and as baskets of bread and pots of stew were set down, people rushed for the seats, and men—fathers—raised their fists and their voices in a dozen languages while setting out places for their children. Elderly women spat out insults in perhaps universal languages as they seated their more decrepit husbands or sisters. Beal did not know that the territories being claimed would stand as assigned seating for the rest of the voyage, and that after this free-for-all there would be only occasional rough words if someone innocently counted off the wrong number of places from the head of the table and sat in someone else's seat.

Beal didn't care where she sat, and as she waited, the groups making a dash for the table became smaller and smaller, less and less aggressive, until it was clear that the remaining ten or so passengers waiting to seat themselves were each traveling alone. As she watched this process, she'd been slightly comforted that there were several other colored people in the room, one family with a gray-haired patriarch, three boys not much older than she was and, from the look on their faces, not much more at home. But as she waited to sit, she became aware that one man had sidled over to her, perhaps in the expectation that these last stragglers would simply form a line and file into place. He was very tall and quite formally dressed, with skin so black that in the shadows of the gaslight she could barely discern the shape of his nose or the point of his chin. When at last it was her turn, he jumped forward to a seat and swiveled it around for her with a gesture of his open palm, which, like his eyes and teeth, was one feature she could really make out. She did not know, even then, whether she liked him treating her as his charge, but she allowed herself to be seated in this way, and when he took his place beside her, she turned to give a nod of thanks to him. He was not through with serving her. He reached one of his very long arms out to grab the pot of stew, and he held it while she ladled a little into her bowl.

"Thank you," she said, not at all sure he would understand English.

"You are welcome. There is no need for anyone to fight for food," he said, beckoning with disdain toward the other tables. "I am Monsieur Diallo Touré." He spoke precisely, enunciating every syllable as if a little unsure that he would be understood. He was not like any black man, any man at all, that she had ever met.

"This is your first crossing?" he asked.

She said it was.

"You are domestic?"

He had made the assumption he was supposed to make, and really, she'd never minded her job a bit, but for a reason she could not yet discern, she was wary of disapproval from this man. She answered, "I am *a* domestic, but that don't make me *domestic*." Her brother had once made a joke of the word, teasing her that if she were domesticated, she'd be like a cow.

M. Touré was confused by this, but then he realized it was his grammar that she was correcting. "Oh yes," he said. "*A* domestic. English is not my first language. I am more comfortable in French, though I was raised speaking Wolof, the language of my tribe."

Beal couldn't imagine having all these different words in her head. "I'm sorry. I didn't mean to be fresh."

He smiled; he had regained the upper hand. "Not at all," he said grandly. "You are correct. In French one does not use the article when stating one's profession. *Je suis diplomate*," he said, apparently illustrating his point.

She nodded uncertainly, hoping she hadn't gotten into something here. She took a spoonful of stew and found it delicious, not too greasy, a sort of sweet flavor to the broth. She reached for a piece of bread, which, fortunately, did not require M. Touré's help.

"And what is your business in France?" he asked.

She had no idea how to answer this question and took herself to that surest of all places of refuge, a state of ignorance: she didn't know why they were going to France; no one had told her.

"An intelligent girl who can make jokes about grammar should ask more of herself. You are no longer in America. American prejudice has its missionaries all over the world, but you are leaving the worst of it behind." Touré paused here, as if swallowing a bad memory. For a second the cocky demeanor wavered, as if the thought of America were too much to bear, and he continued to stumble a bit. "In Paris there are Ethiopians, singers, troubadours, who revel in mocking themselves and our people for the amusement of the ignorant. Shocking." One more slight pause, and then he ended this on a firmer note. "But you will find things very different in France."

She didn't understand the early part of what he said— missionaries? Ethiopians?—but the last part was what she had been led to believe, though honestly, she couldn't imagine how her life was going to be so different, except that she would be with Thomas and away from her family.

"I am Senegalese," he said proudly, puffing up his chest a bit. When he saw that she didn't understand, he added, "From Africa."

"I don't know anything about Africa," she said. "My Granddaddy told me that Maryland once tried to move us all to Liberia, even us who was free."

"A shameful episode, but if it had come to pass, you would be living a very different kind of life today." A better life, he meant, not one where you could be taken across the Atlantic Ocean without knowing or asking why.

Beal tried to imagine this, but she had no idea how people lived in Africa, how she might have grown up if her parents and grandparents had all been forcibly relocated. Were there really no whites there? Did they have real houses, like her family's two-story house in Tuckertown, or did they live in huts made of straw? What clothes did they wear? She knew it was stupid of her not to know anything; how hard her mother had tried to make her attend to her studies, to maybe go to college like her brother, but she was a silly girl, a pretty girl, and then before she knew it—as if from the day she was born, born into this—she had agreed to marry Thomas. Beal thought it was love, or maybe something less breakable than that.

M. Touré broke into her thoughts. "You should come to Africa to see how our people are rising."

She could think of no way to respond to this, so she stood. Most of the passengers had already left, headed into their cramped staterooms or into the steerage lounge or onto the fantail of the ship, where they could see the sun set over the horizon with a sudden burst of orange and then watch the froth of the propellers disappear in the moonlight. She didn't like the way this conversation was going. "Going to France is all the traveling I am fixing to do."

He paid this no mind; he made his face blank, as if she'd said nothing.

"Thank you for helping me get on," she said.

He had stood when she did; he was all frame, with skin stretched over his high cheekbones, hands with sharp, darting fingers and powerful claws. "I look forward to more conversation with you. I hope to learn more about you, and I will tell you about our homeland."

Beal climbed back to first class. On the way down, she had not had to explain herself at the gates to second class and then to steerage, yet on the way up she was challenged by stewards to say precisely where she was going, what was the name and suite number of the family she served. All this subterfuge pained Thomas far more than it pained her; before they left Virginia, she'd overheard one last argument between Thomas and Mary about the plans for their escape. Thomas argued that they should just book a stateroom in steerage as the man and wife they were now, and no one would care, no one would bother them. But Mary had said, "Please, Thomas. We're so close. Just do this for me. In nine days it'll all be over."

Beal was allowed to eat her breakfast at a special seating for servants and crew early in the morning, and lunch was irregular enough for her to avoid M. Touré for the most part, but he'd find her taking some air on the fantail from time to time, and at dinner he was always beside her. He gave her no quarter, and after a few days she did not resist so much; no one else said a word to her. He told her that his tribe was one of the ancient and powerful peoples of the area, that he was the chief aide to one of the two Senegalese deputies in the French National Assembly. Did she know that the Senegalese had seats in the National Assembly? He and his superior often went abroad to promote trade in agricultural products and groundnuts. He said that Senegal was to become a French colony; soon, he hoped, it would further cement its position as one of France's great provinces. If that happened, he hoped to gain a major post, with homes perhaps in Paris and his native city, Dakar. How would she like that, he asked, to be the wife of a man with homes in Dakar and Paris?

This had been a rather long lecture, and she wasn't listening all that attentively. But the word *wife* brought her back into the moment. They were sitting on the deck, leaning against a hatch cover, when he asked her that. He'd found her there; he always found her. She was thinking that the easiest way out of this was to say that she couldn't be the wife of such a man, as she was already married to someone else.

"Ah," he said. "You have been untruthful to me."

"You didn't ask."

"I did not expect to be misled." He was angry and made no effort to conceal it. "And where is this husband you have been willing to leave behind, as if sold to another master?"

"You have no call to speak to me like that."

He flicked away her protest. "I am not required to acknowledge this marriage if I am not apprised fully about it."

Beal felt herself being subsumed by this man, by these demands and these rights he seemed to be claiming. One minute he would be complimenting her, showing himself charmed by her jokes; at other times he seemed to berate her. He called her a "stupid American" from time to time, pretending he meant it as a joke, but he did not; he said this only when she tried to assert herself. She did not understand this power he had gained over her, the way he was trying to twist her mind. She felt his desire for her and was horrified that she felt it working on her. She was being tugged somewhere by him. So when he insisted one more time that she tell him who this husband was or he would simply refuse to believe it, she told him that she was married to the man she was pretending to serve, Thomas Bayly.

His eyes became huge orbs of astonishment and horror. He said nothing for a few moments. She thought he might get up and leave her in disgust—that was one of the outcomes she'd hoped for in telling him the truth—but he did not. Finally he said, "He may have married you, but he's still just the white master taking his privilege. *Droit du seigneur*, we call it."

Beal wanted to slap him across his face, but she could not, partly because this was the same argument her brother had made before he died, Randall arguing that even though Thomas had been for many years his closest friend, whatever Thomas may have believed about himself in his heart, in the end he was making her into his whore. Others had said that too, though in nowhere near as awful language. They'd said that Thomas wouldn't think of it as a real marriage; that when he tired of her, whatever vows he made could simply be withdrawn, forgotten, citing some law passed somewhere that said a white man who married a black woman could back out at any time he liked.

"And your children will be so pale that they'll disappear in the sun," said Touré. A few days earlier he had ridiculed her skin color as "mongrel skin." Her tone was not actually so faded as all that, but she was brown, not black, not remotely as dark, as pure, as he was.

"Why do you care about me? Why do you follow me around this boat? I don't owe nothing to you. Leave me be, if I'm such a stupid American. Go back to Africa where everybody gets along right nice."

"This is not a real marriage," he repeated. "In time you will understand that."

"And then what?"

"Then I will be there to make you a real husband."

"I will be wife number three to you?" He had told her about his two wives quite casually the night before. "Do you think I want that?"

"My other wives will be no concern of yours."

At this, Beal finally got up and left him on the deck, and in the evening she told Thomas she was feeling a little seasick and would not be going to dinner. But the following night, their last before reaching Le Havre, she went back to the dining salon, and he was there, showing her to her place as if nothing had happened the day before. None of the people who sat around them had been to France, and he told them about Le Havre, where the train station was, how to send a telegram back to their families, ways to avoid being robbed. Looking at Beal, he said he would be boarding the first train to Paris, where he had a room in a flat with fellow Senegalese deputies. When the meal broke up, Beal lingered. She could not help it; she could not extricate herself from this man without some parting. She swiveled her chair toward him. "I want to thank you for helping me."

"You know very little of the world, but you do not need help. You are leaving the protections of our race and entering the white world, but you will not have difficulty in Paris. On the contrary. *En garde, Paris.* As Monsieur Balzac says, '*À nous deux maintenant.*'"

Beal did not know who this Balzac was or what he had supposedly said, but she got the point. "That's crazy talk," she said.

"Paris will lay itself down for you."

"For my husband, you mean."

"Not at all. I have observed your husband, and he is not a strong man. Paris will devour him. When you are ready to leave him, I will be waiting."

This time Beal came closer than ever to slapping him. "You are wrong. People been putting Thomas down since the day he was born, even his own daddy. What they don't see is that when he sets his mind to something, he doesn't let it go. I don't know what he intends, but whatever he decides to do, I will be at his side. If you are waiting for my marriage to fail, you will be waiting until the end of your days."

She stood up during this, and when she finished, he stood up also. She stared her defiance into his eyes, but instead of anger or contrition, she saw an unnerving kind of patience. He took her hand, kissed it, and said, "*À bientôt, Mademoiselle Beal.*"

When Beal got back Thomas was, as usual, still at dinner. She looked into his French–English dictionary and was not really surprised to learn that *à bientôt* meant *see you soon*.

They pulled into the great city just as the dusk light turned a sort of purple, the color of Lent, a solemn time, but not without the promise of joy. Years later, when Thomas thought about those days, it was the metaphor of Lenten light that came to mind first, so strongly that in his memory he'd get the dates wrong, thinking they arrived in midwinter rather than November. It got dark early in Paris, his sister Mary had told him that at some point; he remembered her saying that the city was on the same latitude as Newfoundland.

At each high point of land or river bluff along the way, there seemed to be a town clustered around a steeple or two, but now the train had dropped onto a rather dismal plain, and as they approached the city, each town began to bleed into the next. When once again they crossed the Seine, perhaps for the fifth time—they had been slicing along and across its serpentine course all afternoon— Thomas caught the first full sight of the city, and if Eiffel's tower immediately grabbed his gaze, the teeming city at its base is what held his interest. It was on a scale he had never imagined: the place Mary had described was largely confined to the convent and the commodious park around it. His impulse was to nudge Beal, to direct her attention, but maybe this daunting tableau was not something he wanted her to see. In the twinkling activity of dusk Thomas could imagine thousands, millions of people, all working at some purpose, or at cross-purposes, a crush of traffic on the boulevards, the exhausted march of dusk in the simple streets, a knife being wielded in a back alley. As vast as it was, the city seemed too small to contain all that must be happening there. The river itself up to then had seemed crammed with vessels, skiffs and dinghies, lighters loaded with coal or grain, and barges mounded with what appeared to be apples, but oddly, on this final approach, the traffic had disappeared and now the river appeared as a majestic, unsullied thread winding unhurriedly through the tumult. It was a month before Thomas got to the bottom of *that* mystery, discovering that Napoleon had ordered canals built through the northern part of the city in order to divert commerce from his beloved broad avenue of water.

Thomas might have hoped that this first view of the arena he would soon enter would elate him, as if the roar of the crowd could be counted on to raise him up, but the fact was, he had never heard the roaring of a crowd and he did not expect to hear it now; no one but his harried sister and Beal's bereft parents had dispatched him for this fight. *If you* must *do this*: that was Mary's sole benediction; to make it complete, all she needed was a basin of water in which to wash her hands. Well, given all she had done for them, that was unfair. But forget his father, now dead, who had preferred Beal's brother, Randall, to him from the day the two boys learned to walk. *Why can't you be more like Randall?* was written on the banner under which he'd been raised. Thomas's father had arranged for the two boys to do their schooling side by side in a back room on the Retreat, but once Randall was dead, murdered—no one except the murderer knew by whom or why—Thomas himself became even more unnecessary, a dangling sequela of an experiment gone awry.

Except that something none of them expected had happened: he had fallen in love with Beal, and for years the Retreat and the little enclave of Tuckertown had revolved around this immutable fact. It was odd that this surprised anyone, not just because she and Thomas had become almost inseparable as friends, and not just because Randall, for one, had been warning people that this was happening, but also, when Thomas considered the state of the game as it now stood on the Retreat, his falling in love with Beal was about the only thing that made sense, the only solution, the only path forward for any of them. Even now, as he glanced over at her, sitting expectantly beside him, lost in her own thoughts, Thomas's devotion to her was so absolute that he could not begin to articulate why he loved her, why she and she alone gave him comfort and joy he'd never experienced before, why it had seemed to him fore-ordained, why there had been nothing—*nothing*—that anyone could have done to convince him to end it. Thomas was not stupid; he was not unaware. He understood all the arguments against it, it pained him to cause hurt and fear to her parents, he had earned loathing on the streets of town, and he cut himself off from almost every comfortable path that his privilege offered. Every path except for the one that would always be open to him: the privilege of his white skin. It would be some years in his life with Beal before he recognized fully what a privilege that was. He, finally, simply cast aside his own free will and mortgaged it in full to a love affair. It was unseemly, not very manly, when he thought about it, to be so helpless in the face of mere passion—like Aeneas falling for Dido, Thomas recalled from his days at the university (*"if you will not shoulder the task for your own fame"*). Men, his father would have said, understand that their calling and their fulfillment lay in the great designs they forge with other men. To his sister, Mary, his love for Beal was just selfishness, as she had pointed out again and again and again. As if falling in love could ever not be a selfish act; it was either an act of courage or of cowardice, a supreme show of strength or a pathetic display of weakness, but it belonged only to him.

The train was now scuttling through the dark streets, like a rodent with business of its own. There was no going back. With each rattle of the train carriage he was both leaving everything farther behind and conjuring something to take its place. Madame Bernault was stirring, gathering in her cloak, and Thomas had to admit that he was extremely grateful she was there to guide them. Paris had been useful as a place to head toward; otherwise, they were simply heading to the edge of the earth. But this was only the first stop, just a portal to their new lives, not a destination. He'd reminded Beal of this every chance he'd had since their wedding, as if all the challenges they faced were bundled onto these streets, as if once they got through this trial, the rest would be easy. He had no idea what that "rest" might be. None. Not even the shadow of a plan— even a vague interest; Beal had been his young life's sole focus. It was almost indefensible, most especially what he was making Beal do. He had made, silently, a solemn vow that whatever this city threw at them, he would protect her. He'd throw himself in the path of any oncoming runaway coach; he would ease her way through the mysteries here because, by default, maybe only by default, this was his world and not hers.

Which would have been fine if Thomas had been a man of this world. He had money enough, but in no way was he raised in this manner. Yes, the fiction on the ship that she had been his servant was disgraceful, loathsome, except . . . except that it made things simpler. No, said Thomas to himself, I must admit the truth: it was a tremendous relief. It was as if they had taken the cloister of the Retreat, of that bench by the stable under the pecan tree, along with them; the lie was the wall they used to protect themselves. The first night on board, she had already left to find her supper in the deep tub of the ship and he had dressed as he knew he must and found himself with no difficulty in the first-class dining salon, where he was greeted with relative indifference by the waiters and the five other passengers assigned to his table, and as he lowered himself into his seat, he had one of the most unwelcome thoughts of his life: Thank God Beal isn't here. He would never have dreamed of subjecting her to this, but even so, the thought had come to him in a more selfish guise. Thank God he could slide in under the cover of these incurious gazes, confront all the forks and knives and glasses, and listen to the first of eight days' worth of complaints about the service, the food, the weather. God, why didn't they just swim to Europe, or fly, if that's how they were going to behave. But imagine how they would have scattered if he had shown up with Beal on his arm.

When he got back to his stateroom, she was in her little inboard cabin. He knocked, and she yelled through the door, "I'm okay," and he thought that maybe it was better to leave her be, even though he wasn't sure that she wasn't crying. He didn't want to have to describe dinner in the first-class salon, and she wouldn't have to tell him anything about steerage, so he yelled back, "Me too. Good night," before tiptoeing to his own room. Yes, this had all been Mary's idea—"Think, Thomas," she had said, "what it would be like. It's a French ship, but most of the passengers will be American. I don't even know if they would let her in the dining salon"— but maybe not a bad one after all.

The days had passed with roles all nicely laid out, and Thomas had become aware that Beal was slowly becoming more comfortable at meals and on deck; the whole fiction required that they show themselves topside alone, and Beal seemed to like that, being up in the weather, and there seemed to be people, families, whoever, who had welcomed her. Thomas was passing the time in these insipid and boring conversations about people in New York he knew and cared nothing about, and she was acquiring whole packets of hints and facts about France, which she spilled out to him in his stateroom. "*Sou* is the word they use for a penny," she said. And then, "The clocks in railroad stations are kept five minutes slow all over France, so people won't miss the trains."

"That doesn't make any sense. When is it ever real time?"

"When you're in Paris," she answered, and then later that same day she said, "People take baths in barges that float in the river."

"I think we'll have a bath in the hotel," he said.

"I don't know about that," she answered. "That's just what someone said."

"Who was that?" The fact was, his own dining companions directed almost nothing to him, certainly nothing about clocks and baths or life counted out in dollars and cents.

"Oh, just a man at our table," she said, and volunteered nothing more.

So that was the way the days passed, and by the time they'd arrived in Le Havre, Thomas was sufficiently bored with his fellow first-class passengers—all Americans, at his table—not to care what they thought of him, and Beal was sufficiently reassured that in some way she could survive the next few days. The assurances he had been giving her seemed, finally, to sink in, to the point that Thomas almost wished he believed them as unconditionally as she did. When it came time to debark, they approached the gangplank with her walking a pace or two behind, but he stopped at the top, waited for her to catch up, and offered the loop of his arm to her. She slid her hand through it, and they joined amid gasps of shock and dismay, and in part because Beal stumbled a bit stepping up off the deck, they marched down together as one. Thomas had never felt so proud; he wished his sister had been there to see them, but her nun would do.

And tonight, tonight, in a little hotel on a quiet street, after years of waiting, years of nighttime dreams and daytime fantasies, he would share a bed with his Beal as husband and wife, he would make love to her, she would make love to him. He was grateful, and he knew Beal was too, that their week on the ship had provided this other kind of transition, a slow approach to intimacy, but now it was upon them, their unlikely wedding night. He could not imagine what it would feel like when she opened her body for him, but she would, and they would never again be apart. The breath fluttered in his chest, a cause for wonderment.

When they departed the station, the glow of purple had given way to a grayer sky, but the air had not yet turned cold. The evening reminded him of Novembers at home, when the fall warmth lingered before the wind off the bay became steely and unforgiving. It seemed a shame that it was a landau sent to pick them up—the Paris convent's worldly effects were several steps up from Le Havre's—but once they were seated, he appreciated the comfort and privacy, and he put his arm around Beal. Madame Bernault had closed her eyes the instant she reentered the protections of her Society, and worn out by everything, she had fallen fast asleep. Her veil was squashed against the seat back, her mouth open, and Thomas smiled at Beal: *a nice lady.* "No wonder Mary liked her so much," Thomas whispered.

"She has been right sweet to us."

"More than that. Imagine if we had to do all this ourselves."

"Thomas, you would have done fine without her. You would have got us here just fine. You're a strong man, and I trust you."

Thomas was a little surprised at the vehemence with which she spoke—this seemed to be part of some wider conversation—but she'd always believed in him just a little more than anyone else had. That was one of the many reasons he loved her; he *was* two years older, and as children, it was natural that she looked up to him, but even as they became young adults she still defended him against all his detractors. But yes, if he'd had to, he would have gotten them off the ship and to Paris without any help whatsoever.

He glanced over at her. Her tight waves of black hair, uncontained by her hat, seemed to caress her cheeks; her thick eyebrows seemed an impossible luxury above her pale eyes. From the moment they entered the carriage in Le Havre, people had been gaping at her; maybe they thought she was Andalusian, or a Creole from the West Indies, or a tribal princess from Africa. Thomas had seen this happening all his life. The first careless glance from the white man, or even a white woman, that saw only her blackness, and then, as if a deeper truth suddenly landed in that dim brain, the second helpless gape that watched her face move for a second or so, a moment of surprise, or disbelief, and then the stare, from the men, that settled despite itself into a hunger. *The pretty nigger girl of the Retreat*, that's what they said in Queen Anne's County, but that's because they couldn't account for her beauty. The truth was—as Thomas figured out later—as a child, Beal was beyond race. Anyone could see in her looks what they wanted to see; no one had to think of her as anything but a child. And now that she had matured, she was in every way a woman of African descent, but to the lover, the beloved's features remain unplaceable, they were born with her. Those eyes, sure, Beal's eyes adorned her face like jewelry, but there was also something sculptural about her profile, her brow, her chin; something joyous about the broad smile that came and went in an instant. Thomas would never tire of looking at her with a kind of wonderment.

It was dark now, but the streetlamps were bright and there were a surprising number of people out walking in the chilly evening air.

"I am in the place I really want to be," he said. "I only ever wanted to be with you. Isn't that what you feel?"

She squeezed his hand, gave him a nudge with her shoulders, which meant, *you don't need words from me.*

"Look," he said, pointing out the glass. "See up there?" She leaned over his lap and looked up the glittering avenue toward the towering stone arch at the top. The traffic proceeding up and returning down the hill were like twin rivers of light, their lamps twinkling as they passed under the bare branches of the horse chestnuts. "The Arch of Triumph," he said.

"Gee," she said. "Is that a house? Do people live in there?"

He tried not to laugh, but did. "No. It's just a monument. Like the Washington Monument."

She heard the suppressed laugh. "I don't know about no monuments," she snapped. "People could live there. People live in lighthouses," she said, but when she righted herself, she took a place even more curled up at his warm side. Yes. She had never expected in her life to be in France; neither did he. A better place for her? Maybe. Farm girl. Maid. Answers to the name of Beal. Strong and reliable. Cuffee. Nigger. A long way from all that, maybe. That's what Thomas had been promising her, but really, none of that had ever seemed to bother her so much; it was just the way things were. They were here for other reasons than that. *Who cares?* Beal would say. *Don't matter to me.* Maybe it mattered more to him; his whiteness, not her blackness.

Once again they were crossing the Seine. This seemed a city of bridges, and again Thomas could not help taking notice of this river; he would not call it broad and powerful but something of its appeal, or its myth, came to him. The way it hollowed through the heart of the city between its ancient stone walls—it seemed a thing, a being that had been captured. Still, the river seemed to permit the city, as crazy as that seemed. Once on the other bank, they were driving the length of a park, and to the right was an enormous gilded building with a dome that seemed to float over the whole district. Though down some alleys they could see and smell the humble foundations of this city, Thomas began to understand a bit of the grandeur. The greatest city on earth. At every street corner there was something remarkable, a church, a bridge, a park; the top of the Eiffel Tower seemed to be tracking them everywhere they went. For a moment, with this neighborly sleeping nun across from them, with a melodic chatter from the driver and porter coming from the seat above them, with Beal now pressed against him, Thomas thought that things would turn out all right. Life had a way of turning out right, if one trusted the hours, if one trusted tomorrows.

As if her thoughts had just come through the same pathway, Beal said, "I'll do better, Thomas. I've just been so scared. I'll do better by you."

"What do you mean? What says you haven't done amazing things already?"

"I says it," she said. "I'll show you." And when she said that, they both knew what she was talking about.

The porter reached his hand back along the side of the carriage and tapped on the glass. "Madame Bernault?" he called. She slept on until Thomas tapped her knee. "Madame Bernault," the porter called again. "*Nous allons au Lion d'Or?*"

The sister was still a little woozy.

"The hotel?" said Thomas. "He's asking about which hotel?"

"Oh yes," said Madame Bernault. "Good for you," she said to Thomas, still the old teacher. She called out a longer, less intelligible set of directions or instructions and then leaned forward toward Thomas and Beal to point to her left. "The Hôtel Biron," she said happily, and it was quite a building for a school, with a gate and towers with conelike roofs. Thomas had been tutored in a back room off the kitchen of the Retreat, and Beal had done most of her schooling in an old tobacco barn with her sister Ruthie as the teacher.

"All that is just a school?" asked Beal. "That's where you live?"

"The best of it is for the girls. We live in the servants' quarters and off the stables. Simplicity is in our vows."

Beal nodded. She knew about living in servants' quarters, and she'd choose one of those cozy nests over a master bedroom any day.

Madame Bernault continued. "When I was in Louisiana, we had nothing like this. I won't say that everyone in our Society approves of the Hôtel Biron. It was an old aristocrat's château before the Revolution."

"Hmmm," said Beal. "My brother told me about the French Revolution. The people had risen up, they killed the king and took over the property of the rich."

"If it had happened in America, they would have killed all of us in the Mansion House and taken the Retreat," said Thomas.

Beal jabbed him in the side. "Oh now, don't say anything as awful as that."

Madame Bernault seemed a little shocked at that turn, but it was the first time Beal had said anything more than yes and thank you, and she smiled at their play. "Thomas will see the Hôtel Biron tomorrow when he comes to talk to Mother Digby. Perhaps you'd like to come along, and I will show you around."

Thomas remembered the planned interview with Mother Digby. He expected the full grilling about his plans and intentions, and perhaps the exercise would be useful. Still, what could he say? His first intention was to learn some French, which had seemed to come easily for Mary and so might for him if he could find a good teacher. They would set up in the apartment Mary had found for them—it came with a cook, which Beal found hard to accept. Then, well, something to do. A life, really. And some kind of living. He did not have enough money to do nothing, but he wouldn't want to do nothing anyway; during harvest at the Retreat he worked from dawn to dusk like everyone else. So farming was a possibility, maybe, but what did they grow in France? He'd seen vast apple orchards just outside Le Havre, but fruit trees seemed an unlucky choice for him. Before he entered into a panic, he reminded himself that they had set aside the winter to get established, and he had time. He'd read; he'd study. That's what his father had done. But then, a new anxiety: What would Beal do during this time? Learn French also, he supposed. But what else?

They arrived at the hotel a few minutes later. The door was heavy wood reinforced with iron, as if this were the gate of a castle, and above the doorway was some sort of beast—half lion maybe, but half goat—carved into the pediment. A small plaque to the left of the entrance announced it as the Lion d'Or, a respectable but modest place, nothing like the grand seaside hotels in Newport News and Norfolk. "The golden lion," said Thomas. Now that it was deep gray dusk, all this stone was beginning to feel cold, almost medieval, but once they were inside, in the yellow light of the gas jets, Thomas felt a hospitable good cheer from the man at the desk, who seemed to know Madame Bernault well and to like her very much. They chatted away, and he could make out words like *dîner* and *bagage*, which seemed to refer to what they sounded like, and then he was surprised and almost shocked but finally amused when their conversation took on the sort of bawdy tone one used to hear from old Uncle Pickle, the mule skinner on the Retreat, and even Madame Bernault let out a nasal snuffle, which she stifled when she turned back to Beal and Thomas.

"M. Richard has given you their nicest room, on the top floor. He wants to make sure you are"—she couldn't help glance quickly back at him—"completely comfortable during your stay. From your balcony you will be able to see the river." She added that they could come down to dinner as soon as they were ready, and that the carriage would come by at ten in the morning to take them to the *Trente-Trois*. "It has been my pleasure," she said when Thomas thanked her. "It has been my honor."

"Mary said you would help us, but I really had no idea that you would do all this."

Madame Bernault seemed ready to accept this with a nod and to take her leave, but she lingered for a moment. "It has been God's will that you two young people have had to do so much in order to come together." There was no more bawdiness in her voice. "Your love will be tested; otherwise, how will you ever know its depths? None of us knows what lies ahead for us. But you are brave and in love, and perhaps that's all you will need in the end."

Madame Bernault was looking, it seemed to Beal, more at her during this than at Thomas, and when she said they would be tested, she seemed to be addressing Beal exclusively, which seemed unfair. But yes, Beal was already being tested in some way by, well, that man from the boat. She was being tested for being an American Negro, the daughter of free blacks but the granddaughter of slaves; she was being tested for her ignorance of the history of her people and of her continent; she was being tested for being smart and for not having attended to her studies, to her reading and to history; she was being tested for marrying a white man—the "white devil," as old, crazy Aunt Zoe had so often said. She was being tested, finally, for her beauty, which would open countless doors for her, including a few she would have preferred to remain closed. She and—she supposed—the wise Madame Bernault both knew that she would have to pass each one of those tests in due time and that thus far, she may not have been doing all that well. But before that, she would first have to become a wife, a grown woman.

They ate in the small dining room off the lobby. For months, the idea of entering a restaurant had terrified her. That game on the boat about her being a maid . . . she'd gotten wind of that plan with nothing but relief: she'd eat with the help, where she belonged. She wished they could continue with it tonight; there must be a place back in the hotel kitchen where the waiters and maids ate. Why couldn't she just get her supper there and then meet Thomas back in their room? She debated refusing to come with him, pretending she was sick or something, but there was now a new voice in this conversation, and that was the voice of Diallo Touré, and he had told her that she would encounter surprise, even shock, but that she would not be rebuffed. He told her she would prosper, and strangely enough, she had the feeling that she would, that this was all a kind of play, with roles that wouldn't be so hard to figure out. A strange kind of self-confidence came upon her. That is, she would prosper, if she could just get through this evening, the restaurant, and bed with Thomas.

The only other diners were an ancient French couple who seemed to be squabbling and a man not much older than Thomas who was probably American but was pretending he hadn't noticed their arrival. Beal hardly tasted what they ate, though Thomas kept telling her how delicious it was. M. Richard served them and came by offering wine, and Beal couldn't imagine that anyone would want to do that, drink wine with food, to have that smell in your face. The idea was faintly disgusting to her, and she was relieved when Thomas didn't take any either. M. Richard did, it seemed, take slight offense with this, snatched up their wineglasses, and smacked them and the bottle down on the sideboard.

As they were leaving, the other diner came up to them, a sandy-haired, freckled boy with a slight stutter. "I am Stanley Dean of Pittsburgh, Pennsylvania," he said.

Thomas shrugged a bit at Beal and gave him a slight bow.

"I am here studying painting at the Académie Julian. Previously

I was a student of Thomas Eakins at the Academy of the Fine Arts in Philadelphia. Miss Cassatt, as perhaps you know, grew up in Allegheny, just across the river from Pittsburgh."

Beal glanced at Thomas, and he shrugged again; neither of them understood much of what the young man had said, or why, but Thomas relented and introduced himself, introducing Beal as his wife and saying that they were both from Maryland. As Thomas finished, Beal realized that Stanley Dean was staring at her and was not really listening.

"Yes, I assumed you were American, but I wasn't sure about Mrs. Bayly."

Beal did not like what he was implying and didn't like that he seemed to be studying her, his eyes darting across her features. He even took a step back so he could see her better. She wished they would get done with this person and move on, but he made no sign of letting them go.

Thomas said that he had attended the University of Pennsylvania and knew Philadelphia passingly well.

That seemed to force this man to break off his gaze at her and turn to face Thomas. "Well, then. We have a great deal in common. Don't we?"

Beal could feel the loneliness seeping out of him and grasping them in its needs. A weak emotion, thought Beal, really, not something to give in to even a little bit. Homesickness: yes, a yearning for something, but loneliness was just giving in to the emptiness, into fear. This was one thing she understood from the moment they put her in the carriage at the Retreat to begin this escape: if she gave in to fear, fear about anything at all, she would not survive. Besides, she wished Thomas would cut this off, get them free of this man. Wasn't it their wedding night? She gave Thomas a slight nudge in the small of his back.

"Yes," said Thomas. "Well. Glad to meet you."

"You just arrived from Le Havre?"

Thomas confirmed that they had landed in Le Havre, from New York, and were actually quite tired.

"I have been here for three days," said Dean. "I am planning on moving onto a fellow's spare cot soon. There will be five of us. If I am careful with my money, I can last through next summer. As you know, we all leave in the summer. I eat very little, actually."

Beal glanced over at his table. There seemed to be only bread crumbs on the place mat in front of him, and a small tub of butter, scraped clean.

"Be careful what you put on the hotel bill or they will charge you double."

"Thank you for that warning," said Thomas, "but I still don't have a single coin of French money in my pocket. We have been guests of some nuns."

"Yes. It seemed you were in the company of a nun when you arrived. I am a Presbyterian."

Beal could see that they would never be rid of Stanley without some exchange, which Thomas clearly understood as well. He tossed in a concession. "Tomorrow we hope to see a little of the neighborhood," he said. "Maybe you could show us around a little."

Stanley Dean almost shouted his response. "Splendid," he said. "Of course. The Latin Quarter is where we all live. It's not too far. Here on the Left Bank. I can introduce you to so many fine fellows."

Thomas agreed that they would meet at two o'clock, and added that Beal—"Mrs. Bayly"—would be busy planning the move into their apartment, which they hadn't discussed but did seem reasonable, even necessary. With that they were able to take their leave from Stanley Dean. Beal took Thomas's arm as they walked up the five flights of stairs, and she waited patiently while he worked the heavy iron key in the lock. Their luggage had arrived, the covers on the two small beds had been turned down, and her nightgown and Thomas's pajamas were draped on each pillow. Beal was not sure she was comfortable with anyone going through her things, though she herself had unpacked other people's bags many times—guests of the colonel, the colonel's nasty sister-in-law. The ceilings of this top-floor room were low, but the room felt airy enough, with two sets of tall glass doors opening onto narrow balconies. There was a small chaise and an armchair in front of one of the doors. On the walls were engravings of country scenes, distinguished-looking men in uniform, families gathered around the hearth. There was a sink and a washstand in a small alcove, and down the hall, they had been told, was a water closet and a bath.

They stood at the door, which Thomas had not yet closed behind them, as if they could still back out of this conjugal chamber if they wanted. Beal didn't want to, but she waited for Thomas to lead them into the room. At last he said, "This is it. This is what I dreamed of. This is what could never happen for us."

Beal laughed, a nervous giggle, an unthinking response. "This room is what you dreamed of?"

"No. Not this room," he said, slightly hurt. "But any room we could call ours."

"Yes," said Beal. "This is ours for tonight."

"It's just the first of our rooms, our beds, our pillows."

She smiled for him; this talk of rooms and beds, she had to admit, unnerved her but also aroused her. "You asked me once to believe this could happen, and I never did, not until this moment. But I wanted to. It just seemed there was too many rubs against us."

Beal wasn't really sure why she was unburdening herself at this particular moment—nerves, a heart beating too fast to hear herself think—but Thomas turned a little darker, silent. He conveyed them both through the door and closed it behind them. She walked into the center of the room, which was lit only by the streetlamps and the moon, and after surveying what was in front of her, she turned to face him.

"I'm sorry, Thomas. I didn't mean that the way it sounded."

"In Philadelphia I used to go crazy sometimes, thinking of you, thinking of losing you. I knew how much you liked Hampton, how you were moving away from the Retreat and into the world, and I was stuck. Every day we drew a little more apart. Every day I had to make myself believe, and it got harder to do. That's what all those letters were about. If I had stopped writing for a single day, I think you would have left my life forever."

"Shhh. I never stopped wanting you. I never stopped hoping." But Beal knew there was truth to what he was saying. Yes, once she had left the Retreat, the world seemed to open up for her, and if she hadn't come back for Thomas's father's funeral last year, she very probably would have moved on. There were boys, college boys, in Hampton. But. Well, sometimes out of the greatest doubt grows the greatest certainty. "I'm sorry I didn't write back. You know I feel bad about that. I just couldn't."

"It doesn't matter," he said, but Beal knew it mattered a lot then, knew it would take some years for him to get over it. She'd sit down to write a letter to him and find that there was no place in her world for this back-and-forth through the mail; she told herself it was what white people did, ignoring the fact that her mother wrote her weekly. That's what she told herself at the time, but now it was very simple: he had overwhelmed her with all those words, and besides, she would have been a fake in those letters, she would have lied when she said, as she supposed she should, that she couldn't live without him.

Thomas threw the heavy bolt on the door; it landed with a thump Beal felt in her abdomen. "I waited for you," she said. "I kept myself whole for you. All that is gone."

"Yes. I'm sorry. You're right. I love you," he said. "All of that is gone," he repeated. "It's just us now."

"Just us." She liked the sound of it, even if it still scared her, even if it didn't seem like quite enough on her side, even as she depended on him to be more than half of the "us." She walked across the room to the windows and, with a little fumbling of the hardware, opened one of them and stepped out. Paris, France. It rumbled like a machine; there seemed no limit to its powers. She could see the top of the Eiffel Tower, the tallest structure in the world.

"What do you see?" he asked.

"That tower. Maybe these French people are some kind of genius race to be able to do that."

"We can ride a lift to the top if you want. You can see the whole city."

Beal kept her place on the balcony but turned her shoulders to look back at him. "Are you crazy?" she asked. "Ride up to the top of that thing? I bet people die all the time up there."

"Die of what?"

"I don't know, Thomas. Is there air up there? Something like that. The heat up so high, so close to the sun. Old Martin, he just died of the heat one day. Remember him?"

"That's silly. The government would never allow that."

Beal supposed that was true, but there had to be some danger; otherwise, why would they build it? She turned back to the street, resting her hands on the iron railing, tracing the filigree of grape leaves with her fingertips. The street below was dark and quiet, but at the end of it the boulevard was brightly lit with the yellow of streetlamps; she could see carriages crossing the opening at a lazy pace, and then suddenly—when it was gone, she could hardly recall what she had seen—an automobile darted past, leaving a trail of smoke. There seemed no real end of wonders here.

She left the window but stayed at that end of the room, and Thomas was at the foot of the beds. He had picked up his pajamas and her nightgown, which he held out to her. "I'll go down the hall," he said. "Why don't you change?" She took the nightgown and smiled.

Four years earlier, on the night before Thomas left to go to college, they had met at the old peach dock on the Retreat to say goodbye, and they had taken off some of their clothes and had done *something*. There had been the smell and stickiness of Thomas's wetness on her thighs, and as she ran back home through the dying peach orchards that night, she stopped to rub off the flaky residue with some tall grasses, but in the years since then she had heard the talk of other women, the other help at Colonel Murphy's especially, and she concluded that she was still a virgin, and that her first time might hurt. That she might bleed, the way Mandy had done, or not, the way Esther had not done, their first times. That she would have to guide him without hardly knowing herself where he should go. That she should relax and let herself become slippery. That he would find pleasure in it and she would most likely not find any at all. That it wouldn't take very long no matter what. But pleasure could come for her, in time. She'd heard her parents, Abel and Una, in their bedroom, trying so hard not to make noise, whispering, shushing each other, but at the end of it, her father was always silent, but her mother moaned and purred, and from the sound of it, it seemed to feel good.

Yes, they had done something like this before, and even before that Thomas and Beal and Randall had swum and played on the beach in their underwear or even naked countless times, so it was not modesty about her own body or about his that seemed to stand in the way, and not the prospects for pain or pleasure, but simply about doing it right. Would they—could they do this right? She didn't want Thomas to fumble or fail, as what was about to happen pretty much rested with him. She thought this as she undressed. Mary had given her a "trousseau," as she called it, along with a little speech saying that since they didn't know when or where they would be setting up their first house, this trousseau was mostly for Beal. What it was, mostly, was undergarments, and Beal laughed, remembering how curious she had been as a child about what white women wore under their dresses. Since then, as a maid in the colonel's house, Beal had plenty of opportunities to learn what white women wore under their dresses, plenty of opportunities to wash these soiled garments and attend to other women's monthly necessities. She had been expected to wear proper undergarments, but she held the line against anything with steel in it or bone—no bustle or hoop. Never. She didn't care what ladies wore; she wasn't anyone's lady.

When she had shed everything, she stood in the middle of the room taking note of herself, as if her nakedness had been let out of a cage. She loved being naked; she always had. When she swam with Thomas and Randall on the river shore, she was the first of them to strip and the last to get dressed again. She didn't mind that Thomas always stole peeks at her. But now, when she heard Thomas turning the key, she hurriedly slipped her gown over her head and stood in the moonlight to greet him.

"Do you want to lie with me?" he asked.

"Yes."

"Are you nervous?"

"A little. Are you?"

As if in response, she noticed the movement of his erection in his pajama pants. She supposed that was all the answer he needed to give. Suddenly she had a vision of them from outside their window, the two of them standing face-to-face in their nightclothes. From outside the window they looked like a very young man and an even younger woman, but a man and woman in love. Exiles for love, meeting in a foreign land in this rented room. This sudden

out-of-body view took just an instant, but it was strange, as if someone or something, an angel maybe, had put it there for her to see.
It helped. The city would now let them be; Mama and Daddy and
Miss Mary and Madame Bernault were gone; there was no one else
in Beal's world. She took his hand, and in the darkness of this French
night it didn't seem any paler than her own, just a hand.

He led her to the bed, the one that had been turned down
for her. She hiked up her nightgown, and he dropped the trousers
of his pajamas, and they seemed to do it all just fine; they kissed
and hugged, and Thomas explored her body with his hands, which
to the surprise of them both made her jolt spastically. He stopped,
as if he had caused her pain, as if she were saying she didn't want
him to touch her there. "It's okay," she said, feeling breathless. "Don't
stop." Her own hand brushed against his penis, and she was horrified by how big it seemed; it would never fit into the firm folds between her legs. But then he took a position above her, aligned his
body with hers, and by some sort of magic or design he was entering her in a way that was very right—*yes*, she breathed, right in *there*.
Before this moment she had never conceived of a *there* in her own
body, a place somewhat apart from the day-to-day, but Thomas had
surely found it. It did hurt a little, though in the morning there
was only a tiny rose blush on the sheet, and when it was done,
Thomas was holding her and saying her name the way she loved to
hear. Not so much to it, really. Even in Paris, France.

3

The interview with Mother Digby had gone just about as Thomas had expected. One thing he did not want to hear was some nun expounding on the challenges he faced, on the barriers Beal would encounter as—he had expected her to use this word and she had—a "Negress." But of course, expounding on challenges was what she had done. Thomas could take refuge only in the fact that she clearly held him in no higher regard than she did Beal. In fact, if he discerned correctly, she was no big fan of Mary's either. When he said he was exploring various possibilities for a career in business, she acted as if this were code for doing nothing at all. She looked at Thomas and saw idleness; she thought he was stupid. He was supposed to think she was treating him perfectly properly, but he was also supposed to feel bad without really knowing why, to go away with a gnawing disquiet. He'd seen this performance from his mother dozens and dozens of times: *how perfectly fascinating*, she would say. And Mrs. Bayly would, Mother Digby supposed, "have to find some way to pass her time"; the thought made her flick her hand into the void. Thomas wanted to strangle the old witch, but that morning he had seen some of the challenge. They had slept in each other's arms on that small nuptial couch, but as soon as the dawn began to break and the roosters, swallows, and pigeons began their racket, Beal was awake and up and dressed, because that is what she had done at dawn every day of her life. What was she supposed to do then? The evening before, Madame Bernault had mentioned to them that the next street over was the market street for the area. Beal knew plenty about early-morning markets. Thomas was still half asleep when she said she was going to see what French people ate, and it seemed proper enough to him for her to go see it while he roused himself, bathed, and got dressed for breakfast. She came back in the cheerful company, in fact, of the hotel owner, who was carrying six long loaves of bread, but how long would that remain interesting to her?

Now, on the way out, as a sort of parting shot, Mother Digby said, "I think you will find that a number of young Americans are taking up residence here. Artists," she said, once again curling her lip, "in many cases."

"I do not expect to be seeking out either Americans or artists," he answered. "I am here because I am trying to get away from Americans, and I don't think any artist would have much interest in me."

"Quite," she had answered, but after lunch Thomas was indeed heading off in the company of an American who called himself an artist. The sun was already low, and as they wound through the twists and turns of these ancient streets, Thomas was intermittently bathed in light from the sun behind him and groping in the darkness of shadow. Some of the buildings, five-story apartments, seemed modern; some of them seemed nothing more than peasant cottages sandwiched in between. Every few blocks there was a whole new line of shops, their fronts plastered with signboards advertising wonders that seemed unlikely in these dreary little hovels. Stanley and Thomas had to keep stepping up onto the stoops and sidewalks to avoid the drays and wagonettes hurtling down the middle of the street. The whole purpose of all this vastness, it seemed, was to cram more than two million souls into the tightest, dingiest spaces imaginable. It seemed like the life of moles; any people Thomas could glimpse in these gloomy caves stood as black silhouettes. In the midst of all this, Stanley Dean kept up a continuous stream of facts and details: here's the café where all the medical students go after class; here's where we buy paint and canvas;

there, you can see the towers of Saint-Sulpice; here's where my friend has a room. The closer they got to what appeared to be Dean's destination at the center of the Quarter, the dingier it all looked and the more Thomas felt out of place. As a child of the flatlands along the Chesapeake Bay, the two elements that were irreplaceable for him were light and wind. Beal felt the same way. Light and wind: when you have been raised in both, you cannot live without either. That's what Thomas believed. Struggling down these cramped, airless streets reminded him of being all but lost in the miles of his father's peach trees, where you could be overcome by the oily fragrance of the blossoms or the buzzing of bees and wasps. But just as it used to occur when Thomas finally reached the edge of the orchards, Thomas and Stanley Dean rounded the last corner and burst into the light of a broad intersection of boulevards and a large open plaza in front of a largish church. Thomas exhaled with relief. There were cafés on two of the corners, and they seemed to be filling up. Dean suggested that they might sit for a lemonade or a beer.

"That would be fine," said Thomas, assuming that Stanley was angling them into one of these, where there seemed to be an ocean of chairs and little tables with groups of two or three hunched in conversation.

"Oh no," said Stanley, turning Thomas around the corner toward a humbler establishment at the bottom of the block, the Café Badequin, the sign said. "That is where we go," he said proudly. The sidewalk was narrower here, just wide enough for a single line of tables. Two old gents were playing cards at one end, but at the other there did seem to be a larger group convening.

"In fact," said Dean as they walked down the block, "one of my friends at the Académie here is a Negro from Hartford. He was planning to go to Rome, but found he was quite at home in Paris. He might be here. Perhaps your wife would like to meet him."

"I'll ask her," said Thomas. "Perhaps."

"I hope I am not overstepping, but your wife is quite striking . . ."

From the way he trailed off, Thomas assumed he was about to say "for a Negro," which at home had been the obligatory suffix to her name. But in fact Dean had something quite different in mind.

"Do you think she might like to sit for a drawing sometime? A charcoal? A pastel?"

"That's something people do?"

"Yes. We talk about it all the time."

"Talk about what?"

"Finding people to draw, to paint. Women really, to be honest. Men are boring to paint."

"Why Beal?"

"Because she is so unusual looking. Do you mind me saying that about your wife?"

"I don't know," said Thomas. "I don't know what married people are supposed to mind, or not mind."

"Do you think she would agree to sit?"

"I wouldn't know, really."

"Would I have your permission to ask her?"

Thomas said yes, and in fact, he was charmed by the idea of having a drawing of her, a painting even. He could not begin to form a real opinion of this man—whether he was simply open and friendly or slightly pathetic; whether as an artist he had any talent at all; whether this interest in Beal was something Thomas welcomed. But they had arrived at the end table, where Thomas was introduced as "just off the boat and looking for a place to live," which wasn't exactly right, but was truer than Stanley Dean knew. Thomas noticed that none of these men seemed to be the promised Negro, unless a Negro from Hartford had extremely light skin.

"Are you joining the Académie or the École for your lessons?" asked one alarmingly pale and unhealthy-looking man.

"Donald Makepeace, from Chicago," said Stanley.

"Well, neither," said Thomas. "I'm not an artist."

"Neither are we," said another of the group in a thick and cultured Richmond drawl. "So said le Maître Rodolphe this morning," he added.

"But he's willing to take our money just the same," said Donald.

"After all, the Académie *is* on Dragon Street." They all laughed, a joke of some sort.

"Thomas and his wife are relocating," said Stanley. Clearly, he was pleased to have made this catch.

A heavier, dark man in the corner had been reading and did not bother to look up when Thomas was introduced. His forefingers were yellow with nicotine, and his stringy hair curled over his collar. He seemed very much the oldest at this table of students. When Dean used the word *relocating*, he glanced up and curled his lip. "Must be nice to be rich," he said, and returned to his reading.

"Arthur Kravitz, from New Jersey," said Stanley.

The Virginian—Fred Shippen—broke in. "Arthur, give the man a chance. We know nothing about him, do we?" It passed as a defense of sorts, though Thomas didn't love being spoken of as if he weren't standing there, as if any additional information about him could tip a judgment against him. Arthur did not respond. "So what *are* your plans?" the Virginian said, beckoning for Thomas to sit beside him.

"Moving here was actually quite sudden. We haven't had a great deal of time to plan. I am not sure we know exactly what we are going to do." Thomas realized as he was saying this how feckless it made him sound; the image of Mother Digby came to his eyes. But he didn't have anything truly more impressive to say. "I will be investigating my options this winter." This earned nothing but another snort from the dark man behind the newspaper in the corner; Thomas couldn't fault him.

"You make it sound as if you are on the lam," said Fred.

"I wouldn't say that, really," answered Thomas, and he didn't elaborate on his "really," though Stanley was harmless enough and Fred seemed a friendly and well-mannered person. There was a moment of silence, and then Stanley introduced the fact that Thomas was looking for a tutor in French, which elicited the final disagreeable snort from fat Arthur. "Oh yes. First step. Master the language. By all means."

The waiter brought their drinks, and Thomas had a chance to look around. This was indeed the student quarter, as Stanley had promised, and what was on view was not high fashion, but the freedom that seemed to be in every garment, every gesture, every meeting of friends, male and female, on the sidewalk. Here in this rather carnivalesque bustle, Thomas had simply no idea what he'd gotten into, what he and Beal faced. He wanted to see her now, and he truly wanted to avoid walking the long way back to the hotel with Stanley and then perhaps being forced to invite him to join them at dinner, and when Fred the Virginian stood up and announced he had to go, Thomas jumped up to join him. Stanley seemed torn about loosening his grip, but finally the pleasure of staying behind and gossiping about him, about Beal, won out. That's how Thomas figured it. He and Fred walked single file up the street, and when they reached the boulevard, they stood for a moment to introduce themselves more formally like the well-raised Southern boys they both were. "Why are you here, really?" Fred asked. "In Paris."

"There's no reason for us to be in Paris. It's just where we're getting started. I'm not that comfortable in cities, actually. I grew up on a farm."

"I grew up at a college. My father is a professor of anatomy at the University of Virginia. He thinks drawing nudes is a fine thing to do. He just thinks I should dispense with the skin." He laughed, seemed to encourage Thomas to see the humor of the thing. Yes, thought Thomas, Fred Shippen's father did sound like a man with a wit; his own father had not wasted time on jokes.

"But . . ." said Fred.

"I'm sorry," said Thomas. "But what?"

"But then, why in France?" he asked, as if he had been purposefully thrown off the scent by his own disclosures. "Why have you left the United States and come to France?"

Thomas didn't blame Fred for being a little exasperated by what may have seemed his evasiveness. Thomas was not one to evade, but from his earliest years he had the habit of answering questions with a precision and a literalness that a lawyer could admire; he gave no one the benefit of implicatures. It frustrated him as a child to be scolded for being fresh; *You didn't ask that*, he would say in his own defense. But at last Fred had asked the right question and got a direct answer. "I am in France because of my marriage. It's a long story. We had to leave Maryland. My wife is colored."

For a moment the good Virginia boy had nothing to say. At last he said, in a strangely admiring tone, "Just as I thought. Running from the law, in a way."

"Maybe it's better to say we were exiled. But what we did was illegal in your home state. I'm not really sure about mine, but it didn't matter what the law said. Our families tried to stop us."

"Hers too?"

"Of course. Why not?" Thomas may have answered with more keenness than he intended; he was trying to be likable here.

"Well," said Fred, slightly bruised. "I'd think it would be quite a step up for her. Why wouldn't her parents want that?"

"Her parents wanted only what was best for her. If I'd been in their place, I wouldn't have let her go with me without a fight. Her brother used to be my best friend, and our friendship ended over it."

This time the pause in the conversation felt more fraught. "I'm sorry," said the Virginian. "I didn't mean to be insensitive."

"It's all right. I know that wasn't what you intended. Beal and I have seen it all." Thomas said this and hoped it was true, though he wasn't sure. "She risked a whole lot more falling in love with me than I did. It took me a long time to figure that out, even though my sister had told me that over and over." They had reached a corner where Fred announced he had to branch off. "I have enjoyed meeting you," Thomas said. "I'm sorry if I sounded belligerent."

"I deserved it," Fred answered. "I think she'll be fine here. I think it will turn out all right for you. We're a very long way from the Confederacy."

The next day, M. Richard helped them move into their suite of five rooms on the avenue Bosquet, just around the corner from their hotel. It was a simple and somewhat charmless place, but the avenue was broad enough to let in plenty of morning light, and the river was a short walk away. The apartment had fireplaces with marble mantels in the parlor and the bedroom. The parlor came furnished with a threadbare Oriental carpet, two equally worn chairs upholstered in red velvet, a love seat, and an upright piano. The cook, a Mme Vigny, seemed a disagreeable sort. There was a room for a live-in servant upstairs under the eaves, the quarters for all the domestics in the building, and Thomas blushed when the concierge insisted on showing it to them. Beal didn't mind: *Sure,* she seemed to say, *this is what a maid's room looks like.* The apartment was on the fourth floor, and the bedroom window opened onto a court-yard, where the concierge had a toolshed, and two little girls in rumpled white pinafores played games until their mothers called them in. The high voices echoed in this stone court, and Thomas and Beal learned their names one afternoon when they heard the little blonde say *"Gilberte"* in a very stern voice and heard the one with curly red hair answer shyly, *"Oui, Monique."* They seemed very sweet, Gilberte and Monique.

Once they had moved in and Beal turned her attention to getting settled, Thomas started in with his French lessons with M. Richard's daughter, Céleste, sitting beside her behind the hotel desk; when she was doing business with guests, Thomas listened carefully, and after the business was done, Céleste found a way to tell Thomas what was being said. In that way Thomas's first French lexicon was the language of the hotelier; what the guests wanted and needed was almost always predictable, and within a month he took over the desk when Céleste was needed elsewhere. This was a good family, M. Richard and his wife, Céleste and her sister, Oriane—a family Thomas envied, just as he envied Beal's family, her parents Abel and Una, her sisters. He envied any family that seemed to be loyal to one another.

Thomas had failed mostly disastrously in his three years at the University of Pennsylvania, and as the days and weeks began to pass, he assumed that the reason he was picking up things rather quickly was that Céleste was a phenomenally good teacher. His Latin helped, but as time went on, even Thomas had to admit to himself that he was good at this; and years later, as he reflected on his rocky youth, he recognized that learning French had been perhaps his first success, and that if this had not been so, all the other successes that followed might not have happened. Some afternoons Madame Bernault would drop in, find them both huddled in front of the array of heavy iron keys dangling in the pigeonholes, Thomas conjugating verbs. Madame Bernault always bustled in with great cheer, came around the desk to greet Céleste warmly and shake Thomas's hand, and then took up the single chair in the lobby for the afternoon, often falling asleep and snoring loudly. Céleste had Thomas conjugate the regular verb *ronfler*, which meant to snore—*je ronfle, tu ronfles, il ronfle, nous ronflons, vous ronflez, ils ronflent*—and Madame Bernault woke up during this and asked, *"Est-ce que je ronfle?"*

"Oui, Mère Lucy. Vous ronflez," said Thomas.

Beal visited Madame Bernault often at the Hôtel Biron; she was welcomed by the sisters and the kitchen staff, and many days she simply sat in the comforting bustle of the back halls. She could still not imagine that this mansion was a school, but she did observe that the girls and the teachers lived a simple and austere life in these halls. An unkinder life than she had lived growing up in Tucker-town, that was certain. Beal did not know very much about Mary Bayly, but from what she did know, it made sense that Miss Mary would fit in here, where everything was ordered, where everything seemed to have a top and a bottom. Two of the sisters were black: one from Brazil and one from Africa, but neither of them had any English, so all they could do for Beal was encourage her with their smiles.

In the mornings she often joined Mme Vigny for the trip to the markets on the rue Cler. Thomas had no idea what this rather disagreeable woman thought of it, but it was clear from the beginning that the shopkeepers and merchants were very taken with Beal. They called her "Mademoiselle Beal" and also *"la belle noire,"* and she didn't mind; it all sounded like poetry to her, she said, and besides, their protector M. Richard was often there at the same time, and he roundly cussed out—so it sounded to Beal—anyone who tried to give her anything that was less than pure or fresh. The chatter and commerce of the market were well known to Beal, well known to any domestic in America. Any young black woman could be at the grocer at six in the morning or on the pier at Hampton at five in the evening buying a nice fat rockfish and no one would pay it any mind, but here on the rue Cler, they knew she was buying this food for herself, for her husband. They teased her about Thomas, Beal told him, pantomimed him sleeping on flattened hands, and when she took him there for the first time after a week or so as they were closing up their stalls, the men—the fishmonger, the butcher, the greengrocer—winked at him lustily, and the women, the baker's wife, the cheesemaker, patted and stroked Beal on the back and arm, saying that this was how he must treat her. "*Comme ça, M. Thomas,*" they said.

A few weeks later, after they had begun to acclimate themselves to Mme Vigny's comings and goings, to the unfamiliar rhythms of city life, to their own slightly numb disbelief that all this was happening, Thomas and Beal sat at the window balcony overlooking the avenue, saying very little, holding hands. The sun had set over the rooftops and spires, and the calm of twilight was settling all around them like dust. Up and down the street, people were opening their shutters for the evening; before he understood the French custom with these shutters, Thomas had assumed that most of these buildings were closed up for the winter or abandoned. Mme Vigny had lit the gas jet in the kitchen behind them, but there was still a gleam of dusk on the teapot in front of them, and Thomas was in no hurry to break the charm of this restful Paris evening. Beal felt warm and precious at his side.

"It really is beautiful, don't you think?" he asked.

"Yes," she said. "I don't even want to tell you what I thought it would be like."

"You always said you had no idea, that you'd just have to see."

"Well . . ." she said.

Thomas laughed and gave her arm a jiggle. "What? You have to tell me."

"Oh," she said. "I thought it would be too dangerous to be outside without soldiers to protect us. I thought we would be robbed, killed maybe. That's all I'd ever heard about France, that the roads were unsafe because of robbers." The truth was, she wasn't entirely over that fear. "I thought there would be factories everywhere—I mean, that it was a city of factories making iron things and stuff. And perfume. I couldn't imagine what all these people would be doing here if not working in factories. Of course, I still don't know what people do here."

"They go for walks, it seems."

"Yes. I thought the only people we'd see outside, besides robbers and policemen, would be old widows and men missing legs from wars."

They sat quietly for a few more minutes as the last of the evening dusk withdrew from the room. All around them were the flavors of cooking; neither of them had ever imagined that food would be attended by such fragrances. On the streets the smells were far less agreeable, but up here at the rooftops, everything seemed to have the fragrance of wildflowers, even in winter.

"This afternoon I walked to the river," she said. "I sat on a bench and watched. So much going on, so many people walking by, the boats in the river. Monique and Gilberte were there chasing each other around a fountain. The girls call their Mamas *Maman*," said Beal, forcing the *m* sound through her sinuses. "One of the *Mamans* spoke to me, but of course I didn't know what she said."

"Well, did it seem she was saying something nice?"

"Not really nice or not. Not anything really. I think she was asking whether the girls playing in the courtyard bothered us. I just smiled. The girls seem sort of afraid of me. Maybe they've never seen a colored person before."

"They seem like very polite girls. I think here in France people don't talk to strangers on the street. People are polite, but not friendly." As if to cast doubt on this thought, a clang came from the kitchen and then the sound of something being pounded.

"Did you find that library?" Beal asked. That's what he had set out to do that day, to find an English-language reading room on the rue de Rivoli that Fred Shippen had told him about.

"Yes, a library, but also sort of a bookstore—I think it will be useful to me."

She gave a murmur of assent and he watched her reflect for a moment on the word *useful.* Yes, some sort of utility, which meant some way to begin to pierce this land, to find beneath the sheen of beauty and monument something firmer to latch a life onto.

When Thomas had arrived at the library, he was shown to what a young Irish girl called "the den," and in this rather musty space he found newspapers and guidebooks and illustrated magazines in English, and before he could stop himself, he was hungrily devouring those homey sounds and words. After about an hour of this, he began to wander around the edges, into the book stacks. The Irish girl took him for a quick tour, pointing out that this was one of the most complete libraries in English on French culture and industry, with sections—she pointed to some as she mentioned them in alphabetical order—on ceramics, steelmaking, textiles, wine. Thomas thanked her; her name was Eileen Hardy, and on first glance she was a bit sad-faced, but she was pretty and as copper-haired as Thomas's mother—a favorite, not surprisingly, of the male clientele.

Thomas stood in front of the tall bookcases, eyes darting, as if this were a magic maze of sorts, a labyrinth of ideas; he had, for a moment, a hallucination of these shelves of books opening like a door, each section of volumes a path, a future, and him stepping through. Could he read himself into his own life? The idea quite shook him; this was the way his father and his sister had confronted the world—worlds of peach trees and dairy cows—and it was a way he had roundly rejected because, at least for his father, the results had been tragic. But on the way out, the girl smiled a lovely smile at him—she seemed to dart from sunshine to shadow—and said she hoped he'd be back. Oh yes, he said, he would be back the next day.

Thomas had momentarily lost himself in this recollection—he felt a slightly elated tremor in his chest at the thought that he had the beginnings of a plan—and Beal brought him back. "For us," she said. "Useful for us."

"Yes," said Thomas, but he kept the slight tremor of elation to himself, as if he doubted that she would take comfort in a future got out of a book. He did not want to say that a very pretty red-haired girl had shown him around.

"The strangest days of my life," he said in order to change the subject. "So happy and so strange at the same time. Don't you think?"

"There's nothing strange about us," said Beal.

"No," he said, giving her hand a squeeze. "We're just ordinary. Ordinary love."

"That was my point."

"Everyone keeps saying we will be happy here," said Thomas. "That people won't be mean to us."

"Yes. There was a man on the boat who told me that, and he was right—" She stopped quickly.

Thomas knew she hadn't meant to say this, but it had come out in the lazy pleasure of this moment. "Who was that?" he said.

"Oh. Just nobody. Someone I ate with in steerage."

"That tall, African-looking man?"

"Thomas, I don't remember who it was who said it. That African man, he helped me get settled that first night. There were other colored on the boat. African men look all the same to you, I bet."

The last of the light was fading now, and whether they wanted it or not, Mme Vigny would soon come in with a taper and ruin the mood. Everything had to happen just so with her; she seemed to be the guardian of all things French, perhaps not a bad thing as they tried to get used to this life.

"You're really getting on here, aren't you?" he said.

"Oh. I'm not doing so much. You're learning French. You're planning our lives. Besides, maybe it's easier for women. Even for a little colored girl like me."

To Beal's relief, Stanley Dean had found his cot in the Latin Quarter very soon after they moved into their apartment, but before he moved from the hotel, he asked if he could draw her picture. Beal didn't know exactly what was being asked of her, and he explained that all she would have to do was sit in a chair someplace and let him copy her. "Just pastels," he said, holding up a chalky-looking crayon. "On paper. Just a sketch."

The whole thing struck her as odd, but Thomas told her that Stanley had already mentioned it, and it seemed all right to him. Stanley sat her in a chair in the lobby and then set up a little stool he had brought with him. He lay the pad across his knees, and even though he was drawing her likeness, it seemed that he quickly forgot she was there. Céleste's sister, Oriane, came to run the front desk, and she giggled. Stanley finished one and held it up to the light. "No," he said. "No. No."

"Why no?" Beal asked. "Did I do it wrong?"

"Wrong?" Stanley wasn't really listening, but he finally took note. "Wrong? You? No. Your skin tone's too dark in this one." He let it saw back and forth to the floor. "I've never done a Negro."

"Oh," she said.

"More red in your skin than I thought," he mumbled, mostly

to himself, and went back to work. A few minutes later he laughed faintly to himself. "Your hair is fun," he said, moving his crayon wildly. Beal wondered what kind of crazy person he'd make her look like. When he was done, she expected him to give the pictures to her, at least to show them, but he did not; instead, he rolled them up and tied them with a piece of black ribbon.

"Did they come out well?" she asked, but now that he had put away his crayons, his paper, the tools of his trade, he became once more the awkward bumbler she was familiar with.

"Oh. Gee. I don't know," he said. He clutched the roll to his side protectively. "I never know until I live with them for a few days. Especially . . ." He trailed off.

"Especially what?"

"Well, I'm sorry, because you're so pretty."

Beal didn't know exactly how she felt about Stanley's saying that, but what of it? It was as if, for Stanley, there were three people in the room: herself, him, and the version of her he had put on paper, a version that treated her beauty as nothing but a layer, like her clothes. Stanley still seemed pretty silly to her, but she saw that there was something firm in him; the awkward boy who sets out on an arduous quest has to have special sturdiness within. A couple of times she and Thomas had sat with his group at the café, and it struck her that the other boys, especially that scary Virginian whom Thomas liked, had seemed to recognize this about Stanley too. All except for the dark presence who was always there, the man named Arthur, always in the same seat, never joining the conversation but instead sniping in from the side whenever it pleased him.

As the December afternoons became shorter and shorter, Thomas and Beal took long walks on routes that crisscrossed the river on the innumerable bridges. Beal was surprised that walking was such a pastime for so many different types of people; at home, no one would walk anywhere unless they had somewhere to get to. But here, there was so much to see—the people, of course, but more oddly, each time they strolled along the quai or entered a boule-vard or square, it looked different; it was the light, the color and height of the sun, the way shadows played down the facades of these stone monuments, the way the streetlamps fluttered in the fog, the way the bridges seemed to float when the air was slack. It seemed to Beal that she could live here for decades and still not see these scenes in every one of their costumes.

Often they boarded an omnibus and got off randomly in some other neighborhood, going as far as the Île de la Cité, crossing the river on the Pont-Neuf and landing on the Right Bank, and one day they found themselves at the edge of the great market, Les Halles, where, Beal had learned, all the shopkeepers and stalls got their wares, their produce and meat and fish. A writer had called it "the belly of Paris," Beal had been told by Diallo Touré. And as they stared across the vast ground under the iron-and-glass roof of the market, which was mostly deserted at this hour, Beal remembered—she'd never forgotten—that Touré had said his apartment was in this district and that he often went to a café right at the edge of the market called . . . Well, she couldn't remember what it was called until she looked up and saw a frosty door etched with the words CAFÉ SALY. The words brought back the memory of him speaking to her, how mean he was to her sometimes, how he liked to belittle her, how he insinuated himself on her, and Beal thought at this moment that if she walked into this favorite spot of his on Thomas's arm, if Touré were there and could see that she had no fear of him, that she and especially Thomas were doing right good here in this Paris, then that would be the very last of Diallo Touré.

All of this was wrong, beginning with what Beal told herself were her intentions. She recognized that as soon as they walked in, with Thomas slightly surprised by her insistence that they stop and then slightly discomfited to see that almost everyone else in the café was colored, black like Africans or brown like Arabs, and that all the waiters were taller than Thomas, giants, really. With all that, there was no mistaking M. Touré sitting in a corner, unmoving, like a cat. Their eyes met, and he let out the same smile she'd seen through the railway car window in Le Havre as she and Thomas and Madame Bernault rushed past to first class; it felt like a slap, this meeting of the eyes, and she staggered enough so that Thomas thought she had tripped. Instantly she realized that she had fallen into the trap Touré had laid for her; in horror it came to her that if she had not come here, she would never have laid eyes on him again, but that now she would never be rid of him. Thomas found them a table, but as soon as he headed off to find the WC, there was Diallo Touré, standing above her.

"Mademoiselle Beal. What a pleasure to see you."

"Go away."

He ignored this. "But you have come as I directed."

"We didn't. I was walking with my husband." She looked nervously in the direction Thomas had gone and realized that even that was a mistake.

He smiled. "I see," he said. "Perhaps you will come back another time, and we can continue our discussions at more leisure."

She did not respond to this, and by the time Thomas had returned, Touré was gone, almost as if he had disappeared.

Thomas had gone back to Galignani's the day after his first visit. He'd had a dream about those book stacks. In the dream they were numberless, slightly terrifying, and then, of course—who else?—his father appeared at the end of a corridor, wagging a disapproving finger. The person who might have appeared as another member of this stacked jury was Mother Digby—he woke almost daily with her contempt for him on his mind—but in this case his father needed no help. In the dream, Thomas could not discern exactly what he was being scolded for: selecting the wrong volume or, well, just being his own feckless self. What could a son do with a father like that? In almost any way that counted, Wyatt Bayly had been without flaw, a visionary, a reformer, a person driven by the quest for scientifically proved certainties. He'd married Thomas's mother at the very end of the war and taken on her moribund Eastern Shore farm, had led that whole part of the state into a booming peach industry in which everyone got rich only to watch it all die twenty years later. The "yellows" is what they called it, the blight that wiped them out, an unstoppable and malevolent force of nature, a cyclone that ravaged the county, and not with the suddenness of catastrophe but with the slow accretion of despair. There had been times during his earlier youth that Thomas took pleasure in the way his father's plans were falling apart, but in the end it was all just too ghastly, too soul-destroying to do anything but sympathize. Thomas would find him late at night in his study, staring not into, but at the large microscope sitting on his desk amid a jumble of roots and leaves, gnarled pieces of twig, and rotting bits of fruit, staring at it in a rage for not producing the answers he sought. The brilliant brass microscope became the centerpiece of Wyatt's resistance, a line in the sand from the first day the yellows arrived on the Eastern Shore. They had been chasing the poor peaches from the Hudson River Valley down through New Jersey and into Delaware and Maryland; each time the industry moved south, the yellows followed, and as far as Thomas had been able to tell, the whole doleful caravan was now marching through North Carolina.

The microscope had taken over the room, but the whole thing started with the books. Thomas knew this because his father had sermonized to him on the subject of books, of research, of knowledge. In the months before he and Ophelia married, Wyatt had conducted exhaustive research into the possible uses—crops, resources, amenities—of Mason's Retreat and had decided, first, that grain had no future, for the revived Baltimore and Ohio Railroad would soon be shipping in wheat from Ohio, but that fruit, especially the fragile little peach, could not be shoved onto a railway car as if it were a bag of grain. Wyatt knew about the yellows before he even started, but here he made the fatal mistake— here is where, so Thomas believed, the books had led him fatally astray because there was something in there that made Wyatt believe he knew how to stop the yellows. And he didn't. The books didn't, as it turned out, have a clue.

But here, years later, was Thomas heading off after lunch to confront the bookcases of Galignani's. He walked down the Quai d'Orsay and crossed the river on the Pont de la Concorde, marching *tout droit*, as they say, toward the Obelisk and the Madeleine. The French loved things that lined up—that had been clear to him from the first day. The Baron Haussmann had simply obeyed the will of the people. Thomas half hoped that this trip to Galignani's would turn out to be a pointless and useless gesture—books!—but the thing about books was that they were often the last chance, the last stop along the way to the abyss. What other option did he have?

In the months to come he would make this trip many times—at first just to Galignani's but later to the library on the rue Tronchet, and even in the bitterest weather he enjoyed this half hour along the banks of the Seine. In his waterborne youth he'd gotten used to the rivers of the Chesapeake as highways of commerce; during harvest the steamers called at the Retreat every afternoon and swept the peaches to market. But here in Paris, at this point in the mighty river's flow, except for the laundry and bathing barges and an occasional lighter with some high-priority cargo, the passage was reserved for the *bateaux-mouches* or the barges of the rich; even as Thomas admired the French for making this sacrifice to beauty, it did seem wasteful to him. His father's son, he did not think that utility was ugly. Nor did he know then that in years to come, he would once again rely somewhat on a watery highway—the Canal du Midi in Languedoc—but at this point in his research he'd never even heard of the Canal du Midi or, for that matter, the whole region of Languedoc.

When he returned that second time to Galignani's, he was disappointed not to see the Irish girl at the desk. He'd wondered about her the night before, why she was in Paris, why she had this job. It didn't seem very jolly. He'd overheard her speaking French, and even to his ears she wasn't very good. But on the way over he had composed—why he thought he might need it was another question—a small explanation of his interest in the collections: He was relocating, he would be making a study of certain industries, did his two-franc-per-month membership allow him to withdraw unlimited volumes? But it was a dour, dyspeptic middle-aged Frenchman at the desk, and therefore only the last topic seemed worthy of effort and Thomas figured he'd face the issue later. Instead he wound through the reading room, where men of all stripes—maybe the presence of a rougher sort explained why, as Thomas had learned, the English and American ladies tended to prefer the reading room at *The New York Herald* up the street at l'Opéra—studied their newspapers and periodicals, smoked and dozed.

He stood facing the first of the stacks. A wall of books, and there happened to be some groups of lighter-colored volumes that stared back at him like two eyes. Thomas had fun, for a second, placing his father's face over them, but the joke quickly paled, followed by a moment of panic: What did he think he was doing here in this library, here in France, following this doomed strategy? His spirits flagged. Yesterday this wall of books seemed full of the future for him, a trove of possibilities; today the whole thing seemed a last stop on the way to Hell. He wandered a bit through the stacks, his eyes darting over the prominent section labels: GLASS, PERFUME, CERAMICS, TEXTILES ("see: fibres"). Why not just go straight to STEEL and learn how to make a Bessemer furnace? He returned to his original spot, feeling his heart race: yesterday this had seemed like salvation, but today perhaps it was all just a near miss, as good as a mile, as Hattie's Mary, the woman who had largely raised him, often used to say.

He must have stood there for quite a long time, as the next thing he heard was a pleasant voice from behind saying, in a thick Irish accent, "Are you all right, Monsieur?"

He turned and without doubt revealed far too much—his state of fear, his pleasure—when his eyes settled on Eileen Hardy. "Miss Hardy!" he said.

"I thought that was you." She was quite short, but that hair! Remarkable. She took a step back so she could address him better. "You seemed quite excited yesterday."

It rushed to Thomas's mind to say all sort of things to her— that his mother in America had copper hair like hers, was famous throughout the county for it, and other things. He might also have said that there was a large family of Hardys in his town at home, and in fact he had just that second been remembering one of them, Hattie's Mary Hardy, but then he would probably have to explain the reason for her odd—to European ears—name, and he didn't want to do that. The lines he had composed on his walk over about relocating seemed idiotic now. He pondered all this long enough for her to repeat her first question.

"You seem," she said, "quite . . . well"—she pursed her freckled brow, searching for the word—"confused." It was a slightly forward thing for this woman to say to a library patron, but it was delivered with a mordant twist, a sly humor, which Thomas liked.

"Yes. Perhaps that is so," he said, making sure to sound rueful and not in full-blown panic. He went on to say that he had some research in mind but wasn't entirely sure where to begin.

"Can I help?" she asked. "Is this research in a certain industry?"

Thomas glanced back at the case in front of him: it went from AGRICULTURE ("see: crops") to CERAMICS. "I'm not quite sure yet."

She looked at him with appealing disbelief; she might well have thought he was crazy, disturbed, but instead she took it all for a game of sorts. "Well then, I'll leave you to it," she said, as if it were the opening gambit.

Thomas was left alone, and it did not take him long to recognize that he must start with what he knew—sage advice, after all—and as if guided by the most self-destructive of urges, he sought out and found a section on peaches. It did not surprise him that there were twenty or so volumes on the subject—his father had liked to say that peaches were the fruit preferred by Louis XIV—and furthermore, he recognized most of the titles from his father's own fateful collection. But as he thumbed—it was necessary, it seemed to him, to show some focus before Miss Hardy really did dismiss him as a *fou*—he found one volume on walled orchards right here in Paris, in a neighborhood called Montreuil. He quickly became lost in this fascinating tale, how the *murs à pêches* absorbed the sun's heat and sheltered the trees from the winds, which meant that Louis XIV himself could enjoy thin-skinned beauties from June to November. The walls would probably do nothing to slow down the blight, but the yellows was an American disease anyway.

"Well, now," said Miss Hardy, who had come to tell him that the establishment would be closing soon, "you have found a place to start."

He was sitting at one of the tables, with four or five books on peaches arrayed in front of him. He held up the one he was reading for her to see. She cocked her head sideways in order to read the title.

"Oh, yes. The orchards at Montreuil. They used to be quite something, I am told. I live not far from Montreuil."

"Used to be?"

"I think more peaches are now shipped here from the Midi."

"The Midi? The South? The middle, or something like that?"

Yes, she said, as far as Parisians were concerned, the Midi was anywhere south, a sort of uncivilized center. She added, "Are peaches of interest to you?"

The question was so innocent, yet so grotesque to Thomas that he couldn't help laughing, laughing quite hard. She was used, it seemed, to offering up her own brand of cheek, but this laughter took her aback and clearly hurt her feelings.

"No," he said as she began to walk away. "No, please. You don't understand." And in order not to lose her, he began the briefest possible version of his family's story, of the Retreat, which ballooned a bit into the catastrophe of the yellows, his father's desperate and doomed attempts to find a cure, and before he knew it, he had admitted to her that he was now living in France and hoping that this library could help him decide what to do with himself—how, really, to start over again. He said nothing about Beal; he did not say he was married.

He had remained seated during this blighted tale, and she had remained standing next to the table, with her hand on the chair back opposite him, and as he was winding down, she looked behind her to see that the reading room was now empty and her disagreeable superior was glaring at her. "Well," she said. "Perhaps not peaches then. We Irish know all about blight, after all." A polite smile, for a moment, disappeared into a flutter of pain. "Apples?"

"This may surprise you," he said. "But there are certain rivalries among orchardists. My father thought apples were a crude and uninteresting plant. Apples would be disloyal to my father's memory. He doesn't have much else, to tell the truth." She flinched a little on that. Thomas had not wasted much time on the family dynamic during his quick history, so perhaps this mean note surprised her, but in fact, he took her reaction to suggest that there was plenty of family drama in her own story: people came to Paris for all sorts of reasons, but of the Irish, of whom there were many in Paris, Thomas had gotten the impression that most had fled here, escaped here, not unlike himself. "My father is an even longer story," he said.

"They usually are." She gathered up the books in front of him and was heading to the stack when she stopped and turned. "Then how about grapes?"

"I'm sorry?" Thomas was busy speculating about her story and had to be reminded of what they had been talking about." You mean, growing grapes?"

"Yes. You'd be right at home."

"Why is that?"

"Well, for one thing, they've been almost wiped out by blight, but they are coming back. It's your chance to succeed where your father failed."

She walked him around to the section on grapes, an entire wall of books. Thomas stood back. Grapes, wine: he could imagine absolutely nothing that seemed more French and therefore more impossible for him to pierce. The sight should have been over-whelming; the old Thomas would have been halfway home by now, but a strange new sensation had been creeping into him these past weeks. He looked up at the challenge of these books and said to himself, this is big enough to bother with. How remarkable to recognize in a single instant that he had been going about every-thing in his life, everything but his love for Beal, with exactly the wrong objectives. Not *small enough for me to succeed*, but *large enough to keep my interest*. His fingers tingled, as if they wanted to begin pulling volumes from the shelf. How extraordinary. Eileen was looking at him intently; clearly some of the scale of this stranger's moment was evident to her, and she seemed pleased that, as a good librarian should, she had nudged him into a new topic. From behind them *monsieur le directeur* was complaining at a high pitch. Thomas looked at Eileen and smiled. "Yes," he said. "Perhaps I'll look at grapes next time."

It was now a few days before Christmas, and Stanley had arranged for Beal and Thomas to be invited to a dinner with a few of his fine fellows and two of the women students, Hilary Devereux and Colleen Sullivan, who studied in the separate wing at the Acadé-mie Julian. Hilary's mother had moved over from Boston for the winter to accompany her daughter, but Colleen was in Paris on her own, living in a "most respectable"—said Stanley—establishment for female students run by two maiden sisters, the Mesdemoiselles Rostand. They would be dining at a restaurant called Prévost's, on the river. The only problem, said Stanley, was that Hilary's mother would be there. "A terrible snob," said Stanley. "But Hilary is loads of fun."

Beal had been dreading this turn, this public outing, but Thomas was pleased. "I'm glad you will be meeting some girls," he said. "Maybe you could be friends."

Beal could not imagine this. Artists? White girls? Not people who would likely want her as a friend. Almost every time she and Thomas went out for a walk, they attracted some sort of attention— looks of scorn from large, buxom *dames* or some sort of mingled rebuke and curiosity from men of almost any age. Maybe recently it had been happening less, or maybe Beal was noticing less, but it was still there. They had dined out only at the Lion d'Or, where any complaint about them would have been stifled by the effusive warmth of M. Richard, his wife, or Céleste and Oriane. The cafés, in the afternoon, tended to serve the same clientele; if there were those at the nearby Café du Pont who still found them objectionable, most had given up paying them any notice at all. Except, of course, if an American happened to drop in. Yes, Beal could always spot the Americans, the "missionaries," as Touré had called them, and lately she had taken to flaunting her relationship with Thomas—putting a hand on his arm, leaning her head into his—just to irritate them. But she and Thomas knew nothing of this place, Prévost's, and of these girls, and of this mother.

"You should go," she said.

"And not you?"

"Thomas, they don't want me."

Thomas simply laughed at that, and Beal, stung, waited for him to explain himself. "Don't you understand?" he said. "Stanley's pastel pictures are posted on the wall at their school. Stanley says they all want to meet you. I bet that's the real reason for this dinner. I'm the afterthought here, not you."

Beal could not argue against that, because it seemed to be true;

not the "afterthought" part, but the way Stanley, embarrassingly, fixed on her every time they met. She knew that people tried to sit beside her the few times she had visited the Café Badequin; this wasn't very subtle. And so it seemed to her that this dinner was worth a try, and if she was turned away at the door or if there was a terrible scene, then Thomas would never again be able to ask her to do something like it. It was a wedding night all over again, but, as with her wedding night—as she counted off the days before this dinner with dread—she also could not still a tiny flame of interest. Imagine! she said to herself. Well, I'll be!

The night was cold; neither Thomas nor Beal had winter coats yet, but when they arrived at Prévost's they were greeted by a blast of heat and light, conversation and instructions among the staff. Beal had seen this welcoming bustle many times in restaurants as Thomas and she walked by—voices and laughter, colors and stylish clutter, lamps pouring out light. In truth, she had from time to time wished they might go in, and here she was. She stood at Thomas's side as he announced them to the maître d', and she looked around for the disapproving looks, the stares, and didn't see any. No one seemed to notice them or care about them; this was a sort of raucous place anyway, perhaps not totally respectable, a place where artists might mingle with bankers, where older men could entertain younger women, actresses, even.

They were shown up a narrow flight of stairs, following a waiter in a white coat who navigated the tight turns with an enormous tray balanced on his fingertips. "Ah!" exclaimed the watchful Stanley from a long table over in a corner by the windows. The glass was foggy and frosted, and through it, the light from the street outside broke into more color, more ornament. Quite a few fine fellows seemed to have shown up, which made sense, as Hilary Devereux's mother was paying for this, and little Stanley Dean, such a lonely sight a month ago, was ebullient. "We've saved you places of honor."

One of the places of honor turned out to be at the center of the table, directly opposite the hostess. Thomas was placed there. A good choice, thought Beal. This woman, with her tight jaw and jewels, reminded her of Thomas's mother, Miss Ophelia. No one at the Retreat, even Thomas, ever saw much of her, as she lived mostly in Baltimore, but still, he would know how to talk to people like that. Beal was placed toward the end, near the window, beside Stanley—naturally—but on the other side was a plump and unscary girl named Colleen Sullivan, sandy-haired and freckled, and across from her was Hilary.

Hilary jumped right in as soon as Beal sat down. "*You*," she said. "*Beal* at last." She turned to Colleen, as if she needed a cue. "Thomas and Beal," she stage-whispered.

"Yes, Hilary. I can see that."

Beal found this a little odd, to be spoken of like this, but there was nothing about it to give offense.

"We've all seen Stanley's pastels," said Colleen. She turned to look at Beal more directly.

Beal raised her hand to cover her mouth.

"They're quite good," said Hilary, her eyes slightly narrowed, a slight squint. "The best things he's done."

Stanley let out a small cough, but he did not dispute it.

"You inspired him," said Colleen. "Actually, he's talked a lot about you."

"Oh now . . ." said Stanley, reddening.

"You have to forgive painters," said Hilary. "We're always look-ing for models. I'm tired of painting my mother." She leaned her head toward the center of the table. Beal felt a slight tremor of fear, but the lady was engaged with Thomas, so perhaps all would be well. "Do you like portraits?" Hilary asked Beal. "Colleen doesn't," she added.

"Well," said Colleen. "A sort of long discussion . . ."

Beal had seen plenty of portraits in her life, the portraits of Masons on the walls of Mason's Retreat and the Lloyds at Blaketon, the estate on the other side of Tuckertown. Men in furrowed col-lars and women with lace in their hair; soldiers pointing behind them to the battlefield where they were killed; little white boys in silk suits with their pet dogs. In one or two family portraits a ser-vant or slave was in the background, an arm out in the universal posture of service. Aunt Zoe used to talk about those pictures: *White men*, she said, *slave drivers. What was they thinking while folks died in their fields?*

"I guess I've never really seen the point of them unless they're your kin," Beal answered. "I don't mean any disrespect."

Colleen laughed, said that there was no offense taken; most people where she grew up, in Brockton, Massachusetts, thought art was a waste of time. "Shoes," said Colleen. "Everyone in Brockton is in the shoe business. They think the reason the North won the war was because they had better shoes. My father thinks civilization began with the invention of shoes."

"He might have a point," said Stanley. He stamped on the floor as if to show off his boots.

"Yes, Stanley," said Hilary. "I am sure Colleen's papa would approve of your footwear."

When this joke died, all three of them turned to Beal; she couldn't imagine what to say. "I don't know noth . . . anything much about shoes or art. Maybe a little about something in between," said Beal, which everyone liked.

"Come with us to the Louvre tomorrow," said Hilary. "It's the museum," she added with a shrug; Beal already knew what the Louvre was, but Hilary had said it in a way that did not imply that Beal was ignorant. "We go there to copy master paintings. It's kind of silly."

"I don't think it sounds silly at all," said Beal. "To be able to copy a famous picture. I can't imagine such a thing." She'd never been to a museum, though when she lived in Hampton, her employer insisted that all his staff go to the library at the Hampton Institute once a week.

"Thomas could bring you to the entrance to the Pavillon Denon at ten," Colleen announced. "And then he'll go do whatever he does with his time."

Waiters appeared with small plates of fish, and the one who served Beal reached down and placed the correct fork on her plate. She did not mind at all; she noticed that he did it for the others, except for Hilary, as if it was evident that she knew which from which. When another waiter came around and poured Beal some wine, she watched the glass fill with alarm. She glanced up and down the table to see if people were drinking it yet, and because they were, she raised the glass to moisten her lips. The pale, astringent drops took her breath away, and she put the glass down hastily. If anything, it tasted like spoiled milk.

"Don't worry," said Colleen. "I don't like wine either. My father drinks whiskey."

"We never drunk anything except some peach wine from time to time. There was an old lady in our village who made it," said Beal.

"She was raised on a farm in Maryland," volunteered Stanley.

"An orchard, actually," Beal said.

"And now you're here in Paris."

"Yes. It still feels very strange to me."

"That's the thing about this city," said Colleen. "We're all from somewhere so different. See that boy up there with the red cravat?" She pointed down the table. "He grew up in Iowa. How did he even know Paris existed? To get here, he took a boat down the Mississippi to New Orleans and then a steamer to Portugal. It's crazy."

"None of us belongs here," said Hilary. "I mean, look at Stanley. He's from *Pittsburgh*."

"Oh no, Hilary," said Stanley. "*You* belong here. You act as if you own the place, and you probably do."

This was the way the conversation went. Everything these people said was meant to be funny in a way that Beal had never encountered, a sort of joking about others, a teasing that would not have gone over very well in Tuckertown, or on the Retreat either. Hilary and Colleen: these were women with schooling, from wealth, people in her former life she might one day have been working for, but they acted as if nothing mattered all that much, that you could make fun of the thing you cared about most in life.

"Stanley! You have scored a point, I believe," said Colleen in a sort of officious, deep voice. Her normal voice was quite high and squeaky. She reminded Beal of the little girl Gilberte in their building, and perhaps it was just the charm of this sweet little face passing before Beal's eyes, but suddenly she felt her whole body relax. Her shoulders, her neck, her forearms and hands—all, it became clear, had been clenched with fear, and now she became light-headed with an obscure kind of joy: she could do this. It was as if, she thought, a miracle was working within herself, that she had recaptured a sense of being just herself, of being just a girl back at the Retreat, just a maid in Hampton, and now just a woman at dinner. She fought this as some kind of illusion, but then relaxed into it. For a second or two she worried that it was the wine, that she was drunk, but she looked at her glass and realized she'd had only that one sip, and surely it took more wine than that to make someone silly. Yes, she had settled in far more than she realized. She had found in this world a place that was good to her. She finished her fish, surprised by the succession of dishes to come, and felt she must finish it all despite the fact that Colleen and Hilary sent their plates back hardly touched. How strange life is, she thought. How can this be happening to me?

At the middle of the table, Thomas was having a very different experience. Mrs. Devereux—oh yes, he knew her well. Any one of his mother's friends would do: Mrs. Benton Lloyd, with her limp and her fear of hot weather; Mrs. MacAlistair in Baltimore, one of his mother's Catholic pack, so determined to hold her high position. Thomas did not mind their pretensions, really; everyone has to make his or her way in the world. What he disliked about them was their frailty, an adopted manner that seemed designed to appear just slightly infirm, and Mrs. Devereux had lots of ailments; consulting famous physicians seemed to be a good bit of the reason for her winter sojourn here.

"But you have a family connection here?" she was saying to Thomas.

"Oh yes." He snapped back to attention. "A small one. My sister went to convent school here ten years ago."

"So I gathered. A Catholic school?"

What other kind of convent is there? Thomas wanted to say. He knew where this was going and tried to head it off. "My mother is very proud of the fact that our family is descended from the earliest Catholic immigrants in Maryland. 'English Catholics,' she would say."

Mrs. Devereux didn't see much in this distinction. The only Roman Catholics she knew in Boston were her maids and servants. "And you went to such a school in Maryland?"

No, Thomas said, he had studied at home. His father had been a technical man and had overseen Thomas's schooling, an experiment that included Beal's brother, Randall. Mrs. Devereux recoiled at this.

"I would have thought there would be something more suitable for old families. If not, you could have been sent away. To Phillips Academy, perhaps."

Thomas shrugged.

"You have heard of Phillips Academy, of course."

"No, I haven't," he answered, but he had; one of his classmates at the University of Pennsylvania had gone there.

"I would suppose not. It is a school for Protestant boys, after all."

The conversation died there, which seemed more than fine to Thomas, except that it would soon become awkward, and she was staring at him. He tried a less controversial tack. "My mother spent most of the year here when my sister was in school, as I remember. She lived on the Quai d'Orléans."

"How fascinating. I have also taken a large flat on the Île Saint-Louis. I find it quite primitive."

Thomas glanced down at Beal; she was laughing. She had rarely looked so beautiful. The men, the painters, at the other end seemed lost in ambitious talk: the Salon, *la vie moderne*. His spirits crashed; maybe here, in the middle, talking to this awful hag was the place he belonged.

"My wife and I are very satisfied with our quarters on the avenue Bosquet," he said. He wished he were there at this moment.

"I'm sure your mother never imagined that her son would be here in—well, your circumstances."

"I'm not sure I know what you mean—'in my circumstances.'"

"You left America because of your marriage."

"Yes."

"I don't understand it, myself," she said, lowering her voice only slightly. Out of the corner of his eye Thomas saw a sudden alertness on the face of her daughter, who had clearly been monitoring this conversation with one ear.

"My marriage?" he asked.

"It seems like an unnecessary risk." She waved away a waiter offering a lemon ice. "You could never be sure."

"Sure of what?"

"Well, they can't be trusted, can they now? It's not their fault. Everything was provided for them."

"Mother," said Hilary. Between Hilary and her mother was a young Englishman, one of the few at the Académie. He had only a vague idea of what she was talking about, but he understood that he was caught in the middle of something unpleasant.

"I can't imagine a Christian vow means all that much to them. How could it?"

"Mother," said Hilary again.

"I'm not saying anything so scandalous, am I?"

Thomas had his napkin poised to be flung down; the artists at their end had stopped their conversation and had all their eyes on him. Fred Shippen, Thomas's friend from Virginia . . . in his heart, he probably would have agreed with this woman, at least before he got to know Beal a little. The maître d' had caught a tremor from the corner table and was angling over to see whether trouble was brewing. Only Beal and Stanley and the other girl had heard nothing of this and were still talking, laughing. Thomas wasn't sure he'd seen Beal laugh like this since they were children.

He could picture how it might go if he flung down the napkin—the hasty departure, the apologies at the top of the stairs from Hilary, the assurance that they would get together soon despite all this misunderstanding, though they never would. A cold and tearful cab ride back to their flat. Or . . . Or Thomas could do what he'd seen Beal herself do a hundred times: take it. Take it for her as she had been doing for him. Look through it, beyond it. Protect her dignity in a world that was determined not to let her have any. Go home the victor. Oh, how much Beal could teach this woman and her ilk about bearing and carriage. Such integrity was not something others gave you, it was something others—like this woman—tried to take away, for sport or out of fear and hatred. Thomas returned his napkin to his lap. Mrs. Devereux still wore that wounded little look, as if she couldn't possibly imagine what all this stir was about, but the delicious pleasure of it, so ripe in her eyes, faded as she observed Thomas relaxing his arms, leaning back, taking a sip of water.

Hilary appealed to him one last time, and he waved her off

reassuringly. "I'm sure you will be relieved to hear that my wife is a person of the strongest moral caliber. Perhaps in Boston you are not aware of what being freed from slavery can do."

"Perhaps not," Mrs. Devereux said. She was already turning to the Englishman at her side, who looked like a mouse being eyed by a cat. Thomas glanced back at Hilary, who in turn glanced at Beal, still engaged, unsuspecting, and then mouthed a *thank you*. Thomas smiled at her; he shrugged, meaning he'd heard worse, much worse, worse indeed from his own mother—yes, he felt the shrug communicated even *that*—that he could handle this, that this was a small price to pay for his happiness.

On the way home in the cab, with Beal snuggled at his side in her thin pelisse, she asked about the commotion she thought she'd heard, something that happened while that funny girl Colleen was telling a story about her brother being chased by a pig.

"Oh," said Thomas. "Hilary's mother is a real specimen."

"Was it about me?"

"No. Of course not. It was about me. It was about Catholics, I think. And about the South. Hilary was a little embarrassed."

"I liked Hilary. She can't be anything like her mother, then."

"No. All of us here in Paris are trying to become something new, something our parents might not be able to imagine."

"Yes. We are," said Beal.

4

Arthur Kravitz did not like her. The reason he didn't like her was that he believed he understood her. She could claim no privilege of discrimination with him. Not that she would, but that was the point: she wouldn't. She and her husband could escape the bigotry and hatred of America, but he had news for them: France was no Eden. He knew. He was a Jew in France, not a great place to be in 1892. He didn't have to understand a word of French to get the drift of the headlines in certain papers he saw almost daily, *juif* this, *juif* that. He'd sit at a café and he'd hear, *blah, blah, blah, juif, blah, blah*. That the *juifs* were hatching something was one thing the monarchists and republicans, the Catholics and the anti-clericists could all agree on quite nicely. The question was, What Jews were behind all this? And, of course, what was *this*? Well, nobody actually knew what *this* was, but that's the nature of the Jewish conspiracy: fingers into the banks, shipping, the military, all ready to be clenched into a fist when the time came.

Arthur had first seen her at the Café Badequin a few weeks after they arrived, and now that she was coming to the Louvre with the girls, he saw her quite often. He wasn't sure what she was doing there, and this did, in fact, intrigue him, but probably she was just trying to take on a little of the sheen. Arthur hated sheen. He had seen Stanley's pastels, and yes, they weren't bad in a sloppy, Renaissance sort of way—that's the way he thought of them—but Arthur had no interest in angels, even if they were black. Besides, she had poor old Stanley well wrapped around her finger; they all knew that this was absolutely the worst possible situation for a portraitist. Dislike, disdain, contempt, that was better; why else had Sargent made Madame Gautreau look like a whore? Okay, maybe not everyone would agree that he had done this. The women, Colleen, Hilary, Vivian, just couldn't get enough of the romance of the girl and her boy husband, the two child lovers escaping in the dead of night, carriages with the curtains down, something out of penny dreadfuls, something about female beauty, but Arthur had no interest in romance, and no interest in female beauty, as a subject for his work anyway. If that was all portraiture had to work with, to express, Arthur would have been on the first boat back to Newark, back to his father's dry goods business, where he'd worked on and off since he was twelve. If his father would have him back, that is, which he doubted. Arthur was thirty now, though he looked even older because of his balding head, his dark, sagging skin.

Arthur lived alone in a single room on one of the more squalid back alleys in the Quarter; if Haussmann's remaking of Paris hadn't been cut short by the arrival of the Prussians twenty years ago, this would have been the next block to be demolished, Arthur was sure of it. His room was freezing cold, but for all that, it was a big space and had top-floor light. If he had had more money, he would have rented this room only as a studio, but as it was, his tiny cot and small chest of drawers took almost no space away from his paints and supplies, his easel, and the one chair in the room that sat empty but waiting for someone, for some kind of human being from whose body—head and face, trunk, two arms, two legs—his brush could nurse out every truth, every shred of anger, every secret yearning for love that had been bottled up in Arthur Kravitz since he was old enough to hold a pencil. He'd been trying for more than a year, bringing home half-finished canvases from the Académie and working and reworking those boring and bored female figures until the paint was so thick it cracked, but there was no truth to be had, just flesh. This was the injustice of painting. You had to wait for a subject. It was like fishing but far less restful.

Arthur took his meals at two or three cafés within steps of his building. Another man would have revolted at the gristly, unchewable meat, the greasy broth, the never-ending mealy potatoes and wormy cabbage, but Arthur didn't mind. He had come over to Paris with $900 in his pockets, every penny of which he had earned, and in his first year he had spent only $395. He figured Thomas Bayly spent that much in a month. Arthur's father's business was successful; his father had stored in his bank account probably as much as the families of most of his fellow students, but it was a different kind of money, money that was counted carefully, money colored by its sources, not genteel money. It was not money that would be given to anybody, especially to a son who hadn't earned it.

In the late afternoons he'd take his seat at the Badequin, trying, but not always succeeding, to feel superior to his fellow American students, and sooner or later one of these inferior beings might buy him a beer. Here he had apparently first met the boy-husband sometime late in November. Thomas hadn't made much of an impression, but Arthur did remember Stanley Dean gossiping about them after Thomas left, describing this "Negress" he had just met. This slave girl, this noble savage. Arthur figured it was the first time in Stanley's life that he'd actually sat at the same, or adjoining, table with a colored person, but then again, as Arthur thought back, he wasn't sure he ever had either. Even on that first afternoon Stanley had been talking of her sitting for him, announcing that he had her husband's permission. So he claimed, and later, others backed him up. *Stanley asked first*, they said, like the obedient little schoolchildren they were, as if the first person in line couldn't be removed by a good pummeling in the far corner of the playground.

But Arthur did remember well the second time he saw the husband, because that was the first time he saw *her*. Oh, he thought, so that's her. She had at least six inches on him, he figured, but he was not immediately impressed; it was a cold day—only the artists were sitting outside—and her nose was running. There was a slick of mucus on her upper lip. Her eyes, yes, that *was* an unusual color; where did she get those eyes? Arthur mused. She had pretty good posture. Throughout his childhood, Arthur's mother had tried to get him not to slouch, as if such a refinement would win them the place their money should have earned on its own. The young gentlemen fell all over themselves to offer their chairs to her. Had anyone, *anyone* ever made way for him? No. Arthur wondered for a moment what that would feel like; in his mind, most women—like *la Bayly*—who got this treatment figured they deserved it. As Arthur reflected later, no one was making much fuss over her husband; he got pushed a little to the side, almost onto the street, yet seemed not to mind it so much. Hmmm, thought Arthur, maybe there's more to the boy-husband than I thought. The funny thing was that the person who ended up closest to her was that Virginian, Shippen, and he looked as if he had been seated next to a cannibal. For twenty minutes they fell all over her; even Shippen got into the act. But okay, by the end of this little episode Arthur was intrigued. But not because he liked her.

The next time he saw her, she was arriving at the Louvre with Hilary Devereux and Colleen Sullivan; Arthur didn't mind Hilary too much, but that little fat Irish loudmouth reminded him too much of himself. The girl seemed on friendly terms with many members of the group; Arthur must have missed her introductions. Sometimes he had to take a few days off, to keep away; he had these . . . spells when talking was hard. Among all these spoiled rich children she seemed perfectly at ease; he kept his eyes on her just to make sure that this impression was correct. Oh, she was trying to be liked, as anyone would. She was eager, but not afraid. They were all milling about, juggling their easels and paint boxes as they waited for the gallery doors to be opened, and she stood in the center of all this with a kind of nerve that surprised and irritated Arthur, who was short, unsure of himself in crowds, always tending to the edges. It came to him in a sudden burst of revelation: this girl had had it *easy*. That's what Arthur decided; she'd been pampered and flattered her entire life. She had been spoiled to a unique kind of rottenness. Never beaten. Never overlooked. She'd swum naked and innocent in a pool of adoration. No question about that. Yeah, yeah, yeah, a Negro: a soul that has been putrefied by kindness doesn't know it's black. If he painted her, he'd want that savage piece of ironic truth in it. An innocence out of ignorance. He

studied her standing in the crowd and caught a few words; she spoke
softly, but her clear voice carried across the mumble of conversation:
*thank you . . . Thomas doesn't think so . . . yes, I've had it since last
week.* He looked at her in profile, watched her mop her nose with
her handkerchief. Found himself thinking that he would not paint
her in profile: an okay nose, but no feature, no *beak* like Madame
Gautreau. Africans have lousy noses. But those shoulders!

The big gallery doors opened, people leaned down to put out
their cigarettes and take up their things, and she followed Colleen
Sullivan through the portal, a surprisingly short gait for someone
with such long legs. Arthur couldn't see her feet, but he figured
they were long and narrow, like her hands. As Maître Rodolphe
would have it, her hands would be the key, the absolute first thing
the viewer would notice, but not in some fey gesture. No ballerina
here. But no fist. And no open, empty palm. This was the palm of
someone who had been *handed* absolutely everything a human needs
without even asking for it. Her husband could buy anything he
wanted, but he still had to ask for it. No need to pose a model like
that, just catch her unobserved, dressed carelessly and heedlessly.
A knee exposed? The knee and the hand the first thing the viewer
noticed. By the time she had disappeared in the crowd, unaware
that he had been scrutinizing her, Arthur decided two things: first,
in spite of himself, he was hooked by this pampered little American
princess, and second, when the time came, he, and not that squir-
relly little Stanley Dean, would paint her portrait.

He did not approach her, try to win her favor. He just kept an
eye on her. Renoir did this in Montmartre, so he had been told,
scouting out models, following them to see how they walked, how
they gestured. A fairly innocent thing to do, for an artist. One
day he followed her home into the swanky Seventh, and when she
doubled back unexpectedly to look at a storefront, he did not try
to hide. "Oh," she said, recognizing him.

"Yeah," he answered. "Yeah, Kravitz. Arthur Kravitz."

"Yes. Hello Mr. Kravitz. I didn't know you lived around here."

"Around here? Uh, no. Too expensive for me."

She was a little defensive, which he liked, and instead of asking
what he *was* doing around here, she said, "We're not paying so
much."

Stanley shrugged: 250 a month, easy.

"We live here because we have a friend in the neighborhood."

"One of your nuns?" She was surprised, and it was a mistake to let her know so much, but really, all Arthur knew was that part of her story seemed to involve some nuns. Nuns were not something Arthur cared much or thought much about. Still, he had to answer. "Stanley Dean said you had friends who were nuns."

On hearing Stanley's name, all was explained, and she smiled affectionately; she clearly liked Stanley, which could present a problem. "Oh, Stanley thought it was so amazing that my husband's family knew these nuns."

"Catholics?"

"Sure. Are there any other kinds of nuns?" she asked.

"I wouldn't know. I'm Jewish."

She shrugged: she could play that game too. He'd get no points from her for difference. We're both something, was what she was saying. "Well. Nice to see you."

"Yeah."

She walked off, assuming that whatever he was doing here, their business was done, and in fact, she was right. He watched her go and was pleased to see her turn back, look over her shoulder when she reached the corner. Yes, he thought, maybe catch her like that, mostly turned away, looking over her shoulder at someone following. Pretty good shoulders after all, but not looking back fearfully. Looking back exactly *without* fear; for someone like that, being followed is something she would expect, not fear. Of course, if he posed her like that, he'd lose the knee.

A few days later he was talking to Makepeace, who had appointed himself one of her palace guards, and Arthur didn't mind at all that the girl had told Don about this incident, that in some way he was being warned off, when in fact he had done absolutely nothing for anyone to get exercised about. "I don't know what you're talking about," he said. They were setting up at the Académie, dozens of them crammed into the atelier. He, like most of the other students, was putting out his last cigarette before getting to work, and the air was hazy with smoke. The wall behind them was nothing but windows, and the smoke would be gone soon enough, replaced by the frigid chill. On either end of the room, paintings *le maître* had blessed were hung five or six high. Way at the top, at the far right, was one of Arthur's, something he'd done practically his first week there—and since then, nothing. And since then, two paintings by, of all people, Stanley Dean!

The model, a malnourished, probably absinthe-addled woman of indeterminate age, stood up and dropped her robe. The appearance of her rib cage made people around him gasp with dismay and revulsion; they paid the Académie good money for instruction, but this was the sort of cheap goods they'd been given to paint. Arthur had no problem; sure, a lousy model, but this was the kind of female body that aroused his desire. This was a woman he'd bear in mind.

Makepeace broke up Arthur's very brief erotic fantasy; Don was still on the issue of Mrs. Thomas Bayly. "She wasn't sure you weren't following her."

Arthur loved the way these people talked, all these negatives dancing around their true intent. Fit right in with the French, all their *I would like*s rather than *I want*s. As far as Arthur could tell, the French had invented an entire verb tense just so they could do that. Arthur had been raised in the land of *I want*. He hadn't come to Paris because he *would like* something, he came because he wanted what they had to give him, these techniques, these impulses. "I *was* following her," he said. He punctuated that by squeezing out a big bloodred blob of paint on his palette. "Is that such a problem?"

"Here now, Arthur. Of course it's a problem."

"I don't think any harm I caused by following her for a few blocks is much compared with all the talking about her all these people do." He waved his hand around the atelier. The real culprits, he and Makepeace both knew, were the women, but they worked in a separate studio. "Tell her and her husband not to worry. Arthur Kravitz won't follow her again."

In her first visits to the Louvre, after Colleen and Hilary had set up their easels and stools and set to work, Beal was left to wander.

After a while her eyes would spin a little, and not just because she spent so much time with her head back trying to look at the paintings on the top row. What was this all for? For these weeks in Paris, beginning with their first night with Stanley, she had heard talk about art, about making art and understanding art, that was completely new to her. Why art? That's what she didn't quite get. There was nothing like this at home. A pretty picture of a sunset or a scary one of a storm at sea, she'd seen these here and there; her mother, Una, liked to stop in the street of Cookestown in front of stores to look at advertisements or posters. She'd say, *Now isn't that a right peaceful scene*, or *Well, I declare, I wouldn't ever want to be seen in that.* Her mother took these images for what they were, some sort of fact—a place, a hat, a famous person. But here, with hundreds, thousands of paintings of all sizes hung up like miles and miles of laundry, you were supposed to do more than that; you were supposed to feel something or think something, otherwise why would they all be here together? Why would all these young artists be here copying paintings brushstroke by brushstroke unless there was something in them, wholly contained in them, that couldn't be found elsewhere? "It's like those fairy tales where people are under magic spells or something," she said to Thomas that night. Mme Vigny had prepared them a chicken in wine, which Beal didn't like, though she found she didn't mind that Thomas had taken to drinking a glass of wine with his food, that he had begun to take interest in this drink. It made him more talkative, for one thing.

"I don't think I really understand it either," he said. "Half of what Stanley says seems like nonsense to me."

Beal laughed and then turned reflective. "But it's not, is it? The biggest building in Paris is filled with art. That means something."

"Of course," he said.

"Colleen is just a normal girl and she's doing this."

"Well," said Thomas. "I hope you go back. I hope you learn everything in the world you can about it and can explain it to me."

"Oh, Thomas. I'm not good at learning."

"If your mama or Ruthie could hear you say that . . ."

It was supposed to be sort of a joke, she figured, but there was something in the tone that reminded her, well, of Diallo Touré, and really of Colleen and Hilary, of people telling her she should ask more of herself, and when she thought about it, this place— Paris—seemed to be asking her the same thing. It seemed to be *offering* something to her, not standing in her way as she thought it might. So she went back to the Louvre the next day, found Colleen in tears because Maître Rodolphe had said that her Raphael was *affreux, épouvantable*, which was clearly not good. Hilary and two other women were consoling her, and Beal could add nothing to this. She set off wandering again, came around a corner, and there was Stanley Dean. "Beal!" he said. "Everyone said you were here yesterday."

"I'm not sure why anyone would talk about me."

"Oh," said Stanley, blushing a little. "I've said I hope to do an oil of you."

"Fully dressed, I hope," she said. She'd been surprised about all this nakedness on the walls—bare breasts, round abdomens, fleshy thighs, all this white flesh; it seemed pretty overdone. So what, she thought.

Stanley blushed so deeply she felt he might get light-headed. She reached out and steadied him by the arm. "Oh, Stanley. It was a joke."

Stanley regained his composure. "You'd be sensational dressed just the way you are now. Your broad shoulders. Your coloring. Look at your hands," he said, holding out his own rather stubby fingers and square palm. As ordered, she held out hers, smaller than Stanley's but longer. Her fingers were slender, and there was a hint of coral in her palm. "See?" he said. He took her hand into his, ran the tips of his fingers on her flesh. "Hands are everything in a portrait. They're the hardest part. You can't make them up."

At home, white people talked about whether you were colored, not about your "coloring." If they said anything about your body, they'd talk about your strong back, not your broad shoulders; your brawn and not your slender neck and fine hands. And then there were those who said *Step over here out of the sun and close the door after you*, but Stanley wasn't saying that either. He wasn't talking about her beauty, but about what made her beautiful, at least in his eye.

"Promise me," he said.

"Promise you what?"

"That if you let anyone paint you, it'll be me."

"Who else would want to?"

"Hilary. Arthur Kravitz. Believe me. Others. Believe me."

How interesting: Arthur Kravitz. Maybe that was why he had been following her that day. "I'll have to talk to Thomas," she answered.

"Sure. Sure. But promise me that if it's up to you, you'll let me."

So she promised, and for the next few days, as she met more and more of these young American students, people would say, "Oh yeah, Stanley says you'll sit for him," or just "Yes, I know, Stanley's model." The only person who warned her that she might be getting into something more complex than she realized was Alvin Tower, the black student from Hartford. "They all want to own you," he said. She'd had no idea that agreeing to be painted by someone meant that he owned you, but she was beginning to understand all these painters and their little competitive world; she liked them and didn't take Alvin's warning all that seriously. People called these students lazy, but she saw no laziness. They seemed to work from first light to dusk. Beal knew about long hours of toil, and she was also acquainted with laziness. She remembered those men—almost all of them were men—on the Retreat and in Tucker-town who suddenly sprang to action whenever the boss drew near, but no one was ever fooled. Toil is toil, and these students, painters and sculptors, they did it. None of them questioned for a moment that this thing they were after in Paris mattered, that they could find it only in Paris, and that they had a duty to bring this life-changing thing back with them to America. She liked the idea that she might have a tiny bit to do with it.

One night Thomas gave her a package wrapped in the paper of Le Bon Marché, and when she opened it, she found a student notebook—CAHIER, it said on the front—and a fountain pen. "What's this for?"

"Maybe you could write down what you're thinking about all this art you're seeing."

"Write in this book?" She flipped through the blank pages. She could hardly imagine making marks on them; in her house, paper wasn't used frivolously, just for stray thoughts, hen scratches.

"Yes. It's yours to write in. It's your book to make. I want you to write down what you think," said Thomas.

A book. Her mother had made her read at night, even after she'd left school and started to work for the Lloyds at Blaketon, but usually she just pretended and then jumped ahead so she could answer her mother's questions about what was happening in the story. But she'd never been given a blank book and told to write in it. She flipped through the pages, empty lines waiting for what? Her thoughts?

"Oh, Thomas," she said, glancing up at him with dismay. "What am I supposed to say about art? I don't know anything about it."

Thomas came over and sat beside her on the threadbare love seat. He'd said that at the Retreat he had seen enough threadbare upholstery to last several lifetimes, but the two of them liked this little couch facing the fireplace; they liked that it had been there so long that its feet sat in their own dimples on the parquet floor, like the hollowed-out marble steps at Notre-Dame and La Conciergerie. They sat on this love seat often, all entwined.

"Just write down what you say to me every night."

"That's just talk. That isn't writing."

"It's writing to me. I don't know how you know all the things you tell me."

Thomas had come with her to the Louvre a few times so she could show him things she liked, and yes, Beal had to admit to herself that she had loved trying to explain it to him, not the art—she knew nothing about the art—but about what the pictures made her think of.

"It'll just be stupid things."

"No one is going to read it but you. Besides, I don't think they're stupid when you tell me. Am I stupid?"

"Of course I don't think that. You love me. That makes it different."

The next day, still dubious, she packed her notebook and pen along with her lunch, and when the painters all began to set up, she found a stone bench, pulled out her notebook, and wrote her name in the center of the first page. "Beal Terrell," she wrote without thinking, because the whole exercise made her feel like a schoolgirl again, but then she added "Bayly," hoping it didn't look crammed in like an afterthought. She held the book out to see how she had done with these first hen scratchings and was suddenly astonished by what she saw. *Beal Terrell Bayly.* Three names. She'd noticed that both Colleen and Hilary used three names when they signed things, but she didn't know why. Beal Terrell Bayly. Who *was* this person? Her pen seemed to have discovered a person she had never dreamed existed, somebody between Beal Terrell, which was who she was on the Retreat, the girl, and Mrs. Thomas Bayly, a name she could not get used to and honestly didn't believe in at all. That person in the middle was in this notebook—only in this notebook, perhaps—and when her arms got tired holding it out to admire the name, she dropped it to her lap and hugged it against her breast, like a gift.

As January went by, Beal continued to spend a few days a week at the Louvre, working through its vast spaces room by room, collection by collection. Some days she had lots to scribble about, not just about the paintings, but about the people, the artists she knew and the museum visitors wandering from painting to painting, and sometimes even about herself and Thomas. Sometimes she wrote down thoughts she had about home, as many of the paintings depicted farm scenes, a life that seemed recognizable the world over. Other days she had nothing to say and felt stupid. She tried to put down a few thoughts in the mornings when Thomas was off to his French lessons with Céleste, but it didn't feel the same at home. Beal Terrell Bayly seemed to be present only in the Louvre, which was fine with her.

On one of those days when her pen seemed to have no mind of its own and the sheets of paper offered no insights or delights, she looked up at a person lurking nearby and saw that it was Diallo Touré. She jumped a little, let her pen fall, where it splashed a blot of blue ink on the white marble floor. As usual, he was dressed formally, but his long body seemed more filled out, more muscular than she remembered. He was not pretending that this was delightful serendipity to run into her. He was not smiling.

"What are you doing here?" said Beal.

"You did not come again to the Café Saly."

"I told you I didn't want to see you."

"Then why did you go there? Why did you bring your white husband when you knew I would be there?"

"I don't know," she said.

"Of course you know. You came to see me."

"Okay. I saw you, and I knew that was the end of it." She closed her notebook with a snap, as if to emphasize the word *end*.

Touré looked at the notebook with contempt. "What are you writing in that book? You're not a schoolgirl. Why do you keep coming to this place with all this decadent art?" He beckoned around to the immense tableaux in the room, the myths, *The Raft of the Medusa*, with its lone Negro crewman off in the corner, where in the portraits of American families, the black servant would be. "This is off the coast of Senegal. This is what the French think of my country. This can teach you nothing."

As unnerved as Beal was at being confronted, she noticed that his tone seemed to have changed; perhaps all was not going well for him here in Paris. "I thought you wanted your country to be part of France," she said. "Why would you want that if there is nothing here to learn?"

"My country and all the other provinces of France will meet as equals. I will show them how little they know about our world, about Africa. It is they who have much to learn, to understand their place. When they cease to be colonial occupiers, they will realize that they have no idea what the world really is."

The whole thing seemed unlikely to Beal, a sort of madman's delusion. There were people at home who talked like this from time to time, talked about the Eastern Shore of Maryland becoming a black state. But there was no argument to be had here. "Africa is not my world," she answered.

"You are wrong. You have Africa's blood and Africa's skin, and you can never escape it. And why should you try? You came here on that boat because there is no place for you in America. This husband of yours can give you no life in France; otherwise why would you be here scribbling like a schoolchild with all these spoiled white Americans?"

Beal could see through the archway into the next gallery that a couple of the students at their easels had noticed her talking to this man. No one would have thought this was a casual chat between strangers; anyone would have observed her distress. "I don't want to talk to you here," she said.

He looked over his shoulder through the archway; he seemed to know everything on her mind almost before she did. "Then meet me at the café. Or I will announce myself on the avenue Bosquet."

She might have been surprised that he knew where she lived, but she was not. She cast another nervous look toward the painters at work, and nodded. "I'll come in half an hour."

Touré left, and Beal tried to go back to her notebook, to make a show of it, anyway. Fred Shippen and Donald Makepeace were in the next room, but she did not think they could have seen her talking to Touré. She did not know why she was so certain that any of these people would assume more than the simple, innocent truth here, that she was being harassed by an acquaintance. Yet from that first instant on the boat Touré had been more than an acquaintance; any time he was in her presence, she immediately believed she had something to hide. She did not know why she felt guilty, why as soon as Touré even entered her thoughts, unbidden, her first response was to ask herself, What about Thomas? There could be no sort of rivalry between Touré and Thomas unless she herself contrived it—which she knew, in fact, she had done. She looked down at her notebook and wrote one word under the day's date, January 27, 1893: "Why?" Why what? she asked herself. Why did he appear so certain that she would give in to him? Was he right that she and Thomas could never really be joined—because she was black and he was white?

He was full of charm when she found him at his corner table, his petulance and bad temper banished. He stood up, seated her as he had done in the dining salon, and ordered tea for her. She didn't like tea—it gave her headaches—but she said nothing.

He asked her what she had been doing when she was not at the Louvre, and she refused to answer him. "You seem to have been following me anyway," she added. "You tell me."

"Going to the market. Playing with two little girls. Going for walks with that husband of yours. Shopping in the stores. All comme il faut for a rich American tourist."

"But not the proper life for a wife."

"Ah." He wagged his eyebrows at her, a supremely unattractive male gesture: he knew everything there was to know about her. He might have to endure some of her resistance, but in the end it was decreed that he would be her master. "I see your husband has been spending time with a young woman at your old hotel."

"She's teaching him French. He's paying her. Our friend Madame Bernault is often there."

"And, of course, there is that red-haired *fille* at Galignani's. So much more suitable for him. Their skin is the color of—" He stopped, realizing that she knew nothing about this woman. "Oh yes," he picked up, suggesting that her distress was a trivial by-product of wisdom. "An Irish woman. They have had tea on the rue de Rivoli, just as we are now doing in less fashionable surroundings." All was in order, he suggested; *just as I predicted*, he might have added.

The waiter brought her tea and said something to Touré in a language that was not French. Beal took a hot sip and immediately her head pounded; she'd sucked the tea in with a huge inrush of air. She coughed, and he waited.

"Why are you doing this?" she demanded, finally.

"Doing what, Mademoiselle Beal?"

"The avenue Bosquet. Following me. Following Thomas. Don't you have anything better to do? Selling your peanuts, or whatever it was. Making a whole new world. Or is that not going as well as you hoped?"

He ignored this dig. He knew that he had caught her unawares, and did not mind at all that she lashed out in anger. He waited for the petulance to clear, like a wise parent. "I am only asking that you allow me to introduce you to the part of your life the Americans have stolen from you. They have stolen it so shrewdly that you don't even know it is missing. Have you not felt the difference here in France?"

"Of course I have, but it's not like the French are perfect."

"Exactly. We may visit here in some comfort, but sooner or later, we go home."

"My home is in America."

The eyebrows again: *We both know that isn't true.* And, of course, it wasn't true.

"I have to go." She glanced at her cup of tea; she was pleased to leave it practically untouched.

"Then you will meet me here again? Next week at this time? I have so much I need to teach you."

In the Louvre, Arthur had been standing a hundred paces away when that tall African came up to Beal, but from the way they were gesturing, the imperious way the man loomed over her, it was as if Arthur were listening to them through a voice tube. The man was imposing himself on her; she remained sitting, resisting, sort of. If she'd really been confronting him, she would have stood up. At least that's what a man would do. At one point, first she, then the African, looked right into the gallery where Arthur was working, but they didn't seem to notice that he was staring at them, one set of eyes in the clutter. The African left, and she pretended to be working, writing in her little notebook; then she left, and Arthur was up and out of his stool in a second.

She was walking upstream along the quai, toward the towers of Notre-Dame. She reached the Pont Neuf, did not pause to admire the view, as so many did, but kept walking. Arthur had not expected anything like this, this kind of intrigue. Whatever else you might say about the girl, she was as virginal as they come, a prude, like most country people he'd ever met—good, God-fearing, decent folk. Arthur didn't mind being indecent. Instead of turning right, back toward the Quarter, a path that had been worn into the stone by the footsteps of thousands of art students, she veered left toward the markets of Les Halles. This was not a part of the city Arthur knew anything about; he didn't cook, after all. Halfway up the block she hesitated outside a café, glanced around nervously, folded a tight lock of her hair under her hat—a pretty charming gesture, thought Arthur—and went in.

Arthur rested where he was for several minutes, smoked a cigarette while he decided whether to wait until she came out or to risk being exposed by looking into the café. A look was all he needed; when she came out, she'd be headed straight for home, that was clear. Nothing to be learned there. So he dumped his cigarette and ambled past the café. The windows were completely misted over, as he expected, just an occasional brush of clarity where someone might have backed onto the glass or run a hand through the moisture to get a better view of something on the street. Through one of these little portholes he might have seen the African in the back, in a corner, but it really didn't matter; this was what, back home, even in Newark, would be called a "colored" establishment, and it all fit too well to need further confirmation.

Arthur continued up the street, went around the block, and in fifteen minutes was back on his stool at the Louvre. The whole thing left him deflated, disappointed, depressed. He wasn't sure why. He could not care less about the husband, this little fairy-tale romance, but it seemed so frail, all of it. What was the point? He looked around at all the paintings on the wall and at the assemblage of students peering up so intently, then so desperately back at their own canvases, their mouths drawn in such fierce purpose and desire. Despite his unkind thoughts, he didn't feel ill will toward any of these people, he really didn't. He wanted every one of them to find whatever it was they came to Paris to find, even if they all knew that only a fraction of them would succeed at anything close to the levels to which they aspired: paintings in an exposition or at the Salon, a medal, a buzz of comment here and notice in the right circles back home, a return voyage to New York transformed. Most of them would go home broke, without prospects; their mothers would applaud their efforts and their fathers would either beat them—as Arthur's father would—or just write a check for God knows what new fluffy pastime: a saddle horse, ballet lessons, a sailboat.

He looked down at his palette, on which his paints, so carefully dispensed a sou at a time, were hardening. The life force of defeat, the familiar miasma of despair was now presenting itself to him, had taken on a visible vaporous form, like a cloud of color, the same cloud that had seemed to trail behind the girl as she made her way to this assignation, whatever it was. With supreme effort he reached up and gave his brushes a good swirl; he couldn't afford to ruin them. He didn't want failure for himself or for any of them; he wanted to, well, denote. He just wanted a painting to denote, and at that moment, full of disappointment and anger and sorrow, he was sure only that a portrait of her was it. It was worth anything he had to pay in order to make it happen, to avoid failure. That was his future, but for now, he knew he was heading into one of his black moods and he had to get out of there fast and into his room, where, if he was lucky and he didn't starve to death first and he didn't freeze, he could wait it out.

A few weeks later, thinner, still wobbly, Arthur found the girl sitting on a bench in the *salle d'ethnographie*, writing in her notebook. A new notebook, in fact. Scribble, scribble. Arthur "found" her there, in its remotest possible corner, because he knew she often went there to sit among the indifferently displayed Indian headdresses, African masks and totems, and Polynesian grass garments. He'd seen less of her these past weeks, which didn't surprise him. For one thing, he'd lost that last week in January, when all he did was hide in his room and draw self-portraits, each one more frightening, more frightened, than the last. Whether this was out of self-love or self-loathing Arthur could not tell. Makepeace was gone, back to Chicago to work in a bank; Hilary Devereux was also gone, taken to Italy by her mother and sister; and as far as Arthur could tell, the girl had not formed friendships to replace those. Was Arthur the only person who understood why she had withdrawn somewhat, why, indeed, to this collection? Was he the only one who could see the confusion and fear roiling in those opal eyes?

"I would like to ask you a question," he said.

She looked up, startled that he was speaking to her, and not particularly pleased about it.

"I would like to ask if you would sit for me." There, couldn't get more *indirect* than that, but still, she recoiled a bit at this, pulled her hands and notebook deep into her lap. Arthur was not daunted. "I know others have asked you."

"I really don't know why."

Arthur gave a shrug, as if he didn't know why either.

"What difference does it make to all of you who you paint?"

"It makes all the difference. Painters don't invent, even when they are imagining the scene. They don't create. They look. They see. They record. We don't doodle around with things in our heads, like you writers."

She dropped her eyes to her notebook, seemed to read the last few lines of her current entry. Here in this gallery of curiosities, no one could argue with what he had said. She'd probably just finished saying something like that to herself.

"I promised Stanley I would sit for him."

"I know."

"So?"

"I want you to sit for me. I think you should. It would be a favor, in return for a favor."

"What favor?"

"I know about your African boyfriend. I'm not the only one who has asked questions, but I put an end to that. They listen to me. So I'm asking for something in return."

He was not looking at her when he said all this. He had rehearsed lighting this bomb, wanted to have the explosion well contained. Arthur was not a bad person; he was simply someone in need. He was delighted when he came up with the idea of introducing it as a quid pro quo, which seemed to characterize the spirit of the proposition. This bit about others asking questions was not true, but the "others" weren't the issue here anyway. Just a softer way to express it. He caught a glimpse of the horror that immediately came over her, and he didn't want to see the tears he assumed were coming. Out of the corner of his eye he saw that she was rigid, except for her hands, those beautiful hands, clutching her notebook. At length, the hands stopped, and she exhaled, shifted in her seat. "You are wrong," she said finally. "He's not my boyfriend. I have done nothing improper."

"Sure. Yeah. Of course."

"Why are people doing this to me?"

He might have supposed that she was referring to his purported gossip and chitchat, but he heard more than that. "What do you mean?"

"Why can't people just leave me alone? What have I done to deserve all this?" She reached into her bag and took out a handkerchief, wiped her eyes and blew her nose. "When will it stop?"

This was going only partly the way Arthur expected. Yes, he'd played the African pretty much right, and it got her attention, but he'd scored no clean victory. He needed to keep his focus on the prize. "I just want you to sit for me. I don't want to make trouble for you. Maybe letting me paint you will help with whatever it is," he added.

"How would it help?" There was anger in her voice now; she was not without guts.

He had no idea how it would help. But he knew well enough, and she did too, how it would hurt if he revealed her secret to anyone, starting with her husband. "You might like my painting. I just want to paint you as you are. Whatever pose you want. I could even paint you with your husband," he said, suddenly electrified with that idea—Mr. and Mrs. Thomas Bayly, the couple, with this secret between them, this fearful dark presence hanging over them from shadows. *Is that a figure you have drawn in the background, M. Kravitz? No. I don't know what you think you are seeing.*

"You leave Thomas out of this," she snapped.

"Okay."

"What about Stanley?"

"I don't care about Stanley. He's the one who wants you just for himself. Do what you want about Stanley."

"Where would you want to do this?"

"In my studio. It's right around the corner. Not the *septième*, but it will do. In the spring, when it warms up enough not to freeze my palette. Bring whoever you want to chaperone. I know you like things to be proper." He liked that, using her word, keeping all this decorous, correct, even if it was being built on a foundation of lies and secrets. They weren't *his* lies and secrets.

"My husband would never agree. He doesn't like you."

"No. I don't suppose he does. I don't know why you'd have to tell him, anyway."

Arthur didn't learn for some months what, if anything, she had said to her husband, but he did not imagine that Thomas Bayly would stop her from doing what she wanted to do. Now that he had had a few more chances to observe the man, Arthur had actually begun to admire a certain quiet mettle in Thomas, a self-assurance that seemed not to need to fight meaningless battles. For Arthur, Thomas's demeanor suggested a third way of getting what you want. Wouldn't have thought it. Arthur knew that Beal had agreed to sit for him when, a few weeks later, Stanley Dean confronted him on the boulevard, furious, surprisingly confrontational. "Everyone knows that I found her, that she is mine. You ask anyone. You keep your hands off her."

Arthur held up his hands, turned them front and back. "I'm not touching her. See?"

"You know what I mean. You follow her all over the place."

All over the place? thought Arthur. Hardly. That first time, yes, that was following; the second time, when she went to the café, that was detective work.

"You are a person with no honor," said Stanley.

Arthur thought that was unfair, but he could see how Stanley could think it.

"I don't know why she is willing to do it. She promised me I would be the only one," Stanley added, letting out a small squeak of pain. "What did you tell her about me?"

"I told her that you may be the best painter of all of us"—he hadn't told her that, but he was coming to believe it, the best technically—"but that I understood her and could give her a painting that would show who she is. That would speak for her."

Stanley had been mollified a bit by the compliment, and the truth was, as Arthur knew, that Maître Rodolphe had been moving Stanley away from portraits anyway. "You mean about the hardships she has faced? About the cruelty? About the South?"

"Yeah. Sure," said Arthur, but of course, he didn't mean that at all. He meant exactly one hundred percent, one hundred and eighty degrees the opposite. He would show her that she had been blessed, that she had been favored, that she had been held up for all to admire. How could this not help her? Arthur could see clearly the painting Stanley had in mind, neck collar and ankle chains and all. The horror of the innocents. How was that supposed to do anything but keep her shackled into eternity? The painting would be a fraud and a failure for two reasons: first, it would be boring, and second, this girl knew nothing about being enslaved, being crushed, being thwarted. Put that in this girl's eyes and it would be a mask, a cheap party favor.

"Look, Stanley. Your painting and mine wouldn't look anything alike. No one would even guess that it's the same girl."

That would have to do for Stanley.

5

The depth of the winter had arrived, and what had seemed a cozy apartment in the fall was now revealed as drafty and frigid. Ice formed in the washbasin. Thomas and Beal were both accustomed enough to being cold in the winter; the Mansion House on the Retreat was so big that each room was its own tundra, and Beal's family's house in Tuckertown was built to accommodate but not necessarily shelter farmworkers and domestics; in the winter they were on their own. The warmest room on the avenue Bosquet, even if it had no fireplace, was the attic maid's room, and often at night after Mme Vigny went home they would go up there and lie on the little iron bed and talk until it was time to retire. Thomas held her under the blankets as they talked, and he knew that every day seemed to bring new challenges to her, not all of them uncomplicated, but it was just the same for him. If she wasn't saying absolutely everything to him, he wasn't saying absolutely everything to her about the audacious plan that was forming in his mind. As he recorded all these memories years later, Thomas thought of this cold, locked-tight winter as a winter of waiting, waiting for spring, when they would have to decide how they were going to live; he thought about trusting the hours and trusting each other even as, on somewhat separate tracks, they were each discovering who they were and what they wanted. Occasionally they went to the hotel to eat supper with the Richard family, and as the weeks passed, Thomas was surprised by how well both of them were doing with French, especially how much Beal seemed to understand. They went to the theater sometimes, to the Gymnase on the boulevard de Bonne-Nouvelle generally, but ventured a few times to the Comédie-Française, sitting high in the loges where no one wore evening dress: that was Thomas's one inflexible demand. Still, it was fun for him to watch Beal studying the crowd, and in that, she wasn't all that different from the various *duchesses* and *comtesses* in their boxes who also seemed to be doing anything but watching the play. Thomas didn't mind a bit to notice that just as often they were looking at her, the only African in the house, and that sometimes men tried to catch her eye, that the men in their top hats and evening dress hanging around the stage door would turn and watch her as she and Thomas walked past them. It was all theater, harmless invention, nothing for keeps, and years later, as Thomas was remembering these days, it seemed to him that this was where the true legend of Beal got its start.

By the end of January he had worked his way almost to the end of Galignani's sections on grapes and its much larger sections on wines, wine regions, and wine making. He could have checked out many of these volumes and studied them at home, but for one thing, Galignani's was the best-heated space he had thus far discovered in the whole city, and for another, he wasn't ready to tell Beal that this was where his thinking was headed. He understood his own reluctance from the very beginning: every single day that passed, she became more a *parisienne*. Even her accent was more Parisian than his, and every time she came back from Le Bon Marché with a little piece of ready-made—he almost had to force her to buy things—she seemed to be growing into a person who would never have existed anywhere but here. And Thomas, in his considerations of the future, was diving ever farther away from this place, south, through the Loire Valley, past Bordeaux, across the Massif Central, and into the real wilderness, a region the vignerons of Bordeaux regarded with horror, where it seemed to him that a man with somewhat limited resources and a solidly considered plan could make a mark.

His guide through most of this voyage had been Eileen Hardy.

That was another reason he liked to do his work at Galignani's—because she was there, Tuesdays through Fridays from ten to closing, which so perfectly matched Thomas's own schedule that he found his time with her slightly preordained. They had come to expect to see each other for most of these appointed times, and neither of them tried to hide their pleasure. This was new for Thomas, having a girl for a friend, especially a girl—a woman—who took such delight in the jape and jest. Beal would like her, he figured; he could easily imagine Eileen as a farm kid, though it was clear that she wasn't. By now Thomas had realized that she knew far more about wine than he would have expected from a Dublin girl; it had been no accident that she put him onto grapes and wine making at the beginning. He put this right to her one day when they were having their afternoon *goûter* at a teahouse just a few doors down on the rue de Rivoli.

"It seems to me, Eileen," said Thomas, "that you have been holding your cards back. You have been foxy with me." From that early day when she called him "confused," this was the way they talked to each other.

She reddened, which, given her hair and her complexion, meant that she looked as if she were about to explode. "About what?" she said quietly, as if she expected to be scolded.

"About wine. You know as much as any one of these books I have been reading."

"I don't. I just hear things."

"How does one just 'hear' about the difference between Petit Verdot and Cabernet Franc? No one has ever breathed such a thing to me."

She took up her napkin as if she could dust away the violent blushing of her cheeks. Thomas wished that this gesture did not move him so, delight him, make him want to take the napkin from her and finish the job.

"My father," she said.

Thomas had not expected this, the father that had seemed to be a mystery best left unprobed. "He knows about wine?" said Thomas. "He's like one of those English lords buying vineyards in Bordeaux? The ones you have been telling me about."

"Well, yes. He is like one of them."

"You mean," said Thomas, getting ready to make all sorts of fun with this, "he *is* one of them."

"Irish. Not English. But yes." There was no jesting here. "One day he just announced to my mother that he had done this. That he was moving there without her. And he didn't tell her about Mme de Bose either."

"Oh," said Thomas. "*Her*," he added, a joke.

Eileen smiled gamely.

"Why didn't you tell me about this in the first place? There's almost no family secret of mine that I didn't pour out to you the day we met."

"No. It was the day after we met. The second time you came in."

Yes, thought Thomas, she was right about that; the second time he came in, that Thursday, the first of December. "But—"

"Because I don't like to talk about him. That's why I am here in Paris. So I don't have to talk about him. It is still a scandal back home." The blush had gone. "Besides, you *like* to talk about your family, as much as you try to pretend you don't. The Retreat. See? I even know what your farm is called. Everything for you seems to grow out of that place."

Thomas might have argued that this must be true of almost everyone, that young adulthood grew out of the places of youth, but maybe it wasn't so. All these painters, these friends of Beal's: where they came from was just a way of telling them apart—part of their names, like Stanley from Pittsburgh and Kravitz from Newark. And he might have argued that here in Europe, land of aristocrats and thousand-year-old names, surely a family's past marked one for life. But he knew what she was saying; the Retreat was so present in his daily thoughts that even here, in a tea shop on the rue de Rivoli, he could conjure up the smell of Mason's Creek just before a rain, the sound of the locusts at noon in July.

"Not that I think you have told me everything. Just a lot."

No one was joking now, and Thomas understood what she was saying, what her eyes were saying, which was that she wished she did know more, that maybe there were some things here that didn't line up. He still hadn't told her about Beal, hadn't hinted that he was married, which had become worse and worse, meaner and meaner, because he knew this friendship of theirs was no longer as simple as it should be. There was never a right time, but she must have guessed, must have figured out that for all the tales of the Retreat, there was a very big hole. She must have figured it out and decided that she didn't care.

"I came here to get away from the place," said Thomas, avoiding her eyes. The tearoom was quite full, mostly American and British ladies, a safe place for innocent transgressions. He had asked her, on one of those early days in the reading room, where he might take a short break, and she said she would show him if she could come with him. No one, especially no woman, had ever said such a thing to him.

"Then we are here in Paris for the same reason," she said.

"That's why any mention of Bordeaux makes you curl your lip."

"Do I? Does it? Well," she said—the arch tone was back—"it's not the place for you. You don't pretend to anywhere near as much as you'd need to do there. Trust that."

Beal was late getting home that day. The worst of the freeze was over, and at least the days were getting longer and it wasn't completely dark when she returned.

Things were starting to feel a little odd; his own guilty voice spoke to him. He made unnecessary and elaborate excuses to Mme Vigny and went out to the landing on the stairs as soon as he heard the door open four stories below. He took her coat from her, hugged her especially hard, the solidness of her, his one true love. "I was worried about you," he said.

"I knew you would be. I'm sorry. I sort of lost track."

"Where were you?" Thomas knew that the students in the Louvre had to pack up and be gone by three.

"I just felt like walking. My back gets so sore when I'm sitting on those benches." One of the artists had lent her a little folding stool of the kind they all had for painting, but it was so low and her legs were so long that her knees jutted up practically to her shoulders and she had no flat place to put her notebook. "I went to

Printemps to see the silk. Not that I'll ever be able to sew. But it sure is pretty."

"I wish you'd treat yourself more, for all the time you spend in those places. Things to show how beautiful you are," he said, giving her buttock a caress.

She slapped away his hand, too abruptly, too harshly. He drew it back too quickly, surprised. "I'm sorry," she said. "I guess I'm tired."

She greeted Mme Vigny and then followed Thomas to the table. Lately Thomas's French lessons with Céleste had included more and more talk about food, and Mme Vigny resisted his interest in cooking far less than she resisted Beal's presence in the market. Apparently, in France, men cooked sometimes, or maybe, finally, one of these Americans had shown the proper level of respect for her and her country. She was taking them on a slightly involuntary tour of the food people ate in the provinces: *pot-au-feu, ris de veau, caillettes.* Usually they had no idea what was in them.

"I was in Egypt," Beal said.

"The sphinxes? The caskets? I thought they scared you."

She laughed. "They do, but they've been dead for four thousand years. If they were going to jump out at anybody, I reckon they would have done it before now."

"Besides, they're about half your height."

They were waiting at the table. Usually Mme Vigny would serve them and then leave. They had no idea where she lived, how she came to be their cook, what she would do when they departed. Beal could hardly get used to being served by a cook; a maid would have been impossible for her. Besides, she had told Thomas years ago that the sounds of her mother and father in the kitchen at the end of the evening, doing the last dishes, talking, sharing their days, had been a sort of magic music of care she wanted to have in her own life.

While they waited, Beal recited the words for the bowls, spoons, glasses, napkins. "*Un bol, une cuillère, un verre, une serviette,*" she said.

"Very good. *Pas mal,* as Céleste says."

"No. *Très bien.* She always says you've done *très bien.*"

"Céleste is a nice girl."

Mme Vigny brought out the pot of stew and set it in front of Thomas. "Cassoulet," she said. "De Languedoc, de Castelnaudary," she added, with enough emphasis to make Beal ask what she meant.

"Languedoc," said Thomas cautiously. "It's a region way in the South. Almost in Spain. It's the heart of the Midi. I was talking to Mme Vigny about it the other day, and she said we must try the famous cassoulet. It has duck cooked in its own fat, and sausage and beans."

"Seems a little mean. The duck. Its own fat."

He took her hand and gave it a squeeze. "Yes," he said. "Most of cooking is mean, even to the vegetables."

He spooned out the cassoulet, taking a bite while Beal took a sip of the broth; it was smoky, tasty, reminding him of the stews Aunt Zoe cooked, which always started with a pig's foot or a rind of ham.

"Fred Shippen is leaving," said Thomas. He had heard this the day before. "His mother is ill, and he has to go back to Virginia. I know you don't like him very much, but I'm going to miss him." Yes, Fred had been courteous to Beal in a studied way, but he remained a Virginian at heart; no question which side he'd have been fighting for in the war. But then again, Thomas's grandfather, the famous Duke, had been one of the most notorious Confederates on the Eastern Shore, had spent a few months locked up in the Union prison at Fort McHenry, and both of Thomas's uncles, his mother's brothers, had died fighting for the South.

"I'm sorry," Beal said.

"It's all right. I don't want anyone else in my life but you."

"Oh, Thomas. I'm just your wife. You need more than just me. What about those men in the reading room?" He had mentioned a couple of brief conversations he had at Galignani's, though the truth was, he'd said hardly a word to any of them. The crew at Galignani's was really the worst of the lot, the people Mother Digby despised, the kind of idle and worthless Americans she had figured him for.

"It doesn't matter. Come summer, we will be gone from here. We can't afford it anyway."

"Yes. Sometimes I worry about that," she said.

Thomas knew well that this was a brand-new sensation for her. For her family, what they could *afford* had never been an issue at all. "Don't," he said.

She took a few bites. "But where will we go?"

"To the Midi, I think. By the Mediterranean. That's why I was talking to Mme Vigny about it. I have been reading about it." He was paying out a lot of rope here; he tried not to make it too obvious how far along all this had gone. Yes, he thought: they would go south, and that would end this adventure.

"What would we be doing?" she asked.

"Well. Farming. Maybe grapes. It's what they do in the South. It's what we know how to do, right?"

"I guess." It was what they were born into, but the farming they knew about had been a disaster; things planted and harvested seemed to be about dying. "I'm sure you will tell me about it when the time is right."

"Yes. Of course." It was obvious to him that she did not want to talk about the future, to face it, any more than he did. He took her hand, and this time, having rebuffed him, she clasped his with both of hers.

"I'm really proud of what you're doing," he said. "All your writing. Randall would be proud of you too."

"My husband," she said, a slightly odd comment, as if she were saying this to herself.

My husband. For some reason, this simple phrase kept returning to him as he slept, and he woke with it on his mind. He set out as usual in the morning. By now he was working at another library, yet he often stopped in to say hello to Eileen, as her boss did not come in until noon and there were never any readers in the den. But as he crossed the rue de Rivoli on his way to the rue Tronchet, he glanced down the arcade and thought of Eileen sitting there, waiting, and all at once the whole spot he had put himself into broke his heart. Because of course he let himself think of her the way lovers do: How could *anyone not love her?* Because he would do almost anything to keep her in his life, as one cherished so dearly, except hurt her. At that moment he did not reflect on any hurt that

Beal might experience; she was not part of this equation simply because she would have no role in hurting Eileen. He stopped in the street abruptly enough to force a man to jump to avoid smacking into him, and because he needed something, anything, to give him a pause, he forced his gaze up ahead at the Madeleine, a Napoleonic embarrassment no one really knew what to do with, a building, like a life, born into confusion. He had been evil, he had been cruel. He had known for weeks that she hoped blamelessly that there could be more between them, that at night, in her apartment not far from the peach orchards on Montreuil, she had imagined a life together. This had never been possible, would never be. He had the love of his life with Beal, a love that had literally, for him, moved continents, but there was something so plain and easy about Eileen—no continents being moved here, just two people washed up together in Paris—that a few times he had absently imagined the same thing. This life he and Beal were living seemed to allow this sort of illict *rêverie*; Paris allowed it, even encouraged it, and it couldn't be. Sometime soon he would speak to Eileen, but for now, Thomas decided as he stood on that spot on the rue Royale, it was time to get serious, time to cut out this fey research and move on to the future, time to leave this city before it destroyed them.

Beal had not agreed, but she had not refused. She had not agreed to do this painting with Arthur Kravitz, and she had not agreed to meet Touré at his café. But she had not refused either. It seemed that neither of them would let her go, no matter what she said or did. Touré would go back to the café the following week, she knew that now, and she schemed that she would not, that she would make him wait all afternoon in vain, and she counted down the days, telling herself that she would not give in, that it would be fine come Tuesday afternoon to imagine him drumming his fingers angrily. He'd come looking for her, she knew that, to the Louvre, to the avenue Bosquet. A couple of times she came close to telling Thomas about him, *this man from the boat, that African you noticed, he's bothering me,* but it seemed late for that. She should have told Thomas about him after that first dinner, but even then Touré seemed to be her own problem, something confined to the steerage dining salon, a private affair. And besides, she believed that Touré would never reveal himself to Thomas, that in many ways to do so would be, for Touré, to admit a disadvantage. He wouldn't come to their door; he'd stand at the head of the avenue—his hands on his hips—and Thomas wouldn't pay him any mind if he noticed him, and Beal would know he was there.

But then there was the red-haired girl. Oh, Beal remembered well enough Miss Ophelia's red hair; they called her "witch," they called her "the red Devil." What could there be to this? Beal wondered. Thomas had made it clear enough that he didn't really like her friends, Colleen and, especially, Hilary; something had happened at that dinner, but more than that, he just didn't seem to notice other women. On their walks she'd say, *Now isn't that lady right pretty*, and he'd glance but do no more than that. He had told her a good bit about Galignani's but had never mentioned much about the other people there, and when, at one point during that week, she asked him straight on who he talked to, he said he just talked to the librarians. And then she said she'd love to see this place where he was spending so much time, and he answered that these days he was spending more time at the Bibliothèque Universelle and he'd be happy to show it to her. So maybe that was that with the red-haired girl, and maybe it all meant nothing, but Beal could not get that moment with Touré out of her mind, and it made her angry that Thomas had given him more power over her.

This winter, it seemed to Beal, was in some way out of time, a kind of adventure time that wouldn't count on the calendar or against her lifetime, and after all, she deserved—*they* deserved, she corrected herself—this winter of change. Who was she? The farm girl who had come to the great city of Paris: it sounded like some of those books she'd heard Hilary and Colleen talking about, by Balzac, Zola. But still, this struggle seemed uniquely hers, not Thomas's. Beal knew that he had some project going, that he was doing what, as she understood it, his father had done all those years in his lonely study in the Retreat: reading, researching, looking for answers to the yellows. She'd asked Thomas what he was studying, and he told her he wasn't ready to talk about it. She'd asked him,

as straight as she could, about the red-haired girl, and he had said
nothing. So maybe they both had secrets, and maybe that was fine
in a marriage, to have secrets.

So, that next Tuesday, she met M. Touré. This time he was neither angry nor ingratiating; he seemed simply pleased to see her.

"I wasn't going to come," she said.

"I wasn't sure you would, but I knew you had nothing to fear
from me. I mean to give you only pleasure."

She took off her gloves and coat and sat down. The café was
almost stiflingly hot: a joy. This was the warmest she had felt in
weeks, and with the strains of the tobacco of many lands mingling
and twining above the tables, the air was almost herbal, lavender
and rosemary. As soon as she sat, she wanted to abide in this comfort forever.

Touré had brought along a book about Senegal, which was
in French, but he told her about his life as he thumbed through
the photographs of the city of Dakar, the broad Senegal River, the
mosques and markets, the beaches, the groundnut plantations. The
land was flat, like the Eastern Shore of Maryland, but in some of
the photographs Beal could see distant mountains, and on the coast,
the sea seemed endless and restless and deep, unlike the brackish
and confined waters of the Chesapeake. The people all looked
extremely content with their lot and their work, and nowhere was
there a white boss or foreman or overseer. Touré was boyishly proud
of this little country; he missed his home. Beal understood that
without any difficulty. Here he was in Paris, in this freezing, biting
wind, so far from the fragrant breeze, the soul-reviving heat, a man
alone in a harsh land. She looked over at him, and in this mood his
features appeared soft; he even seemed a bit confused, less certain
of everything. She felt bad for having plotted all week to stand him
up. How would he have felt, bringing this book to show her and
then waiting for her in vain? She exhaled, a breath drawn from deep
in her chest, and with it went the coil of tension that had been
inside her all week. She'd really thought of little else at the Louvre,
at home, falling asleep beside Thomas, and here she didn't have
to look over her shoulder in fear, because Touré was right in front
of her.

"I would like to continue seeing you," he said after he had closed the book and after she said she must go. "This will not be difficult for you to arrange."

It was delivered in the form of an order, like so much of what he had been saying to her since that first night in the steerage dining salon. A crude demand that brooked no dissent. Except that this time Beal heard a different tone, a kind of awkwardness that may have been the result of speaking in his third language, or it may have been the way men talked to women in his country, or it may have just been that this was a lonely man who didn't know how to ask nicely. How to say please. As quickly as that, her ire could melt into tenderness. If he had been offering and asking for friendship in some nicer way all along, wouldn't she have returned it willingly? Wasn't she curious about this unknown part of her being: Africa? How could she not be curious? "Okay," she said. He looked confused at the word. "*D'accord,*" she said, and he brightened.

"Ah."

"But you will not threaten me. You will keep away from me."

"Of course. As you wish."

She wanted to say something about loving Thomas, about being faithful to him, but she knew that if that were an issue, she should end this right now. So she didn't say anything about Thomas, and with that, she could feel that a great unknown had taken over the part of her life outside her marriage, like stepping on one of those trapdoors in the barns at home and falling through, landing not with a soft bump on a pile of hay below, but far away from the Retreat, farther away than she had ever imagined. "I do wish it," she said, which, in the absence of anything more steadfast, had to do. She had the sense that if she pushed harder, he'd lose the softness, and for the moment, she had decided on a different path. She would encourage this better part of the man and see where it led. There was nothing disloyal to Thomas in that. "I will meet you here next week," she said, standing up, and he rose to help her with her coat.

"You delight me, Mademoiselle Beal," he said, a whisper from behind, close enough to her ear to feel the warmth of his breath.

A week later, after meeting in the café, she went to Diallo's rooms. He wanted her to see how a real African lives in the city; they were just around the corner from the café; there was no bother to it. For reasons she did not understand, she accepted. When she got there, she found nothing African about it, nothing but the same bare washstand, meager table, barely warm stove, empty larder that she knew was in every other apartment of this type all over the city, all over Europe. And the same narrow bed. She was not naive; she wasn't even blameless.

On the way, she had asked herself if she was willing to let him make love to her, whether she would use that door to step into this promised land he kept insisting was waiting for her, a place beyond her constricted, Americanized, enslaved ability to imagine. She knew he believed that sex with him was her duty, but also that it would purify her, wash her of that white man—not her husband. He refused to accept that Thomas was her husband—whom she lay with night after night. She knew he believed that taking his semen would cleanse her blood of the whiteness that had seeped into her family in America.

When they climbed to the top of the stairs, he went ahead and then turned to greet her, as if she were paying a call. He was charming, once again revealing that childish sense of pride, which was confusing, because, in truth, what he was proud of was not what was African about these rooms, but that they were Parisian, that out of the front window he could see the roofs of the great belly of Paris, Les Halles. He denied this pride. "We must make do, after all. But these are not the sights I will show you in Senegal." There was no one else in the apartment. He walked her to the kitchen, suggested that she warm up next to the stove for a few minutes. *Yes*, he was saying, *let's warm our hands and feet before we undress.*

He had not showed her his room, though the door was ajar and through it she could see the foot of his bed. This bed. It seemed to Beal, almost as a hallucination, that this bed was Africa itself, or that this was the way Touré saw it—that this bed where an African slept was the Africa he wanted her to see. Then he was standing over her, as he so often did, and what came to her was not the *no!* she wished had come, but rather, the mealier *not yet.* The *not yet* that could get her out of this apartment intact but not completely free; the *not yet* that offered a decision by way of not deciding anything. Still, it was enough to give her the determination to resist.

"Now, Mademoiselle Beal, I will make you my wife."

"No," she said. "I'm leaving." She turned from the stove and moved toward the door, and he placed one hand on the wall in front of her to block her way.

"You know you want this. You have agreed."

"I haven't agreed. Please put your arm down."

"You cannot do this to a man. An African woman does not do this to a man."

"Then you would force her whether she wanted it or not?" she asked, suddenly calm and very certain of her argument. "You would force me? How is that different from the white man you say must have forced a mother of mine way back? How is that different from the slavers who brought my people to America?"

"This is not about these silly words," he said. She had twisted his arguments and intentions, and he was angry; he seemed to be fighting his own arms, as if the contradictions she was feeding him could make him explode. "You have been coming to me for my counsel and guidance for months, and now I am telling you what you must do."

And here something further happened to her, when the *not yet* became, at least provisionally, *never!* Never was somewhere between yes and no; it was the answer to a different question altogether. *Never* did not really require a choice, it was simply a fact. And now she was ready to put up a fight. That much of the farm girl was still within, the part of farm life where everything gets decided by physical means—a chore, a desire, a conflict. She took him on, looking straight at him. "You don't have any idea why I have agreed to see you. You don't know nothing about me."

The thought that he should know anything about her beyond what he had imposed on her seemed to give him the barest moment's pause, as if, despite the fact that he was dismissing her defense as mere rhetoric, there was a flaw in his logic that he must address. He did not put his arm down, but he relaxed it, and she ducked under it.

"All right," he said. "We will go on as before. You will determine the time and place."

In the beginning of April, when spring had finally arrived for real and a season's worth of chill had begun to dissipate in Arthur's studio, Beal appeared at his door. She had brought a companion with her, a French mademoiselle named Céleste. Arthur was a little disappointed that it wasn't her husband accompanying her; he wanted that edge of subterfuge in the air, but this plain, mousy Céleste brought in a clueless and unsuspecting innocence, which was good too. In either case, a chaperone made everything vastly easier. The girl was dressed in proper daytime attire. There had been no discussion of costume, of formal gown or mythic drape, no mention of necklines, no suggestion of disrobing of any kind. Arthur knew that if they ever got to something more staged, it wouldn't be this first time, and he didn't press it. He invited them in, straightened his cot so the French girl could sit on it without coming into contact with his filthy bed linen, and then pointed over at the chair. Beal went to it as he settled onto his stool, charcoal and drawing paper in hand.

"Okay," she said. "Here I am. You win." Arthur assumed that Céleste spoke no English.

"I'm not trying to win. I just want to paint you."

She shrugged. This whole relationship was turning into a contest of shrugs, and he liked this latest one especially: imperious but powerless. "What do I do?" she asked. "What does a model do?"

"Just sit still. It's pretty easy."

She sat, put her hands in her lap stiffly and impatiently, as if she were in a depot waiting for a train. Okay, thought Arthur, picking up his charcoal. I can work with this. And over the next several visits, he did. He had her stand, posed her this way and that, waiting, hoping. He showed her nothing even though he knew she was curious. Who would not be curious? He didn't care what they talked about. On the first sitting, after she had settled in a bit, she asked him why he was doing this, and he understood that she wasn't asking about painting her or blackmailing her, but why he did art, what was he after? What tiny purchase on truth did he think he had in the very point of his pencil, the fleece at the tip of his brush, what to be found there? She uttered none of this, but that was what she meant, in a rather hostile way.

"It's about capturing," he said.

"Are you trying to be cruel to me?" she asked.

He appreciated the fact that as she asked this freighted question, she made every effort not to disturb her pose.

"No. I'm trying to answer your question. It's about subjecting life to the least possible shrinkage even while shrinking it."

She didn't respond to this concept, which Arthur had come upon quite some time ago but had never had the opportunity to express. Odd, he thought, that it would feel so easy, so natural, to say such a thing to her. It set a pattern. She often didn't respond; exchanges between them ended in silence, without the usual empty mopping up, which was fine for Arthur, as he had only half his mind on talk anyway, and evidently fine for her, because she liked to reflect on things, try them out, ponder. She never started speaking before she knew what she was going to say; she was almost always after something, and when she got it, she stopped. This was something he began to understand about her, a style of learning. Arthur had not had a whole lot more formal schooling than she had—he gathered that she had some opportunities but no interest—but her style of conversing, like her many hours in the Louvre, had the nature of the autodidact, as if the function of conversation was to fill the voids of knowledge. Over the hours he spent with her he found himself choosing his words more and more carefully: he knew he'd get only one chance. He began to feel a bit intimidated. He wasn't sure where to put her intelligence in the mythos he had created for her, but he liked it. A couple of times during intervening days he found himself storing up an aperçu or two to run by her. It was worth the bother and effort to express things to her because she was on his level, she thought concretely, as he did; she thought with a purpose, the only way he had survived.

She sat for him four times, and he had yet to pick up a paintbrush. He had a deal with her, and he knew it wasn't open-ended. Whether she was still seeing the African, he did not know, but if so, she had a fair amount of absence to explain to her husband. Of course, one occasion for absence could be explained away by another, more benign occasion. Thomas was a mystery to Arthur—in some ways, he didn't exist; he was a concept, part of the mythos, but not part of the scene. Arthur began to think that his first impulse, to paint them together, was probably right, and in any event, he couldn't paint her unless he knew something about her husband. Arthur was losing ground; his drawings were dull. The more he became aware of her intelligence, the stupider she made him feel and the stupider he made her look. He had bludgeoned her into this, and now all he was doing was wasting her time. Somehow he had lost a power over her, and he realized that without this upper hand, the portrait painter is just playing catch-up. He could see that Beal was getting tired of this; in fact, she did not seem totally well, even as April passed, when everyone is supposed to sparkle. He could hardly express concern; he, after all, was one jaw of the vise that must be closing around her. He was ready to thank her, tell her the favor had been repaid in full measure, and quit, go back to Newark, a mode of painterly failure he'd never imagined existed: defeated by his model.

But then one day she arrived alone. "Where's Céleste?" he asked with some alarm. The studious girl, sitting on his cot devouring Zola, had become a consoling fixture: at least someone was accomplishing something.

"She's busy helping her father."

"Then why did you come?"

"Because this is getting nowhere. You're just sketching." She was taking off her hat, one hand holding the brim, the other pulling out the pins.

Right enough, thought Arthur. Nowhere.

"At this rate, I'll never be done with you." As she said this, she was unbuttoning her collar, and she kept going, working down her front. "I'll never be done with any of you."

"What are you doing?" he asked stupidly.

She pulled her shirttails out of her skirt, reached behind to unbutton the waist, and let the skirt fall in a circle around her feet, looking at him the whole time. "This is what you want me to do, isn't it?" She dropped her petticoat, then loosed the stays on her corset and let it drop too. No pleasure in any of this, and no flirtation either, just shedding the unnecessary layers. She was now in her drawers and her chemise, and Arthur was thinking, Okay, her in her toilette, underthings draped on her torso, that knee peeking out of the petticoat, this was really what he had in mind all along.

"You don't have to do this. I never asked you for this."

"I'm not afraid of my body, but you're afraid of it, aren't you? You're afraid of my skin. That's why you can't paint me."

"I'm not afraid of your body. You don't have to bare yourself to me to prove it."

"What difference does it make whether you see me naked?" she asked. "Why does everyone care so much about my body? Believe me, I got used to the sight of my body a long time ago. So here. I give it to you." She held out both hands, as if handing him a folded blanket. She was attempting to project defiance and was doing a pretty good job of it, but now something else was going on: she had started to cry. She was still in her underthings; Arthur hoped she was going to stop there. "Everyone else wants to have my body, why not you?"

"Hey," he said. He should have used her name, but he had never used it before; he didn't think he had earned the right. "Hey. Forget the painting. Maybe I can help you."

"That's what you said when you blackmailed me into this. You said your painting would help me. Well, paint me. Paint my body." With that she turned away from him, shrugged off her drawers and hiked off her chemise, and stood with her back to him, naked. "How do you want me to stand?" she asked.

A beautiful back, but a back in pain; her shoulders rose and fell with the deep, miserable breaths she was drawing in. In the silence, in her nakedness, she seemed to appreciate this moment to compose herself; Arthur had never played a part in a drama of such complexity. Fully recovered but still facing away, still preserving her frontal modesty, she put her right hand on her left shoulder and turned to face him. He could see the fingertips of her hand on her shoulder, holding this slightly uncomfortable pose in tension. She looked at him without warmth, yet, for all her nakedness, without alarm, as if she were leading him into another room, but not because she wanted anything to do with him. He thought, This is about sex and it is not about sex, at the same time. He wondered whether it was what he had been missing all these months with all those naked models at the Académie. He didn't know what to do except what he had done growing up, when life was too mean or sad to bear: he picked up his pencil.

"Just like that," he said. "But turn your head a little farther to the left? Okay?"

The next time she came, Céleste was with her once again, but that didn't matter. He didn't need to do any more nudes of her. By the same token, what she wore was meaningless. They agreed that the clothes she wore that day—the same clothes she had shed two days earlier—would be the costume for the painting. He now knew what he was painting, knew that her body was not like everybody else's. Her waist was high, her hips quite square, her buttocks and breasts full, even if a little heavy for Arthur's taste, but not fatty. For the past few weeks he had been copulating—well, yes, that was the right word, as he was paying her for the privilege—with his skinny model, and the brittleness of her body, the way he could feel her sharp pubic bone jabbing into his lower abdomen, that was what Arthur liked. Except for the fact that she had these narrow, birdlike shoulders. Mrs. Thomas Bayly's shoulders? Oh, a provincial seamstress given such shoulders to adorn could dress a queen. You could hang the crown jewels across those shoulders. You could build a civilization on those shoulders.

It was almost May now. The brutally short Paris winter days were spreading out into the long light of summer, and the cafés were full. On the promenades were old soldiers and their wives arm in arm, secretly bankrupt counts with their *courtisanes*, all there on the streets of Paris. Teenagers giggling in love; one could not be very serious when one was seventeen and bathed in this light.

In recent weeks Arthur had actually spent some time at the café with Thomas Bayly, who seemed to be taking a greater interest in this society his wife had passed a good bit of the winter with, which seemed to Arthur a wise if overdue move. Arthur found to his surprise that he liked Bayly, found him quiet and thoughtful, but not bland. Maybe it took getting to know him through his wife; Arthur could see now how alike the two of them were. He pictured their quiet evenings at home, with not much chatter, and he could feel something very private about them, a history shared right down to the core of their beings. He couldn't imagine anyone intruding, being able to insert himself into an organism so self-absorbed. Arthur didn't know how much Thomas knew about his wife sitting for him, and neither of them brought it up at first. It seemed an odd though workable discretion, but now things were tightening around the girl, and something had to give. Really, Arthur owed her something. One thing he could do would be to remove at least some of the subterfuge.

"So," he said to Thomas one afternoon. "I think the painting is almost done. I'll work on it for a while, but she doesn't need to sit for much of that."

Thomas looked at him with the same unrevealing equanimity Arthur had gotten used to from his wife, except for the afternoon of the nude drawings. For all the reaction Thomas showed, this might have been either the first time he'd heard of the project or the oldest news on the Continent. "Good," he said. "She says it's tiring."

"I'm sure it is." The topic seemed to be exhausted with these stray remarks, and in the silence Thomas ordered beer for both of them. Arthur was impressed by and envious of Thomas's French, and as that thought passed through his mind, he recalled that the girl Céleste had been Thomas's teacher. If the nun had come along one day, that would have completed his sweep of Thomas's world. At times during the previous weeks, Arthur had believed that he was invading this private man's life; he realized now, with shock but also with some relief, that he had been subsumed by it.

After their beers were delivered, Thomas resumed the topic. "I was surprised when she said she was going to sit for you. As far as I knew, she had an arrangement with Stanley."

"I know," said Arthur. "Maybe I pushed her too hard. I feel bad about it. It was probably unfair of me, but I thought I could do something Stanley couldn't. That's what I told her."

"You thought?"

"Yeah. I don't know. But your wife—" He coughed; he still couldn't use her name. "She is a remarkable person and has done everything and more than I could have asked for. I hope I've done her justice. Her beauty, but more than that."

"What's the 'more'?"

"I really couldn't say. I guess if I could say it, I wouldn't try to paint it. I don't think I've done a very good job, either way. This is hard for me to say, to you of all people." Arthur said that honestly; by now he knew not to expect Thomas to offer flatteries and encouragement.

"Interesting," said Thomas. This was what Arthur expected. Thomas Bayly glided through life on the wings of every manner and politesse ever devised, but he was a person of fact, not nuance. He would think that if this was what an expert said about his own work, he was probably right. But then Thomas added something Arthur did not expect. "I'm glad she worked with you."

Arthur had to light a new cigarette on that. This man would not be glad if he knew the truth. He wouldn't be glad about any of it, and he was owed the truth. The truth felt like a bucket of water balancing on edge, ready to tip, ready to release a flood. "I'm not sure why," he said finally.

"Because you're tough. You're not a very nice person, Arthur. In case you didn't know that. I mean, your manners stink." Thomas said this with good cheer.

"You should get to know the people I grew up with. Compared to them I'm the most courtly son of a bitch you ever met." Arthur let this sit for a minute before asking exactly why the fact that he was ill-mannered made him a good person to paint Thomas's wife.

"Beal hasn't been around too much toughness. She's been pretty sheltered. I'm sure my saying that seems crazy to you."

"Believe me. It doesn't seem crazy. It had occurred to me."

"Considering?" said Thomas.

"Considering what? I don't know enough about your lives to consider. Considering that her brother was murdered?"

Here Thomas did show a slight discomfort; Arthur wasn't sure exactly how he had learned of it.

"No," Thomas said. "That made everyone shelter her even more.

If that hadn't happened, I'm not sure either of our families would have been willing to let us have what we wanted. To help us escape."

"Huh," said Arthur.

"She's never known anything but love and kindness."

"And you?"

"I have had nothing but privilege. You know that."

Arthur spent the next few moments mulling that over, wondering if Thomas, who seemed among the least self-pitying people he knew, really meant what he said, that he had been given privilege and nothing else. Arthur had never, in his life or any life that had touched his, imagined that such a statement might contain a tiny packet of sorrow. Privilege had its consolations: this café, Paris. Arthur had spent a considerable amount of time this winter envying everything that privilege allowed Thomas to afford. But nothing else from anyone but this girl he grew up with? What a pair. They fit together like a jigsaw puzzle, each piece alone just an awkward and intricate muddle of needs waiting to be filled, arms waiting to grasp; once joined, they were seamless. If she was sheltered, that made them both stronger; if he had spent his childhood more alone than not, that made them better prepared for loneliness and solitude. This, Arthur reflected, was the unique power that allowed them to reach across the divides between them.

"I wanted to ask you a slight favor," said Thomas.

"Sure," said Arthur.

"I'm going away on business for a few weeks, and I wanted to ask you to keep an eye on Beal. Make sure she's doing okay. Maybe check in with M. Richard and Céleste to see if she seems okay. It would mean a lot to me."

Arthur didn't hear much of this last bit, not that it would have surprised him. He was still wondering about that phrase *keep an eye on*. Painting a portrait of someone was about looking at her, but he still felt like rubbish about the way he'd behaved; he regarded this as a "bad time" in his life. Lately he wished he did know more about Beal, and about this African, and whether there was anything going on, and if so, what was the nature of his hold over her. He wished he knew why she cried when she was getting undressed; in the absence of knowledge only one supposition made sense. And as all this was going on, her husband had seemed to be seeking him out, as if he too had something he needed. From the beginning Arthur had thought of himself as the barbarian outside their gates, and now he discovered that he was in the middle, in the heart of it. How, he asked himself, had that happened?

But he could say none of that, of course. "Business? I know you've been up to something in Galignani's. Your wife says you did a lot of research there in the winter. I'm not sure she said what sort of research."

"She didn't say because she doesn't know."

"That doesn't seem entirely like you. You seem incapable of answering any question without all too much candor." Arthur thought for a second about that word, *candor*. Before becoming friendly with Thomas, he could hardly have imagined why such a word had ever been invented.

"She didn't ask."

"And you wouldn't"—he paused again, about to use another strange word when speaking about family discourse—"volunteer anything?"

"It's for a kind of an odd reason."

"Well. What is it? What's the plan?"

"Wine."

"No. I'll just have another beer," said Arthur.

Thomas laughed, beckoned to the waiter, and ordered two more beers. "Actually, I'm thinking about grapes. I've been reading about wine and grapes. A fair amount of it in English. Some of the texts are in Latin, which I know pretty well, but most of them are in French. Some in Italian. It's been slow going for me."

"You mean you're thinking about growing grapes. A winery? Something like that?"

"Yes. In the South, in the Midi. A region called Languedoc."

"Huh," said Arthur. He could play this game of monosyllables too, not that it came naturally to him. Having mastered the way Beal conversed, he was now getting acquainted with Thomas: first this ritualized little dance, a kind of throat clearing, waiting to be asked the right question. Unattractively coy, really. Back in Newark,

you might as well cut your tongue out if that's the way you expected to be given the floor.

"Do you know anything about phylloxera?" Thomas asked.

Arthur did not. Never heard of it. No idea what it was. A kind
of flower? He tipped his head forward encouragingly, impatiently.

"Phylloxera is an aphid that kills grapevines. It attacks the roots
and kills the plant. It's native to America, and it's the reason that
for two centuries every attempt to grow European wine grapes in
America has failed. Now it's gotten over here. In the past twenty-
five years it has pretty much destroyed the French wine industry.
In many regions there isn't a vine left."

"Certainly sounds like an ideal time to get into the grape business," said Arthur. Their beers had been brought, and he took a
long gulp.

Thomas smiled: yes, he implied, an ideal time. "There are two
camps on how to treat it. They're called the chemists and the Americanists. The chemists have developed sprays that help a little, and
they're trying to perfect them. The Americanists have been bringing over rootstock of native American grapes that is resistant to
phylloxera and then grafting French varieties onto it. Most of the
varieties take to the graft pretty well. It's the right way to do it.
Simple, really."

"I guess. We didn't do much grafting of plants in Newark.
Graft, yes, we did that."

"This was all decided at the International Phylloxera Congress
in Bordeaux in 1881."

"Gee," said Arthur. "I was busy that weekend."

Thomas laughed. Arthur had never seen him so happy; this trip
was changing things for him, it seemed. "Beal and I grew up in
this world. *Rootstock* may have been one of the first words I learned.
At one point there were more than a hundred thousand peach trees
on my family's farm, every one of them grafted either by Beal's
father or under his supervision. Then they all died. It was living
hell for all of us. For years all you could smell in the breezes was
burning peachwood."

"Perfect," said Arthur. "I can see why you'd be planning this
on the sly from your wife."

"The odds of success are better than those for painting."

"Yes," said Arthur. "Those odds are getting longer every day."

Beal's final sitting was the week before Thomas left for Languedoc. Arthur didn't know what Thomas had said to her about his plans and still had no idea what he was supposed to do for her in Thomas's absence. Once again she came to the sitting without Céleste, but their greeting was as formal as it had always been: Beal heading straight for the spot on the floor where he had chalked in the outline of her feet, Arthur keeping behind the demarcation described by the plane of his canvas. There was no bare knee in the portrait and only the tips of the fingers of one hand.

There had been no real reason for this sitting, maybe even for the last two or three. Arthur would keep working on the painting for months, but releasing his subject represented a jump into the unknown, a place where he could either perfect or destroy what he had set out to do, and he was more than a little reluctant to go there. In this he was not unlike every painter he'd ever known.

"Are you really doing anything over there?" asked Beal.

"No," he said. "I'm staring at my canvas in fear." He meant it as a joke, though he didn't think she would get it.

"Then we're both afraid."

Arthur was so absorbed in his own anxieties that it took him a moment to hear what she said. His eyes darted back to his canvas: Is the fear there? Should it be there? But suddenly, unexpectedly, perhaps belatedly, it registered on Arthur that after all these weeks, none of this was about—or simply about—a painting. His model was reaching out to him; she was asking for his help. He wasn't sure what a painter was supposed to do in that situation. He put down his brushes and came around from behind the easel. She was still in her slightly contorted pose, but when she saw him come forward, she relaxed it, let her right hand fall off her left shoulder and hang at her side.

"Beal," he said.

She gave a start, hearing her name from him for the first time. "You said your painting would help me."

"I think I was wrong. Maybe a painting makes nothing happen. But maybe I could be your friend. Would that help?"

6

Thomas was late getting off to the station to catch the train into the deep South of France, to Toulouse, almost in the Pyrenees. He'd ordered a cab in plenty of time, but Arthur was coming to accompany Beal home after the train left, and then Madame Bernault decided that she too must join the party. She made up some excuse for this, but the real reason was that she had never approved of Arthur, thought the idea of sitting for a portrait indecent even with Céleste along as chaperone; she was shocked that Thomas had asked Arthur to look in on her while he was gone. "I don't think he's suitable," she sniffed.

"He's a rough sort," said Thomas, "but I've come to trust him. He's very fond of Beal."

"Exactly," said Madame Bernault.

"Have you ever heard or observed anything that makes you think there is more to his feelings than that?" Thomas asked.

No, said Madame Bernault, she had not, but what did one know about these Americans, these American youths in Paris who lived a life so apart from the normal population, whose comings and goings seemed to obey no particular standards of behavior. Madame Bernault had lived all over the world serving the Society of the Sacred Heart and had always felt it her calling to enter into the local community, not to remain cloistered. But one maintained one's carriage. "I can't imagine what the parents of those young women are thinking, allowing them to come here alone to live only God knows where."

"Oh, Mother Lucy. You know Hilary was here with her mother, and the rest of them live with the demoiselles Rostand. Your novices live a freer life. You said that Colleen and Hilary were *gamines et captivantes*. You said you admired their resolve."

Still, Madame Bernault insisted on coming along, and she was to be hurried less and less these days. So after the frustration of waiting for Arthur to help him carry his luggage to the street, Thomas had to endure further minutes waiting for Madame's large black-and-white form to round the corner from Les Invalides.

"Don't fret," said Beal.

Céleste was there too, still the French teacher: "Remember, in the Midi some say *oc* instead of *oui*." When at last they made it to the Gare d'Orléans, there was time only for Thomas to give Beal a parting hug and tell her that he hoped that when he got back, the path forward for them would be clear. Beal didn't add anything to that—he had not expected her to, for what could she say?—but Thomas understood full well that what had once been a promise—*Don't worry, I'll find something for us to do*—had become more of a warning: *Someday very soon we're going to be packing up.* Because by now Thomas was more aware than ever that it wasn't going to be easy for her to go back to the farm after living so fully in Paris.

The conductor was waiting impatiently outside Thomas's compartment, and as soon as his luggage was loaded, the train lurched with a clang and thud and a screech of the whistle. The train gathered speed as it passed through the suburbs and towns just outside the Paris purview, and soon they were on flat tableland that reminded Thomas of the Eastern Shore, except for the clusters of stone villages and the imposing hubs, the *mas*, of the larger farms. As the morning wore on, they passed through rolling hills where there seemed to be mills and forges of some size. In Argenton, while the engine took on water and coal, Thomas descended to the platform to eat the lunch Mme Vigny had packed for him. In the hills were the ruins of a thirteenth-century castle "destroyed by Louis XIII," as one of his several guidebooks informed him. This was a theme of the French landscape that Thomas had begun to notice: so much built by human hand for some purpose or cause, so much destroyed by other human hands under the banner of other purposes or causes.

Back on the journey, they entered into that sparse heartland of France called the Limousin, an ever-changing vista of hills and rivers and fertile farmland, and as they reached the city of Limoges, they were in the midst of one of France's greatest industries, porcelain and enamel known the world over. Thomas had skipped over the vast number of volumes on the subject at Galignani's; he remembered his mother, Ophelia, exclaiming with a kind of feverish rapture that the new set of china at the Retreat was *genuine Limoges*, not some cheap German imitation. How odd is life, Thomas thought, that he might have just passed the factory where that set was made, that he could see in the very air of the city the light haze of dusty kaolin, the headspring, really, of his mother's delight.

Thomas could have booked himself on a mail train that had dining and sleeper cars, but seeing the sights of this country, of his new home, seemed as much the point of the trip as anything, and so it was that he spent the night in Limoges at a rather plain but comfortable hotel not far from the station. From his accent, the proprietress thought he was Flemish. The city, the hotel, the chatter of business people in the dining room reminded him of Baltimore, and for a moment he thought of all those years when his mother and Mary were living across the bay in that city and he and his father were on the Retreat. He went to bed that night, his first night without Beal since they'd landed, with his arms closed around her absence. He did not minimize the stakes for this trip, but here in this new bed his heart pounded with eagerness for what might lie ahead.

Thomas had once considered taking a route farther to the west and spending a day or two in Bordeaux, where he might one day have some business. But then he had decided not. Yes, Eileen Hardy was the angel guiding this trip, and there was no way for him to think otherwise; it was as if she ran alongside the tracks like a clear mountain stream. It was her voice in his head that told him not to waste his time among the British and Austrian aristocrats; it had been her voice telling him to get on this train in the first place. Back at the Gare d'Orléans, in the rush, he had for one second thought he spied her red hair in the crowd, and it was a moment of panic but then of sad delight, the thought that from a distance she would be there to see him on this quest. She *was* there, in his mind; he'd told her that she would be when he said goodbye to her a few days before he left. For the past month, all had been very businesslike between them. "Good luck, then," she said. "I am glad our collection has served you so well." He wanted to tell her he would miss her; he almost wanted to tell her that everything was riding on this trip and that depending how it went, the situation might be very different when he got back. But he had not said any of that, only that he would be sure to let her know how it all turned out, and she turned away with a proper smile to the work at her desk, as if he should certainly not disarrange himself on her account. That smile would remain in his mind, in his conscience, to the end of his days.

After a night in Toulouse—less comfortable, with indifferent welcome and service—he caught the Perpignan branch line, across the dry rubble land of the Haute-Garonne and the wild rocky hills of Aude, along the route of the Canal du Midi, and finally into the old Roman capital of Narbonne. This was his destination: *lenga d'òc*. Below the southern limit of metropolitan France, as the Parisians thought of it. The *paysans* were dirty, coarse; they talked without stop, as Céleste had told him. The wine was not fit for the Parisian table, so said M. Richard. Why in the world would he want to go there? Worst of all, in Languedoc many people didn't even speak French, but clung to their own language, Occitan, the Langue d'Oc. It was the land of the Cathars, a twelfth-century heresy that had taken two centuries to wipe out. People thrown off cliffs and ramparts; four hundred men, women, and children roasted alive on a single day; defeated soldiers left with their noses, tongues, eyes, and ears cut out. That sort of wiping out. It was a land of steep mountains and deep crevasses, but also broad plains and high meadows. A yellow land, with dots of ochre and obsidian. The land of schist, of limestone and shale, of chalk rubble. A land on which grapes flourished because it was so inhospitable to them. How odd, thought Thomas; this was the sort of orneriness in the natural world, the sort of melodrama of plant life that his father would have enjoyed. Grapes like to be mistreated, forced to search for water and nourishment. If they're fat and happy, they make a luxurious and indolent leafy mantle; if they're hungry and worried about the continuation of their species, they skip the ornament and make seeds—not a lot of them, but a few bursting with vital juices. They had been doing this for thousands of years quite happily, until the arrival of phylloxera, a different kind of wiping out.

Thomas knew all about fighting a desperate, endless, and finally unwinnable battle against the peach yellows, an enemy one couldn't see that would show itself only after it had completely infected the plant. He remembered walking in the orchards with his father and Abel Terrell, Beal's father. They never said anything to each other; they didn't have to: the leaves, the fruit, the bark said everything for them. *We are ruined.* For Thomas, as a child, it felt as if his own body would be the next to be attacked, that he would wake up on some not-too-distant morning with the suckers of diseased branchlets sprouting on his arms and legs, just as they did on the peach boughs. He remembered the dozens of theories and treatments, each one loonier than the last, which were extolled loudly and emphatically and then quietly dropped when the deaths continued. Blight had a way of reducing owners and professors and senators and farmworkers and former slaves and immigrant fruit pickers to a single class, to a genus of baffled humans who had no idea what was hitting them. It all ended in cemeteries distinguished by a unique brand of tombstone: the endless lines of blackened stumps that marked the places where a tree, or a vine, had once lived.

The difference here was that a solution was at hand. So Thomas had picked a name out of the list of *négociants* in Montpellier, Béziers, and Narbonne and written to him, asking whether there might be land for sale in the region, and if so, could M. Fauberge serve as intermediary for him. The return was immediate. Yes, said M. Fauberge, there was certainly land suitable for growing grapes available in the region. But, he asked the writer—who was obviously English or American—why not Bordeaux or Bourgogne or Champagne? Why Languedoc, a region not of legendary domaines and wine caves, but of simple table wines? His tone was defensive, protective: Did Monsieur have any idea what he might be getting into? Thomas could well understand why M. Fauberge asked this, and his reply was straightforward: "I know nothing of wines, nothing about how to make them and how to drink them. I know only about farming. I was raised on an orchard and am familiar with blight."

So he found himself, all ironies intact, the following morning, waiting for M. Fauberge in a pleasant sidewalk café under the palm trees just a block from Narbonne's modest but picturesque Place de l'Hôtel-de-Ville. High piles of firewood, flocks of sheep, mounds of coal, and, over and over, casks and casks of wine bobbed almost magically in front of him, the cargo piled atop canal boats that he could not see from where he sat.

"M. Bayly?" said a man behind him. He pronounced the name "buy-lee," which Thomas had heard from time to time in Paris.

Thomas stood up and found that M. Fauberge was an extremely handsome and robust man with a mustache of remarkable breadth and luxuriousness; anyone who ever saw him would remember the mustache first. Thomas found it a little untrustworthy. Fauberge was wearing the obligatory black serge suit, but his straw boater was tipped back on his skull and he had a welcoming, winning smile despite the facial hair.

Thomas introduced himself, and they sat down.

"I am hoping . . ." M. Fauberge began in English, but Thomas waved him off. "*Excellent*," M. Fauberge continued in French, relieved, seeing Thomas already in a new light. "I hope you are enjoying our city."

Thomas was. It was a lovely and relaxed town, full of charm, he said.

"Your M. Baedeker has said that we have 'emphatically seen our best days' and that visiting Narbonne is a disappointment to 'those who bear in mind its former importance.'" M. Fauberge quoted this in English, but with good cheer.

Thomas had the feeling that M. Fauberge, and other town

leaders, could recite the entire hurtful entry from the guide, which, in fact, Thomas had read on the train just the day before. "I think Karl Baedeker is German. No?" he said.

"Quite so. I should not have blamed America for what he said."

"Yes. Especially since you can rightly blame phylloxera on America. No need to add to our sins."

The dreaded word caused M. Fauberge to flinch, but Thomas knew that by using it he had won a tiny bit of respect, that the more he could remove the unsaid from this man's prattle, the better things would go for them both.

"Oh, but America is the source of our salvation as well. We all have our roots in America now." He laughed at this common joke. "Here in Languedoc we think that the plague was a blessing of sorts. It gives us a new chance while Bordeaux and Burgundy try to recover. That is, if we plant the right grapes."

"By which you mean something other than Aramon?"

M. Fauberge's mustache danced with surprise at hearing Thomas say this, and he looked around with alarm to see who might have overheard. He lowered his voice. "As you Americans say, the wines of the plains, the Aramon wines, are my 'bread and butter.'" He said this in English, with a self-satisfied cock of his head. "But this is not where we will compete with Bordeaux."

"Grenache, then? Carignan? Syrah?"

M. Fauberge was still a little nervous to be having this fraught discussion in a café full of his friends and competitors; Thomas was doing little more than parroting words he had read in a book, but he understood the magic of some of them.

"I see you are very well acquainted with the challenges that face the vigneron. And"—and here, for the first time, M. Fauberge entered into the sly, slightly arch but finally more candid tone that Thomas was to hear a good bit of in the coming weeks—"that you understand the opportunities for a man with a vision such as yourself. Eh?"

Thomas didn't know if he had a vision, but the facts and figures and the science, the botany and agronomy seemed to add up to the same empirically proven conclusion: Aramon was a lousy grape that made a lot of lousy wine, wine that no one outside the

Midi would consider drinking for one second. That was a vision, as far as Thomas understood it.

"A vision," M. Fauberge continued, "to show the world that we can make wines as fit for the table in Paris as those from Bordeaux. That Languedoc is the sleeping giant of French wine no longer. That we can produce more than simple *vin de pays*. Am I correct?" M. Fauberge was almost rising from his seat in excitement.

Thomas had been in this strange land only a few hours and was hardly ready to take up its causes, but he acceded to M. Fauberge's take on the matter. Yet he did this with enough diffidence to induce M. Fauberge to delve further into Thomas's personal history.

"Could I ask," he said, "why you chose to leave America? At this time?"

"Certainly," said Thomas. "France seemed to offer a better opportunity for my wife and me."

M. Fauberge allowed some surprise, and relief, at hearing this. "Ah. Such a young married man. It's good to be married. Is Mme Bayly with you in Narbonne?"

"No. She is in Paris with friends. I'll return with her when everything is settled."

Here M. Fauberge's brow furrowed; it was remarkable how expressive his face was, how it brightened and darkened, how his mustache amplified his smiles and accented his concern. "A vineyard is a calling for an entire family. It needs children. But the wife must be prepared for the simple pleasures of work and hearth."

"Don't be misled, M. Fauberge. My wife was raised on an orchard just as I was. We are used to, as you say, the simple pleasures."

"Well then. All is magnificent," said M. Fauberge.

Thomas had passed the several tests put before him, and at that they agreed that he would accompany M. Fauberge on his annual tour of the brokers and the vignerons with whom he did the bulk of his business. Between appointments, they would take such detours that allowed Thomas a survey of the more unusual opportunities. They would leave in perhaps a week's time. M. Fauberge's man Léon was already in Carcassonne with his carriage. "Must keep up appearances, especially in these times," said M. Fauberge. They would take the train to Carcassonne. Thomas admitted to M. Fauberge that he had hoped to travel on a *barque de poste* on the Canal du Midi.

"Oh, there hasn't been passenger service on the canal for thirty years, but it could still be some use to you if you ship to Bordeaux. I'll arrange for you to take a day on the canal while I prepare for our trip. A wonder of the world, of course."

Once they got to Carcassonne, they would head south, toward Limoux—"Saint-Hilaire, the abbey that invented Champagne, Blanquette de Limoux, as I'm sure you know," said M. Fauberge— because M. Fauberge had immediate business there. "Fine hillsides in the upper valley of the Aude. There are some splendid *nouveaux châteaux* in various styles for sale there, but they would not be a suitable situation for a serious man."

On the way back north they would cross the alluvial plains, the heartland of the Languedoc winery. "Fine, rich soil, well-drained, somewhat resistant to mildew, excellent for our beloved Aramon grape," said M. Fauberge at a heightened volume.

After they had crossed the broad plains and visited the small number of growers who had survived the plague, they would work north and enter the garrigue, the rocky herbed hills of the Minervois region, where Thomas and his young bride would find their fortune. "Right under the shadow of *la Montagne Noire*. Eh?" he said. Thomas nodded. They would stay for a day or two at especially comfortable hotels in Caunes and La Livinière, maybe in Minerve itself, though the terrain around that little town was perhaps too *dramatique*. Thomas had seen photographs of Minerve, and even on the page the cliffs and gorges made him tremble. "Thin lands," continued M. Fauberge. "Microlithic and pyroxenic. Very little depth. Calcareous fissures right up to the surface. The soil decides everything, after all. The yields are especially low, hardly worth all that work. A drop in the bucket, as you Americans say, but what a drop! Perfect," he added. "We'll see Carignan, Morrastel, Terret Noir, Aspiran. Even several hectares of Cinsault that survived the plague." M. Fauberge was practically singing at this point. And finally, clearly a sentimental choice for M. Fauberge, they would complete the tour on the dunes and sands of the Agde coast, where they would have a chance to drink quantities of Piquepoul and gorge on *les fruits de mer.* "We shall have a splendid time . . . Armand," he yelled to the waiter, "we will have lunch now." Thomas was, indeed, famished from all this travel, all these dry soils and vast plains. "You will never forget me," said M. Fauberge, giving his mustache a comb and a caress with the tips of both index fingers.

In Paris, the morning after Thomas left, Beal awoke in an un-earthly quiet—she had never before slept in an empty home, which thrilled and frightened her. Imagine being alone, waking up like this for the rest of your life. Yes, these were the sort of stakes that seemed to be attending her thoughts these days—never this, for-ever that. She recalled the extremely rushed and completely irregu-lar process of her conversion to Thomas's Catholic faith, and the one session of discussion and counseling prior to marriage with Father Langlois back in Newport News before he married them and sent them clattering down the road for their escape to . . . here. To France. There had been so many momentous aspects of her mar-riage to Thomas, so many legal considerations, so much secrecy, that the more ordinary questions, the more ordinary assumptions and commitments about the future, about the future until Death, did not come up. Not really, until now.

Beal stayed in that day, tried and failed to write a letter to be mailed somehow to Thomas, tried and failed to write in her note-books, which had now become a diary, a journal, something. She stayed in the next day, took the little girls to the Champ de Mars in the afternoon, and ate dinner with Céleste and her family at the hotel, and when she awoke the following day, she knew that she was supposed to spend these days and weeks of her husband's ab-sence in just such a manner. It had a comfortable and simple rhythm and would be the proper way to protect herself from distrust, but she was *not* living a simple life, and she had to venture forth into the heart of her confusions.

So after lunch she went back to the Louvre, where Arthur found her. "Am I some sort of devil?" he asked. "Did the Jew need to be cast out?" After Thomas had gotten on the train, Madame Bernault had made it clear to Arthur that he was to go his own way.

"Oh," said Beal. "Mother Lucy is just a hen guarding her chicks. This isn't about religion."

"That's good," said Arthur. "If it were, I'd be shtook."

"Shtook?"

"Oh, I keep forgetting who I am dealing with here. I'd be in deep trouble."

Beal laughed. Thomas's friendship with Arthur had at first terrified her—what would Arthur tell Thomas?—and then confused her, as they seemed to have nothing in common but herself, which did not seem enough for a manly relationship. But through Thomas's eyes she had begun to see a different kind of man, an honest and guileless sort of man whom Thomas would indeed like, and with that new image in mind she found she could forgive Arthur for the way he had treated her.

"So," he said. "Am I going to have to keep my eye on you, as Thomas said?"

She was sitting in a window well in the portrait gallery; she had been looking out at the courtyard in front, at the Tuileries down to the left, as a way of avoiding all these faces of worthy people, of dutiful wives—all these eyes already on her. She sighed.

"You know I will do anything to help you. That was our deal anyway, wasn't it?"

"Maybe. If that's the way you think of it now."

Arthur dropped his eyes in a moment of shame. "This guy. Nothing about this makes you feel good. You're happy when you're with Thomas, isn't that right?"

"Thomas is the miracle of my life. You'd have a better idea than most people how miraculous the change is. Less than a year ago I was a maid in an army colonel's home."

"Sure," he said. "Then why do you let this guy, whatever his name is, come between you?"

"Because he is between us. Because he's in my way. Because he's asking questions I have to answer. Just because a Jew might fall in love with and marry a Methodist, does everything that stood in their way just disappear? I don't think Thomas made the mistake of thinking this way about us, but I did."

Arthur had nothing to add, but Beal was grateful that he knew as much as he did; if he knew nothing, he would not know that she needed him at her side. In secret wars there are no allies, just casualties.

"I've been working on the painting. It's almost done. Will you want to see it?"

Except for some glances quickly pulled away, in the whole process of sitting for him she had seen nothing of the portrait. More than anything, she was afraid it would embarrass her, though in exactly what way she didn't know. Maybe she was afraid that it wouldn't be good, that it would look nothing like her. That was what a portrait was supposed to do, wasn't it? Or was it? Arthur's insistence that a portrait of her by Stanley or Colleen would be "a waste" made her wonder what would be wasted, what would be missed or dropped along the way.

"Will I like it?" she asked.

"What a question," he said.

"I don't see why it's so strange to ask that. It's supposed to be me, right?"

"Well, I think it captures who you were when you were sitting for it."

"Who was that?"

"Someone with a whole lot more strength and power than she dreamed."

"At home they'd call it uppity."

"There's you in the portrait, but no home."

"Then I hope I never see it."

"No. You're wrong. You don't need to cling to 'back home,' and you know it."

Beal left him with the answer that she might look at it when the time came, or she might not. That was the way she felt about almost everything. She was bored by the Louvre. The truth was, she had been bored for the past few weeks, months maybe, had turned her attention inward in her notebook. Colleen had gone home, and Stanley was still hurt by her betrayal—and why wouldn't he be?—and the few of the new crop of painters she met she didn't much like. It was a beautiful afternoon, beautiful outside. This city life—so much of it inside houses, in rooms, in one's own head. Not that she really objected, but sometimes, like today, she wanted to be in the air and the light. She walked home wondering when she could expect a letter from Thomas. He'd showed her where he was going and explained all about why he had picked this region off the map of possibilities, but as she had no way of knowing what the place looked like, she could only imagine Thomas floating somewhere barely out of her reach. There was so much about him she did not know. Those years when he was in college in Philadelphia—he'd tried to tell her about them, about the rooming house he lived in, about the table he sat at night after night, writing forbidden letters to her that he could not mail, about the boys he had been friends with, sort of. But Thomas himself, in Philadelphia, didn't make that much sense to her. The only place she could truly fix him in her mind was on the Retreat, so that's what she did, but it didn't help to remember that the Retreat was the one place he had given up—that he could probably not return to—because of his love for her.

Thomas never got his day trip on the famous Canal du Midi, but the train to Carcassonne followed the same route from time to time, and in this flat terrain the miles and miles of linden trees on the banks were never out of sight for very long. He'd gotten used to seeing lines of women hunched over their laundry on the banks of the canal, the towropes passing over their heads, or in towns, side by side in long sheds, *lavoirs* with stations where they could set up their tubs. This path between two seas, the invention of a seventeenth-century visionary, or crackpot—*entrepreneur* was the term they used at the time, though the source of his fortune was the less savory tax farming—climbed mountains, crossed rivers and gullies on aqueducts, tunneled through solid rock, bisected towns, and overcame the last hurdle to the Mediterranean with a massive seven-lock ladder at Béziers. Listening to his late father or his erstwhile professors at the University of Pennsylvania, Thomas might have believed that Americans invented civil engineering on the Erie Canal and the Union Pacific Railroad, but that seemed not to have been the case. While his Mason family forebears huddled in pestilent shacks in the tidal swamps of the Chesapeake, dying of the fever by the hundreds, the French were building this canal.

Thomas had spent the morning on the train writing a letter to Beal. How far away she seemed, in Paris, miles and years away. M. Fauberge was sitting across from him with his account books and his escritoire; as he had promised, they were heading into a different life. It was perhaps, as he had said, all a matter of the soil, and what they were passing through seemed to bear no relation to the heavy black beast that was the top mantle of the land in Maryland. At a stop at a station by the edge of a village Thomas walked out into a field. Even the sound of his footsteps on this land was different; this soil seemed to crumble, at worst to crack. This was a world made of stone: the buildings and the towns could seem like nothing more than elaborate outcroppings of yellow limestone and white schist; except for the clay tile of the roofs, everything was the color of this stone, even the cattle and the sheep.

He began his letter to Beal trying to express some of the wonder of this, the dislocation but also the fascination; for all its unfamiliarity, Thomas was—he hesitated with his pen—"drawn" to this life so far removed. It didn't take many sentences for him to realize that he was choosing his words more and more carefully: "if" we come here, "oddly appealing," "not uncomfortable." Far too cautious for a husband supposedly recounting a business journey to his wife at home. As he watched his pen struggle, the whole effort began to anger him, anger not directed at Beal—oh, this slow wooing of her would have to continue, he felt sure of that—but at all the times in his past when he thought dissembling in this way was required of him. These past several months, so filled with joy, had taught him how lightly he had landed anywhere in his life so far. It was something Beal's brother, Randall, once Thomas's best friend, had challenged him on: *Don't you care, Thomas? Don't any of it matter to you?* That had hurt, hurt deeply; of course things mattered to him. As a child, he had cared so much, but he had so little way or reason to express it that he thought he would explode in his bed. It was as if he were always in the doorway, with Beal in the center of the room, and she was looking back to him with love, beckoning him to come in and join the fun, even if all the people standing around her were all men.

"We shall be coming into Carcassonne soon," said M. Fauberge. On the evening before their departure Thomas had worried that M. Fauberge's enthusiasms and hyperboles might make him an exhausting traveling companion, but they had been reading and writing together all day in the most companionable way. "You will be amazed, I think, by the restorations."

Thomas shared with him the thought he had had on the train several days earlier, about this being built and torn down, and now being built up again in an endless process.

"Interesting," said M. Fauberge, giving Thomas a Gallic shrug. "I've never thought such matters of history were in any way remarkable. Two empires. Three republics. A restoration. A war." M. Fauberge could hardly shrug and *pfft* enough to express how insignificant this recent political history was, how distant such Parisian matters were here in Languedoc.

Just as he finished speaking, they rounded a bend, and there, as if magically transported from the library at the Retreat, were the walled ramparts, turrets, and towers of a castle right out of *Waverley*. "We have arrived," said M. Fauberge as they slowed for the station at the base of the hill leading up to this extraordinary vision. The hotel in Carcassonne—in the modern city, below the walls of the restored castle—seemed fine to Thomas; he was not there for hotels, and besides, especially when he was paying for his own room and, by agreement with M. Fauberge, for Léon's more modest quarters and, of course, for the horses in the stable.

In the morning they started on the route M. Fauberge had described, on the first day stopping for lunch at one of those large farms Thomas had seen through the train window, with their massive stone barns, their dwellings arranged like fortresses that showed blank walls to all who passed. M. Fauberge paid no attention to the buildings. "Mauzac, mostly. Very nice grapes. Late ripening," he said to Thomas with the affection reserved for a hardworking but dim nephew. "They make pleasant sparkling wines. Did I mention that we will be visiting the abbey where double fermentation was discovered a hundred years before Dom Pérignon claimed credit for it?"

He had, but Thomas did not say so; even if M. Fauberge repeated himself a dozen times, even if Thomas's hasty scribbles in his notebook were legible, he worried that he would understand or retain only a fraction of what the man said. The world of grapes and soil: Thomas felt as if he were standing at the portal of Western civilization.

As M. Fauberge had promised, in the days to come they worked north, and after they had recrossed the canal, they were on the plains. These were mostly small, single-family farms, a vigneron and two sons in the vineyards, women working in the *mas*, the ancient quotidian drama. Much of this life had been destroyed by the "beast"; fallow sections dotted the land like missing teeth. But what Thomas also gathered was that the area was reawakening quickly, with more and more vines being planted. Here and there were a few fields of wheat, but clearly these farmers were now all in for a single crop, which hadn't worked so well back home. Thomas could begin to identify the cultivars, especially the Aramon of this region, with its bulging clusters and weeping vines, and he had begun to share M. Fauberge's disdain. "Disgusting," whispered the *négociant* as he chatted in the most flattering and complimentary tones with the growers. "These aren't vignerons," he said, getting back into the carriage, "they're fruit growers. Might as well be growing apples." But then he apologized to Thomas, remembering that orcharding was where he had come from.

"No apologies to me, but my poor father would fight you for saying it."

"You speak of your father in so many contradictory ways," said M. Fauberge. During these long days side by side their conversation had become more and more intimate, at least on one side.

"He was a contradictory man."

M. Fauberge considered this for a few miles. This was another reason why Thomas was growing to trust M. Fauberge, to be so fond of him: for all his volubility, the wheels were always turning; you could almost hear them. He reminded Thomas of himself; the cadence of their conversation intermixed flawlessly.

"Could I ask you something?" M. Fauberge asked.

"Of course."

"I had gathered that your wife's family were growers in the same region, but I've come to understand that they are workers on your farm."

"Yes. Her father was the head orchardist. He works for my sister now in the dairy." Thomas had told M. Fauberge all about Mary's trying one last time to give the Retreat a reason to be as a model sanitary dairy.

"And most of the people who worked on your estate were Negroes?"

Thomas gazed out on the surrounding sights. To one side, at a considerable distance, there was a town clustered around a single steeple, or a single keep—it was a little hard to tell which sometimes. On the other side, not far from them, was an elaborate walled cemetery in a grove of poplars, with crypts and mausoleums that seemed a miniature version of the town—a town for the living and a town for the dead.

"Yes. That is correct."

"Ah," said M. Fauberge. He let another mile go by and then said, "That is what I thought." Another mile, and then, "Your love for your wife has seemed so protective."

Thomas could say nothing.

"Only the love that has faced high barriers feels that way." M. Fauberge paused, as if he were reflecting on his own marriage, to a daughter of a family that had come from Basque country. "I understand now."

"Does this make difficulty for you?" Thomas asked.

M. Fauberge put his hand on Thomas's arm. "There are few Africans in Languedoc, but as you have seen, we are all a little bit of everything else: Gauls, Basques, Jews, Arabs. We are all people of the Mediterranean. You will have difficulty because you are outsiders, because you are Americans, because even though you speak fine French, you have a Parisian accent. They will call you a *parigot*, which is not a nice way to refer to our countrymen to the north. But you will not have much difficulty simply because of your wife's race."

It took them a week to get across these lands, which were the

source of M. Fauberge's "bread and butter." Alternating between
the rather tiresome repertoire of flatteries and bargaining ploys in
French and in Occitan when doing business, he shared his real con-
cerns in the privacy of the carriage: too many grapes here, the
wrong kind, no good for Languedoc, they were filling a lake full
of wine that would never be drunk, and it would ruin them. They
should be planting wheat here; that's what these plains were good
for, wheat, animal feed, mulberry trees to feed the silkworms. But
these lands, these holdings were bruised from the battles, and whatever side anyone was on, phylloxera was on their mind. M. Fauberge
counted the losses like the old Confederates on the Eastern Shore:
here, in this very sandy patch, the attack had not been so bad; here
they had flooded the vineyards in the spring to good effect . . . for
a year or two anyway. Here M. Imart went mad and killed his
children; there, M. Delmas's son had spent a decade trying to mix
a recipe of poisons that would kill "the beast." Here was a once
quite adequate winery that the warring sons would let go for a few
centimes.

But there were hills in the distance, just as in Maryland there
was always a finger of the bay reaching to your side, across your
path. This was the garrigue M. Fauberge had promised, steep crags,
arid, inhospitable disturbances on the earth's surface, a tangle of
rough life. Centuries ago this had all been forest, said M. Fauberge,
but once it was harvested, the trees, except for the occasional stunted
oaks and Aleppo pines, did not come back, and now it was land for
vines and olives, for rosemary, thyme, juniper, and laurel. M. Fauberge found this all much to his liking.

On one especially clear day Thomas caught the outlines of real
mountains.

"Oh yes," said M. Fauberge happily. "Here is where it gets
interesting."

It was already interesting to Thomas, and not just as a matter
of business. As these languid days passed into a third week, with
the skin of his hands and arms darkening in front of him, his neck—
despite the broad-brimmed straw hat and neckerchief M. Fauberge
had provided—becoming dry and tough, Thomas could feel Paris
receding, as if it were being shed. He wrote to Beal every night,

but each time he sat down, he felt he had taken another step away—not from her, but from a chapter in which she had been, he thought, happy. All he wanted was to give Beal a home, that's what he said to himself, but it wasn't true, and he didn't really think it was. This land he was in was wilderness. Early in the trip, the vision of the Great Plains and the foothills of the Rockies had come to him and had remained on his mind ever since; this land seemed wide-open and savage, maybe even dangerous. M. Fauberge had told him that Roussillon, the last region before Spain, was full of brigands and highwaymen. But it was full of life, and Thomas had decided that he could, if he worked hard, make a mark here; he could, finally, amount to more than the sum of his inherited parts. His strength, on these gigantic uplands, would spring from being small and focused and free.

On the sixteenth day of the trip, they at last arrived, as if finally reaching the summit of an Alp, in the bustling foothill village of Azay-sur-Cesse. In their final approach they had left the verdant plain for the steepening hillsides, for the stony ground and dried gullies, but the village itself occupied an easy promontory, with a broad, sunny view. The hotel was opposite the *mairie*, and the public space between was full, at this hour, with men playing *boules* and children playing hide-and-seek behind the ancient, massive plane trees. There was a letter awaiting M. Fauberge at the hotel, and over dinner—they had fallen into a routine of dining together every two or three days—he said that what he had been hoping all along was that the owners of a property just outside the town, on a northeasterly slope in front of *la Montagne Noire*, would be interested in entertaining a bid from the young American. "The moment your letter arrived in January, M. Thomas, I thought of this for you, the Domaine de St. Adelelmus."

"Then why," said Thomas, "didn't we go there directly?" He was thinking, in part, of all the hotel bills he had been paying.

"Because I had to make sure you were to be trusted. After all . . ." He didn't need to elaborate.

"And?"

"You are a serious young man," he answered.

As always, the dinner was accompanied by several wines—

M. Fauberge could go nowhere without people pouring from a *pichet* or opening a bottle for him, and he was always polite, even if some of the wine was pointedly left undrunk. All these grapes, the varieties—Thomas's head was spinning, but each evening he recorded the new *cépages* with growing satisfaction, like a birder maintaining a life list. He had even begun, he believed, to understand some of the vocabulary of taste and sensation involved in this trade, the full experiences of time and tongue that transpired with every sip. "Taste the minerals here, but also that surprising little *pincée*—should I say—of nutmeg?" said M. Fauberge, handing him a glass.

As they sat down, M. Fauberge had warned him that there was no lack of alcohol in the wine of the Minervois, unlike—he could not help himself from adding—the thin, insipid wines of the plains, but in the course of this meal, here at the end of the trip, he ignored his own warning. "You are a serious man," he said, picking up the earlier thread and speaking with a candor that Thomas now recognized as entirely un-French. "Otherwise you wouldn't have come here. But here is my question. Are you too serious, M. Thomas? Not all Americans are like you."

"Well, yes. I would assume they aren't."

"You are often lost in thought."

"There's much for me to learn. I'm trying to take it in."

"Hmmm," said M. Fauberge, not buying the answer. "If you come here, you must work hard. I know you will do that, but you must also take your pleasures. An unhappy man makes unhappy wine." He took another sip of what must have been wine made by a happy man, wiped away the droplets in his mustache with a forefinger, but he could not resist touching his finger to his tongue. "You are marked by *la mélancolie*, but that does not mean you must be *triste*. Tomorrow you will be given a great opportunity. I think this will be a good turn for you."

The Minervois, Thomas had learned, was a semicircle facing south, with the center hard against the slopes of the Black Mountain and the lands at either end limited by the mountains of Hérault and Aude. Every one of the soils M. Fauberge had rattled about in Narbonne these weeks earlier was to be found here. In the morning,

M. Fauberge was full of joy, as if he were still drunk, exclaiming on each geologic transition as if—which, of course, turned out to be true—he could taste the difference. As the carriage worked its way up the mountainside, M. Fauberge called out greetings to all they passed, most of whom acknowledged him with a slight tip of the cap and some of whom came to the side of the carriage to converse.

About this time Thomas became aware that there was interest being shown in him, and it dawned on him that the word had gone out that the distant and not very well liked owner of the Domaine de St. Adelelmus was investigating a sale and that an American was coming to look it over. More than a few of these well-informed souls gaped at Thomas, his slender face and delicate features, and then turned away, as if this callow youth was not the savior they had hoped for. The carriage continued, and then Léon brought them to a stop on a ridge above the most beautiful hillside Thomas had ever seen, a perfection of textures and shades of green and yellow, where pasturage and vineyards interwove as the land bucked and heaved, and where the usual but now impossibly lovely assemblage of barns and dwellings occupied the slight hillocks at the center.

"St. Adelelmus," announced M. Fauberge, unnecessarily.

Thomas hardly heard him. There was a slight wind, a distant clang of cowbells, the barest aroma of rosemary and lavender. The deep thickets of scrubby oaks and mulberry trees were broken here and there by red and white horse chestnut blossoms. They drew closer, passed by the bustle and activity of the central farmyards, and continued a few hundred yards farther to the house, not a fake château, but, as M. Fauberge had referred to it, a "bastide," a grand but in no sense elegant home for a "serious" family. It was a solid two-story building, the same hues of yellow as the surrounding buildings, but it was built of quarried limestone blocks and not the rubble and mortar of the barns and more modest workers' dwellings. The house was bigger than it looked from the ridge, with appendages at both ends, and a gravel drive to a circle in front of a green door gave it just the suggestion of stateliness. The shutters were closed, as they always were in the daytime, but it had been long enough since they were opened that vines had grown onto them. As deserted and abandoned as the house looked as they drew closer, Thomas's heart beat wildly. It felt to him as if he had drawn up to this entrance a thousand times before, as if he had done it as a baby in a mother's arms, as a child, as if it would happen in the future thousands of times more. He felt this place closing over his life, occupying spaces left empty until now. He got out, gave the green door a shove, and walked into a large hall with an enormous fireplace to one side and a surprisingly grand stone staircase on the other. The air was cool—mineral and vegetable, marble and sage. Slats of sun showed through the shutters on the other side of the room.

His search was over. At that moment he knew that falling in love with Beal and being forced to leave Maryland was simply part of a plan to bring him *here*; when Eileen Hardy nudged him south, across the mountains, this was where she wanted him to go. To land in this stone hallway, listening to a primordial drip-drip of water somewhere deeper within. Thomas knew that this hallway was the center of his center, that this was where he wanted to be, and if Beal would come with him, it could be their heaven on earth.

7

In Thomas's latest letter he wrote, "I have seen a farm in Languedoc"—he had started to write another word, but then crossed it out and wrote "farm"—"that seems workable for us, and I am in the process of purchasing it." Beal wondered what the other word could have been—maybe it was something in French— but it probably didn't matter. In any language, a farm was a farm. She knew it was going to be a farm, that's what Thomas had been saying, that's where they both came from, that's what they did. But though she could not admit it even to herself, when she read that word, she felt the dull thud of hope dying, as if her luck had just run out, as if she were being reeled back to a former life. She could imagine none of the freedoms she had enjoyed as a young woman in Paris being available to her on a farm. She still missed her family, she missed the pleasures of her youth, but the Retreat was an unlucky place. Its plagues and blights and thwarted dreams seemed to be recompense for its histories, not that Beal knew all that much about them. Compared with Tuckertown, the little settlement where she grew up, compared with anything Beal had ever known, the Mansion House was like an unfriendly world, with each room its own continent.

"The house is simple," he wrote, "but commodious, and the dependencies seem in excellent shape." A farm. Her thoughts went back to the first day she woke up in Hampton, Virginia, in Colonel Murphy's house and looked out her little third-floor window onto the shady street, where even the deliverymen and domestics doing their early-morning chores looked elegant, even the Negro maids looked sophisticated. She'd been sent there to get her away from Thomas, and the separation had had its way with her. She felt she could be someone new there, someone she could never be on the farm, and she was. On holidays she went with her friends to the park along the river to listen to the music, and men who were too old for them pulled up in wagons and carts and flirted with them. In Hampton she wasn't the only pretty girl, the only pretty black girl; everyone else seemed beautiful and full of romance. A silly boy named Hiram, a student at Hampton, often called on her on Sundays, presented himself at the kitchen door; at the end of the year he went back to Roanoke to read law. Hiram was so polite and so innocent that he never even tried to kiss her—which she would have allowed, and perhaps more, because her friends talked of almost nothing but lovemaking. She had been thinking of him from time to time lately, how her life might have turned out with him: a lawyer's wife in Roanoke? This was all to play out in the future, but that first morning in Hampton she knew, whatever else happened in her life, that she was never, ever going back to the farm.

"I don't want to promise too much, but it is a savage and beautiful landscape, mountainous and dry, and some of the vineyards are planted in fields of white chalk stones. Even on hot days it is cool under the branches of the olive trees, and the air is scented with rosemary and thyme." She knew that Thomas was telling her that where he proposed to move them was nothing like the Eastern Shore, for that had seemed to be *his* one certainty. He would never return to those flat lands and tepid waters, that rich black loam soaked in blood. "I believe there is much that a person of ambition can do here. Until now it seems that few winegrowers have approached this challenge with sufficient regard for science." Science, thought Beal; science ended you up under a gravestone at the Retreat like Thomas's father. *Scientist*: that was the one word of identification or praise that he had decreed for his own epitaph. "The purchase is taking longer than I want, but if all goes well,

I will be back in a fortnight, and we can move on to this next part of our adventure together."

Beal put the letter down. It had arrived two days earlier, along with another letter. Two letters, one addressed to Mrs. Thomas Bayly, the other to Mlle Beal Terrell. One mailed from Narbonne, France, and the other hand-delivered. It was June now, unexpectedly bright and hot; she had gotten used to Paris as a chilly and rainy place, and the dry, dusty early-summer heat wave came as a surprise. She was sitting at the little writing table they had borrowed from one of the rooms at the hotel; in the winter, from where she sat, she'd seen these rooftops covered in gray snow and smoke, a monochrome display relieved only by the red of the chimney pots. It was a cold, almost primeval memory, but today she looked through the fresh leaves of the lindens and chestnuts, and every balcony seemed to have its own pot of begonias, poppies, roses. From three or four rooftops, flags were flying, though she did not know what they celebrated or signified. It seemed impossible to her that she had been here only eight months.

She was pretending to write, but she was only counting down the hours. She had pulled her skirt above her knees and was fanning her face and neck with the Chinese fan Thomas had given her at Easter. Mme Vigny clanged away in the kitchen; she was a noisy cook, unlike Beal's mother, always so silent, so strong. Beal couldn't bear to think of her mother, couldn't shake the idea that somehow she was looking over her shoulder still. Beal had learned that Mme Vigny's husband was in the army and had been stationed in Algeria for the past ten years, that he had another family with an Arab woman; she seemed to warm up after Thomas left, as if wives on their own were the proper order of things, a sisterhood that understood the challenges and temptations of a marriage where the husband had gone missing.

In all Beal's months at the Louvre, she had never picked up a paintbrush, which she had no interest in doing. More and more it was clothes she thought about, wrote about in her journals, and toward the end of her Louvre visits it was the dresses, the simple Roman tunics and the Elizabethan monsters that she concentrated on. She liked to think of the painters painstakingly rendering the textures and patterns as if they were weaving them anew. If she thought anything about sitting for Arthur—and it wasn't something she liked to think about—it was that she regretted what she'd been wearing. She often found herself wandering through the aisles and galleries of the Bon Marché, where everything that happened in the parks and boulevards seemed instantly to find expression; that was what she loved about clothes, how subtly they *expressed*. Recently a whole new department selling cycling clothes had sprung up. Just the day after Thomas left, there had been a gigantic sale at the Bon Marché; the whole vast central gallery had been swathed and shrouded with linen, like a Persian tent. Floating in these airy spaces, hovering like dandelion thistles, were hundreds of umbrellas and parasols of the strangest colors. All through that spring these Bon Marché colors were the rage. Beal wouldn't admit this to anyone, but all those months at the Louvre had not given her the thrill, the visual delight that these floating umbrellas hanging by the handles in midair had offered.

She still loved taking the girls out to play, and a few times they went on outings to the Champs-Elysées for the *guignol* shows at the marionette theater, and then she watched them as they played tag with the other children, almost all of them under the eye of someone of dark complexion, Arab, Iberian; Beal fit right in. Gilberte was turning into a little bit of a bully, and when she was tagged, she pouted; she was mean to a shy little round-faced boy who seemed always to be there, wanting to play with them. Beal did miss going to the theater, which was one thing she could not do alone; she had made no real girlfriends since Colleen and Hilary left, and there was no way she could go with Arthur. Besides, he hated the theater. She missed Thomas. Of course she missed Thomas. She missed their intimacy; she could make desire bloom just by thinking about it.

She reached for the other letter on the table. It had appeared two days earlier, an escalation, an insinuation that brought this battle right into her home. Another week had gone by and she had not visited him in his rooms. But she had returned to the café as always. What was the meaning of this? he demanded. In six weeks he would be returning to Senegal and he had to know whether to tell his household, his other wives, to prepare a suite for her. This was all so *ennuyeux*, so *inutile*; she knew he was right, that her future lay in Africa. He had been patient beyond any acceptable measure. As one could see, he was willing to look beyond her bad American manners. Until now, he meant. She would stop this. At three o'clock on Wednesday she would come to him and she would accept his offers.

This was all getting very complicated. She had seen Arthur the day before, had snuck out the back way lest Madame Bernault be at the hotel keeping her eye on things, on her. She had wanted to tell him about this letter, because by now she had very few secrets from Arthur and he was a wise person, but he had not been at any of his afternoon spots; no one had seen him for a few days. A bad sign. She went to his building, trudged loudly up the stairs to warn him that she was coming, and he met her at the top, unshaven, unwashed, dressed in a grimy gown. His black despair seemed to be increasing; this time he didn't even try to hide it from her. "I thought it was you," he said. Her visit seemed to give him no pleasure.

"Can I come in?" she asked. It was the first time she had been there since she stopped sitting for him. When he stood aside for her to enter, she noticed that the canvas was still at his easel, with a cloth over it. "You haven't finished it yet," she said, tipping her head. She was trying to make it into a little joke.

"No," he said. "I don't think I ever will." He pointed her to the chair where she had spent so many hours, and he sat down on his bed.

The air in the apartment was awful: sweat, sewer gas, fear. "Can I open a window? Wouldn't you like some fresh air?"

"Sure," he said.

She turned the latch and tipped the window open; a light breeze entered the room. "Arthur. Are you all right?"

"I'm fine. I just didn't want to see anyone."

"Do you want me to go?"

"No. Tell me about your happy life."

Beal thought she might tell him about the letter from Thomas, the farm in Languedoc. Arthur had been talking up Thomas's plans to her, saying how he envied them, getting out of this stifling, malodorous swamp, away from the pestilence of Paris. Thomas, he had said not long ago, was "unfinished," by which he meant he had some kind of potential that no one could imagine. Beal knew she couldn't paraphrase what Thomas had said in his letter without revealing that she didn't want to go, that she had risen above her life as a farm girl, that she had risen above her parents, above any expectation anyone had for a little black farm girl in Queen Anne's County, Maryland, which was just what her mother had worked so hard to make happen. She had risen above her own *people*. There. She had said it to herself. She would say it to Touré. But not to Arthur, who was trying so hard to rise above his own background. That's what these despairs were about, his feeling that as his centimes played out and the portrait remained unfinished, he was entering into the long, painful slide back to Newark.

Instead, she nodded toward the shrouded portrait once more and asked Arthur why he had wanted to paint her so badly. "What you did to me was awful, but now I know you did it because you were desperate. You did it because you needed to paint me."

He shrugged. "Everyone wants a pretty model. Renoir prowls the streets of Montmartre looking for a pretty model."

"I am getting very tired of hearing people say that."

"I know. It shows how boring and unimaginative painters are. We're really very stupid."

Beal didn't say anything in response, because she had begun to think there was a drop of truth in it. She stayed on the portrait, which made Arthur uncomfortable. "My looks had nothing to do with it. I bet you didn't make me pretty in your picture. You were too mad at me."

He sat up as she said this, his eyes wide. "How do you know that?"

"That you were mad at me? That you hated Thomas and me?" She aped an expression of astonishment.

Arthur grimaced and shook his head. "No. Not that. What makes you say I didn't make you pretty?"

"Well. You would have showed it to me otherwise. You can't even look at it yourself, now that I am your friend. You don't like what you did to me."

Arthur slumped, his back curled against the wall. He said nothing for a full minute, and she let the silence settle.

"I didn't make you unpretty," he said finally. "No one, nothing could do that. In some ways I wish I could. Your beauty is your curse." It was Beal's turn to be disconcerted. Before she could say anything, he continued. "Look at me." He raised his arms as if to show off his fine figure. "No one cares about me, no one wants me. I am the very essence of free. Look at the way your nun treats me. Compare that to your . . ."

Beal had leaned forward, and as soon as he began that sentence, she bored her pale eyes into him and forced him to desist.

"Yeah," he said. Once again, a silence.

Beal wished she had never come, almost the way she felt the first time she sat for him, but once here, she was going to follow it through.

"Okay," said Arthur about nothing in particular. She nodded, allowed him to go ahead. "I could have just as well compared the way I treat you. That's what you said once, that we all want a piece of you. You know I love you."

"You do not. I'm too fat for you. My chest is too big." Beal had seen him once with an alarmingly thin woman, taller and flatter than he was, in every way his opposite, and she had instantly recognized that this was Arthur's sexual preference, the sort of body that excited him. When she posed for him naked that one time, she had not felt a single blood pulse of desire from him; before she saw him with that consumptive model, she had assumed that what put him off was her skin, but she realized now that it was the ampleness of her flesh.

He laughed a little. "That doesn't mean I don't want more of you than you want to give."

She had been handling this well, she thought, concentrating on cheering him up, but this comment grabbed her by the throat. *More than you want to give.* Sometimes, even now when she had so firmly renounced home, she was frightened about how very far away from herself she felt. New things had been thrust into her life, but old things had been torn away to make room. It was like the baron and his new city. Through the window she could hear the sounds of late afternoon, the medical students coming back to their flats after a long day with their cadavers, the omnibuses rumbling by, heavy with passengers. She should be on one of them, going home.

"I've had a letter from Thomas," he said.

"Yes. He would have written you about his farm."

"*His* farm? That isn't the way he sees it."

"No. It isn't," she said. "He thinks he's buying it for both of us."

"Well, he is. No? He feels the clock is ticking, but you are the one controlling the hands."

Beal felt she was controlling very little.

"So what are you going to do?" he asked when she said nothing.

"About the farm?"

"Maybe."

"Or about Diallo Touré, you mean?"

He opened his hands in a gesture of dispassion. "Only if you want to talk about it."

"I love Thomas. I know that more every day."

"See?" he said. "There's more to any or all of this than love."

"He wants me to come to his lodging."

"You mean you haven't been there before?"

It took her a moment to understand what he had said, to understand that Arthur had assumed, in some way, that she had already been there, and since it was true, Arthur's assuming it meant that no denials could ever work with him, or with anyone. What she had done, or not done, so far contained its own undeniable truths. Yet one had to resist. "Arthur. How would you think that? How dare you say that to me?" She wheeled around to reach for her hat, her gloves.

He looked genuinely sorry. "I am just trying to understand you."

"You don't know anything about me." Beal knew this wasn't true. In some ways, Kravitz was the first person she had ever met who seemed to read her with no difficulty whatsoever, who seemed unconfused by his love or by her beauty.

"I'm sorry," he said. "I just want you to know you're not alone. That I'm willing."

"So you keep saying. You keep saying you want to help me;

Thomas keeps saying he wants me to be happy. Is all this well-wishing part of my curse?"

"Yes, I suppose it is."

She did not put her hat down, but she relaxed her wrist. With her heart still beating in anger and surprise, she realized why she had come here: because it was safe. Her most shameful and carefully guarded secret, that she had gone to Touré's flat and probably would again, was nothing in this room, even as it remained a secret. This awful little hovel felt like the safest place in Paris. If safety was what she wanted, she could find it here.

"Is this all in my portrait?"

"Yeah. You see the problem. I wanted deep, but I haven't found a way to pile it all in the layers of paint. Even ten layers isn't thick enough."

She laughed at the idea of layers and layers of paint, but she understood what he was saying. She had seen this in some of the paintings in the Louvre, some of the canvases made from a paste so thick it seemed one could fall into the light and space of their cracked surfaces. "I don't want to see it. Not until it's done. Not until I'm done."

"What are you going to do?"

"I'm going to be faithful to Thomas. This man means nothing. But he won't allow me to ignore him. He won't let that stand as my answer."

"But won't he just go back to Senegal? Isn't that what you said he had to do?"

"I suppose."

In the course of the conversation Arthur had pulled himself out of his depressed shell and was sitting forward at the edge of his cot, his elbows on his knees, fixing Beal in his gaze. He felt better, Beal knew at least that had been accomplished, at least one of them felt better.

"Then, Beal . . ."

"What?"

"That means you can just ignore him. Doesn't it?"

"I think it means I haven't found a way to answer his questions. I have to do that, don't I?"

"In his rooms?"

"I was there once and came out unspoiled." She let this out a word at a time, an admission that felt better and better as it progressed, especially because where it ended, the unspoiled part, was the truth.

"Ah," said Arthur. "As I suspected."

That was yesterday. Tuesday. By the time Beal got back, Mme Vigny had gone home and Beal paced around the little suite of rooms in the gathering darkness. She recalled the cold of the winter, the way it drove her and Thomas together on the love seat, in bed. *I have seen a farm in Languedoc*: the words came back to her as a sort of curiosity. Languedoc. Why would he think this would mean anything to her? "*Langyduck*," she said out loud, a churlish little joke. She pictured the ducks on the Retreat, the way they swished their tails when they waddled out of the creek; she pictured old Uncle Pickle slaughtering them, their unsuspecting round heads lying smoothly in the grass below the chopping block. Thomas could just as well have said he had found a farm on the moon. But then she reflected that almost three years ago, back when no one could have dreamed what was coming, Thomas had said they could run away to France, and that had seemed farther than the moon. She sampled from the pot of Mme Vigny's chicken in apples and cream. Mme Vigny had told her that she grew up in Normandy, where they made almost any dish with apples; they made sandwiches with apples and Camembert cheese, which Beal could hardly touch. They didn't drink wine in Normandy, they drank *cidre*. Mme Vigny had left rural Normandy when her husband was sent to march on the Commune of 1871, and whatever the modesty of her situation in Paris, she had no desire to return.

Beal walked into the bedroom, with its simple brass bed, its deep pile of down coverings. The walls were bare, but textured with water stains and plaster patches in a way that reminded her, happily, of home. Someone was singing, humming maybe but with a sure voice, in the courtyard. *The house is simple but commodious.* She undressed, got into her nightgown. She reached for the covers but stopped, her hands outstretched; maybe each night that Thomas had been gone, there was just a little less of him in this bed. But she would be faithful to this room; she would protect it with her life. She couldn't just crawl into it like an animal in a cave, without faith or will. She thought of the little maids' rooms on the floor above them. There were several girls in them, and she had seen them many times on the stairs, at the markets; they greeted her, but rarely spoke of anything other than the weather. Beal knew they would be fast asleep very soon—in her former life she would have been—so she waited for another half hour, then crept up the stairs in her night-gown and bare feet and crawled into the little cot. It was just right, and in the morning she crept back just before Mme Vigny arrived.

She stood in front of her armoire. She did not have many dresses, despite Thomas's urgings and her frequent browsing at the Bon Marché. For her, buying a garment was a surrender to its appeal, a giving of oneself that had to be done with certainty. She'd hesitated all winter over a satin dress in the ready-made department—the salesgirl Denise Baudu looked lovely in it, but she was more slender than Beal—and by the time she had decided it was right, the sea-son had changed and it was gone. Her hand lingered over her new-est, a champagne color that matched her eyes, but it was too gay, too lighthearted. In the end she settled for something slightly un-seasonal, a maroon skirt, over which she would wear her new dark gray jacket. Perhaps the epaulets were a touch too military. She dressed, wondering with each button and tie what would happen to her today, ate breakfast, wrote in her journal, took some soup for lunch, and now was sitting at her desk. It was a little after one.

Coming home from Arthur's yesterday, she had reaffirmed that she would confront Touré in his rooms. She felt that Arthur had given his assent. To confront him. *I'm going there, I'm going there tomorrow*, she'd said to herself, to the rhythm of her footsteps. It seemed to help. Then, *I don't know what's going to happen, I don't know what's going to happen*—which helped even more in ways she did not want to analyze. *I love Thomas, I love Thomas*, she tried, but that didn't help at all. It had so little to do with this, which was perhaps a convenient thought, but it seemed to Beal, in the earnest center of her self-understanding, to be the truth. Besides, this re-peating of phrases was kind of silly.

At two she stood up, hobbled on a sleeping leg to the bedroom, where she put on her hat, grabbed her gloves, and slipped out the door. Mme Vigny had said nothing about Beal's late return the day before, so maybe she wouldn't mention it if it happened again today. She could not worry about Mme Vigny or Mother Lucy or her mother, or anyone. She had planned to walk all the way to Touré's building, but an omnibus with several vacant places was just about to depart when she passed by, and she guiltily paid her fifteen centimes and climbed to the second level. She looked down at the poor horses, just three of them pulling this immense wheeled structure, and felt guilty all over again. All these guilty feelings were feeding off her real transgression; Beal knew that she wanted to lie with this man, that this desire she had been feeling for weeks could be truly quenched, would be truly quenched, and all she had to do to make it happen was say yes. *Yes.* She wanted all that, but didn't think she was going to do it, believed instead that the warmth she felt between her legs riding in the omnibus would be gone the moment she entered his flat and she would walk out not a few minutes later "unspoiled" once again, as she had said to Arthur.

Because she had ridden the omnibus, she was early, and she passed a few minutes in Les Halles, where most of the trade was long over, except for farmers and fishmongers trying to unload the last of their stock. The streets were a mass of carts and wagons, some almost medieval in design. A little girl in a dirty pinafore stood tearfully in front of an immense pile of cabbages and begged her to take some. "*Emma,*" a sharp voice called, an order to make her work harder. Beal gave the girl a five-centime piece but took no cabbages. In the fish stalls, the last of the sea creatures, in all their unfamiliar shapes, iridescence, and unblinking eyes were arrayed in melting ice; in one stall, two women, a seller and a less-than-prosperous-looking customer, had a shouting match over a turbot, and Beal sensed that neither woman was in a very good position: the seller needed to get something for the fish before it spoiled, and the customer was hungry. Two people, each trying to get the upper hand: Was this not what she was there to do, to get the upper hand over Touré? This person who had been haunting her, stalking her, spying on her, testing her at every juncture, judging her, desiring her? Desiring her and desiring her and desiring her, ever since he'd laid eyes upon her in the dining room on the boat. She wanted to hurt him for that, all that lust for her body, hurt him with sex, give it to him and then deny him, deny him, deny him.

Touré's apartment was off a small courtyard; from the street, the arched entrance looked like the mouth of a tunnel. Just like the last time, there were dogs sitting in the stony shade, chewing on things stolen or retrieved from the markets. "Shoo," she said warily, but they didn't look up. In the courtyard there was a bit of light, but it was an unforgiving place, a sort of prison yard just big enough for an execution. The only door opened into an airless stairwell. She climbed the stairs, and when he opened the door, he behaved exactly as she'd expected. Charming. Feigning slight surprise to see her at his door, delighted to show her in. "Mademoiselle Beal," he said. "You have accepted my invitation at last."

She walked past him without a word, stood in front of the mirror over the fireplace to withdraw her hatpins and take off her hat. Through the triangles of her arms she saw him appraising her in a questioning manner; he had no idea how she was going to behave, mostly because she herself didn't know. Everything about him was obvious; everything about her was concealed, dimly sensible.

She turned around after she had finished. He was in his suit; she'd never seen him in anything but. Both the waistcoat and frock coat were a little short for his long torso. If he ever wore a top hat, he'd look like one of those stick figures in a Bosch painting, but he never did. She was satisfied with her own dress, so proper, so unfeminine, nothing to reveal the state of her body.

"I have made tea," he said. He pointed toward the pot on the table, with two cups arranged. "In case you came."

Still, she said nothing. It seemed strangely unnecessary because she knew now that she would allow this man to make love to her this once, and just this once, God help her.

He knew this as soon as she did. Not the "just once," but the "now," which was all that mattered to him. He pulled out a chair, and she sat, and then he poured the tea and for a few minutes they drank. She still didn't like tea, but took it to be polite and also to give her some time, because now there was a lot going through her head, a jumble, shards of memory vitalized by the flashes of desire. She remembered swimming on the river shore at the Retreat with Thomas and Randall, remembered how much more beautiful Randall's body seemed, with its velvet shine, compared with Thomas's freckled paleness. Yes, she thought, she would need to make love once with a man of her race in a way that Thomas would not need to make love with a woman of his, because . . . well, because a man could do pretty much what he wanted anyway, white or black didn't make much difference. Wasn't that the way of it? Or because Touré had said that she could never be sure that her womanliness was being honored and treasured, not just taken. Because in America that was all white men cared about.

She took a sip of tea and looked at him. Expectant, yes, but not a hint of triumph. That would close this thing down right quick if he looked smug, looked as if he had won over anybody, starting with Beal herself. He hadn't won over anything, but his arguments had; she didn't need or want him the way he wanted her. Any random black man would do, she told herself. He was content to let her gaze at him neutrally, to cast her eye lazily around the bare apartment. In a few weeks he would be in Africa and she would be in Languedoc, wherever that was, and all this—her apartment on the avenue Bosquet, this flat, Arthur's squalid room, yellow omnibuses and theaters and cafés, walks along the Seine, the Louvre, and the Bon Marché—all would be memory, some of it good, some of it bad, but all of it gone.

"I've come to say goodbye," she said. They were the first words out of her mouth.

"Ah," he said. He did not try to debate this.

"You will not need to tell your wives to set up a suite for me in Dakar."

"Too bad. So beautiful in my country."

"I have also come to thank you."

This did surprise him, she was pleased to observe. He raised his eyebrows: *For what?*

"You have helped me understand questions about myself that I never imagined. You were right about me. I *am* an ignorant American girl. I wish it had been possible for you to meet my brother.

You would have liked him, but also, you would have met your equal with him. Not for one second would Randall have been willing to renounce America. Not for one second. If he had lived, he would have changed it."

"You have listened to my words. I am a politician, a diplomat. Having someone listen is all that I can ask."

She had run out of things to say. She hadn't planned to say any of it, but she meant every word.

"And now?" he asked.

She nodded. He stood up, walked to the door of his room, and opened his arm into it. She remembered the last time, when that arm had been placed across her path and she had ducked under it. She followed his gesture into the room and saw the fresh lavender on his dresser; she'd been aware of a fragrance from the moment she entered the flat but had been too distracted to note what it was. She was unbuttoning her jacket as she passed. He had set up a chair for her to put her clothes on, and while she undressed, he was in the main room doing the same. She turned, and there he was, naked in the doorway. She glanced down his body. He was slender but not frail; his shoulders, his joints seemed powerfully structured. His chest and stomach were taut, and his penis was partly erect.

As she looked at him, he was looking at her, and finally he came over to her. "Turn around," he said gently, and she did, and he came up behind her, closed upon her almost, it seemed, worshipfully. He rubbed her shoulders, massaged her jaw and cheeks, then dropped his hands to her breasts.

"Ooh," she said, an escape of sensation.

He led her to the bed and turned her around. She felt like a puppet grateful for its strings, for what its strings were making it do. When she was stretched out, he kneeled on the floor and leaned over her body. He seemed in no hurry to enter her, as Thomas usually was, and each new way his fingertips grazed her skin made her shudder. He could do this forever. She thought of him pleasing his wives and maybe many other women—yes! another shudder—and she guessed he had learned many caresses because each woman liked to be touched differently. It seemed to her that this knowledge was the price he paid for his own gratification and that he was very willing to pay it. Many minutes passed, rising and falling, and when at last he climbed on top of her, she was more than ready, and his penis seemed no different from Thomas's, just right in fact, but this time she was so aroused, so loose, so wet, that the moment he was fully inside she reached a point she had never reached before. She held on as long as she could.

M. Fauberge had sent Thomas a note earlier in the day that the owners, Belgians as it turned out, had accepted Thomas's final offer. If convenient, he should come to M. Fauberge's office on the Quai de Lorraine at three o'clock to meet with the banker who was serving as intermediary. Thomas was beginning to doubt that this was ever going to work, although, in the end, two weeks of negotiation, at such great distance, did not seem so bad. He had been out to St. Adelelmus twice, had met M. Murat, the manager, and his family. M. Murat did not seem much impressed by Thomas, which was fine; Thomas had always preferred to lead from behind. His wife was rather hostile, but that was beginning to seem the way Frenchwomen acted. The rest of the names of the laborers and tradespeople of the estate would take a while to master, since most of them spoke only Occitan. Thomas had gone on two complete tours of the vineyards, the pressing rooms, the cellars; there seemed plenty of space to expand, even to set up a bottling room, if that's where this all went. His sister, Mary, was now in the process of setting up an operation very similar on the Retreat—for milk. Pure milk for babes. It began to seem to Thomas like a small, undeclared competition, their two very different beverages, their two enterprises. Mary's looked into the future, toward modern standards of sanitation and purification; this was a business their father would understand, and Mary had always been her father's daughter. Thomas's project reached deep into the past, to the terrors of superstition, out of which ancient processes had developed over a millennium—sulfur candles, sprinklings of bentonite, the blood of black hens—all of them revolving around a singularly mysterious plant, the grapevine. Perhaps, for the second time in his life, that made him his mother's son, caught in the inexplicable mysteries of her Catholicism. About the other time, when each of them, for their private reasons, renounced the Retreat, there was no mystery at all.

Even though Thomas was not yet the owner and might never be, he asked that the house be completely cleaned, the furniture polished, the linens washed. On the first day, he followed the women from room to room as they made their first pass, tramped through the dust, disposed of the dead birds and mouse droppings, threw open the shutters; on one exposure there was a fiery mountain brook that feathered out into pasturage and a vegetable garden; on another exposure he saw nothing but white chalk rubble with lines of grapes that seemed almost biblical, drinking their water out of the stones. At one end of the house was a gravel terrace bounded by a low, semicircular stone parapet, with a fig arbor on one side and on the other a large horse chestnut tree, at this time heavy with white blossoms. It was under the welcome shade of the chestnut, on a stone table, that he wrote a letter to Beal describing the place as best he could. On one side the terrace seemed to hang over the village; beyond it, the broad valley ran all the way to the Pyrenees. The other side of the terrace looked over the domaine, the tangle of stone buildings and clay roofs that seemed completely without plan but had certainly evolved out of current needs. Some of the farms Thomas had visited with M. Fauberge were tightly packed into urbanlike warrens, but St. Adelelmus, on its hilltop, was more spread out, more like an American farm, more light and more air.

An enormous, friendly Basque woman was revealed as the cook, and pantomiming in several languages, she brought forward her family to be introduced. She and her stick-thin husband made a comical pair; their daughter Gabriella, Thomas could not help but notice, was the pretty girl of the estate. There was always a pretty girl on these farms, even when and if she wasn't all that beautiful, but in this case, she was *très, très belle.* Work stopped in the farmyard, in the vineyards, when she appeared.

One night M. Fauberge had arranged for him to meet a couple not that much older than himself, the Milhauds, Theo and Léonie, who owned a vineyard the next ridge over on the mountain. They were, like Thomas, not of the region: his father was a lawyer in

Marseille who twenty years earlier had bought the property in Languedoc as a sort of investment, an investment in prestige among his fellow notables more than anything; apparently this had been a fad for a while before the arrival of the beast. Theo and Léonie had met when they were students at the university in Montpellier, and for whatever reason, they wanted to take over the task of rebuilding La Fontaine, which Theo's father was more than happy to let them do. Mme Milhaud was a stylish woman with luxuriant brown hair and a slightly arch manner; she immediately asked Thomas to call her by her first name, which surprised and charmed him. The husband offered no such gesture, which struck Thomas as equally appurtenant. They were both quite short. Beal would dwarf her. Who knew what they would make of her?

"M. Fauberge says you and your wife make an exotic couple," said Léonie suggestively. They were dining at the hotel in the village, but it was hot now and they were outside in the garden under the plane trees.

"M. Fauberge hasn't met my wife," said Thomas. "But that was handsome of him to say. If he meant it nicely." It was clear that M. Fauberge had told them that Beal was black.

"Oh. He's very excited about you," said M. Milhaud. "The de Bergs were not a good turn for Domaine de St. Adelelmus."

"No one seems to have liked them very much."

"Well," said Léonie, glancing at her husband for some sort of go-ahead, "they had no idea what they were getting into."

"It was her," Theo said. "She was the problem."

Thomas listened while they debated this: M. de Berg had been unrealistic about the work required; Mme de Berg was unprepared for the rudeness of the life in the garrigue. If that idiot had listened a little more carefully, been a little more alert to her struggles, Madame never would have done what she did; no husband, however doltish, should have to endure such *scandale*. Thomas pieced together that she had run off with an Italian who came ashore from a yacht at Sète. The Milhauds thought this denouement was funny, the Italian and the yacht, but Thomas didn't love much of the story: a naive husband overwhelmed, a beautiful wife bolting.

"Forgive us," said Léonie. She had noticed that Thomas's attention seemed to have turned inward.

"Oh," said Thomas. "I don't know how prepared I am for any of this. It's really quite mad, my buying this property. Both my wife and I grew up on a farm, on an orchard, but we are many miles away from there now. I pulled the name Languedoc out of a text in Galignani's reading room in Paris. It's because of a librarian that I am here."

There was a flicker of alarm between the Milhauds. "M. Fauberge spoke very highly of you," said M. Milhaud, attempting to reassure himself as much as Thomas. "He said you were remarkably knowledgeable. He believes you are a serious man."

"Too serious, in fact, or so he said to me on the night before my first look at the farm."

"I wouldn't pay too much attention to him," said Léonie.

Thomas turned to her; she was lovely in a sharp, angular French way, and deeply tanned; he wondered how deep into the daily labors of farm and household she got. "I think I have been very lucky on this trip. In a way I am coming home here. I am an exile, really, but a willing one. It's a long story. I won't bore you."

"No," she said. "You wouldn't have to worry about that. Tell us."

So Thomas told them a little about his life. About parents who were mismatched in every way, who lived apart on separate shores of the Chesapeake Bay, the mother with the daughter on the left-hand shore, the father with the son on the right. About the aftermath of the Civil War and the end of slavery and his father's dream of peaches. About the boom and then the tragic disaster of the disease known as the peach yellows. "There is still no solution to *our* blight," he said. He told them about his love for Beal that grew out of childhood and had driven him, had driven them, finally, to this place and time.

"This is like a novel," said Léonie.

Thomas had never spoken about himself in this way. He had never imagined that one would, or could, talk this way for any reason except egotism. That his life made a *story*. Once started, he couldn't stop, not that Léonie would have let him. He realized as he spoke that his life really had been unusual, that this story was uniquely his own, that the classmates at the University of Pennsylvania who so bored him had lived no life at all, had never been tested as he had. He realized as well that all those painters in Paris were running from similarly boring lives. The revelations poured into Thomas's brain as he spoke: I am not the person I have always thought I am. He would go back to Paris, reclaim Beal, and over time she would see that the adventure being offered to them here was real, was even—at this point the wine must have been clouding both his thoughts and his speech—*epic*. By the time he was done, they were very much the last diners in the garden; the Milhauds' carriage had been brought around, and the horse, a beast of enormous size, was asleep on its hooves.

Theo bid Thomas good night and went off to pay the stableman. Léonie stayed behind. She gave him her small hand, a gesture that surprised him and meant more to him than he could then imagine. "The garrigue is not for everyone, but I feel it will be right for you. I will do everything I can to make your wife feel at home here." She laid down her napkin, and when she stood, Thomas realized that she was quite pregnant. She followed his eyes to her stomach. "Oh yes," she said. "Our third."

Thomas reddened; he didn't know what to say, and she seemed to enjoy his discomfort. "Beal and I hope to begin our family very soon," he said finally.

"Good," she said. "Playmates next door. All the cousins are in Marseille."

He thanked her again, gave her an arm into her carriage, and watched them depart down the winding main street. The moon was full, and in that light the stone of the buildings and the streets glowed. The stream in the gulley roared; Thomas assumed that by August it would be little more than a trickle, and as he reflected on this, he realized it was fed by the mountain torrent that ran through his property.

The next day, he returned to Narbonne, and at three o'clock on Friday, the ninth of June, 1893, he walked into M. Fauberge's office on the Quai de Lorraine, met the banker and the lawyer M. Fauberge had hired for him, presented the bank draft that had been wired to him from Baltimore, and emerged the owner of the Domaine de St. Adelelmus. Up and down the quai the casks were piled three high; the canal boats, in this slack time of the wine year, bobbed in the slight ripples. Thomas was in this business now; its challenges and complexities awaited him. Back at his hotel, he arranged a wire to Beal: DOMAINE DE ST. ADELELMUS PURCHASED. BACK TO YOU ON SATURDAY. OUR NEXT STEP AWAITS.

8

From the moment Thomas spotted her on the platform, he knew that even one more day away would have been more time apart than their young marriage might bear. She was dressed for the summer heat; this was the way he liked her best, white shirt, a skirt that blew in the wind. Take away the slightly mannish jacket, the straw boater worn at a cocky angle, and she'd look just as she had back at the Retreat, the Diana of the orchards. But this was no farm girl or farm wife awaiting her rough-hewn husband back from the day's market; the woman greeting him was a *parisienne* through and through. She had heard the private song of Paris and had made it her own. She was waving without self-consciousness. *Welcome home!* her wave said. *I have a cab waiting!* Other people greeting passengers were more reserved; a few of them seemed to be focusing on Beal more than anyone they were meeting. Nothing about her betrayed any doubt, any change in her heart; to Thomas, she was acting as if her life were simple, but that was a problem. Her life wasn't simple: their marriage was balanced upon miracle and illusion. That's what he had always understood. He was astonished by the miracle, haunted by the illusion, but aware, always aware, that anything could tip the balance.

He waved back, but his hand felt unconnected to his arm, a thing going through its own motions. It had been only six weeks, but the person returning was not the person who had left; it was as if he had been unfaithful to her, or as if he expected a different person to be meeting him. He did not overestimate the change; he did not think he had suddenly become a Frenchman of the Midi, even if he had adopted some of the swagger. That morning, without giving it a second's thought, he had tied his cravat in the Midi manner, loose around his collar, as if it could double as a handkerchief or a rag if needed. But Thomas did believe, had always believed, that just as a man and a woman fall mysteriously, uniquely in love with each other, so can a person find a place where he could be uniquely and completely himself. And he knew he had found that place.

"Thomas," she called as he approached. They had not yet taken to using any endearing terms for each other. He stifled the hollow feeling and reached out his arms; they embraced. Her body against his felt right; the soft sensation of her breasts put his body to rest. He lingered there, telling himself that all was well, really, this is Beal and all should be well.

"Look at you," she said, drawing away. Thomas wasn't sure what she meant; she was the one with the new clothes; she was the one with a radiant smile. "You're so dark," she said, putting her hand on his cheek as if to compare hues and then letting it drop down to his neck and chest.

"The sun is very bright in"—he wasn't sure what to call it—"in the South."

"Almost Africa," she said.

"Well, almost Spain, maybe."

"Yes. That's what I meant."

"I feel I have been gone a long time," he said. "You look beautiful. More beautiful than I remembered. Different."

"Don't be silly," she answered. "Do you like my hat?" It was a boater, with a narrower brim than a man's hat, and it was black.

"It's perfect for you." He glanced around: the other women in their billowy sleeves and fussy ruffs and flowered hats all looked like overdressed dolls next to her.

She took his arm, and they walked up the platform, with the porter following. When they came out into the sunlight, Thomas had to blink, and for the fraction of a second that his eyes were shut, the landscape of his new home, the garrigue, seemed imprinted on his eyelids. When he opened them, the cityscape surprised him, as if it had been misplaced.

The porter located their cab, and when they were inside and settled, he said, "I don't know where to begin." She had her hand in his, waiting. What was different about her, he suddenly realized, was that she looked older. He had never noticed the change, but he saw now that in the past six months, the teenage childishness of her face was gone. "It's like we have to start all over."

"Oh now, shush with all that," she said, but he was not going to shush.

"It's like those years when I was in Philadelphia," he said, "and all I had of you were the words on my own letters. As if I had invented you."

"You're making me nervous, Thomas. You've been gone for so long and I have missed you every day and now I have you back and you're talking about Philadelphia." The word *Philadelphia* had long meant trouble for them. "I'm sorry I didn't write back more," she said. She was apologizing for both times, then and now.

"It was okay. I was hard to reach," he said. But he wasn't that hard to reach. He hadn't expected long replies, but he had wondered whether, after her winter of scribbling in her notepads, she'd want to express herself to him in writing more. Apparently not.

"You'll tell me all about what you have found," she said.

"Oh, yes. But what about you? Has Arthur been helping you?"

"I haven't seen that much of Arthur. He was in one of those moods of his for a good while."

Thomas wasn't sure why, but he wished she hadn't said that. "And Mother Lucy?"

"Of course. She has kept her eye on me," she answered, but then she put her finger to his mouth. "All was fine when you were gone. Céleste was ill for a few weeks, and I took over her place at the front desk for some of it. It was fun. Everyone was very nice to me. The girls now call me *Tante* Beal. Mme Vigny is a little nicer when you aren't around. I don't think she likes happy couples."

"I'd sort of forgotten about Mme Vigny. Not my favorite thought."

"Well, you won't have to worry about her this afternoon," she said with a wink. "I've given her the afternoon off."

Thomas heard that with a thump; when he moved to the idea of making love, all the tensions and uncertainties of these minutes fueled a surge of desire that drowned him. He paid the cabbie and waited impatiently as the concierge made three trips up to the flat with his luggage. The rooms were bright in the afternoon sun. They went immediately to the bedroom and undressed, and in the midday heat, for the first time, they lay on the bed without any covering, so freely naked. In his ardor he was slightly surprised when she held him off from entering the first time, then was intoxicated to discover that she wanted to embrace more, kiss more, touch more, and that she even pulled away the second time in order to prolong each sensation. Her desire seemed to redouble, to match his own, and when at last neither of them could delay a second more, his relief felt as if weeks of doubt were flowing out of his body. For several minutes they lay side by side, a little out of breath.

"I met a couple that own the vineyard next door," he said finally. "I think you'll like them. They have three, I mean almost three, children."

"She's expecting?" she asked.

He reached down and patted her naked, taut abdomen. "I have been wondering when that will happen for us."

She removed his hand. "Not yet. That I know of."

"Tell me about you. Tell me everything you have been doing since I have been gone."

"Oh," she said. "I'm boring. I'm not the one who has been traveling. Let's get up. I want to take my farmer husband for a walk in the city." She got to her feet and walked over to the washstand and leaned forward to inspect something on her face in the mirror. She had one foot cocked behind the other heel, and the way she had her arm out for support he couldn't see her breasts, just this simple pose, the line from her shoulders down to her buttocks and then to the back of her calves. It was like one of those paintings she liked, something new and scandalous because it was so intimate and unforced, but he couldn't remember the title, *Le bain* maybe. "Stop looking at me," she said, pleased to be looked at.

"Has Arthur finished your portrait?" he asked.

"No. It just sits in his room under a wrap. He's very down-hearted over it."

"You've been there?"

She reached for her drawers and pulled them on. "I was worried about him. No one had seen him for days. It's not as if I hadn't been there many times." He still hadn't moved from the bed, was still uncovered. The brown of his lower arms made his pasty white chest look comical. "You're not disapproving of that, I hope. It was your idea to have him watch out for me, but in the end, I was watching out for him. It's sort of the same thing, isn't it?"

"Of course," he said. Nothing in his recent life seemed more extraneous than the visits to the Latin Quarter, the Académie Julien, the American artists and their dreams. "All those painters. I understand them even less, now that I have been away."

"Arthur is different."

"Yes. But our saying that might not cheer him up."

She nodded. "And Stanley's different, really. It seems that he's the one of them who knows what he is trying to do. I guess I feel we're sort of moving on from them. But they were good to us, taking us in the way they did."

"Of course," he said. "That's what I was thinking." As she was pulling on her underclothes and beginning to appear the stylish and proper lady who met him at the station, the thought of what that proper lady had just been doing aroused him again. She was buttoning her shirt. She glanced over, and she stopped, dropped the clothes in a pool around her feet, and came back to the bed.

This time it was Thomas who got up first. "Now I *am* hungry," he said. "Perhaps we can get an early dinner."

The light had begun to take on a little color, but the day was still hot; they walked along the shady side of the avenue Bosquet. Blazes of yellow sun were beginning to dress the buildings in patches. All seemed restful, even to Thomas; carriages still rumbled by, and there was enough odor of sewage and manure to offend the nostrils of the country dweller, but the scene was gay and bright. She took his arm, and in this familiar neighborhood there was no one new left to gawk at them; instead, two ladies greeted

Beal and an elderly gentleman tipped his hat. "That's M. Tallent," she said. "He and his wife live in the building with the white marble stoop. He reminds me of Colonel Murphy."

They settled in at the café by the river, and Thomas negotiated a meal for them, even though the kitchen was closed for the afternoon. With his French so recently acquired, he knew his accent had probably been bent by almost six weeks in the Midi, and he liked the confusion on the waiter's face. "The *paysans* speak a different language in the South," he said once they were alone. "That's what Languedoc means—the 'language of Oc.' It's not hard to learn, I think."

"I guess I'll have to learn everything all over again," she said. For the first time, there was a tartness in her tone.

"No, you won't. The old language is dying out."

"Hmmm," she said.

He patted her hand. "Do you want me to tell you about St. Adelelmus?"

"Of course," she said. The smile was brave; Thomas almost welcomed the wariness of it, as if it meant that after the forced gaiety of their greeting and the mindless passions of their lovemaking, they were getting to the heart of it.

He did his best: the bastide, the brook, the terrace and the fig trees, the winding road to the village. The Mediterranean, just a few miles, really, from St. Adelelmus. He described Narbonne, with its broad promenade along the canal and restaurants that were the equal of Paris, and Sète, where yachtsmen and fishermen tied up alongside each other and young couples took boat rides in the basin. He told her what M. Fauberge had said, that they might face resistance because they were outsiders, but for no other reason. He told her what Léonie Milhaud had said, that she would do everything to make Beal comfortable.

"You sound very excited," she said. "I'm glad. You deserve this, Thomas."

"But what do you think? How does it sound to you?"

"It doesn't matter what it sounds like to me. You are my husband."

"But it does matter, to me. You're happy here."

"No one ever said we were going to stay here. Was that ever a plan? Us in Paris, France?"

"You're not really answering my question."

"Well, I don't know what you are asking. I'll follow you to this place, this farm. You can't ask for anything more than that."

"No. Of course not," he said. He tried to take a bite of his trout.

"When do we leave?"

"In a few weeks. As long as it takes to put everything to rights here. There's no reason to rush, but I'd want us to be settled in time for the harvest."

"Yes. Of course. *Les vendanges.*"

Thomas was surprised to hear her use this French word; he wondered where she got it. One might have said *récolte*, but when it came to wine, the generic would not do. The word settled upon them, the one word more than any other that described the life they came from and the life they seemed to be heading toward. The harvest, the *récolte*, the *vendanges*: in any language it spoke of the brutal regularity of farming, the ancient clock. But there was also a strange, festive joy in this final accounting of a year's worth of toil and worry. On the Retreat, when the pickers, whole families at a time, began to arrive, all schedules and routines fell by the wayside. Even when the year had been bad, when frost had wiped out most of the peaches, when the yellows had killed half the trees, the harvest was the way to put the bad luck behind them and hope for better next year.

The next day, Thomas went over to the Quarter to find Arthur. The cardplayers were there as always, but the faces in the Café Badequin were mostly new, this year's crop of aspiring artists affecting last year's routines. They seemed younger, more frivolous, more like mere tourists, though Thomas knew this was unfair. None of them had seen Arthur in the past few days. Most of them seemed to know who Thomas was, who Beal was; a couple of them mentioned Stanley's pastels, and what surprised him was the evident regard—*awe* might not be too strong a word—they held for little Stanley Dean from Pittsburgh. Thomas had seen very little of him since Beal began to sit for Arthur, but apparently he had sold something, or something had been accepted into an exhibition. If Arthur had been, as Beal said, in more of his darker moods lately, this might well be the cause.

Thomas had never been to Arthur's room. He hadn't wanted to see the place where Beal was sitting for him, in that intimacy of light and paint, though Céleste had always been there with her. Céleste liked Arthur, which was for Thomas the first indication that one day they might be friends. In years to come, Thomas would see that Arthur loved young people, that a manner that seemed surly and unpleasant to adults came across as gruff to children, which they loved in return. Still, as Thomas climbed the stairs, he did not like the thought that Beal had been there, in this slum. When Arthur let him in, without much welcome, Thomas saw the room for what it was: a painter's studio, quite in order, spare, filled with sun. It could have smelled better, but the air in the streets in this district wasn't much better.

The first thing he noticed was the easel, with a cloth over it.

"So. You're back," said Arthur. "I was wondering."

"It took longer than I thought."

"But you did it?"

"Yes. I am now a *vigneron*, as they say."

Arthur looked at him through this new lens, skeptically at first. "You look good," he said finally. "You look like your real self."

"Not that you had ever seen my real self, but that's what painters are supposed to do. To see below the surface? Right?"

"Right," Arthur said. He was standing at his food cabinet, eating a piece of bread and ham. "I'd offer you some—" he said, waving it.

"Uh. That's fine."

"I figured." He crunched through the rest of his meal. "Beal did fine," he said. "Nothing to report."

"She said she hadn't seen much of you. She said you'd not been all that well, and I guess you don't look that well to me either."

"You're seeing my real self."

"I am not. I don't accept that."

Arthur shrugged. "Summer in Paris is not a great place to be, I'll tell you. All the real painters are long gone."

"I have just agreed with Beal that we will be leaving quite soon. It's going to be hard for her."

"Well," said Arthur. "You've asked a lot of her, if I can say so."

This was similar to an odd phrase she'd used yesterday; it was as if she and Arthur had agreed that this term described everything about her plight. "Is that what she said to you?"

"No. I mean, maybe. Maybe in so many words. But she's not complaining, is she? Not to me—about you, about your life. That's just the way it seems to me. She's barely twenty years old—that's the part of this, of her, that amazes me. Look how far she has come. But she still has a lot to figure out, is all I mean."

Thomas had been standing, but as they were talking, he'd been backing toward the single chair, and now that he was in front of it, he sat. He looked up and saw the stretcher of the canvas on the easel. "Let me see the portrait," he said.

"No."

"Why not?"

"It isn't finished."

"I don't care."

Arthur had not moved away from his kitchen cabinet. To look Thomas in the face, he had to lean around the easel, and it occurred to Thomas that this was exactly where Beal had sat—if indeed, she had been seated—and this was the vision she had of Arthur, his peering—leering—around the edge of the frame. Thomas could not imagine this as a pleasant experience; he could feel the brush-strokes, like insects palpitating on his face. Arthur shrugged, wiped his hands on a dish towel, and got on his hands and knees to rotate the easel by the base. When it was facing Thomas, he stood up and, without any ceremony, certainly without any flourish, withdrew the cloth.

She was standing, and her body was turned three-quarters away; Thomas could see that Arthur had not missed her beautiful broad shoulders or the suggestion of her strength. What the ladies of Paris did with their corsets and bustles, Beal did in her skin. Arthur had let her body, in all its features, glow through the folds of cloth; there was more of the shape and cleft of her buttocks than would be allowed out in the world. Thomas did not love the image of Arthur making such a meticulous likeness of Beal's rear end. Her head was turned back almost directly at the viewer, and the finger-tips and thumb of her right hand could be seen cupping her shoulder. Her left arm hung down at her side, like a frame around her body. Arthur had lavished attention on the places where her dark forearm peeked through the slits at her cuff. Maybe her posture seemed a little contorted and awkward, and maybe that was a flaw or maybe it was the point—that she was heading away from the viewer but had turned herself around somewhat uncomfortably to confront whoever or whatever was scrutinizing her. Her eyes glowed; Arthur had made them uncomfortably bright.

She met the viewer, Thomas, head-on; anyone eavesdropping or snooping would be stopped dead in his tracks. *His* tracks: this portrait was about a woman and a man standing somewhere outside the frame. What had he just done or said? The man could have been anybody—the portraitist, the husband, the rival, a brother: *Don't marry him!* Arthur had not allowed her to be heedlessly beautiful in this painting. In fact, he had given her looks a harder edge. If she was striking-looking, it was the beauty, the depth, of the beginning of the second act. Just what Thomas had noticed yesterday at the train station. Her lovely eyebrows were just slightly furrowed; that sensuous, fluent mouth was set firm; she wasn't going to let anyone off the hook by speaking. So there was defiance here, of a sort, but really—and this is what finally knocked Thomas back into his seat—what she seemed to be expressing was irritation, as if this dramatic moment caught in paint would soon pass, but how tiresome that it had to happen at all. In the end, she seemed eager to leave the room, the canvas, to leave the viewer behind.

"Gee," said Thomas.

Arthur stood up and came around to stare at the canvas; it seemed he hadn't done this in some time. "Yeah," he said again, gloomily. "The eye moves the hand and the hand moves the brush, so the brush is the eye, if you see what I mean."

"I feel I need to go grab her, not let her go. Turn her around. To make her stay whether she wants to or not."

Arthur grunted.

"Has Beal seen it?"

"No. She . . ." Arthur stopped.

"I know she came to see you here last week. Don't worry about that."

"Right. But no. She said she didn't want to see it until I told her it was ready. She did say that she guessed I had made her 'unpretty.' She knocked me out with that. Sometimes your wife is scary."

"I know," said Thomas, looking back at the portrait. He speculated for a moment about what Beal would think of it. It didn't seem to be an image that one would like or dislike or a view that one could argue with. It was just the truth, or *a* truth. *Oh, that awful portrait*, she might say years later, but not now.

"I guess—" said Arthur, then stopped himself.

"You guess what?"

"I guess I think this whole project—my painting her—caught her at a moment in her life when she should have been allowed to be invisible. Invisible to anyone but you, Thomas. Really, you came to Paris to hide. But that's the thing about Paris: it swallows up ordinary people, mediocre people—but the happy few, well, it roots them out and puts them on display whether they want it or not. It spots them before anybody else does. Like Stanley, maybe. You heard about him, right? The Salon? I should have let Stanley paint her. He would have made her beautiful and virginal, and people would have been falling in love with her for a thousand years."

Thomas stood up, took one more very long look at the painting. "I don't care about Stanley and the Salon. This is good. It's a painting, maybe, for us, just a painting. We don't care who Beal really is, we care about the moment and about whatever is happening on the canvas. Right?"

"Yeah, that's what we're supposed to do if we're any good. As a painter."

"I believe in the painter that painted this."

"Thanks, but that painter is at the end of his leash. I think I'll run out of dough by November, and then Newark, New Jersey, will be calling."

"Don't answer. Don't go back to Newark. Come to St. Adelelmus."

"Where's that?"

"My farm. In Languedoc. There must be half a dozen small buildings, or houses, where you could live. Come for the winter. Don't painters go to the South for the winter, the light and all that? Open air?"

"No. They stay in Paris in the winter and go south in the summer. If they're lucky."

"But?"

"You think Beal would want me there, hanging around like some kind of mongrel?"

"She doesn't think of you that way. In fact, maybe I could use you as an incentive. Arthur will come! He'll paint the garrigue! Won't that be gay!"

"I don't think anybody, especially Beal, would describe me as gay."

With all her being, Beal knew that she was only partway through the door to womanhood, to her life, to herself, and that she would be useless to everyone, but most especially to Thomas, like this. Or so she told herself in moments she thought were more detached. *Useless to everyone*, she repeated. *I'll just get done with this*, she told herself; *it's something I have to do.* When she thought of their relocation to this place in the South, she became desperate, short of breath, because all this would be only half done. In moments when she allowed her thoughts to wander, her whole body felt as if it were on fire. She and Thomas made love every night in these weeks, and together they gave each other license to be more and more bold; she'd be embarrassed after it was over, but the next day, ready for more. Thomas didn't question the cause of any of this; he seemed to have determined that she had awakened after six weeks of chastity and was now on a journey, and he had no reason to complain. She wasn't the only one who had changed during their time apart. That was perhaps the only good part of all this confusion. He had come back stronger, more confident, more manly, and that should have been all she needed. He was busy all day with meetings; just like his father before him, he was probing the minds of the academics about grapes, grilling wine merchants and sommeliers about vintages, *cépages*, terroir, appellations. At the end of a day of this, in bed, there seemed more of him to confront, more than just his love for her.

But still, even as this was happening, it drove her desire to go even further, like a game of I Dare You. What she had wasn't enough. No, that was wrong: not about *enough* or *too little*, because she had so much. It was about *now*. About these last days and weeks, when everything she had created was beginning to be disassembled, lodgings let go, goodbyes said, trains and boats departing. These were the last few weeks of this time-out, this Paris time, this "adventure time," as she had thought of it, when her clock was racing years into the future while everyone else's ticked slowly into July . . . and for just these few days or weeks, there was other business to be done. To be finished with. Business that would never count. *I'm losing my chance*, she'd think, as if it were her youth that was being lost. She hated thinking this.

And of all things unexpected, of all things not to be imagined in a million years, she'd feel frantic with a kind of jealousy: Who was he with now? Which one of his wives did he prefer? She had defeated him, she knew that: no more talk of Dakar, no more imperious demands, just one note put directly into her hand by someone swiftly and silently, like a pickpocket. "Come to me." She wanted to do it. This war of wills all winter had been won by the less likely combatant, and now she wanted the spoils. She quivered with desire when she thought about him; her eyelids fluttered.

But she resisted. Of course she resisted. She loved Thomas, she was married. But what was *he* up to, this man who had come back to her? She had seen the red-haired girl. Oh yes, one day she had stopped into Galignani's and there she was. It didn't take more than a glance to figure that out, so Beal snuck a quick look. As fast as all that, their eyes met, and then Beal was back out the door in a minute, her heart pounding. If the girl were in a line of a hundred, each one prettier than the last, this is the one Beal would have picked out for Thomas.

When she slept with Touré, she had told herself that this would be the one time, sanctifying the event with her promises to herself, and as long as it *was* the only time, she could believe in her own righteousness. Or at least in her logic. Going back to him would prove the falsity of her resolutions, would reveal all this as nothing but lust. Yes, lust. She was astonished by its power. No one had ever warned her. Her mother's almost silenced breathy *Oh Lord,* coming from her parents' bedroom: that was pleasure, that was feeling good, but it was not this. Was it? When her friends Mandy and Esther, back at the colonel's, spoke of boys and lovemaking, it was like an idle game, a power they had over men who could lose their minds to it, but no one had ever told Beal that she could lose *her* mind to it. That the female body could feel this racking, desiccating desire. Never, ever had that possibility occurred to her, and she worried from time to time that a lot was wrong with her, that she was truly defective and evil, because other women didn't feel this. Otherwise, all the stories she'd ever heard were only half true, all the great literature she hadn't read but knew a little about would have to be rewritten with the parts restored about the princess or the preacher's daughter being driven mad with this craving.

Thomas resumed his routine, reading and studying, but it was with a focus now, and where before Beal bled from time to time for the loneliness of his projects, now she felt abandoned by his purpose. How could anyone, how could he, care about grapes so much? He did his best to paint a picture of their new life, told her that everyone in Languedoc agreed that these farms were about family, wives and children, and Beal understood that; on the Retreat everyone worked side by side, too. It was just the way farming happened. Mail came for Thomas and she'd ask what it was about and he'd explain how this property was managed, what grapes he hoped to plant, how wine was made and sold, where you got bottles and corks, how you shipped on the trains or the Canal du Midi.

"It's funny," she said one morning. He was reading the mail quickly before heading to the telegraph office. "It don't seem right."

"What doesn't seem right?"

"All this about wine. Don't we really think the world would be a better place without it? No one needs wine."

Thomas laughed, which was probably what she wanted him to do. It was sort of a joke, but a serious joke. "I think that debate was over by the time the Romans got to Languedoc. Grapes are better for the land than tobacco, after all. See what tobacco got us at home."

"Oh," she said. "The Retreat would have been there with or without tobacco. Didn't take tobacco to invent slavery."

He looked back at his letters for a moment, then put them down. "Beal, it's a good life, I think. Maybe I am as nervous about it as you are, but I saw something there. I think I found something there that I have been looking for."

She came up behind him and put her hands on his shoulders. *It's hard to be a man*; she remembered saying that to Arthur. *Paris will devour him*; she remembered Touré saying that about Thomas. His neck was still brown with the sun. She gave him a hug. "It just seems so far away to me. Farther away than France did when we left. France was just somewhere Out There, no closer or farther away than Baltimore. This is a place, it's real. You've seen it, slept there."

"Maybe we won't succeed, but we have to try. It was time, wasn't it?"

"Yes," she said. "It was time."

"We won't be able to delay much past the beginning of August."

"I know." She could tell he was itching to get back to his mail.

"We'll come back, to visit."

"Of course," she said. "I'll stop bothering you," she added, but he was already back at work.

Then one morning she sat on the toilet, idly counting days and weeks on her fingers and then counting again. She could not remember exactly when she last had her period, and now it seemed that this was quite a while ago, and she realized it had been several weeks, and suddenly the thought that she might be pregnant crashed over her, threatened to topple her off the stool as she straightened to attention in a bolt. When had Thomas come back, what day of the week was it? That rainy week: Was it before or after the Last Time? She put her hand back between her legs and pushed quite hard, as if to squeeze out a single drop of blood, but none came. Pregnant. Nothing that had happened in the past month was more likely than this, but she had simply not expected it, as if Paris were too ethereal a place for such an earthly event. She wasn't ready for this; she was too young. Plenty of girls at home, younger than she, had children, and that was the way of things, but not here. She stood up, lowered her skirt as if to drop the curtain on a play, after which everyone would return to their real worlds. But this was her real world, this life event taking place in the darkness of her womb.

She walked back to the parlor. Thomas was out doing business; Mme Vigny was, as always, not to be seen during these hot early-afternoon hours. Beal's whole body felt empty, which seemed exactly wrong. If she was right, and two people were now occupying her body, why would she feel so skeletal? She was more alone with this than she imagined, and it seemed to her that this isolation would continue, past the months of pregnancy, past the birth of the child. Down there in Langyduck—or however one said it—who would show her how to care for a baby? She was the youngest of her family, the baby herself; she'd never been around an infant, a new-born, a newborn human anyway. She did not cry, but she did sit down on the love seat, tracking a chill of despair as it traveled up from her abdomen. She didn't even have someone to tell about this! Nobody in the world. It was too soon, much too soon to say anything to Thomas; she'd keep this a secret from him for months, until at last it couldn't be concealed. Colleen and Hilary were gone, and Vivian, the only woman remaining among them she counted at all as a friend, was in no way the sort of person to whom you would reveal such a thing. Céleste? Too young. Madame Bernault? Beal blushed with horror at telling her this, and all that it implied. Arthur? Unthinkable—so unthinkable that as she sat there reviewing her options, she never even thought of him. The little girls?

There was only one person she would really want to tell, and that was her mother, her Mama, but writing a letter, what would that do? Simply sending out a piece of information was not what telling someone you're pregnant is all about. So of all the world, of all the people she'd ever known, there was only one person she could imagine telling, one person available, whose reaction she could anticipate, who could offer some kind of certainties even if they were wrong. There was only one person she could imagine who would care in the slightest, care if she were living or dead. That's the way this moment made her feel. Pregnancy and childbirth were a mortal battle for sure, and if she lost at the last moment and the child lived, would anyone care? Yes, she would go to him, and as part of a more formal and less fraught goodbye, she'd share the news. Thank him . . . well, she had already thanked him, but still. *Oh, and guess what? I'm pregnant.* And he would assume and assert that he was the father, and even though she liked the notion that he would argue this, she would inform him quite authoritatively that this was not the case. That her husband was the father. She considered all this for a few days, when everything she had been thinking and feeling over the past months became roiled, both sanctioned and damned by this new turn. She had a new clock, a new way of telling time. Thomas knew that something was preoccupying her, and a couple of times he asked what was on her mind. Oh, the move, she said. I'm thinking about it. Perhaps we should leave sooner than we planned. Or a week later. This city, Narbonne; show me on the map where it is. Did you really invite Arthur to spend the winter with us? That woman, Léonie, you said she was pregnant? Did she tell that to you—a stranger? Weren't you a little embarrassed when she said it? Did she seem pleased about it? How many months was she, since you said you noticed when she stood up?

So it was that a week after her discovery Beal was back in Les Halles, standing once again among the fishmongers, being stared at by octopuses and eels and mighty halibut and stringy little sardines. This thing inside her, they said it was smaller than a mustard seed, that before it looked like a baby it would look like a fish. There was no sign of little Emma with the cabbages, but a boy was being scolded and cuffed on the ear, and as soon as he could worm his way free, he took off, followed by a stream of abuse. He would end up on Devil's Island, it was shouted. The day was hot and airless; under the pavilion roof the only movement was the swallows and pigeons swooping and nesting. It seemed the entire market had closed down to mark this moment in her life.

Beal wasn't sure why she was there. She still believed that Touré was the one person she could tell about her pregnancy, that as ridiculous as it seemed, telling him would take the loneliness out of it. But she had had time to adjust a little, and the secret didn't seem quite so unbearable, especially because each day, the secret itself became more and more certain and less possible to contain. She might have been there to say her final goodbye, to thank him one last time, because she would spend the rest of her life pondering and trying to make sense of all the things he had said to her over the winter, imagining how it would have been if she had never been challenged in this way, if her very being had not been called into question, and years later, she awoke with a start, wondering how it all would have gone if it had gone differently, more conventionally. She knew that Diallo Touré had in some ways put her on a path that could accommodate both her own needs and her duties as Thomas's wife. Yes, that's how it worked. Both of us. And would she make love to him, if he wanted? She could not be sure she would not, although now it all seemed less necessary and less momentous. A man enters a woman's body and leaves the possibility of life, and pierced in this way, she becomes marked, her body shared, yet all becomes meaningless, pointless, when a new life is actually growing inside.

She walked across the street to the arched entrance. The dogs were asleep, and there was no one in the courtyard, no sounds of cooking or laundry or cleaning. There was a dead rat in one corner. She walked up the three flights and knocked. Okay, she had to admit it now, her heart was pounding; she ran a hand from her chest down to her belly. There was no response from inside. *Come to me.* She knocked again and then tried the door, which was unlocked. She walked in and, not sure she comprehended what she was seeing, went through the kitchen to Touré's room, hesitated at the closed door in case she could hear him inside, breathing, talking, with a woman. When there was no sound, she opened it and found it empty. The cot was there, the cot where she had felt the first real sexual bliss of her life, the washstand, but nothing else, no pajamas on the hook, no spare white shirt on a hanger. No books about Senegal.

She had not imagined this. Her legs gave out, and she aimed herself at the cot as she fell. Slowly, like a wave building far at sea, she felt the crushing approach of breathtaking despair; her saliva was milky, and her hands and feet tingled. She waited for all this to subside, and when it did, Beal Terrell Bayly was the loneliest person on earth. The morning Randall's body had been found; the night she was spirited off the Retreat after she and Thomas had sworn their love; the day of her wedding, when she got into Colonel Murphy's carriage and had the last glimpse of her mother and father and sisters through the hazy glass—in every way this felt worse because, obviously, this was all her own doing. Being unfaithful to her husband, being in this shabby and now empty flat, no one but herself to be blamed for all that. She started to weep, and once the first shudder heaved in her chest, she began to sob, to cry inconsolably, when the only consolation is the goodness of crying itself. She had her handkerchief opened across her face, and she caught glimpses of this place through the holes in the lace, which made the grime on the walls and the streaky glass seem ancient and unchanging. She cried for a while, stopped, and then cried again. *Come to me*, he had written, probably on the day he departed, something one would do surrendering a hotel key before catching a train. His last ploy. *Come to me.* And now she had come to him, only to realize—as he knew she would—that he didn't mean come to this apartment in Les Halles, in France, in Europe, but to Senegal. Follow me to Africa, Mademoiselle Beal, where you belong.

When she could not possibly cry anymore, she stopped and then lay on the bed breathing deeply. The idea slowly began to come to her that she actually was feeling refreshed, liberated maybe. Relieved, of course, that she was not just now in a sweaty state of recent sin, but more than that: this was all completely over. *Tout est fini.* She straightened her hat and walked down the stairs, recalling the times she had been there; there had been more to this than she could ever admit to anyone, more conscious deciding, more subterfuge, but now that it was over, she didn't have to.

When she got to the street, the eerie calm in the markets had passed; they seemed now to be bustling with tradespeople closing down their stalls, loud conversations and laughter from the cafés at the edges. Perhaps she had simply not noticed all this when she came in. She walked down to the Île de la Cité. It was a hot day, airless and sunbaked, and she looked for a piece of shade to rest in, spying the bell towers of Notre-Dame. She and Thomas had popped in there one day, but neither of them felt any pull, any draw to prayer or contemplation in this vast hulk; this was religion of an entirely different sort from any they could ever possibly need. They had not been going to Mass, to Madame Bernault's dismay, but so few French people actually worshipped on Sundays that it seemed okay to skip. Now, with a child coming, they might have to rethink this, as during her conversion she had learned about Purgatory, an unlikely and mean story to her, but others seemed to believe it, even welcome it as consolation for having lived a boring but blameless life. Beal knew she had not lived a blameless life, but it was not a boring one either.

The cathedral looked cool and inviting, so she crossed the square and let herself in. The heavy door boomed behind her, and she stood for a minute or two while her eyes adjusted. In the dark, surrounded by the odors of frankincense and candle wax, she heard a murmur echoing from far away and then a single, piercing smash from an organ, as if someone had accidentally backed into the keys. When she could see clearly, she found her way to the chairs and sat down. The sun shining through the windows at her back sent a rose-colored beam through the dust particles and smoke; two young men, priests, she supposed, were praying at one of the chapels at her side, and then from much deeper, beyond the altar, she heard a baby wailing. She dropped her hand to her stomach and leaned back a little, astonished by all this—herself, little Beal Terrell, little pregnant Beal, sitting in this ancient monument just waiting, it seemed, to find out the real story of her life.

9

Many times since he had returned to Paris, Thomas had intended to go see Eileen. If his trip had been a triumph, it was largely her triumph. He would have no trouble saying that, telling her that come what may in this perhaps foolhardy venture, anything good that came out of it was due to her. He would have loved to say that to her, in the hope that it would give her pleasure, that she would smile, that she'd know how much he cared for her without his having to say it. Anything bad that came out of it would have nothing to do with her, a blameless librarian simply showing a patron through the collections. *Notice that agriculture is divided into crops shelved alphabetically, and then into products. Here, see: grapes, and here, see: wine.* But if he told her anything about his discoveries, about St. Adelelmus, he'd have to, or want to, tell her the rest: that if much of what he had done was driven by his fear of losing Beal, it was Eileen's good cheer that gave him hope. Maybe it hadn't taken so much, a month or so of friendly encouragement, shared teas; maybe that wasn't so much, except that it was everything. Until the day he died, Thomas could not reimagine his life, could make none of it happen without her—and later, her father—in the picture.

But he delayed, and as the weeks went by, it got worse and worse and meaner and meaner; he had long since realized that mere guilt wasn't all that was going on, that this final visit with her would be the end of this affair. So three days before he and Beal were to leave Paris, he looked up from his work, dropped his pen on his desk, and marched to Galignani's. The director, M. Vaucluse, treated him with no more or no less displeasure than usual, but Thomas was not looking at him. Over his shoulder, through the gaps of a full bookshelf, he saw her hair. He greeted the director loudly enough to make sure she could hear his voice, and she turned in a jolt and their eyes met over the tops of the volumes.

"Ah," he said to M. Vaucluse, "there's Mademoiselle Hardy. I had a question for her."

The director was clearly not fooled by this, and he might well have had cause to fire her on the spot, but instead he shrugged. It was not a cold and indifferent shrug; the man had a heart. "Perhaps it is time for her to take tea," he said.

In Thomas's mind there was every chance that she would not want to take tea with him, would not want to talk to him at all; a chilly *And what was the question, M. Bayly?* would not have surprised him. But she told him to wait while she got her hat and gloves, and as he was waiting for her at the door, it occurred to him that she was doing this because she had something she wanted to say. He'd deserve anything, he figured, especially because he had committed no real crime, that he was blameless but also guilty as sin.

"So. You're back," she said when they got onto the sidewalk under the arcade. It was high tourist season, and from each side sellers of postcards and panorama albums thrust their products into Thomas's face. They recognized Eileen and didn't bother.

"Yes," he said. Neither of them had to make reference to what was obvious, that he had been back for weeks without coming to see her.

"I trust it was a successful trip."

He answered that it was, that he had bought a beautiful but neglected winery in Languedoc. "Domaine de St. Adelelmus," he said.

"Who was he?"

"I guess I don't know. I don't know what he did."

"Whatever, it probably ended badly for him."

They passed into the tearoom and said nothing while they were being seated. The headwaiter welcomed them, and Thomas tried to recall how many times he had been there with Eileen. Ten times? More? Twenty, more likely. He settled in his seat and began to prepare himself either to apologize for waiting so long or to tell her that he had been thinking of her, had planned to send her a postcard but didn't know her address. But no rehearsed lines were necessary.

"Your wife came in while you were gone," she said. "It explained a lot. It explained everything. Married, all along. You live a complicated life. It must be exhausting, being you."

Thomas heard this with a shock and a gulp of air; for the moment, all he could do was dissemble. "I've never really thought of my life that way. I just did what I had to do."

She showed no reaction to this disavowal. "I am not so angry at you as I was. She's very lovely."

Eileen's hurt and anger had not been part of their parting these months ago; she'd made it so easy on him that he probably overstepped. "I'm sorry," he said. He looked across the tiny round tea table between them; their knees were practically touching. "You don't know how much—"

She headed him off. "Please. No more. There's no point."

Thomas understood that there was no point for her; the point for him was to be allowed to express something, to say it. But it wasn't going to happen. He took a sip of tea. All those American voices around him, these ladies; how far from them he felt, how he loathed them. They wouldn't last a day in the garrigue.

He got back on track. "Beal didn't mention it. Probably she was curious to see where I spent all that time."

"Beal," said Eileen. "That's her name? Very sweet. A family name?"

"Yes," said Thomas. "I guess so."

Eileen looked at him with a little surprise, as if he should have known better where her name came from, and then, with some irritation, she said, "It wasn't like that."

"What do you mean? What did she say?"

"She didn't say anything. We didn't talk. She was there for perhaps five minutes. Maybe less."

This whole episode was beginning to seem very odd to Thomas, but he knew, as with the story of St. Adelelmus, that this was probably not going to end well. Still, he allowed his confusion to take the lead. "I don't understand," he said. "How did you know she had anything to do with me? How did you know she was my wife?"

"I didn't. Maybe not until this very moment. But I believed you wouldn't hurt me for no reason. You're too kind, too damn polite to do that. I told myself that it wasn't because you didn't like me that you just stopped coming here. Then she walked in with such presence—so, well, indelible. The moment I saw her, I knew she was the cause."

Thomas was trying to think of something to say, to give the story of himself and Beal in the fewest possible words, but the idea of having to go through it all was unbearably fatiguing to him. Eileen's not knowing anything about it was one of the reasons, a big reason perhaps, that he loved her; he'd recognized *that* months ago. Fortunately—he thought, for a second, that it was fortunate— he didn't need to offer anything, because she kept talking.

"Besides—" she said.

"Besides what?"

She had been canted slightly to the side of the table, but now she seemed to intuit how little of this Thomas was grasping, and in a mode of warning she shifted her chair to face him straight on. Their knees brushed. "Thomas. She didn't come in to look at our reading room. She came in to see me. Do you understand what I am saying? She came looking for me. That's how I knew she was your wife."

The details were beginning to close around him like irons. "How did she know to come looking for you?" he asked stupidly.

"How would I know that, Thomas? I assumed you had told her about me, that in some way you had done the honorable thing."

"No," he said. "I didn't." He pushed his teacup slightly away and leaned back. Two young women, probably British, were staring at them, hungry for the drama that was taking place next door. There's no drama when there are no secrets, so yes, there had been a drama going on in his marriage ever since he got back, an act he knew nothing about. "Then what?" he said at last.

"She came in, and I noticed her because she is so striking, and she surveyed the room, and when her gaze got to me, she stopped and our eyes met. We looked at each other, and then she was out the door. She had a tiny smile. I won't tell you what I thought it meant."

Thomas could barely breathe. "Please," he whispered. "Please tell me."

Eileen raised her eyebrows, as if telling herself that none of this mattered anymore, that there was nothing to be lost or gained, that she could admit something to Thomas that she would never, ever breathe to anyone else. "Well. I thought it meant that she found me pretty. That I might have been worthy of her husband. It was that kind of smile, a smile of approval."

Thomas would not disgrace himself enough to say that she *was* worthy of him. Or to say that he wasn't worthy of her, or of Beal. That he was unworthy. Anything he thought to say had the rote hollowness of catechism for him, so he said nothing, which she seemed to appreciate very much. She had certain things she wanted to get said, had perhaps rehearsed this talk in case she ever saw him again, and she moved forward.

"I thought I should tell you that I have decided to reconcile with my father. You took over the whole arc of my time here, and when you left, I realized that I was being . . ." She stopped, searching for the word. "Careless," she said. "I have been so sheltered, I didn't see that I was being careless about a part of my life that mattered to me. That I was risking something."

"The love of family," said Thomas. He didn't know much about it, but he thought of Beal, of her one great sorrow, the loss of her family.

"Yes. That's right. I have cut myself off, living with my former French governess, who I think is a spy for my mother. I was forced to choose between them, and I chose my father. I have been much happier since I came to that. I'm not really a woman of the world."

Thomas screwed his face into a scowl, the kind of disapproving look a brother might give to a sister who was selling herself short, but it was intimate all the same. He didn't need to say anything more, and they sat drinking their tea across a tiny circle of black marble. Finally he asked her what she was planning, when she would be seeing her father. "In Bordeaux?" he asked.

"Yes. Isn't that funny? Me in Bordeaux. But at least it's Fronsac," she said.

"At least what?"

"Fronsac. It's the region he's in. A poor relation. It's not the Médoc, but it's very lovely."

"Well, then Languedoc is an even poorer relation. The girl who was sent away pregnant when she was twenty and has been living on the streets ever since."

"No. It's the second son who had to go out and make his own way. It suits you. I always knew it would. And Fronsac suits my father."

Thomas almost blurted out that he would like to meet him someday; imagine what she might have said in response to that: *And I'll introduce you to him as exactly what?* He took a safer road. "He's still with Mme de Bose?"

She tipped back her head sharply at the name, but then smiled. She put her hand on his forearm. "Yes. She's the one who got in touch with me. It was brave of her, really. I liked her a great deal before she became my father's mistress. It's sweet of you to remember her name."

"A kind of obscure sweetness," he said, and she laughed. They sat in the slow parting of this better moment. Soon they would have to stand up and he would have to say goodbye. With a handshake, he supposed, which would be better than a kiss on the cheek, when what he would want to do was hug her, a good, old-fashioned, feel-good-on-the-arms hug. He'd have some words at the ready, and so would she, but what he wouldn't say was that he couldn't bear the thought of never seeing her again, of never having some strange set of circumstances where they could meet again in a perfectly seemly manner—Beal at his side, her husband and one or two children at hers, something like that, a chance meeting that would belie an immense possible world that did not need to be, could not be, spoken of, a testimony to the value of making the right choices. He could look beyond, now, and see the pleasure that was waiting for him, this delicate moment in the future, as a reward for making the right choices, as proof that as full as one's life can feel, there is always room for more. Perhaps this would happen in Bordeaux, in the wine business, something like that. Yes, Thomas could easily imagine it, and because it was so plausible, he could be certain that it would happen.

Beal had been out all that day, her last day in Paris, and with each errand she felt she was saying goodbye to a place or a person she'd known for much longer than just a few months. She felt that it was fine to be making these rounds—lingering for the last time on the Pont de la Concorde, tea with her friend Denise in the Bon Marché employee tearoom—fine also getting all these sights and memories in mind, as if the next time she was in Paris, if there was a next time, all would be different. For one thing, if she survived the delivery—these days Beal was regarding almost everything in her life, including her mortality, with an odd dispassion—she would have a child and thus could hardly be considered a tourist. Not that she had ever thought of herself that way. But it didn't matter very much. They were leaving, finally, and she was glad the moment had come.

In these weeks Beal had become accustomed to seeing Thomas at work at the table she had brought over from the hotel. He hadn't asked if he could take it over, but she did not mind: she was not writing anything in her journals these days. She figured that this writing was something she did only in Paris, and that years later she might come upon these notebooks and feel how silly they were. Where would she be at that moment? On their farm, she figured, even if living there was impossible for her to imagine. In fact, imagining anything—conjuring any alternate reality or possible future from her own thoughts—had seemed quite impossible to her ever since she found herself crying on Diallo Touré's vacant bed. For her, there was no surplus of life out of which to fashion dreams—or nightmares. All winter she had seemed to be floating outside of time, but now the only reality seemed to lie in the ticking of the clock.

She was in this distracted mood when she opened the door,

and at first she did not notice that Thomas was standing stiffly in front of the fireplace, a pose so unlike him, so melodramatic, that she thought he was making a joke of some kind. But then, after their eyes met, she realized that his expression was like nothing she had ever seen in him: not hurt—she'd seen hurt in him as a child many times before—not anger, nor surprise or confusion, but instead she saw in the set of his jaw and brow a mortal sadness, as if there were things wrong in the world that could not be set right. She glanced again at him and saw in his hand a crumpled piece of paper, and though as soon as she noticed it he quickly put it into his pocket, she knew what it was. *Come to me.* She tried to remember where she had left it when she came back that day; it was tattered because she had carried it with her like a key she needed to gain entrance to Diallo's flat. Perhaps Mme Vigny had found it and left it somewhere for Thomas to find; perhaps she'd put it into Thomas's hand. Beal could believe this was true. Mme Vigny had no English, but three words written in an elaborate but very male hand . . . what else could it be but a *billet-doux*? But French, English, whatever they spoke in Senegal . . . none of these languages could help her.

"Thomas," she said. She was clawing at her hat and gloves. She wanted these damn things *off.* "That note."

Reluctantly, it seemed, he took it out of his pocket and peered at it, as if there might be some new message on it, then shook his head at the thought that they would now have to decipher it together, a moment he had been avoiding. "It was given to you, right?"

Beal nodded.

"You know who it is from? A man?"

For a moment Beal thought she might be able to say that it came from Arthur, or even Stanley, or that she might be able to invent some entirely different correspondent. A clerk at the store telling her the items she ordered were ready for her to inspect? *Come to me?* Hardly what a clerk would say to a customer. "Yes," she said.

"Who is it?"

"Thomas," she said. Her stomach, her lungs, her whole body gulping and leaping, she sat down on the love seat and looked up at him. "It's nothing. It's nobody. Nobody you know."

"That African? The one from the boat. The one with the hat. The one you talked to in that café last fall?"

The last detail was the one that knocked everything she was planning to say out of kilter. If he knew so much, why hadn't he said anything earlier? Another test? Tests and tests and tests that everyone knew she was going to fail. How could she not, this ignorant little farm girl from dirt-poor Queen Anne's County, Maryland? Who'd have bet on her? And that was the problem at this moment, because for all his abuse, the one person who had never doubted her, never felt she had to be babied, the person who told her that Paris would lay itself down in front of her, was Diallo Touré.

"Is that who it is?"

"Yes," she answered finally. "He was a diplomat or something from Senegal." She told him about the first night on the ship, about sitting for supper in steerage, and she told him that over the days of the voyage he had pursued her, had told her that she was African, not American, that she would have to come to Africa in order to understand her true past, her true fate. "I told him I was married to you. He was the only person on that boat who knew we were married. I told him so he would leave me alone."

"But he didn't."

"No," she said with a small heave in her throat.

Thomas said nothing for a few minutes. In a few hours they would have to get ready for a farewell dinner M. Richard had planned for them. He'd invited everybody, Mother Lucy, the elderly Tallents, Arthur and Stanley, even the little girls and their mothers. It had sounded sweet, but now, who knew? "Please, Thomas. Please forgive me. I wasn't being untrue to you. I was so confused. Each time I thought I had taken care of it, he came back at me in some other way. He pestered me at the Louvre once or twice. I was too embarassed to say anything to you. Please don't leave me. Please don't send me back to the Retreat. Please, Thomas." She'd leaned forward out of the seat and onto her knees, and with each plea she inched forward until she was right in front of him. If he didn't reach out for her, gather her in, she thought she would collapse into the puddle of her skirts. She didn't try to look up at him, to meet his eye; she couldn't have borne whatever it was that she would see there. She waited and then felt his hand, not touching her, but skimming along the ends of her hair, as if a touch would be too painful. Her scalp and neck tingled; it was enough.

"Did you?"

"Did I go to him? I went to that café." She said that he had told her earlier that he was going back to Senegal and she believed that he wanted to say goodbye to her, that she thought this was fair because he had helped her, really. He had shown her some of the ways of France, and his assurances that she would be treated like any normal person had made her first weeks here tolerable.

"And?"

"He wasn't there. The waiter told me he had already left. It's all over." Oddly, whatever lies and shadings of the truth were in what she said during all this now seemed rather simple. Yes, the end of it. He'd written, she'd gone, he wasn't there. All that was God's truth. *C'est fini.* She felt unburdened; it seemed that everything could now go back to where it was before. They would survive this; she had survived it, she thought. She was still on the floor in front of him. His hand, which had been hovering over her, brushing her hair, idly teasing her sleeve, fell firmly upon her shoulder. Perhaps his arm had gotten tired and he was just resting; perhaps that's all it was, but she felt it like a flow of current from him to her, like a sort of promise to give her another chance.

"I understand," he said, a large statement delivered very quietly. Whispered, mostly just air with enough sound to make it intelligible. He was saying that he had heard enough, and even though he knew only half of the story, the trivial half, perhaps what he was saying was that the untrivial half didn't matter. "I understand," he repeated.

"Do you really?" She sat back onto her calves, and he sat down on the stiff, faded side chair next to the hearth. She could not help thinking that she had gotten off too easy, but he did not answer her question because he had already spoken what he believed. Instead he said nothing, remained silent. Seconds, then minutes, ticked by; her thighs began to hurt. She could bear it no longer. "Thomas?"

"We thought our love would make everything easy, didn't we?" he said. "We had no idea, did we, of what we would face."

Maybe, thought Beal. Maybe that is what he had believed, anyway. But she would not prolong this, and she realized from the tone of his voice that he was now going to move on to the subject that had been hanging in the background of her thoughts, had formed the beginnings of a slight protest even at this hour of her greatest peril. He was going to apologize or explain or confess about the red-haired girl, even though Beal had no evidence, no misplaced note, to incriminate him. That is what he did, but it went a little differently from what she expected.

"You know about the librarian, my friend at Galignani's. I saw her a few days ago. I was saying goodbye to her. She said you came in while I was gone."

Saw her a few days ago: impossible, but true, that she was hurt to hear of this. "Yes," she said. But now that the subject had shifted, she was breathing better, thinking clearly enough to be both hurt and surprised. "But how did she know it was me? We didn't talk or anything."

"She just figured it out, I guess."

"Well, there aren't many girls in Paris that look like me, are there?"

"No. And maybe not that many who look like her."

None of this was quite lining up for Beal: that look she had gotten from the girl seemed to have more in it than simply recognizing the only colored girl in Paris. They had exchanged something that day; it was hard to tell what it was, but there had been, indeed, something to exchange. But Beal didn't want to probe this. For one thing, she didn't want Thomas to ask *And how did you know to go looking for the red-haired girl?*

"Her name is Eileen Hardy," he said. "Isn't that sort of funny?"

Beal had to think for a moment what he was saying, about the Hardys at home. "Oh, I don't know. What do family names on the Retreat mean to us anyway? They're never our family."

Thomas nodded and went on to say everything that Beal had already figured out: that Eileen had helped him in his studying about wine, about Languedoc. Maybe, for that, she was an enemy, but so what? "She was just a friend, but I should have told you. I should have told you that a few times we took tea together. That wasn't right."

"Thomas. There's no need to go into it. We were both just trying to get on, right? There's no need to apologize."

"But there is. Because I never told her I was married."

Beal wanted to reflect on this a little, as it put a very different slant on her confrontation with the girl; her head spun a little. *Then how did she know I had anything to do with you?* Another unasked question. Who knew what when? There was more to this, she knew; scales were starting to hang in a more balanced manner.

"You and me," he said.

"Me and you?" Now he was talking in riddles; his guilt was making him do that. She wished he'd stop, leave it at that rather comforting equilibrium she had just spied.

"That's the reason for everything. People have worked so hard for us. Mary, Mother Lucy, even Arthur, for God's sake. And look what we have been doing."

"What have we been doing?"

"Being disloyal to each other."

Beal's thoughts took a sudden turn at that, a resistance at a moment when she had felt she had no standing, that she could be blown away like a pile of dead leaves. She had never, *never* been disloyal to Thomas. That was the one thing in all this that she was sure of. It was all for him, and for them. If she had been trying to grow up, to learn who she was, to understand her own skin and body, it was for Thomas. The thought arrived like a sudden parting of branches in a dense wood: She had done what she had to do to survive, but she had never been disloyal to him, treated him carelessly, had a mean thought. Never.

"But I have not been unfaithful to you," he said. "The word should not need to be spoken, but I haven't."

This presented a different problem: by his account he had been disloyal, but not unfaithful; by her account she had been loyal, but unfaithful. She did want to tell him the truth; she realized that this was a moment when anything could be said, that even though it might seem their lowest point, perhaps it was a pinnacle. So she did want to say that she'd given her body to Touré, once, but she could not, because that same body had a small being clamped within it and wasn't going to let it go. And that child was Thomas's, of course it was Thomas's, there could be no other way. But he would have no way of knowing it: only a chaste marriage could offer that certainty to a man, a chaste marriage or a lifelong lie. So instead of taking the conversation back to where it belonged, to her, instead of taking advantage of this priceless chance to confess, she stayed on him. "Do you care for her? Do you want to be with her and not with me?"

"No!" They had been almost whispering, but this he shouted so loud it scared her. "I have never cared for her like that. She was just an acquaintance I should have told you about. There was nothing more to it. I'm not sure even now that I would recognize her on the street."

"Then if that's all it was, why should you tell me about it now?"

"Because I have asked you about this," he said, and surprising them both, it appeared that the note was still crushed in his palm.

"Then we are all done," said Beal. "This chapter is over, and I am ready to move on. To St. Adelelmus." It seemed to her that it was the first time she referred to this future by name, pronounced it right, and not in one of her bitter anonyms, *adelypuss, addled mush*, or, the simplest, *moo-moo*. "I'm ready to go. I've told you that. The dream of Paris is over. If you will still let me come. If you still want to be married to me . . ." Speaking this last horrible question made her begin to weep at long last, and as he raised her up, she could see the tears in his eyes. In this second, it seemed their love had grown. Yes, a pinnacle. Yes, the trees parting in the woods. Yes, nine months of life, every day of which, every hour of which had served up new tests for both of them, not just for her, yet here they were, weeping into each other's arms. She wanted to shout this out but at the same time wanted to whisper the moment so that it would remain so deeply embedded that they would never have to speak of it again, never have to live it again. He said he loved only her, and she said she loved only him, and that was that.

Two hours later they were walking on the avenue back to the hotel where this sojourn had begun. It had been a dry summer, and they crunched through the first of the fallen chestnut leaves. A motorcar appeared, and everyone stopped and gaped as it churned down the avenue and across the Pont de l'Alma. Beal felt completely spent. At the end of the afternoon, while she hid in their bedroom, Thomas had discharged Mme Vigny, handing her an envelope with, Beal assumed, a too-generous tip. Mme Vigny—well, she'd played her own role in this drama, probably played it quite well. A sort of nasty, obscure subplot. Beal never wanted to see this woman again; she said this to herself, even though there was no reason on earth that she ever would.

They each allowed a slight smile, hesitating at the door of the Lion d'Or, both recalling the same moment months ago. Maybe Thomas was recalling an earlier, unblemished age, and maybe Beal was smiling back with chagrin at the frightened, ignorant child she had been a mere nine months ago, but either way, this was who they were now. When they opened the door, they found the full dinner party waiting in the lobby. As promised, Céleste and Oriane were there with M. and Mme Richard; Mother Lucy and Arthur and Stanley, now surprisingly reconciled, were there; their friends from the neighborhood were there, the Tallents, and as a treat, because Beal had asked especially, the girls Gilberte and Monique accompanied by one of their mothers, though which one Thomas couldn't be sure. The girls were dressed in similar white dresses with pale blue sashes, and they were both so crazy with delight to be there that they could hardly walk. The only outlier in the group was a young man, an American writer from Boston named Morris Malone, who happened to be staying at the hotel that night and mistook the gathering for boardinghouse seating. And why wouldn't he, given the motley group?

M. Richard seated them, with Thomas at the center along the wall, Beal at his right and Céleste at his left. The little girls and the mother and the Tallents were at one end; Oriane, Madame Bernault, Arthur, and Stanley at the other. A chair was brought without noticeable fuss for Mr. Malone, directly opposite Beal. "I'm afraid I have made a mistake," he said in very poor French. The little girls giggled and were shushed.

"*Pas du tout. Pas du tout*," said Thomas, but then broke into English. "Not at all. You're welcome to join us." He introduced the table to Malone.

"I just landed in Le Havre this morning," he said. Beal glanced at Thomas: this was an almost spooky circumstance. "I need to find a flat, and as you can tell, I need to learn some French."

"Several of us here," said Thomas, "had our first meal in France in this very room. Stanley among them," he said, nodding down the table. "So you are another American who has landed in the best of company." This he repeated in French for the Richards, who took the compliment happily. "In the lobby is where I learned my French," he said, turning to give Céleste a quick hug, as if it were obvious to all why he did that. Céleste reddened slightly—the arm around her shoulder, the implied credit for Thomas's fluency. Thomas would miss her; he wanted her to fall in love and marry, and the slightly illogical thought that she would marry this man, Morris Malone, came into his head. Oriane was the darker daughter, the prettier daughter, but if Céleste wasn't beautiful looking, neither was Malone, with a pasty American-Irish complexion and a small cluster of warts on one cheek. "The Lion d'Or is where Americans come home to France," Thomas concluded.

"And how did you find it?" Beal asked him. Malone looked slightly surprised, as if he hadn't suspected that Beal could speak English, or that she was American, from the South even. Yet he'd been stealing glances at her since he sat down.

He smiled broadly. "My mother found it in a guidebook. She said it was right near the station, but of course it was the wrong station."

"She did well by you, even so," said Beal.

"So if I have forced myself upon all of you, could I ask what the occasion is for this party?" asked Malone.

Thomas said he would allow their host to answer this, and translating back and forth across the language divide, he told Malone that M. Richard had said that a young couple very dear to his heart was forsaking Paris for the South.

"And who is that young couple?" asked Malone, full of good spirits, glancing coyly at Thomas and Céleste.

"Why. It's us," said Beal, taking Thomas's hand.

Malone's mouth fell open; Thomas understood Malone's mistake before he did, and really, he could be forgiven for it. "Oh dear," Malone said helplessly. He was a nice man, it seemed, a most progressive person on his first assignment in Europe, but there it was on his face, the rictus of America. A look of horror and disbelief, followed instantly by a crimson blush of embarrassment, like being caught gaping at a veteran's war wound. Beal saw it, Madame Bernault saw it, Arthur saw it, but M. Richard and Stanley and the other guests had missed it, and M. Richard continued his hostly speech to say he hoped that this young couple would not get eaten by boars or be beset by brigands in the Midi. He laughed, pausing for Thomas to translate.

Thomas watched Malone take his napkin to his forehead and he supposed he might do more to diffuse the moment, to give Malone a break, but there was no opening for it; the best anyone could do was ignore what had happened. Thomas finished his translation and then gave Malone a small questioning nod.

"Really?" he answered weakly. "Boars and brigands?"

M. Richard laughed heartily at this reaction. "No," Beal said from across the table. "M. Richard is making a joke. That's the way many people in Paris feel about the Midi."

"Not much different from the way people in New York feel about Alabama," said Arthur. "Or the way people in Newark feel about Hoboken," he added.

"Ah," said Malone, hearing Arthur's accent: a touch of home. But once he recovered, once aware that his gaffe would be allowed to fade, it was clear that Beal had entranced him. "Then what is the truth?" he asked Beal. "Are you going to Provence?"

"Not Provence," said Beal. "We are moving to a wine region far to the west of Provence. M. Richard teases us, but it's an area that has been civilized since the Romans. My husband has bought a vineyard and we are moving there to farm it." She shook Thomas's hand—she had been holding it all this time. "This has been our plan since we landed."

"And you won't miss Paris?" He was looking at Beal. A born journalist, he seemed to sense a fold in the fabric and put it right into a question. "Nobody returns to Ohio once they've left. Will there be enough there for you?"

Beal let go of Thomas's hand. She thought her little speech about Languedoc and farming had given this man everything and more than he should ask for, this uninvited guest. She glanced down at the girls, whom she had come to love dearly, who were beginning, at age eight, to seem like, well, the next generation of Parisian women. They were here for life, but that was because they belonged here. Paris was nothing so special to them or to their mothers or to all the people on the rue Cler, or to the Richards: it was just where they lived and worked. But Beal still had no place; everything she had done over the past several months began to waver and evaporate in front of her eyes, like memories being washed away one after another. If this kept up, her whole body would start to disassemble, and that would not do. She was a wife and, it seemed, about to be a mother. This was turning into a rather long pause; any second Thomas would break in in his loyal and dutiful way, spare the room and Beal especially any awkwardness, deflect this man Malone who obviously had no idea how correct he had been. To head Thomas off, she said, "Oh," trying a gay little smile. She could not answer Malone's question, but she did have to respond. She felt that the whole table, everyone they knew or cared about in France, was now waiting for her to answer. *Will it be enough, Beal?* Madame Bernault had leaned forward especially, as if at last the predictions of tests and trouble she had made in this very space nine months ago had now come to the moment of resolution. Stanley Dean, of Pittsburgh; everything began to sound as if Stanley, with the first stirrings of success, would not be going back home soon. Arthur, he had his own decisions to make, but they were his decisions; he had gotten himself here; something would come up. And Thomas, who had slightly leaned away so he could look at her more directly, he too was waiting for an answer. He'd been asking this question, in one way or another, for months. *Will it be enough after all you have learned to love here, as far as you have come? Do you want to do this? The time has come to decide.*

"Oh," she said again, "I expect so." She retook Thomas's hand and raised them both slightly, as if in a moment of victory. She felt Thomas resisting this gesture slightly, but she did it anyway. "I surely do expect so."

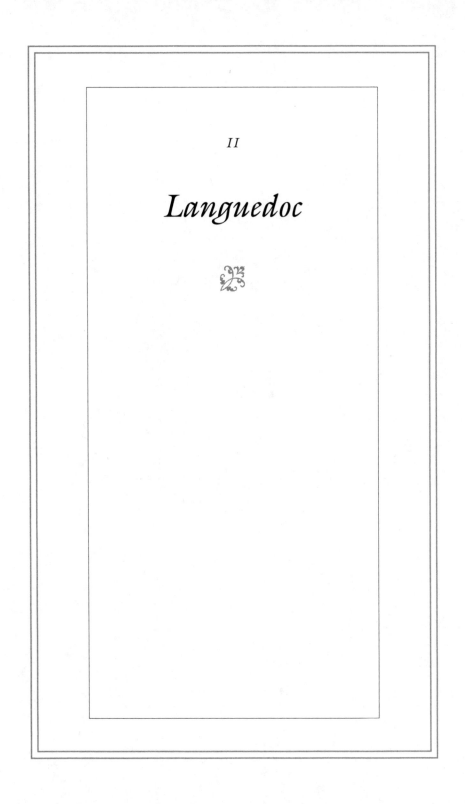

II

Languedoc

10

Years later, when Thomas began to put down his own version of these events, he recalled their first autumn at St. Adelelmus as a descent, a falling into, a letting go. He didn't mind this sense of submission; it was as if a change in the weather had at last shifted the wind to his back and was driving him where he wanted to go. Before, he'd rarely felt anything but thwarted—a thought that might have earned a good laugh, or worse, from his friend Arthur Kravitz, or from Mother Lucy or Randall Terrell. *It's just you, Thomas, puttin' things in your own way,* said Randall one day so long ago. Well, so what. However the thing got there, it was in his way, always something in his way; if it was his own self in the way, that just made it more inescapable. But his own self had no purchase on him here. From the moment they arrived on the property, from the moment Beal and he first walked into the bastide, they both felt a strange welcome, as if they were on a home ground they had previously known only in a dream. Señora Zabala, enormous in girth and enthusiasm, came forward, clucking happily in some combination of French, Occitan, Spanish, and Basque dialect, and took hold of Beal and dragged her off. Beal looked back helplessly; Thomas had no idea what this was about. For all her size—she was not just fat, but big, as tall as Beal—the Señora seemed never to come to rest; Thomas had already gotten used to her as a blur behind him, a figure darting, pouncing. No one of the perhaps thirty men, women, and children who lived at or in the orbit of St. Adelelmus was as loved as she.

For a moment Thomas stood in that hall, with its welcoming fireplace and its oddly disproportionate staircase, both gestures toward a much grander dwelling, as if the masons laid the staircase first and the owner later decided to cut back. The house was dark and still with the window shutters closed tight, and the air was cool and slightly earthen, a fragrance that bespoke not ripeness, not rot, but a sort of drying out. This was the way of the garrigue, an arid land that gave up its moisture begrudgingly and at the end of the season took it back. To his left was a vast parlor, which the Belgians had left furnished in the most formal northern European manner, brocade and carved wood; Thomas wondered if that unhappy and hapless couple had ever gotten to the point of entertaining in this room. He wished it weren't so, but the room reminded him of the Retreat, a place dressed for a party no one much wanted to attend. To his right, through an arched doorway under the staircase, was a similarly sized dining room with a fireplace big enough to roast a whole hog; just as formal, perhaps, but at least here Thomas could imagine some kind of fellowship, some joy. This was the main part of the house, these three large rooms in a line, but to the left of the archway was a tiny door, a sort of mouse hole, behind which was everything else—a warren of kitchens and pantries and sewing rooms and offices—and it was through this door that Señora Zabala had dragged Beal.

Throughout the house were certain large pieces of furniture that seemed almost permanent fixtures, and in one of the offices behind the tiny door was a desk. During the times Thomas had been here as the sale was being completed, he had moved his work onto that desk. Through the room's single small window he could look out over the expanse of drooping Aramon vines, and behind them, a hilltop of the more stalwart Carignan and the more interesting Grenache. At the other end of the house, with a window onto the terrace and fig arbor, was a room he had decided would be Beal's, with a writing table and even an armchair if she wanted. Before they left Paris, he had told her about this room, and she wondered what in the world she was supposed to do in it. "Write," he said, pointing at the notebooks, four of them she'd filled that winter.

Yes, years later, after Beal had died and, at her long-standing request, he read her life's work, her hundreds and hundreds of pages of journals. The earliest—the Paris months and the first few years at St. Adelelmus—were in English, and the rest in French, and as he read the story, its details came alive with extraordinary precision, a tone pinging on a tuning fork. She had captured every fragrance of that first fall, starting with the brown-sugar must of this moment of arrival. Perhaps her memories, her sensations so carefully noted, had now supplanted his own. He did not care. During the long winter after she died, Thomas rationed those pages, allowing himself just an entry or two each late afternoon, after the fire had been set for him in his study by his son Randall, or by the housekeepers, Nalara and Eztebe. He could just as well have rationed Beal's writing sentence by sentence, so much memory was bound there, such long evenings of reflection occasioned. What is truth or lie, now or then, is simply not how one measures a life once it is done. There were episodes in those pages, recorded without varnish, that were painful, almost unbearable, but now at least he understood them with the sort of bruised but burnished wisdom we all hope for at the end. This was good news for the spirit, in place of the gathering storm all around him that winter when he read her journals. To the south, in Spain, the news had been getting worse and worse: by the following June, the fighting would begin. To the north, the Nazi machine was putting the finishing touches on a new Germany; to the east, the Italians were sending troops into Africa. But here, in the sanctuary of his beloved St. Adelelmus, Beal was reemerging to him like the child he (no more than a child himself) had married, and as he gazed head-on into his own past, for him the starting point was that arrival in Languedoc.

That first day, Thomas found Beal upstairs in what was designated as their master suite. After the modest bedroom on the avenue Bosquet, a room that required nothing of them, this was the real thing, the sort of room parents occupy, patriarchs and matriarchs.

Thomas wasn't sure they were ready for it. Beal had gotten up there via a cramped back staircase that Thomas had not noticed before; he could hardly imagine Señora Zabala threading her girth up this spiral, but it did explain how she was able to loom into a room as if by magic. The girl Gabriella was there helping Beal unpack; she had black hair, full red cheeks, and a chin with a slight cleft: the face of a doll. She was perhaps fourteen or fifteen, not that many years younger than Beal. She and Beal were twins in some ways; perhaps they could be friends, girlfriends. When Thomas came in, Beal was at the window, looking out at the ravine and the brook bed, which was dry. From this window one could imagine St. Adelelmus as a castle, strategically placed at the high point, but in fact, on the other side, to the north, the Black Mountain range rose restlessly above them.

"Well?" said Thomas. "What do you think?"

"You said you weren't going to keep asking me that question," she said, but it was in good cheer. Still, what else could she say?

When they left Paris, he had booked them onto the mail train from the Quai d'Orsay, with full amenities, and had arranged to spend a night in Bordeaux and a night also in Narbonne for his last bit of paperwork, as if this stepping down through a lesser rival of Paris and then through a small provincial capital might insert Beal by degrees into the Midi. She had never been in such a place, a place of crags and rocks, of deep ravines and high dry meadows, here thick stands of oak and chestnut, there blasted prairies relentless in their dips and heaves. The tiny train they took from Narbonne, skirting along the border between the plain and the foothills, passed into a new vista with almost every turn. What a place to put farms, no matter what the crop! Beal had lived her first sixteen years on the flat, low banks of the Chesapeake and then had traveled down to the sandy bitter end of Cape Charles to catch a ferry for her job in Hampton. That was it for her, that and the otherworldly Paris, her life atlas: what a strange mélange of place and landscape.

It was on the bustling Place de la Comédie in Bordeaux that she asked him to stop questioning her at every point of interest. "Please, Thomas," she said. "I don't know what you want me to say." She had been doing her best to act cheerful, but it was hard for Thomas to tell what this brave front was attempting to sup-press; there was too much in the air between them for him to parse. Beal could feel it too, Thomas knew that perfectly well, and when she said this—a very minor complaint—it was as if a hole in the arid plaza opened in front of them and they fell in. Maybe they could not do this, any of it—their marriage, this move. Perhaps it was here, in the middle of this brutal expanse of stone, that they were left finally defenseless and exposed; perhaps, years later, Thomas and Beal would agree that here, at this very moment in Bordeaux, was where it had begun to fall apart. Yes, remarked Thomas, reading these pages years later: Beal had felt it too.

He answered, "I guess I don't know what I want you to say either. I'm trying to make this easy for you. Maybe I should just stop."

She tugged on his arm. "No. Don't give up. You can't." She meant: you brought me here and to abandon me here is not an option.

They continued their walk down to the river, where the light-ers floating past were loaded with wine casks and mounds of grapes; *les vendanges* were coming, earlier here in Bordeaux than in Languedoc, where most of the grapes ripened in what Thomas had learned was the "last period." Thomas knew all about such things, the earlies and the lates; he'd grown up where the weeks of the summer and early fall were divided not into months, but into varieties of peaches. But so what?

"I'm trying," she said. "I'm trying so hard," and there, on the banks of the Garonne, she stopped in her tracks and burst into tears. She reached into her handbag for a handkerchief, but Thomas al-ready had his out. Her shoulders heaved with such despair that Thomas forgot everything he was thinking, every angry or fearful thought, and drew her in. "What?" he said. "What have I done that hurts you so much?"

"I'm trying too," she repeated between gulps of air. Two men in bowlers were walking by when she said this, and they paused to express some sort of disapproval, though for exactly what Thomas couldn't tell. Maybe they were simply scolding him for causing this hurt to a pretty girl.

"I know you are. You've been trying so hard ever since we

landed. You have been so brave. I could never have done what you have done. I know that."

"But you're still so mad at me. You'll never stop being mad at me."

"I'm not mad at you," said Thomas.

"I didn't know what to do about that man. He made me feel alone, so apart from you. From the moment I met him on the boat, that's the way he made me feel. That's why I went to find him, to tell him that not for one second could he ever come between us. But he wasn't there. I told you that. Nothing happened."

"I understand. We've put that all behind us. Haven't we?"

She seemed to not even hear him. "He tried to turn my whole life upside down. He said I was ignorant. He said I'd never understand myself unless I went to Africa. That I was full of white blood. As if I should hate my own body."

"Yes. I understand. You know I forgive everything that happened."

"You can't just forgive me; you have to believe me."

"I do believe you," he said, which might have been a lie, since he could not dispel all the suspicious thoughts that had been roiling his brain over the past few days, but he realized in that instant that he could in fact believe her even while these suspicions plagued him. It was a strange equation, but it seemed to work, because he wanted it to work. Doubts, shards of tales of infidelity, these all could exist deep in the mine of one's life without really meaning anything in the light of day. Telling her that he believed her made him feel better, offered a sort of psychic truth going forward into their lives, a state of suspension, and so he said it again.

She had composed herself, but they were still standing at the end of the plaza, overlooking the piers, the bustle of river traffic. It was a comforting sight to Thomas; his own wine, from St. Adelelmus, could end up here on the Garonne via the Canal du Midi.

"I promise I won't ask you again."

"Ask me what?" she said with some alarm.

He realized that he could have meant many things, but he was saying that he wouldn't keep probing her for what she was thinking, whether she liked a view, whether the omelet was too dry, whether she was happy or cold or hot. If she wanted to comment on the sights to come, that was fair, he was saying, but he wouldn't keep chasing her. He explained this to her, and she smiled and accepted the arrangement, and so it was that now, here in their new bedroom in St. Adelelmus, he had broken his word.

"Sorry," he said.

She walked over to him and gave him a kiss, which seemed to both embarrass and please the girl Gabriella. "It's so beautiful here," Beal said to Thomas, answering his question at last, but she said it in French to include the girl, who, like the boys on the domaine—but not the other girls—had been going to school in the village, where the primary objective seemed to be the eradication of Occitan.

"*Oui, Madame*," said Gabriella, in her somewhat stiff schoolgirl French. "*Nous sommes très heureux que vous soyez venus ici.*"

"I just wanted to make sure you were all right," said Thomas, back in English.

"What might have happened to me? Attacked by boars and brigands?"

"No. Nothing, I guess."

Thomas went back downstairs to await a visit from M. Murat, the *régisseur*, the stage manager for the entire enterprise; from what Thomas could tell from his brief experience, the actors in this drama were an expressive lot, but the drama itself seemed a work of improvisation. Last month he had hoped, expected, to find daybooks, accountings, records of the farm—some clues as to what worked and what did not, the sort of thing his father, his grandfathers, and all Masons back to the days of Lord Baltimore had done on the Retreat, but he found nothing. He asked M. Murat if he had any such records for him to peruse, but he responded with a Gallic shrug and a *pfft*, all of which led Thomas to understand that in the commonly held view, nothing that had happened in the previous two thousand years of wine making in Languedoc held any real relevance for the year now upon us. History offered a certain context, an indispensable referent, but no firm guideposts; science, with its causes and effects, its inductions, could only lead one astray, could only obscure the faint signals, the pulse given off by the terroir, by the fruit, by the year at hand, by subtle tremors indicating that the pests and blights were about to attack, or not to attack.

While he was awaiting M. Murat, Thomas went outside and stood in the sun. It was midafternoon, but the light was still white and strong and the buildings seemed to shimmer as the sun's rays caught the facets of marble rubble in the walls; he heard the church bell—so much a part of this landscape that it was almost hard to believe it was a contrivance of man—chiming the hour in the distance. He caught the vague scent of ripe fruit and heard the buzzing of wasps. On the top of the rise, just below the bastide—yes, that was how he had taken to referring to their house, somewhere between a château and a *mas*—were the barns, the sheds and shops, the pressing rooms, vatting rooms, bottling rooms; most of the vignerons, the vine-dressers, lived in the domaine's simple dwellings with their families. M. Esquivel, the cooper, and M. Cabrol, the blacksmith, also lived there with their families, but they seemed to own—in some arrangement Thomas did not quite understand—their houses and shops, and both of them did most of their business with customers outside the domaine. From where Thomas stood, all he saw was the mosaic of red clay roofs and then, radiating outward, the feathery green vines. The vines thrilled him; he was now under their sway. Any day now for the Grenache, M. Murat had said. Weeks earlier they had entered the *véraison*, the vine-ripening period, but Thomas had no idea what would finally tip the balance. It had seemed plain enough in the library in Paris: one harvests when the increase of sugar content and decrease of acidity stop, and before rot begins to set in. That is, the bad kind of rot, and not the *pourriture noble*, the noble rot you wanted if you were making a sweet white. Which they weren't. How one would discern the most favorable intersections of all this was not something Thomas expected to understand for years. He recalled from his research that before the French Revolution the dates of *les vendanges* were fixed by the local worthies—an interference, so said the Revolution, in man's right to live as he saw fit.

When Thomas first stood here months ago, it seemed that this place had reached out to him, taken him into its grasp, awakened with biblical certainty some sort of calling. He still felt that, but he'd faced a bump or two since that small epiphany. He could only admit to himself that he felt daunted. *Why not grapes?* Eileen had said these months ago, and today there seemed no interval between that moment and now. It was as if the first time he reached for a book on viticulture, a wand had been waved and here he was, standing in the yard of a winery he now owned, an idle thought back then—*Well*, he had replied, *I don't know why not*—becoming instantly real. It was as if he had tendered his vows for a priesthood with only the barest and dimmest idea of what he had gotten himself into. Maybe this wouldn't work out. Maybe they'd go the way of the Belgians, with Beal running off with that African and Thomas limping back to the Retreat. That could happen. Maybe some new blight would wipe out these vines, so recently reestablished on their American roots. Maybe there would be seven years of drought and then seven years of rain, and the whole place would revert to the garrigue, these houses and barns just another set of ruins for visitors and tourists in centuries to come.

He heard a thud behind him and turned, expecting to see the wiry and inscrutable M. Murat, but it was Beal. It was the breeze perhaps, the way it caught her skirt and her hair, or the smell of the ripe figs, or the slight murmur of workers' voices from the barns, but for an instant Thomas flashed back to an image of her during harvest on the Retreat, when just the sight of her gliding through the peach trees was enough to cheer up and encourage the pickers. It was her beauty, but more than that, it was simply her way in the world—*aura* would not be too strong a word, as she did nothing to exert it—that diverted the spirits of those toiling laborers. Everyone on the Retreat knew it was a gift that in some way she was condemned to share, that she had to visit each family, whatever the language they spoke, each person, even if she didn't want to. *Come on over here, darlin'*, they'd say, in the tone they'd use for a favorite dog. And here she was now, coming to him in his moment of doubt. Her Mediterranean skin radiated here in its native light. Something had gone on in the house among herself and the girl and the Señora, and she was giggling girlishly. What more would Thomas want to see than that? She came to his side and put her arm around him.

"What is so funny?" he said.

"Oh. The Señora is kind of crazy."

"Good crazy?"

"Funny crazy, I think. Gabriella keeps a close eye on her. She reminds me a little of Aunt Zoe, without her hurts. Aunt Zoe before the day all our people was sold south."

Yes, thought Thomas, everyone changed that day, the day before the war, long before both of them were born, when his grandfather sold practically every enslaved Negro to a man from Virginia in a schooner, including a son of Zoe's. Aunt Zoe was free, like Beal's parents and all the other people in Tuckertown, but these were family and friends being sent away in chains. To hear the stories, Aunt Zoe had always been a little peculiar, but by the time Thomas was growing up, even he could tell that this was a woman being eaten alive by her rage.

"People don't like Basques around here, that's what Gabriella told me. They think Basques can give evil eyes. But they like the Señora."

"And, well, they like Gabriella, I'd suppose. The men especially."

"Oh, now."

"She doesn't remind you a little bit of yourself? At that age?"

She gave him a little nudge, as if that was silly, but she didn't deny it. She settled in beside him and followed his gaze over the barns and down the valley. How odd it was on these hilltops; it was as if they were camping out on the high ground, keeping a watchful eye on the deep gullies below. On the lower hills down the valley they could see four or five farms situated in just this way, like snow on mountain peaks. Off to the south they could just see the tip of the spire of the church in the village. Farther in the distance, on a very clear day, on the next set of ridges, someone with good eyes could see Cathar ruins. No one could dismiss the violent beauty of this place. It would take strong wills to survive here, and even if Thomas could grant to himself that the future was uncertain, could acknowledge all too easily that the odds against a young man from the Chesapeake becoming a vigneron in the Midi were a little stiff, he knew that Beal, if she wanted to, would prosper. She could succeed at anything; she had already conquered the greatest city in the world. She could become a writer, if that's what she wanted. She could marry someone else and become a queen. If she wanted, she could take St. Adelelmus in hand and it would flourish. Thomas and the men and women of the farm would do the work, but she would make it bloom. Just as she had once darted through the orchards like a nymph, a fairy, she could do it here in the vines, and the vintages would fall in line. If that's what she wanted to do.

From a crack in the wall on the parapet above the vats, which in a few weeks would be full of must, M. Xavier Murat caught sight of his new masters, the new owners, this American man and his Negro wife. What sort of disaster might this be? The Belgians had been fine, as they were hardly ever there and had plenty of money to invest; this M. Bayly seemed to have less money but more ideas, very much the short end of both sticks. They were standing in front of the *maison de maître*, a house that once had been his own, or should have been if two hundred years of family history meant anything. Xavier had grown up in that house with his four sisters—*quatre filhas e la maire, cinq diables contra lo paire*, went the old Occitan proverb—and his whole family, including his parents, had found it possible during that time to forget that St. Adelelmus was owned not by his father, but by his wayward uncle, François, who had gone off to dissipate his fortune. When François returned, no one slaughtered a fattened calf for him, for the woman who may or may not have been his wife, or for his miserable, sickly children. Xavier was sixteen that day in 1865, when he and his mother and father and sisters moved their things, their clothes, their mattresses, their pots and pans, their family papers and records, to the *appartement de maître* in the *mas*. His sisters were mostly whimpering the whole time, and it broke Xavier's heart. Each time he passed his father or mother going the other way, they told him this wouldn't be for long, that François would be gone in six months, one harvest, a winter or two, and when they were restored to the bastide, all would pick up where they had left off and they would undo the damage—for surely there would be damage—their uncle had caused and the Murat name would continue at St. Adelelmus as before. But that was before the beast, the *étisie*, the phylloxera, took them all in its grasp.

The Midi was where it first appeared, in 1863, unheralded, the leaves of a couple of vines in the center of a vineyard in Arles yellowing, the edges turning red and then dropping to the ground; in such trivial occurrences does disaster begin. People thought it must be a fungus, like oidium, but it took the great minds of MM. Bazille, Planchon, and Sahut—Xavier mouthed these names with reverence—not long to figure that it was something entirely different: aphids were sucking the roots dry. Later, Planchon deduced that the aphids came over from America sometime after 1858 on infested American grapes, though why anyone would want to import *Vitis riparia* or, worse, *Vitis labrusca* remained a mystery. The aphids came along with those dreadful plants, but the vines themselves were resistant and unaffected. Not so *Vitis vinifera*. No one much liked Bazille's ingenious solution—grafting *Vitis vinifera sativa* scions onto the very American rootstock that had caused the problem in the first place; it doubled the indignity, but it worked. Now there was hardly a grapevine growing on its own roots anywhere in Languedoc, and soon enough the same would be true for Bordeaux, for the Haute-Marne and Alsace, even Burgundy, which had resisted American rootstock to the bitter end.

Xavier himself had put in many hours in the grafting sheds, and there was plenty of trial and error in it, but after a while it seemed that St. Adelelmus might survive. By 1880 they had had enough healthy vines to resume production. Xavier's uncle was nicely out of their hair, as he was occupying himself entirely with attempts to win the 300,000-franc Hérault Commission prize for a chemical cure. His submissions reached such a level of lunacy—a concoction of seawater mixed with the urine of menstruating women was one—that the commission would no longer accept them from him, and at that point he sold St. Adelelmus for practically nothing and disappeared. These Americans were the third owners since then.

The young couple had engaged in a conversation and were now standing side by side looking at the view. Xavier found it a pleasant scene, but his wife, Marceline, had taken an immediate dislike to Thomas when she'd met him in June, which was unfortunately her way, not that she was always wrong. "This is a weak man," she said after he left. "He lacks *fermeté*." They were in their kitchen, Xavier in the chair where he smoked, did his paperwork, kept his accounts. After all these years they had grown comfortable in their apartment, which was big enough for them and their two sons and for Xavier's mother, who had taken to her bed a few years earlier, and his youngest sister, Françoise. When the must was in the vats, the air in the whole complex became a little thick, but this was a small price for having survived phylloxera. Xavier had no interest in resuming life in the bastide, which Marceline dismissed as bourgeois anyway. They both preferred the apartment, which was, according to Marceline—her highest praise—*fonctionnel et efficace*.

"M. Fauberge says he is a serious young man," he had said. "His family are farmers."

"A serious farmer does not buy property halfway around the world. A serious young man does not leave his family's land. Why didn't he stay there, where he belongs?"

"Because of his marriage to a Negro girl. It's against the law in America."

She herself had recoiled at the idea of the new owner's marriage, the idea of the mistress of the domaine being an African, but now she would give no quarter to Thomas just because he came from an insane land. "Oh, the Americans," she answered. "They gave us oidium. They gave us the beast. And now they *sell* us their roots. It wasn't their idea anyway."

Throughout the years, Xavier had kept well informed of the search for the cure, mostly to keep his sanity when his uncle François was expounding his wild theories. He knew that an American agronomist named Riley had been one of the heroes and that the growers in Bordeaux had recently awarded him a statuette in gratitude. But Xavier was never interested in tangling with Marceline when she got like this. "We will give him a chance, won't we?"

She had not answered that day, which didn't surprise him, but as he stood peeking at them through his window on his world, he knew that his wife had simply given voice to what everybody was saying. He wished he had the luxury of finding fault with St. Adelelmus's new owners. But one challenge led to another: Across the plain the growers who survived had planted thousands of hectares of Aramon, and the price of wine was already beginning to fall, which led to even more hectares of Aramon. Madness. His uncle François had jumped into that hole. Most of the growers in Languedoc were so giddy with relief for having survived the plague that they did not look forward and see an even more intractable crisis, a lake full of wine, lurking ahead. And this was saying nothing about the fake wines—raisin wine, sugar wine—and chaptalized Algerian wine!

This young man standing in the wind—the wife had now left, gone back into the house—had stepped into a hornet's nest. He had perhaps no better idea about any of this than anyone else, he knew nothing about wine, didn't even *enjoy* it as far as Xavier could tell; but still, Xavier could not dismiss him. He knew his cultivars, for one thing—had learned from books, but he'd done well at it. And he understood what overproduction could mean, knew that the only way to keep out of a lake of wine was not to go swimming. He had these thoughts about moving up, filling some of the void as Bordeaux reeled, bottling their own cuvée, something *bien meublée* but *aimable*. Plant some Syrah to go along with the Grenache? They had a terroir that could do that—a terroir Xavier particularly loved—if anyone wanted to try.

It was time to learn whether this American had the heart for it. Xavier left his comfortable spot—as his father before him and many forefathers before that, this was where he spent a good bit of time during the harvest and vinification—and walked down and up the dip between the barns and the house. M. Bayly waved as soon as Xavier appeared; Xavier had been told that Americans were always forcing themselves on you, always eager to lend a hand, to hold a door, to "here, let me get that," but he wasn't sure that this was the way M. Bayly behaved. Perhaps the wave had simply been a sign of recognition. Xavier was not sure that what his wife saw as lack of strength was really a more subtle reserve. He supposed that in the American manner, he ought to inquire after the trip, after Mme Bayly's health and happiness, about the state of affairs upon arrival, but it would all be pointless: yes, they had arrived as scheduled, Mme Bayly had seemed just fine from across the farmyard, and if the Señora and Gabriella did not have the housekeeping well in hand, who in the world would have? So Xavier jumped directly to business without a greeting. "The Grenache is almost ready," he said. Immediately he regretted behaving quite so cryptically, thought after he had done so that he might soften it with a few niceties, but to his surprise, Bayly had already turned and was heading up the path to the vines, leaving Xavier to follow.

"A most demanding grape, Grenache," yelled Xavier, catching up. "Some years, too much fruit. Other years, too much leaf."

Bayly turned his head slightly to acknowledge that he had heard, and he kept walking. It was a mild day; Xavier liked this, reckoned that this tiny spritz of warmth was just what was needed, and when they arrived up the hillside at the first of the vines, Xavier could feel that it was time. "A week or two," he said to Bayly.

"How do you know?"

Xavier yanked a *grappe* from the nearest vine; the grapes were a rich purple color, just barely beginning to pucker. He squeezed a few between his thumb and forefinger and pressed some of the clear, sticky juice into Bayly's palm. He encouraged Bayly to raise his hand to his nose, but he did not explain what one hoped to smell—it was rather hard, after all, to describe any smell, especially one that indicated that sugar and acid were in perfect balance—and Bayly didn't ask. This was not a lesson for this year, when the smell would have to be described in words, but for next year, when it could be remembered in the body.

"The year has been good," said Xavier. He reached down to wipe the juice off his fingers on a pile of white stones. His mind ran quickly over the annual high points: steady, fine weather, relatively dry but enough humidity in the soil in the spring. Not a "glorious" summer—this was the word the Belgian had used, as if such weather would guarantee good wine, which it did not, as grapes did not like anything as obvious as glory—but a decent summer. "It is the month of August that makes the harvest," Xavier said. "This year was hot and wet. But now we must act quickly. Before the hail. Before the mildew."

This had all taken Xavier a few minutes to say; he was barely conscious that he was speaking out loud, since every word was merely the mental traffic that occupied his inner being from May to September. Bayly had not interrupted him, had not questioned him as the Belgian had, but rather, he seemed to be recording this information for later use. As much as Xavier approved of the man's manner, he was beginning to find him a little impenetrable, the last thing he'd been led to expect of an American. In fact, he became aware of a slight smile on Bayly's face, as if there were some humor in all this, which there was not.

"You are amused, Monsieur?" Xavier said.

"Oh. Not really amused. Actually, I could see something almost tragic in all this."

Xavier thought for a second that either his French or Bayly's had miscommunicated something here. "*Tragique?*"

Bayly turned to him. His features were fine, maybe a little delicate—perhaps that's what Marceline was reacting to—but the nose was good: a vigneron needed a good nose. "I'm sorry," he said. "I was thinking about the years my father and my wife's father stood side by side discussing the harvest, the same words, the same guessing. All they did was worry, and in the end, it didn't turn out well for them."

Xavier had understood this much in June, something of this history—with fruit, peaches, if he remembered correctly.

"I can't imagine what my father would think about what I am doing," Bayly continued. "Whether it would make him proud or whether he'd decide that I am mad. What happened in the blight destroyed him."

"As for so many here," Xavier answered. "But my papa never lost hope. He lived long enough to see that the grafting was going to work, even though the first few American roots didn't take to our chalk." He kicked the ground fondly. In retrospect, he liked the fact that not just any old American rootstock could come here and take over; there had to be some compromise in all this, some concession.

"My father would have liked that—'didn't take to our chalk.' He'd wonder why. He was a scientist more than a grower."

"Hmmm," said Xavier, meaning some respect—after all, the scientists at Montpellier, Planchon and Riley, had saved them—but also some skepticism.

"But you survived," Bayly concluded. "Me too, I guess. And for all that, our reward is to stand here and worry about hail, disease, frost. It never ends. We could be having this conversation in a thousand different languages about crops you and I have never heard of. Not *tragique*. Rather"—he paused—"as you say, amusing." *Amusant*, this endless cycle of lives.

Xavier had expected nothing like this from Bayly, and somehow they seemed to have ended up exactly where the whole conversation began. But it was not so far from the way Xavier thought of this life: a vigneron needed to have the gift of laughter and a sense that the world was mad. Before oidium and phylloxera, the land of Oc had been a place of laughter, of fêtes and Carnaval—*Carnaval es arribat, le brave, le brave!*—of long stories and twisted reasoning, of the humor of the gallows but also the drollness of the marketplace. One needed some lightness, one needed the carnival of life, and perhaps that had been missing at St. Adelelmus. "*Amusant*, then," he answered. "What we do is *amusant*."

That evening he related this to Marceline. She started to protest—the person we work for now is *fou*—but as he talked, she softened and began to see the appeal in all this. The illogic. Marceline was the daughter of a bookish schoolteacher, and though she was from a much-lesser family than Xavier, she was well educated in the glories of French thought. There was, she allowed, something of Rabelais in what Bayly said.

Beal wasn't thinking about much of anything that day, especially not about grapes and farming and the ironies of the choices Thomas had made. She allowed herself to be led by the Señora from one end of the house to the other, and it seemed that she was pointing out the most positive features of each room, though she was hard to understand. Beal assumed that if she simply listened, before too long she'd gain some access to this private tongue, and besides, after almost everything she said, the Señora burst into laughter, which made none of it seem very grave. To the south was the tidy farmyard, where Beal could see the gentlest view of all, sheep and cows and two enormous pigs, and hay: the things of home. To the north there were no windows at all. The Señora made note of this and then fluttered her arms and hands wildly and made a puffing sound through her lips. "Because of the winds during the winter," Gabriella translated, though Beal had already figured that out.

During that harvest Beal mostly stayed around the house, though several times she went up to the vineyards and watched the men as they worked down the vines, tossing bunches of grapes over their shoulders into the conical baskets on their backs. They never missed. When the baskets were full, the men clambered up onto the back of a cart and tipped their loads, almost somersaulting into the bed of fruit.

Beal didn't remember when, but somewhere along the line of her spotty schooling back in Tuckertown she had come upon a picture of men and women tromping on grapes with their bare feet. She had never said this to Thomas, but it was one of the reasons she thought wine was unclean, one of the reasons she still found it unappetizing to see Thomas drink it with food. But here she discovered that no one did that anymore, hadn't really done it for many years. Instead, the grapes went through rollers to break the skins, and then the whole smashed and gooey mess—grapes, skins, pits—got poured into vats. Which was bad enough, for Beal. She watched this with M. Murat, who fretted and talked to himself the whole time. Sulfur, yeast, temperature, oxygen; too much of one, too little of the other, or vice versa, it didn't really matter. She liked this about him; he reminded her of Abel, her own father, which is what Thomas had told her to expect. Looking down into the vats, which after a day or two began to bubble and spit and then to expel a solid cap of smashed grape skins, stems, and seeds, she realized that the whole thing was simply being left to rot. One day she emerged groggy from the gases.

She kept an eye out for Thomas but mostly tried to let him work. She was proud of him because he knew how to stay out of the way, but still, she knew he was learning and, at the same time, leading. At night she would ask him about the day, content to let him go on and on. It was a relief not to be talking about themselves, the move, the way it had all ended in Paris, about *anything* that had come before this. It was as if she wanted life to simply begin anew, and it would have been possible—she thought Thomas would be disposed to do this—if the new life growing inside her hadn't begun back there, back in what now seemed to be weeks and weeks of confusion and despair. It hadn't seemed like that at the time, but it did now.

One day as she was waking up—these days it was Thomas who was up first, long gone before she ambled downstairs to the kitchen—she realized that it had been exactly three weeks since she had woken up in Paris. It seemed months ago, and the sugary ease of this mountaintop farm made the whole idea of city life seem slightly implausible, somewhere out there, *là-bas*. She thought of Arthur in his studio, the dear girls Monique and Gilberte being woken and washed and dressed for school, the Richards commencing another day, checking guests out, anticipating the arrival of newcomers in the evening. She wondered if that man who had stumbled into their farewell dinner, Malone, was still at the hotel, whether he'd found a flat, whether he was working on his French with Céleste. It made her a little homesick to think of others doing all this without her. She pictured their apartment, now empty, and for a few moments she amused herself by imagining a stroll past the markets on the rue Cler, picturing the crush at each of them, wondering if those merchants had thought of her once or twice since she left. But for all that, she couldn't place herself in the middle of any of it, and she supposed that their time there really was a dream, an experience out of time. But then, once again, it was the child within her that brought her back.

A few weeks after she arrived, she happened to be standing outside the front door when a sporty gig pulled up in a cloud of dust. When it came to a stop and the horse had let out a good snort to clear his nostrils, a young woman wrapped the reins around the brake handle and stepped down; she had her brown hair in a red kerchief, but her shirt and skirt were the indistinguishable gray that all the women here seemed to wear. Beal would have figured out who this was even without seeing immediately that she was very pregnant, a funny sight, really, with such a birdlike frame. "You're Mme Milhaud," she said in her French. "My husband has told me about you."

Léonie smiled back, speaking in her English. That's how these first conversations went, darting back and forth between two languages not that well mastered, but the meaning was clear. She answered, "In the Midi we do not often pay calls, and never at harvest time, but I wanted to see how you were doing."

Beal invited her in, asked Gabriella to bring some tea, and settled at the stone table under the figs.

"It's so lovely here," said Léonie. "A real farm. Not some fake
château built by a banker from Béziers. But that may be St. Adelelmus's misfortune, that it is too pretty for its own good."

"Is that a problem?"

"It means that people have bought it for the wrong reasons. My
father-in-law did not make that mistake with La Fontaine. The
name makes it sound much grander than it is. But don't worry.
St. Adelelmus is excellent terrain. I just mean it makes what we do
seem too easy."

Beal wasn't sure what she meant. "Thomas is working very hard.
He is already very deep into this plan of his."

Léonie blushed. "Oh. I didn't mean to suggest anything. I am
sorry. I was just thinking about this lovely vineyard and how much
it deserves you. I don't mean to sound negative."

"I understand. I know what we are doing seems . . ." She
couldn't find the word, in French or in English.

"Improbable?" offered Léonie.

"Yes. *Improbable.*"

"As you Americans say, *so what?*" She said the last words in English, and they both laughed. "But how are you?"

"I think I am doing all right. It's all so new." Gabriella brought
the tea, and Léonie and she had a brief conversation about la Señora, how she was doing after "last week."

"A lovely girl," Léonie said when Gabriella left them. "Her
mother is a great favorite. You'll see when you go to the market
with her. It's quite comical. She's a sort of queen. The crowd parts
for her."

"Because she is so tall?"

"Yes, but also because they don't know her well, and she is, as
maybe you have noticed, a little odd. She prowls about at night,
sometimes several kilometers away. Sometimes in the morning we
find her and bring her in and wait for her husband or the girl to
come looking for her." Léonie took a sip of tea. "I'm sorry. Perhaps that wasn't very useful. I keep saying the wrong thing. I don't
want to scare you about her. She's always very cheerful."

Beal shook her head. "At home there are always one or two people who get jittery at evening times or at night. We call them"— she didn't try to translate—"walkers."

"*Les gens qui marchent?*"

"Yes. My Mama said that it was slavery that did it to them— they're always trying to find things that were lost. Maybe la Señora is looking for something like that."

Léonie listened to this with a bit of surprise on her face, which softened into a sort of sympathetic wonderment, and they drank their tea and listened to the sounds of the harvest for a few moments. "Your French is actually very good," she said finally. "You've made an impressive start. Some people here will not understand you, but mostly because of your Parisian accent."

"Thomas says my French is better than my English. More proper, he means." Beal didn't know why, but it felt good to open up to this stranger. "We speak a little different at home. My parents always corrected us kids, but when they talk to each other, they always speak the way that comes natural for them. A couple more years away, and I might not even understand them."

Léonie put her hand on Beal's. "This must be hard for you. To be so far from home. I can't imagine."

At some later time, Beal supposed, if they really became friends, she would tell this woman more—she would say *yes, it is so hard for me, I never think about it at all. From the day I got on a boat to come here, I put my home and my Mama and Daddy in a box, and I won't let them out until I can bear it. I can't even write them a decent letter.* But here she said, "Yes, but Thomas and I really had no choice."

"Still," said Léonie. They drank their tea, and Léonie told Beal the essentials about life here, about the markets, and about the people who would be friendly to them and the people who would not. She finished with what Beal thought was a truly kind offer to help her in any way she could, and then, as they stood up, Léonie looked at her with a sort of double take and a quizzical smile. "Are you pregnant?" she asked.

That this woman was the first person to guess this, that she would be the first person Beal told, seemed strangely right. Strangely the very best thing. "Yes," she said. Her ears coppered. "But I haven't told anyone. I think Thomas just thinks I'm getting fat on the Señora's cooking."

"When will you be due?"

"I'm not really sure. I think it happened in the middle of June."

"Yes. We never really know these things. And besides, you're smart to wait. I lost my first one." When she said this, she caressed her stomach, as if reassuring the child waiting inside that all would be well. And it was: two weeks after this meeting, Léonie delivered her third child, her second son, whom they named Gustav.

"I'm sorry to hear that," said Beal, and her hand went to her own stomach. She realized that this was a gesture she had begun to make often, sensing the slight roundness in the cup of her palm. It came to her then that Léonie could not possibly be the only woman who had suspected something; Gabriella had seen her emerging from the bath, and who knew what the girl might have noticed.

"It was very early," Léonie answered. "It was fine. If I hadn't told Theo right away, I wouldn't have had to pay it much notice at all, which I would have preferred. But you seem well beyond that. It's probably time for you to tell him."

"Yes. I suppose there is no reason to delay anymore."

"Is there some other reason? Are you frightened? You can be."

Beal heard this with some alarm; it now seeming impossible to conceal anything from this person, even the things she would die trying to keep secret. She wasn't sure how she felt about this. "No," she answered. "No reason. It's just not something I've ever done before, to tell someone I am expecting. I didn't tell anyone in Paris, though I tried to tell one person."

Léonie might have followed up on that obscure "one person," but she departed without any comment, and Beal stood awhile, her hand on her stomach, following the gig as it raced away down the hill, past the barns, and into the chestnuts before reappearing one last time at the bottom of the ravine. With an empty feeling, Beal watched Léonie go. How long had it been since she really had a friend? The women in Paris, Hilary and Colleen, she was grateful for all their kindness, but she wasn't sure they were friends. She didn't understand why her pregnancy made her feel so lonely; maybe that was the real reason she hadn't told Thomas—though there were others—because she was afraid this loneliness would come in the door along with the child. It seemed completely wrong, but that was the way she'd felt from the moment she realized what had happened, from the moment—again, she wished these memories would forever go away—she collapsed onto Diallo Touré's empty bed. She hoped she could hold off, at least until the end of the harvest.

Beal had supposed that once the grapes finished rotting in the fermentation vats, they would draw off or press out—who knew— the juice, and that would be that, but over the next few weeks she heard all manner of things about fining and filtering, all sorts of ailments being guarded against, from Thomas and from M. Murat, and by the time the wine ended up in the casks, she almost felt sorry for it. "Why not just let it be?" she asked Thomas one night.

"The natural destiny of wine is to become vinegar, and bad vinegar at that."

"Listen to you. 'Destiny.' Is this a religion or something like that?"

They ate their meals in a small room just off the kitchen that had only a slit of window at the top of the high stone wall; in the evening a shaft of light came down from it like a blessing. To Beal, it felt as if they ate in a church, one of those small antechapels in Notre-Dame or Saint-Sulpice.

"For them, it is religion," said Thomas. "St. Martin's Day, St. Vincent's Day. Big days on the vignerons' calendar." He laughed. "Most of the time when I ask M. Murat a question he tells me the answer is a mystery that only the vine understands."

"Do you think that is his way of ignoring you?"

"Yes, but it is also the way he thinks. There's a logic to surrendering to mystery. Just ask Mother Lucy."

Beal looked at him; he was radiant, as if after years of doubt, he had given himself fully to faith. His face was ever browner from the sun; maybe, just as there was white blood in Beal's body, there might be black blood in his. She had never seen him so glad at heart, almost triumphal. "But people do have some idea," she said. "Some people make bad wine. Some people make good wine."

"Yes. They do. That's what I want to do."

"You will. You will succeed at this because your whole heart is in it. You will be famous before you are done." Beal did not know exactly where or why this thought came to her; it had simply come out from nowhere, an idea placed on her tongue, but as soon as she said it, she felt she had seen into the future, far into the future, which was a safe place for her.

He looked up, startled, caught off guard, his private ambitions spoken aloud. He may not have been seeking fame, but he was seeking something that marked its own spot in history, something oddly permanent; a good wine, a *vin supérieur*, could just as well be it. "We will," he said, taking her hand. "*We* will be famous."

The harvest was over by the first week of October. The wine was in casks in the cellar, and the slow season began. On St. Martin's Day, in November—Beal had been hearing about it for weeks, some sort of big holiday—they sampled the new wine; everyone got drunk and then they slaughtered one of the pigs, a sacrifice as if from the Bible. They'd be pruning the vines all winter, and in the *chais* they'd be turning the casks, but everything was doing what it was supposed to do, which was to sleep and to age. The air would be seeping through the pores of the wood, which Beal began to understand was key. Then she discovered that early the following year, in some fancy places like Bordeaux, the opposite strategy would be taken, which was to put the wine into bottles, where it was protected from the air! What a lot of work, but maybe that's what it would take to be famous.

At some point in all this, Beal realized that her life had changed in ways that she could not have imagined permitting just one year ago, before they landed in Le Havre, an anniversary that was approaching. This idleness. That young reporter back in Paris had asked her if she would find enough to occupy herself in the Midi, but what he had been asking was how she would replace the Louvre, the theater, the Bon Marché. That wasn't the problem—wasn't a change in her life that she noticed or cared much about at this point. It was this role, the mistress of St. Adelelmus. When had she ever supposed she would wake up in bed, the sun well up, husband gone, and have to ask herself what she might do that day. In her girlhood fantasies of joy and comfort there had been none of this, this flitting from relatively meaningless activity to trivial task. Yes, she had never seen Thomas so engaged, and she thanked God for that, as if it removed any wrong she had done him. But she could not help envying him. She could not help feeling supplanted.

So one evening—it truly was time, after all—as they were preparing for bed, Beal dropped off her underclothes and stood naked in front of Thomas. For the past month she had been careful not to do this, had been arranging her clothing to cover her stomach, had been joining him in bed in a long nightgown. "Thomas," she said. His eyes were closed on his pillow. "Look at me."

He rolled over. "You are beautiful," he said.

"You see what is happening?" She turned sideways to give him the sharpest profile. "This isn't me getting fat." She didn't know why she was doing this, why this had to be so abstruse. It was almost as if it were a test for Thomas, but it wasn't. It was a desire to intrude in all this in the most physical way possible.

Thomas did as he was commanded, looked at her, following the bow of her belly down to the dark tuft of her pubic hair. "Well, I'll be damned," he said.

"Is that all? Not blessed too?"

He got out of bed and came to her. "When?" he said.

"In March, I think."

She could sense him counting off months, though she assumed that like her, his real understanding of gestation was a little imprecise. He stood back, gazed down her front, ran his hands down her sides, and held her in front of him by her hips. "You've been keeping this from me. You've known since Paris." This was just him counting the days; there was no displeasure in his voice.

"I had to be sure I would not lose it. And you were busy."

He brought her back into him, hugged her tight. Beal was satisfied by this; there was no need for him to say much more.

"Does anyone know? Have you written to Abel and Una?"

She said she had not yet written her parents, but she told him about Léonie guessing, almost a month earlier. "I guess every woman in St. Adelelmus has figured it out. Gabriella and la Señora. Mme Murat was nicer to me the last time I saw her."

"A child," he said. " A little dark child. He'll look right at home here in the Midi."

Beal realized that she'd always believed that their child would be somewhere between her skin color and his, but she didn't want Thomas to assume it. "Hard to say what it will look like. You know those Hardys. Stephen could almost pass as white, and Luke and Tillie look like lumps of coal. No one would think they're full brothers and sister, but they are. Zemirah would take a cane to anyone who suggested there had been some funny business in there."

"Well, I don't care."

"And besides, it could be a girl."

"Fine. Another beauty in the family." She'd thought he might want to celebrate this moment by making love, but she was glad that he, like her, seemed to assume that her body was now on to other things. In fact, since they got to St. Adelelmus, they had not been making love with the desperate ardor of their last weeks in Paris. She finished getting dressed for bed and joined him under the down duvet. He blew out the lamp, and the moonlight took over the room. The moon followed you wherever you went, found you at night—the same moon, but still, so much had changed in its light. Another step along the way taken, she thought, another step in a life, in two—or three—lives. How odd, she thought; how ordinary it all seemed. She wished it weren't so, but she was a little disappointed by Thomas's reaction to her announcement. She didn't know what more she wanted, only that she wanted more. How odd that seemed! To be in this position, where she had more of absolutely everything than she could ever have imagined—more love, more possessions, more power, and more freedom to make choices— where everywhere she went, everywhere she looked simply exploded with plenitude. The next morning she wrote, *I now have so much, and Mama and Daddy, all they have, all they have gotten from their life and love, could go into a single chest of drawers. Yet they are so content with their ordinary happiness.*

When Thomas finished reading Beal's journals that spring of 1937, the Civil War in Spain had started. Thomas was sixty-six years old, and still healthy—he lived for another fifteen years—but Beal's death had taken the urgency out of everything he used to do, and their sons were now firmly in charge of St. Adelelmus and its many other properties. As he passed the hours in his study, he found that he was also writing a sort of memoir, or a story combining his own memories and Beal's. He had other bits to go on: a collection of prayers from Mother Lucy, a set of reminiscences by Arthur Kravitz. More than enough to conjure some multifaceted version of what had happened to them. His life. Her life. He called what he was writing "Thomas and Beal in the Midi," and on the first page he wrote the title and then added "by Thomas Bayly and Beal Terrell Bayly," as if anyone would ever read it—and, if so, would ever care who wrote it.

11

Beal was entering the last month of her pregnancy when Arthur Kravitz arrived. Spending time in the South of France had never been his plan. For one thing, he wasn't a landscape painter, was bored by all the plein air debates of the past two decades. He was a city boy and an urban man, and besides, this whole South of France thing stank of privilege. Gee, why not just keep going to Venice and spend the winter doing nothing but drinking and going to masked balls? Well, Arthur didn't have the money for that; in fact, he was now coming to the end of his savings, and if this kept up, he wouldn't even have the money to sail back to Newark. He'd gotten so used to spending next to nothing that he forgot that sooner or later, next to nothing would mean nothing at all. Which was the scariest thought? he wondered. Going back to Newark or not having enough money to do so. He'd stopped his lessons at the Académie, and it had been months since anyone asked about his portrait of Beal. If it weren't for the reflected glory of Stanley's recent success in the Salon—he still considered Stanley's *Pittsburgh, Winter Morning* shallow and sentimental, but he was sincerely pleased for him—no one at the cafés would have a clue who he was, this dark, heavy Jewish figure at the corner table while the fresh-faced Boston Brahmins and pretty boys and girls with rich daddies occupied the center. Nothing new in all that. Impression-

ism was all played out. As for the Americans, it was still all about
Sargent, who'd left Paris almost ten years earlier, and Cassatt, who
was now painting nothing but fat little girls getting their toes dried
by nursemaids. As for the French, Arthur still admired Caillebotte—a painter who understood cities, who could spend hours at
a window, gazing at the delicious tangle of streets below—but from
what he gathered, Caillebotte was now a full-time gardener who
spent most of his leisure time sailing on the Seine. If all this kept
up, Arthur figured he might as well give up painting altogether and
buy a camera; each time he looked at one of Marville's old prints,
it was as if a world had been brought into his studio. Monet's *Hay-
stacks*: If Arthur never saw the color yellow ever again, it would be
too soon.

So there didn't seem to be much arguing against accepting
Thomas's offer to spend the winter in the South, and after a letter
came, confirming that yes indeed, there did seem to be a stone
dwelling that might suit, he began to think it could work. But in-
action or lassitude or simple fear kept him staying on in Paris
through the fall. More probably it was that leaving Paris, this grand
statement of his ambition—the boy from Newark, etc.—signaled
defeat, but after Christmas he started packing up his things in earnest and crated his canvases. When he laid Beal into her nest of ex-
celsior, he stopped and stared at the portrait in a way he had not
done for months. He was struck, in his despair, with how bad it
was but how true it was: this was a cul-de-sac from which no work
of art, and perhaps no artist, could ever emerge. He was also struck
by how much he missed Beal. She brought him out, that's what she
did, as if in talking to her, he was getting a second chance to be a
better, and wiser, person. He didn't pretend that seeing her again
did not have a lot to do with his decision, and this portrait told him
why. Or, for an instant, he thought that her portrait *could* tell
him why. This was just a flash, a dart of light from the surface of
the work that caught a crystal in his soul, and by the time he tried
to investigate what he had learned, the light had dimmed. Still, it
was as if Beal had come to him in that second, and now—as he
completed the task, covering the front of the canvas with this terrible wood wool and banging home the top of the crate—it felt as

if he were packaging a living thing, not so much a person but a little bit of news from the spirit of that person. Maybe that's what a good painting is, he thought. Damned if he knew what a good painting was. He hadn't planned to bring it with him—all this crating of canvases was simply about storing them safely in Stanley's studio—but at that moment he decided to bring it along, although it would cost a fortune to have it shipped with the rest of his supplies.

As instructed, he had taken the train from Narbonne to Azay-sur-Cesse, and he dreamed but dared not hope for one second that Beal herself would meet him. He disembarked onto a pleasant square in front of the town hall, and in the center there were wagons and carts twisted in friendly knots. She was standing there in a carriage, a Winged Victory with arms, which she was waving madly. Arthur had never seen her look so beautiful, that's what he told himself, though from his distance he couldn't see her very clearly; he'd gotten a letter from Thomas telling him that Beal was pregnant, which might have been part of it.

By the time he worked himself through the animals and the vehicles, she had climbed down and was standing alongside the carriage, a simple open four-wheeler, a country vehicle. The horse was enormous and dumb-looking, a true beast of burden. As Arthur got closer, he was surprised to see that the driver was a girl, a teenager. When finally he stood in front of Beal, he was, as usual, a little discomfited by how much taller she was. And she was very pregnant. She held out her hand to him, and he took it. "Arthur," she said. "How lovely."

He wouldn't have expected that word, *lovely*; he remembered her the first day he saw her, spied on her actually, and she was not awkward—never awkward—but completely without affect, socially invisible. That person wouldn't have said "lovely," would have said "right fine," maybe, or wouldn't have felt the social impulse to characterize the moment at all. "Yeah," said Arthur, taking her hand and holding on to it for a second. She looked a little disappointed, so he added, "Long trip."

"Not happier than that to see me?" There was no coquettish little smile connected to this; it suddenly seemed possible to Arthur that the word *lovely* had been a joke, an acknowledgment of their special bond on the fringes. This time he did look her in the eyes, and he did not see unhappiness or discontent—which would have been the last thing he wanted—but he did see need, maybe even some kind of chaste desire. He saw in her eyes what he hoped was not so evident in his.

"Oh . . . Beal—" He still found it hard to call her Beal, a given name that had always seemed too intimate, a name only family should use. "You have no idea how much I have looked forward to this day. To seeing you. You don't want to know how much, believe me."

At that she smiled. She turned to introduce him to the girl and to ask about his luggage. He held up his carpetbag and shrugged.

The day was fine despite the steady dry wind—cold, but not piercing, as it was in Paris. On the train from Narbonne, when they had left the city limits they were on a flat plain, but soon he could see mountains to the north, and as they wound their slow way into this arid high terrain, he realized that he had been picturing this countryside as if it were the farmland of New Jersey, which could not have been more wrong. They had passed mountainous crags that turned Arthur's hands white with terror and then, at the next bend, a fragrant meadow dotted with winter blossoms. But now, in this open wagon with Beal and the girl, the land seemed milder, as if one could bail out before the whole equipage went over the edge; he was grateful that the old nag—named Philippe, apparently—was a plodder.

Beal wanted to hear every snippet of news from Paris, and he did his best, although he couldn't tell her much about the new clothes for fall. He told her he had been to visit the Richards with Stanley and he understood that Madame Bernault had taken a fall.

"Yes, we heard. She's been moved to the first floor, which she doesn't like. I hope it isn't too much of a shock for her."

"Pretty tough old battle-ax, no?"

Beal wagged her head. "Not tough, I think. Maybe stout." Sure, sure, thought Arthur; either way, the nun still didn't approve of him. "Tell me about Stanley," Beal said, and he did, telling her that his notices and entrées were piling up.

"Here's the thing about Stanley," said Arthur. "He's earnest, but not stupid. There's always a little subtext, a kind of anger going on in his work. It took me quite a while to figure that out, to see it. Stanley would probably have done a better portrait of you than I did."

Beal waited for him to continue, and he wondered whether she would pick up on this reference to the portrait. When he added nothing, she said, "Arthur, anger is not something you lack."

"Yes. But my anger is wholesale. Stanley's is retail. It makes it more interesting because it is selective. He's getting back at all the bullies."

Beal took this in. Arthur could see the thoughts churning, could almost imagine her applying this simple test to herself. The truth was, he understood that defending, even liking Stanley Dean was a sign that he himself had softened. But Beal was not thinking so abstractly. "Yes," she said. "He must have been teased."

Arthur hesitated for a moment. "Well, he's a little awkward, and he's got his secrets. Me? I'm just what you see. No subtext."

"Oh, Arthur. Enough of that. Your baggage arrived. And a canvas in a crate, I guess. Is it me?"

"Yes. I'm not sure why I brought it. Maybe I'll work on it a little. I still don't want you to see it."

She jabbed her shoulder into his, a classic girlish Beal gesture, something he loved, something no other girl or woman he had ever known would do to him. Arthur had never invited warmth, only heat or room temperature. There were other mannerisms he loved, all of which seemed to be little windows into her soul. She held her hand in front of her mouth sometimes as a sort of whisper, which made her completely inaudible. She shook her feet restlessly when she was bored, which had been a problem while she sat for her portrait. In some ways, the times Arthur loved best were when she was completely at ease with Thomas, and with him and their friends, and she let her English slide into the cadences and grammar of the farm and her sentences became long and musical. How funny she could be, but then, when it was over, when she snapped back into the present, there was always a momentary look of sorrow, of loss and forgetting. Arthur had lost and forgotten nothing about his childhood that he wasn't eager, in fact, to lose, so he envied her grief.

When they got to St. Adelelmus, Thomas was standing on the stoop. At least, from a distance, Arthur assumed it was Thomas, if he was this large, imposing, brown-skinned figure dressed in clothes that could only be called peasant wear—a loose, big-sleeved, all but homespun shirt, a pair of trousers gathered at the waist with a brown sash or something. A floppy hat of some sort, a beret, Arthur had heard it called. Thomas looked like an extra in the theater, in *Carmen* perhaps. When Arthur stood next to him, he seemed taller than ever. Perhaps, thought Arthur, I'm shrinking. Thomas gave him a hearty handshake, none of this "lovely to see you," but the heartiness was in every way a comparable act. His friend Thomas, once seeming so uncertain, so retiring, had landed with a firm *thump* and had settled in for the duration. This whole apparition took Arthur's words away. "Phew," he said. "Gosh."

Thomas took no notice. "We're glad you have come at last. We hope it will be good for you. We've prepared a studio. It used to be a goat shed. You'll have a fine view of the Black Mountain."

"The goats must have appreciated the view," said Arthur. In fact, once he got settled in this little building, he draped a cloth over the window with the viewiest of the views; the mountains seemed as if they were trying to bury him, or eat him. The living quarters that had been prepared for him made his old apartment in Paris seem like an outhouse; as far as Arthur could tell, these must have been the best-cared-for goats of all time. It was a palace for goats, with its arching loft above, its expanse of light from the west and the south, its almost overpowering stove, and, of all unexpected things, a WC. Surely not for the goats. He wondered where the goats were living now.

He ate dinner with Thomas and Beal in their house—in, excuse me, *la bastide*. Arthur didn't really know what he was doing here, but it had begun to feel a bit like fate, that his choices and his chances had become intertwined with Thomas and Beal's. Perhaps more than anyone else in the world, he knew that their future, just like his, was anything but fixed. So here he was, sitting at the table in a small room Thomas described as "the chapel." Arthur had encountered la Señora earlier in the afternoon—she had come over to his studio to help him light the fire—and here, finally, after all these cold concierges, judgmental nuns, disapproving art matrons,

and desperate grisettes, he had found a Frenchwoman he could re-
late to. Or a Spaniard. He couldn't tell. He could discern that her
speech was in a tongue all her own, but what she said was as clear
to him as if she were speaking English. She reminded him of home,
those Middle European mothers with uncertain English he'd fled
from so long ago. By the time he came up to dinner, cleaned,
scented, and monstrously hungry, most of his resistance was gone.

"You have met the Señora," said Thomas.

"Oh yes. She's already agreed to take over my life. We discussed
my ethnicity. I think the word she used was *judua*, but I'd spot it
in any language."

"That must be Basque," said Beal. "Most people here don't like
Basques." She had just come in with the soup.

Arthur had eaten almost nothing on the entire train trip down,
and he was light-headed.

"Perhaps that's why she liked me. Even lower in rank."

Arthur took a bowl of soup and dived in. Delicious. Thomas
and Beal also took up their spoons, and Arthur slurped in the silence. He had not expected to be dining with them, wasn't prepared
to be a guest like this. He had eaten with Thomas and Beal in the
avenue Bosquet only once, and Stanley had been there to carry
the conversation, not that Stanley was much of a blabber. But now
there was no one but him.

"So," he said. "This is quite a place."

"We're just beginning to get to know our way around," said
Thomas. "I've been pretty much following along blindly."

"Is it going to work? This wine idea?"

"Well, you can always make wine. All you're doing is harnessing a little part of nature, the part where things rot and decay. The
question is, can you make good wine?"

Arthur was pleased that Thomas—only Thomas would have remembered such a thing about him—had made sure to serve him
beer with dinner. He raised his glass to say that either way, he knew
what he liked to drink. "You don't make it sound very tasty."

"Thomas must work on that," said Beal.

Arthur turned to her, lovely in the dim light of this February
evening, in this stone fortress on top of these summits and precipices.

It felt medieval; she seemed like a character out of a fairy tale. He didn't know whether to feel protected or entombed; maybe he had come here to bury or burn his dreams. Maybe Thomas, with all this new provincial gear, was holding aside the door to Hell. But the soup—the soup was pretty good.

"He looks the part, anyway," said Arthur.

Thomas laughed. "You'll be wearing clothes like this before you know it."

Beal's first son, named Randall after her dead brother, was born in March. She had gotten enormous, she thought; she was too big, or too top-heavy, to climb the spiral stairs safely. A few weeks before she gave birth, Thomas looked at her and said, as some sort of expression of sympathy, "I'm glad this is happening to you and not to me." Her mother once told her that she had been *a little runt,* a *tiny little thing that we wasn't sure would last out the night.* When she was growing up, Beal liked that—that she had fought back, prevailed, that she had begun life "in peril." If the size of her pregnant belly meant anything, this baby was going to start healthy. The Señora was pleased, and even Léonie said it was a good sign, but she did add that she hoped the doctor could be there for the birth, if that was practical, if there was time. Beal wasn't so sure about that: *le médecin,* Professor Cottard, was a pompous little man who was always making jokes and then immediately pretending he hadn't meant to be funny. Of course, his jokes never were funny. He exhausted her. When he placed his handkerchief on her stomach before leaning over to listen to the baby's heartbeat, he said, "Hello, my little monsieur," but then he shushed Beal when she forced a slight laugh. Beal didn't want him anywhere near her when she was doing something as important, as private, as giving birth.

Beal knew her baby's skin tone would be whatever the baby wanted it to be. She was not that dark—brown, she had always thought of herself—but she hoped for just a tiny shade lighter than she was, fawn, like her brother had been. She hoped this not because she thought there was anything wrong with her own color, but because, if it was a boy, she and Thomas had agreed he would be named Randall. And she knew that Thomas also hoped their baby would be a mix of them, his white skin and her black skin; she understood that fathers wanted to see a little of themselves from the very beginning, just to be sure that this person who came out of the woman's body was a miracle they shared. That's the way it seemed to her, for of course, this baby *was* something they had shared. Thomas's body inside her body, somehow, even if that thought struck her as kind of monstrous.

But if the baby was blacker than she? Well, that didn't have to mean anything; her own father was very dark, mahogany—that's all it would mean. *Looks like his granddaddy.* She told herself that, over and over: That's *all* it would mean. That's all it would *mean*. But she could not keep that other thought away. She could keep the memory of a certain June afternoon away, could keep the name away, but she could not keep the thought away. And what was this thought? That if her baby was black, if despite this huge pregnancy he was born long and scrawny, by age twelve he would be taller than even Thomas, and with adolescence his cheekbones would become sharper and his cheeks hollower, and instead of Thomas's broad back he would remain narrow, and by eighteen this fine young man would look like a father no one had even imagined. No one but Thomas, that is. In the midst of all this, the baby was blameless; her baby would deserve nothing but love, protection. But would even her own love come with a question always attached to it? Could she ever be certain it would not?

As hard as she tried, she could not make any of this go away. This was real loneliness, having life-altering thoughts you can share with no one, ever. Ever, ever. But it did work itself into her journals, in a code that would not be difficult to crack. Each time the baby kicked, these thoughts came; in her journal she called these thoughts "doubts." Each time the Señora told her she must lie down, get off her feet, these thoughts arrived. How she envied Léonie, with little chubby Gustav an almost comical version, at four months, of his rather homely father. How she envied every pregnant woman, new mother, even new *grand*mother she saw at the market: You don't know nothin', she would think, dropping back into the safety of Tuckertown where, in truth, at the three shacks at the far end, parentage could be a little iffy, dropping further back into slave times, when being the father, or not, got nobody nothin' a t'all.

So it was that in these last few weeks, when, Beal supposed, women looked forward with anxiety about the delivery but undiluted joy about the child, she even went so far as to imagine that if she died in childbirth, no matter what the result was, she wouldn't have to know it. In the code: the "event," the "outcome," the "release." She wrote her parents the first truly candid—sort of—letter she'd been able to write that revealed anything at all about this new life she had been living, and Una, her mother, understood that there was trouble but missed what was really on her mind. She wrote back the sort of motherly reassurances Beal needed, and they helped. Una wrote that there was no reason to fear a child would have "anything wrong"; there'd been no such thing as far back in the family as Una could recall. They knew a lot about her family, which had been free since the middle of the last century, but about Abel's, beyond Abel's father, not very much. She wrote "barrow or gilt," who would care which, just as long as the child was healthy. She wrote that all her deliveries had been quick, just a few hours, and that this was true also for Beal's sister Ruth. "Don't know why you're being so morbid about it," Una concluded. *Morbid.* Her mother had about four years of schooling but used a word Beal had to look up in her dictionary.

Her labor started in the late afternoon, and though Thomas immediately sent for the doctor, the Señora had already arranged for the local midwife, who arrived with Gabriella not an hour after Beal's water broke and pronounced everything *tout normal.* And then the next thing Beal knew, or that she remembered, was Thomas at her side telling her it was a boy and that he looked just like her.

"What do you mean?" she asked.

"Well, that's what the midwife said. Maybe she says that to everyone."

"I want to see him," said Beal. "I want to see him now."

"They're bathing him. The professor has arrived, and he is checking him over."

"Oh, the *professor* . . ."

"Shush," said Thomas. "He's a boy and his name is Randall and that's all that matters."

Even flat on her back, ravaged by the most climactic physical event she'd ever had or ever would experience—there would be three more to come—she looked deep into Thomas's eyes, almost wondering if he was signaling something, some acceptance, some forgiveness. But when Randall was brought to her, when the midwife laid his naked body on her bare breast, the baby seemed almost to disappear, so perfectly was his silken flesh matched to hers.

"See," said Thomas happily. "He's all you."

"Oh," she said. Darker, lighter; she'd never imagined that the baby would be right in the middle, just like herself, would announce no clues to anyone. That a baby was a person not made up of the bodily parts of his parents, but assembled out of his own image; that from the moment his head appeared between her legs, he was born with this fierce knowledge that he would *be* what he would be. He was no longer a problem, but a blessing. She almost laughed, a sort of drunken relief, like a secret kept.

"Randall Terrell Bayly," announced Thomas.

"Yes," she said, looking down at the little creature curled up on her chest, and the truth was, he looked like *Randall*, her brother, his eyes and nose.

"Oh, Thomas," she said, taking the tiny hand. "Do you love him? Do you love your brown son?"

"Yes," he said. "Just like I love my wife." He kissed her. "Get some rest. The Señora seems rather eager to take him off your hands."

"Really?" said Beal. They had already discussed what Gabriella had said: that her mother was possessive about babies; she seemed to think that newborns came into this world with messages from those who had died, messages that only certain people could understand. Gabriella had said not to worry, but it hadn't been easy for her to tell this to Beal, and she had done it for a reason.

Thomas apparently understood it all. "No. It's good. Gabriella is there. You sleep."

By the end of the week Beal had taken Randall for a tour of St. Adelelmus, to show him to the families who worked there. The

Señora came along to officiate. The women cooed, the men were mostly polite, the children made fun of his color—"*un merle*," they called him before being shushed, which Thomas later translated as "blackbird." Beal didn't mind; the children weren't being mean, and for the rest of her life she thought of Randall as her "blackbird son," in part because the other three children were lighter in tone. The cooper, M. Esquivel, had carved Randall a little horse on wheels with a pull string, the weaver had made him a blanket, and the blacksmith made him a tin whistle. Beal paid a special, more formal call on Mme Murat and was received graciously but without warmth. Mme Murat gave her items for the baby's layette that she had bought in Narbonne, which was quite unexpected, but she remarked that she had expected the baby to be lighter skinned; Beal only smiled. And finally, Léonie came over with her little pale-skinned Gustav, and when they placed these two boys side by side and stood back to admire them, Beal burst into tears.

"Are you all right?" said Léonie, her hand on Beal's shoulder.

"I'm sorry," said Beal. "I don't know what that was about." But actually, she did: it was Thomas and her brother she saw in front of her, the two boys of the Retreat, in that period when almost all the children on the farm were girls. Surely at some point those two infants had been placed side by side just like this, and they had grown into best friends, brothers, until they quarreled over Thomas and Beal's love for each other. On the day Randall returned from his first year at Howard University, he was murdered, his body left in a pile of straw in the mule barn. And the body she saw in the straw at this moment was not her brother's, but her son's. All this was what Beal saw, but she couldn't go into it now.

Léonie looked worried. "You be careful," she said. "You tell me if you start to feel too sad."

Yes, thought Beal, there was a little something of sadness here, but nothing to worry about. Still, after all this, what next? She was twenty-one years old, a mother. Was it all over? Much as she admired Léonie—would, in years to come, love her and distrust her in equal measure, like a sister—Beal wondered whether she was quite ready to live the way Léonie did. Spring had started, and Thomas had told her that the vines were "bleeding," which seemed to be what they were supposed to do, and now, as she cast her eyes over the hectares of grapes that surrounded them, she could see that the buds had started to break and tiny shoots of green were beginning to show. Which promise of new life would mean more to him, his grapes or his son? A silly question, but she knew that in the weeks and years to come, the grapes would get more of his attention, if far less of his love. The chestnuts, *les marronniers*, would soon blossom, a show of red and white that everyone much admired, but, well, it wouldn't be April in Paris. The cherry blossoms, the forsythia and lilacs, the little borders of primrose and cowslip—the magic of those colors and fragrances had taken over Beal's senses just a year ago. The Parisians worshipped spring as a sort of godly visitation, but here, as on the Retreat, spring was little more than the signal to start fretting: late frosts, early droughts. The almighty tree and vine. Except for the odd flash of memory, a sudden tableau across her eyes, she hadn't thought about Paris at all since they'd come to rest here. Even having Arthur here, in every way the conscience of her months in Paris, she had thought of any life outside St. Adelelmus as something held in reserve. She'd been busy, after all, and fixed on this great ordeal and the change to come. Now that it had arrived, she wondered how to fill the space.

A few weeks after the birth, in early April, she went to visit Arthur in his studio, the first time she had done so since he'd gotten settled. He ate with them two or three evenings a week; he rarely showed a smudge of paint or smelled of turpentine, but they had all gotten used to him sketching in pencil and pastel throughout the domaine. For the past few weeks he had been talking to Thomas about photography and had just spent what was for him a good bit of money on a new Kodak folding camera.

Whatever the confused jumble of thoughts in Beal's head these days, she shuddered to recall those weeks, those hours and hours she spent sitting for the portrait in Arthur's studio in Paris. Of all the places she had visited there, including—she could admit this to herself—that apartment in Les Halles, Arthur's studio was the dingiest, smelliest, most vile, yet it had been a kind of refuge for her.

Perhaps at the time she should have reflected more on that odd truth. Now, standing before the handsome ancient doorway of this stone house, she felt relieved that he was out of the place that in the end had seemed so miserable for him.

"Ah," he said, opening the door to her knock. "The new mother."

"Can I come in?"

"Sure," he said, opening the door all the way.

She walked in, observed that the portrait was still in its crate, but then noticed a number of his works on paper pinned to the walls. She recognized several of the subjects; from the look of it, he had concentrated on M. Esquivel, the cooper, and on the activity in the line of shops down by the brook bed. "May I look?" she asked.

"Of course."

"They're nice." They were mostly scenes of people at work, bodies twisted in the slightly awkward postures of their trades—the moment when the blacksmith cocks his hammer above his head and his shoulder looks ready to dislocate; the women sewing, their whole bodies scrunched into a ball over their hands. He had spent time with the shepherds before they departed to the high meadows, and he drew them precariously balanced on their stilts. But even if he made them appear vaguely deformed, anyone could tell that the artist admired these people, the work they did, the lives they were living.

"I've had a good time with them," he answered when Beal remarked on this. "They remind me that I like being around people who make things and fix stuff. Maybe that's what I should have done with my life."

"It already is," said Beal, surprising herself with this kind of assertiveness. "You already work with your hands. You make pictures."

He nodded a thanks. "It's almost as if in recording this, my drawings do something useful, if you can imagine that."

She said she could easily imagine it, even if the subjects might not be able to.

"Well, they like them, anyway."

She heard this with slightly hurt feelings and glanced at the crate. "You let them see their portraits, but not me."

"Right," he said. He moved some supplies off a chair and beckoned her to sit. "Nice of you to visit. How are you and young Randall getting on?"

"Oh, we're fine. The Señora isn't quite as frantic about him as she was."

"And Thomas?"

"He's a wonderful papa. Not that he says it in this way, but I think he is determined to be everything for Randall that his parents weren't for him. If you understand," she said. The truth was, since the last days of her pregnancy, her thinking and her speech seemed to have gotten a little garbled.

They sat without speaking for a minute or two. "Why do you have that cloth across the window?" she asked.

He got up and took it down. He pointed. "Those mountains. They make me nervous. They kind of overwhelm the frame." He traced around the four sides of the window, and yes, now that he mentioned it, there did seem a lot of rock and rill for that small opening.

"It's the Black Mountains. La Montagne Noire. Meadows where hundreds of Cathars were burned. People say there is a Cathari treasure up there, but no one knows what it is. Something sacred," she added.

"Great," said Arthur, putting the cloth back. "Now I'll have nightmares about it." He sat down, and again, they fell silent.

"So," said Arthur. "What brings Miss Beal here to my humble goat shed?"

"Can't I just come to see you, to see your new work?"

"Of course you can. But that isn't the real reason you're here."

She smiled. "Something is happening for you here. Thomas was so certain this was the right thing for you, and I hoped he was right, but I know it would be hard for you to admit. Feeling good, I mean."

"Yes," he said guardedly.

"Settled, is maybe what I mean. You've been here for six weeks and you're already settled." She waved back at the wall of drawings, as if that were all the evidence that might be needed.

Beal knew what he was going to say before he said it. She loved Arthur; she depended upon him because he would never miss an opening, because he would require her to bring the whole thought out of the depths, not just dangle this little strand, which was something Thomas would never, ever do. "But you?" he said.

Still, she resisted; it was part of the dance. "I don't understand what you mean."

Arthur said nothing more; he didn't need to. He looked at her with the same neutral, appraising gaze she had witnessed from behind his easel those many months.

"Well, I'm just feeling a little up and down," she said.

He continued to stare at her.

"Ladies do this after delivering," she added.

"Oh," said Arthur, the equivalent of refusing to enter into the discussion.

Beal ignored this. She told him what Léonie had said, what even Mme Murat had said, that the first baby changed everything, and sometimes it was hard to get used to.

Arthur was unmoved, uninterested in all this motherly chitchat; she couldn't imagine anyone who would be less interested. Beal had known, since her first awful contact with Arthur, that he liked women but didn't care so much for the female in them.

"But?" he said. "It's that and something more, isn't it."

He'd capitulated; she'd counted on it. "Maybe there's something wrong with me," she said. "Do you think? Who ever thought this is where I'd end up, *la maîtresse du domaine?*"

"It doesn't seem to bother you. I see the way you pay your calls. You're the people's queen. You know all about the life they are living because you lived it yourself. Being royalty with them seems to sit pretty naturally on you, if you ask me."

Beal didn't know whether to feel flattered or insulted. Yes, she did try to treat everyone with respect; yes, she had picked up some Occitan, even a word or two of Spanish. "That's not what I mean," she answered.

"I know."

She let out a troubled, raspy breath, ending with a little flutter of her lips.

"Beal, you're at your worst when you have too little to do, you know that."

"Yes. But I have so much to do."

"I guess you don't, really. Or you don't like what you have to do. Something like that. It seems."

"My Mama and Daddy, they went through so much, losing Randall, losing the peaches. Back home, Thomas's sister gives Daddy something to do, but it's way beneath him. I sometimes imagine that if he had been born up North, went to college the way some of those fancy Negroes in Massachusetts do, he'd be a lawyer, a professor. But still, they are happy. They are filled with gratefulness."

"And you're not."

"Oh, I'm grateful. I know what I have."

"What about Thomas? He knows your soul better than anyone. What does he think you should do?"

"Thomas is consumed by this farm. He has earned every second of his joy. You have no idea how much he has earned it. I love him too much to intrude."

"Hmmm," said Arthur.

"I have to go. Randall will be waking soon." She reached for her hat, a deep straw bowl with a black band.

Arthur stood up, walked her to the door. It was a brilliant day, mineral white, but she felt a little reluctant to step out into it. She hoped Mme Murat *mère* hadn't seen her go in or go out, but she was sure she had; the windows in her bedroom commanded almost every vista on this hilltop, and often when she saw something she thought was irregular, she sent her daughter Françoise to investigate. Last week it had been the appearance of an unfamiliar dog that had come along with the lumber dealer.

"Beal," said Arthur. "Just now, you have to let it happen."

"Let what happen?"

"Right. That's what I mean. I say 'let it happen' and you want to know, in advance, what will happen."

"Well, what if what happens is bad?"

"Happens to whom?"

"To anyone. To me. To Thomas. To Randall. To you."

Arthur shrugged. Really, it was obvious to her that he wanted to get back to work, which made this whole visit a terrible mistake. "I don't think you realize how much you have changed in the past year," he said. "As far as you're concerned, your circumstances have changed, but you're still just Beal. Being 'just Beal' is no longer enough. For you. For anybody."

12

In midsummer, Arthur returned from one of his drawing and photography trips—he seemed to do both interchangeably these days—with a handsome, formally dressed young man. The man's light brown skin made him rather indistinguishable in this region of many hues, but as soon as he spoke, Thomas knew that he was American, with an accent Thomas recognized as New England, Boston probably. He'd gone to college at the University of Pennsylvania with some boys from Boston, and he hadn't much liked them, but this little echo of home was not unwelcome, and the intriguing guest had come to do business.

Thomas was in his office when Gabriella knocked with the news that M. Arthur was there with a stranger. It was early August, "the month that makes the harvest," as he heard from almost every mouth on the domaine, in the village, as if it were a private piece of wisdom. *C'est août qui fait la récolte.* This was not said with affection for this most devious month, but rather with fear. It was always thus on farms: the stakes are always the highest at the end, when the fruit is set, the grain is golden, the corn has tasseled, and the farmer has nothing to do but wait. For grapes, extremes of any kind were always a threat, but the *catastrophe* everyone spoke of was hail; in one hour a year's work could be lost and a winter of hunger would follow. Naturally, the kind of weather that brings hail—hot and wet—is the very kind that is best for a good harvest. Not long ago it had come to Thomas that everything he was doing, everything his father and Mason ancestors had done on the Retreat, everything M. Murat and his forebears had done here on St. Adelelmus was rather like fishing: you dropped a hook into the murky depths and if the depths and if the fish obliged, you had a catch; if not, you had nothing. Imagine having your whole livelihood depend on the whims of fish.

The man's name was Frederick Lawrence Goodrum. He gave Thomas a slight bow and handed him his card. GOODRUM & SONS, it read, FINE VICTUALLERS. On the card there was a small engraving, a remarque, of a rather impressive-looking city building. A Boston address. "Well," said Thomas. "Welcome to St. Adelelmus."

"Mr. Kravitz was kind enough to let me accompany him," he said, and explained that he had come on the train from Narbonne, and Arthur had overheard him asking directions—in loud English—to St. Adelelmus.

"Lucky break," said Thomas. They were standing in the hall, and Thomas realized this would take some time. "Go sit on the terrace," he said to Arthur. "I'll ask the Señora to bring some tea." When he caught up to them, he and Arthur were standing at the edge of the terrace and Arthur was describing the buildings below with a sort of proprietary pride. Even more surprisingly, it seemed that Arthur took to this stiff and pompous, but also apparently prosperous, man; Thomas couldn't help but compare this warmth to the snarls and insults he'd gotten from Arthur the first time they met.

"So," said Thomas. "What brings you here?"

"It's very beautiful," said the guest. "One of the most beautiful wineries in the region, I am told."

Thomas hated it when people began with this. "It's really just about wine," he said. He hoped he wasn't being curt.

"Yes, of course. Which is why I am here."

"Ah. How did you hear about us?"

"From M. Fauberge, in Narbonne."

"Of course. Then you know that M. Fauberge has everything to do with the fact that we ended up here." Thomas also assumed that the *négociant* had told this colored man about Beal.

"Yes," he said with obvious fondness. "He thinks we could work together." He went on to describe Goodrum & Sons as one of the finest specialty groceries in Boston. "If you haven't heard of us, you might have heard of our great rivals, the Pierce family." Thomas knew of neither, but he explained that he knew nothing about Boston, had never been there. Yes, Goodrum continued, their store was on Tremont Street, a prime location, and it offered a great variety of the fine foods and sundries from the world over. He mentioned wine, but then listed a dizzying array—Russian cigarettes got Thomas's attention. Why would anyone in Boston want Russian cigarettes? Goodrum explained that their customers were the best families on Beacon Hill, in the South End, and in Back Bay, and that they delivered as far away as Brattle Street. "In Cambridge," added Goodrum when Thomas didn't react. "Almost in Watertown."

Thomas didn't bother to protest again that all these place-names meant nothing to him, but as Goodrum continued talking about their importing business and his own role as the son who went abroad periodically to find new suppliers, Thomas slowly realized that he was wrong about one thing: he had assumed that the "best families," the clientele of this store, were Negroes, the most prosperous, no doubt, of the colored who live there, that the neighborhoods he kept mentioning were where the wealthy colored lived. But the more Goodrum talked, the more it became clear to Thomas that "the best families" were indeed the upper crust, the white Brahmins, that most of the Goodrums' many employees were white: Italian butchers, Irish clerks, French Canadian delivery drivers. Thomas wished it weren't so, but he'd never heard of such a thing, a Negro business with white customers and white employees. This stiffness, this too-formal dress, this dropping of names—the man had a difficult role to play; a single misstep, a muffed line, and the show folded. And yet there was nothing fake about him that Thomas could discern; he didn't doubt for an instant that what he was hearing was mostly the truth.

Goodrum paused. He had come to the end of the introductions, and probably because he knew that Beal was black, it was time to speak of race. "You should understand that Boston is not the South," he said. "Many of our customers don't know who owns the store, and the rest don't care."

"I'm sorry," Thomas said, in defense against what might have been some sort of imputation. "I wouldn't care either."

"I didn't think you would. But at home we forget how it is in the rest of the country. Boston is not free of hatred, but the best families do not discriminate. There is no law against intermarriage in Massachusetts," he added pointedly.

"During the war, when the Federal troops occupied my family's farm on the Eastern Shore of Maryland, it was a Massachusetts regiment. They delivered my grandfather to prison in Fort McHenry."

Goodrum didn't know quite what to say to this. "I hope—"

Thomas interrupted. "He deserved it. From what I heard, he was a complete, vicious bastard. He died before I was born."

There was no need for Goodrum to continue with his interrupted sentence. "We all have our private histories," he said, and Thomas liked this remark, liked the way he said it, but more, liked *that* he said it. They sat quietly for a few moments, enjoying this meeting of minds.

Arthur finished his tea and excused himself. They watched him as he walked down the long flagstone stairway off the back end of the terrace, stopping when he reached the bottom for a second or two while two small children and a dog chased each other around his legs. Suddenly he raised his arms in the classic pose of monstrousness, his hands clenched into claws, and he roared; the children and the dog ran off. Thomas wasn't entirely sure whether Arthur did this to delight them or just to scare them out of his way.

"An artist," stated Goodrum.

"Yes. A friend from our days in Paris. He's doing extraordinary work. We're very proud of him."

"And your wife?"

Thomas explained that Beal was visiting their friends on a neighboring farm. They both had infant sons, he said, and the two mothers enjoyed each other's company while the children amused each other. "It's our friends' third child, but our first, and my wife gets a good deal of comfort from a woman who knows the ropes. At times like this she misses her own mother, of course."

"It must be quite difficult for her to be away from her family."

"Staying with our families was not an option for us, as you already know."

Goodrum nodded.

"So, what's on your mind about wine?"

Goodrum talked for an hour or so, about everything from Boston's Puritan resistance to alcohol of any type; the belief expressed by the châteaux of Bordeaux that Americans would never really be interested in wine; the fine wine they produced anyway; the glut of table wine that was clearly coming to the Midi and the threat of fake wines confusing the palates of the ordinary Frenchman; the feasibility of domaine bottling, even here in Languedoc; the potential for the diverse soils and exposures of the hillsides to make wines of exceptional size and color if only . . . if only they could be made with some finish. Thomas was impressed; he recognized in Goodrum—Lawrence, as he was now calling him after erring the first time by asking whether he could call him Frederick—the careful researcher, the autodidact he knew in himself.

Beal arrived as this was winding down. They heard her carriage clatter up the stone road, heard the bustle of arrival, the cries of an overtired baby, the to-and-fro of the Señora and Gabriella, and at length, Beal came through the door onto the terrace. She was unwinding the light scarf that held her hat in place, and when she removed it, she waved it at her side like a schoolgirl. She stood in a ray of sun dappling through the chestnut leaves, and Thomas could not help feeling proud of her—of her beauty, the moment, the gesture with the hat, her smile in the sun: not an artificial hour but an instant, a sample of their real lives. Having a guest made this all seem both ordinary and miraculous. The two men stood up as she came out, and Thomas made the introductions. Taken with the moment, he did it up perhaps more than he needed to, as if to make sure that she would not be as skeptical as he had been, as if to head off the guest's impulse to self-promote.

Beal ignored his last bits of introduction; she turned to Goodrum before Thomas was finished, cutting him off in mid-sentence. "I hope you've been having a nice trip," she said. "Down here. Off the beaten path."

"Oh yes. I have never come this far south. In Bordeaux they speak of Languedoc as not entirely safe."

"Boars and brigands," said Thomas.

Beal took no notice of this old joke. "You will be able to have dinner with us?" she asked.

"Oh no. I couldn't. I must be getting back," he said.

"To Narbonne?" said Thomas. "You've missed the last train."

Lawrence explained that he had already taken a room in the hotel in the village, and indeed, he was planning the next day to visit another local winery. "La Fontaine. Have you heard of it?"

Thomas and Beal both laughed, and Beal allowed Thomas to explain that this was where she had been that day, the Milhauds were their very good friends. It was decided that they would send to the village to collect Lawrence's things and that he would spend the night with them at St. Adelelmus and be dropped at La Fontaine early the next morning, giving him plenty of time to meet with the Milhauds and catch the two o'clock train back to Narbonne.

"Well," said Lawrence. "If I refused such a reasonable plan, anyone would wonder why."

As she and Thomas were getting dressed for dinner, Beal asked, "Thomas, was that all really necessary?"

"Was what necessary?"

"All that talk about his store. About what an expert he is."

"I just thought you would be interested. He knows far more about wine than I do."

"A lot of people know more about wine than you do."

"As I am the first to admit."

"We see all sorts of experts, and you do not feel you have to carry on like that."

Thomas understood well what Beal was saying, but there was a point to be made on the other side. "I just liked him. I was impressed. I wanted you to know that, and I guess I wanted him to know that. Did he look as if he minded?"

"Hmmm," she said. They went back to their preparations. They did not normally dress for dinner as much as freshen up, but they had no doubt that now that the luggage had been retrieved, their guest would appear formally attired.

"An intriguing prospect for us," said Thomas, starting anew after Beal finished at the washstand. "Of course," he continued, "we wouldn't be ready to ship anything bottled for three or four years at least, but I never dreamed we would sell anything in America, especially in this sort of package deal. The wine has to be first-rate, sturdy enough to make the voyage . . ." He noticed that Beal was glaring at him. "What?"

"A package deal? That's what this is?"

"Beal, I'm sorry I keep saying the wrong thing. The wrong words, I guess. But I meant what I said: an arrangement to sell directly in our own bottles to a store in America. I had never thought of such a thing. An extraordinary idea. That's all I meant."

"Okay," she said.

"But yes," he said, answering the questions in the air. "I didn't know about his family's store." From the moment he had first laid eyes on Lawrence Goodrum, he knew the man was taking them into new territory. There was no reason not to come out and say it. "I didn't know that Negroes, well . . ." He paused, looked at her in an appeal for agreement. "That life for Negroes in Boston could be like that. You understand."

"No, Thomas. I don't understand." She was at her mirror, and her reflection glared at him. "There were very distinguished colored families in Hampton. Professors at the institute. Attorneys. You think we're all just country people, and we're not."

They finished dressing in the echo of this accusation, which Thomas wasn't quite sure he deserved, at least entirely. They found their guest waiting in the parlor. This was the first time they had sat with anyone in this room, the first time they'd had a guest of any kind, if one did not count Arthur or the more informal hospitalities with the Milhauds. It was a fine, rose-colored evening, and this room, cold and unwelcoming in winter, was at its best with the windows and doors thrown open; they heard the magpies outside, noisily gathering for their evening roost. Gabriella brought Randall in to be shown, and Mr. Goodrum—"Please," he said to Beal, "Lawrence"—took him readily into his arms.

"Do you have children?" she asked.

"Oh no. Nieces and nephews. I'm not married. I still travel too much to begin a family."

She asked him to tell them about Boston, and at first he demurred that Thomas had made it clear they had no connection to the city.

Thomas smiled. "I didn't mean to sound uninterested," he said.

Lawrence went on at some length, and Beal prompted him for more when he seemed to flag. His family had lived in the West End of the city, "Behind Beacon Hill," he said, but had just three years ago moved to the South End, a fashionable neighborhood of handsome brick row houses, intimate leafy squares, and broad avenues. His father had been able to buy a fine, mostly furnished building for a surprisingly good price. Lawrence allowed that some people had built houses on the newly filled land in neighboring Back Bay, but that the South End, in its classic French high style, would surely endure as the premier district.

At the end of this they moved to the dining room. As soon as they were settled, Thomas kept his distance while Beal prompted Lawrence anew. "Your family must be very busy," she said.

With the business, of course. His brother and his sister's husband were both part of it. But there was time for more enlightened pursuits. The Goodrum family had recently joined Trinity Church, which was between the South End and Back Bay, in Copley Square. The building was a marvel; the best artists in America had contributed murals, stained-glass windows, pieces of sculpture. "It isn't Chartres," he said, "but it is without question the most beautiful church in America. And as perhaps you know, Bishop Brooks was rector there for many years."

"Catholic?" Thomas asked, to be polite, because it all sounded rather Catholic to him. His mother had always implied that everyone in Massachusetts was Irish, and therefore Catholic: Irish Catholic, as opposed to Roman Catholic, by which she meant English Catholic.

"Oh, Lord no. Phillips Brooks was the greatest Episcopalian preacher, indeed the greatest preacher of any denomination, in America. We are Episcopalians. As I assume you are."

Thomas glanced at Beal. What would she have him say? He

could imagine being faulted for any way he played this, and he waited for her to respond.

"We are Catholic," she said. "At least Thomas's family is. Cardinal Gibbons in Baltimore helped us get married, and we have been helped every step of our way by the Catholic Church. Perhaps you have heard of Cardinal Gibbons?"

Lawrence coughed into his napkin. He was sorry to say that he had not heard of this Gibbons, but Thomas was quick to throw him a line. "We are not regular worshippers," he said. "This dismays our housekeepers, who are Basques and rather strict Jansenists."

"Jansenists?"

"Oh," said Beal. "Just a lot of Catholic stuff. I was raised AME, if anything. We had a building, but we were burned out of it. Then we had services in our neighbor's house, a woman who saw visions and spoke in tongues."

"Ah," said Lawrence. "I of course meant no offense."

Beal took no offense, and she knew that Thomas would not either. What did either of them care about Catholics? Or Episcopalians. Or bishops. But she felt sorry for Lawrence Goodrum that this bit about the church had worked out badly; he was laying down his cards here, and he thought he needed every one of them to count. From the moment she laid eyes on him, she understood him to the core—the way, quite deliberately, he was overbuilding his story. She had never seen this version of the game, this urban, high-society version, but it was all the same to her. She knew all this talk of culture was meant to impress Thomas, and she knew it was having the opposite effect, but surprisingly, she didn't mind that either. Thomas was being irritating. She wanted him out of the picture tonight: Lawrence Goodrum was hers; he'd come to St. Adelelmus, she believed, to meet her. He was handsome, Beal thought; a true American with his light skin and ready smile. Everything Diallo Touré would despise. She knew that their guest would never have bothered to go on like this just for her benefit; he'd say, *Do I really have to play like this with you?* Which was a game within a game that she was enjoying playing with him.

But as dinner went on, with its talk of travel and Paris—where

Lawrence's visits to Europe all started and ended—and more about Boston, a yearning Beal thought she'd outlived returned with an empty thud in her gut; that place in her body where Paris had so comfortably lodged had not gone away. She felt like a landlocked boy hearing tales from a sailor returned from afar; she felt like an exile, not from America, but from all higher things. She felt a desire that was not unlike homesickness, but without the pain. What was roiling in her as Lawrence went on was an ache but also a hunger; it felt good even if the desire was unconsummated. This was the backdrop for romance—city squares and promenades, music from the public bandstand and nights at the opera, images of closed carriages clattering on the way to some private affair, to some intimacy. She had this once, and it had slipped from her grasp. As if trying to overwhelm the pangs, she kept asking him questions, and each answer came like a message sent to a place deep in her soul, and each answer simply inspired more need. It seemed hardly possible that his America was an America that anyone, anyone at all, could actually aspire to, but here was this man as proof. Thomas was wrong—see, see?—but then, after quite a few minutes of this, the wave of her craving crested. She regained control a bit and quickly recognized that *she* had been the one overplaying, that her infatuation was showing to Thomas, so she tried to withdraw, pretend that it was simply dinnertime talk, absent chatter. *Is that a fact?* Just a short walk from Symphony Hall. *Sounds right nice.* "In Paris we lived on the avenue Bosquet," she said, trying to sound a little bored.

"Le Faubourg," said Lawrence. "How nice."

"There were two little girls in our building whom Beal quite loved," said Thomas.

Why was Thomas talking about them? she wondered. "So you have lived your whole life in the city?" she asked.

"Yes," Lawrence said, except for his years at college, a small college in Maine called Bowdoin.

"Maine," said Beal. "It sounds like the North Pole to me."

"Well then, you and Thomas should come for a visit. You might say New England looks not unlike Languedoc, with more trees."

After dinner they took a tour of St. Adelelmus. It was a beautiful evening, the rocks still warm from the hot August sun, though the air, as nightfall approached, was already chilly. The families were mostly indoors by now, half withdrawn, half lingering for a final word or two. From the washhouse came a few strains of a song: it was Mme Esquivel, Beal knew, who always did her laundry at night when she knew she would be alone. The few men still at *boules* in the dusk touched their caps as the three of them passed by. They stopped at Arthur's house, but it was too dark to see any of his works. Thomas let Beal show the way, though when it came to the wine operation, Lawrence directed all his questions to him, and each detail Thomas provided led to a small discussion of alternatives. Beal was proud to hear Thomas speak with such authority; yes, he was definitely allowed to talk about the business here, a sort of practical voice from the rear.

When they returned from the tour, they ended up on the terrace, enjoying the last few minutes of dusk, the mountain looming in its blackest form behind them, but the plain was more purple in the darkness and the Mediterranean air that rose from it was gentle. Thomas announced that it was time to retire, and Beal said that she and Gabriella would make sure Lawrence was settled and then join him. She was not prepared for the instant release of tension when he left, as if the officer had left the enlisted men to their mess. She didn't evince anything, she felt, but Lawrence leaned back in his chair, tipped one arm over the seat back, and crossed his legs, as if he wasn't going anywhere very soon.

"A remarkable man," he said. "I mean that. Your husband is a rare combination of humility and self-assurance. We don't see a lot of *that* in our customers."

In our rich *white* customers, Beal thought, but did not say. "His reticence is his power and his gift. His problem is that he doesn't know it; he doesn't trust it."

"Your husband has a problem? That's a rather odd thing to say to a stranger like me. Another man," he added.

Beal took a start: she realized she said that because she was still angry at Thomas, though just now she couldn't recall why. But worse, she hadn't recognized Lawrence as a man, and now he had offered himself as "another" man. "Oh. Ain't nothin' to it," she said. "We all have our problems."

"What, then, are yours?" Lawrence was enjoying himself immensely, skirting within these confidences; he settled even farther back in his chair.

Beal supposed she had problems, but what could they be? What was wrong with any of this? Well, where to start? In Paris or back at the Retreat, or back in Africa? "Oh," she said finally, "maybe I have too little on my mind to have problems."

"Too little to do?"

"That's what Arthur says about me. Thomas keeps saying he wants me to work with him, but what would I contribute? I don't know anything."

"Is that really the way you think of yourself?"

Once again she was thrown, but now she was saved by Gabriella's coming to the door and asking whether Beal needed anything from her before she went to bed. "We'll take Mr. Goodrum up," Beal answered, but instead of following Gabriella back through the rabbit door—that's what they called it, mostly because Rabbit was Gabriella's nickname—she led Lawrence to the front staircase that they almost never used. She climbed to the top and then looked back and saw him hesitating at the bottom, standing in the moonlight that came through the window at his back. He'd watched her climb from below. He looked slightly ghostly in this light, as if he had always been there but had never been noticed, a Moorish presence. She was holding a lamp, and he read her quizzical look, responding with an equally obscure shrug. Beal had no idea what any of this meant. He took a few steps up and stopped. "I have one question," he said.

Oh Lord have mercy, thought Beal, what's he going to say *now*? "Sure," she said.

"Who was Saint Adelelpuss, anyway? Some guy fed to the lions?"

When she reached their room, Thomas was sitting at her dressing table with one shoe on and one shoe off. He took off the other and gave her the seat. "What was all that laughing about?"

"Lawrence was making a joke about our namesake. He doesn't know how to pronounce it."

"Well," he said. "Full of surprises. Trinity Church, don't you know," he mimicked. "But I like him. This could be good for us."

The next morning, after Thomas and Lawrence spent an hour or so in his office and after Lawrence had insisted that he would walk, Beal drove him to La Fontaine. It was a fine morning. They'd brought up the gig, hitched to Reza, their young, not entirely trustworthy gelding. What Beal really wanted was a motorcar, but that still seemed a good bit in the future. The seat was narrow for two persons, especially for a man and a woman, but Beal noticed that Lawrence was making not much effort to keep to his side as they jolted down the St. Adelelmus hill.

"Extraordinary landscape," said Lawrence. "Savage, really."

"I've gotten used to it. All these rocks and stones. I'm beginning to feel settled on them."

"It didn't sound like that last night."

Beal glanced over at him; his expression was smug, his tone bold. "I don't know what you mean," she said. "I was just making conversation."

"Of course," said Lawrence with a maddening smirk, as if he had drawn a high card out of the deck.

They clopped along; the horse wanted to run and kept testing Beal's hands on the reins, which irritated her; she kept yanking back. Thomas would have scolded her for such awful driving. She'd gone to bed the night before in fine spirits but woken up scratchy, finding fault. Everything seemed not quite right; Randall had been fussy in the morning and she was shocked at how angry that made her. She could not quite figure it out, but the arrival of this guest had ever so slightly skewed the comfort they had slowly worked into at St. Adelelmus. "You've got such a fine life. We're just country here," she said.

"You may mock me," said Lawrence. "I'm proud of what we have but, hey"—this "hey" came from a coarse new place: he'd picked up her mood and was willing to throw it back at her—"it's not as if you've got nothing. Your husband owns a whole village."

"Yes, and the livelihood of each family is on his shoulders."

"That's why I am here. Because of our employees."

Again, the skittishness of the young horse, startled by a hedge-hog or some other beast of the shrubs, provided a diversion. "All right," she said. "I'm being unfair."

He did not respond, which made her realize that he agreed, and then, to her surprise, she blurted out, "You really have all these rich white customers?"

Lawrence laughed. Laughter for him, alone with her, was easy, even after they had snapped at each other. Maybe it was because they *had* snapped at each other. The odd phrase "our first quarrel" came into Beal's head; she had no idea where it had come from, or why.

"Yes. We do. Some, anyway. We are making a new world. You should come to Boston to see it for yourself."

Beal heard this echo of Diallo Touré with a jolt. They had come to the crossroads on the flat, where there was a shrine to some saint, though not to their saint. On her travels the Señora often stopped here to pray, and sometimes she went no farther. They were in a field of boulders, a tumble of rocks green with moss and lichen; over the next rise toward town, they'd be in fields rich with grain. This landscape made no sense at all. God had just thrown dice when He got to Languedoc. To the left, the road continued down to Azay; to the right, up to La Fontaine. Beal stopped to give the horse a chance to chew at the sparse stalks within his reach.

"It seemed like things were getting better for our people after the war," she said. "But I don't know now. The promise hasn't come true."

"My grandfather dealt in secondhand clothes, but even as he peddled rags, he saw the opportunity ahead."

"Well," said Beal. "The times can help us, and they can hurt us."

"Yes," said Lawrence. "But once one has achieved a certain level, it can't be taken away."

Beal wasn't sure of that; a position, a profession, had been taken away from her father. For all his talents, he needed a boom to succeed; in a bust he had nowhere to go. She shook the reins, gave Reza a slight tap with the whip, and he took the turn to the right. The horse knew that La Fontaine offered a cool drink and a handful of hay, even some grain if he was lucky.

"I had heard of you in Narbonne," Lawrence said. "I admit, as much as anything, that was the reason I came up to see St. Adelelmus. It was an impulse. I had no idea your husband was so ambitious."

"Then I hope you liked what you found."

"Well, yes. I did. You are quite remarkable."

"Our wine," she said quickly. "I meant the possibility of our wine."

"Yes. That too. Don't worry. Your husband is very solid. But when I come back, I will be thinking about more than the wine," he said.

"You plan to come back?"

"Yes. My father and brother don't really approve, but I think we can make a good business in wine. No one else in Boston is trying."

"Well, I hope you're right, but really, I think wine is kind of awful. I'll never get to like it, I think."

Lawrence laughed again, but clearly he wanted her to respond to the little intimations he had made about returning. "I hope you don't take offense to hear me say that I will look forward to seeing you again."

I should be taking offense, Beal said to herself. I should not be listening to any of this. I should not. He was being forward—their thighs had been touching the entire drive—but she did not mind. "I wouldn't take offense if you didn't mean to offend me," she said.

"I meant the opposite."

The opposite of what? she wondered. Too many ways to take what he said. "Please. Let's drop this," she said. He said nothing as they jolted around the last bend in the steep road. "It doesn't matter what you meant," she added. La Fontaine, the tops of its roofs, came into view. "We are arriving," she said, and without much further chatter or polite parting remarks, she dumped him in the center of the farmyard and drove off.

Back at St. Adelelmus, Thomas was at his desk. What a night! was what he was thinking: Lawrence Goodrum showing up unannounced and on foot, like the tramps in Maryland looking for harvest work; his intriguing propositions; Beal's anger. Yes, Beal liked Lawrence, but why shouldn't she? Thomas liked Lawrence well enough, and as he reflected on those recent events, what stuck with him was that vision of Beal coming out onto the terrace, her hat at her side. For perhaps the first time ever, their lives seemed settled, their choices proven correct. It was all good enough for him, and for her, for now.

Gabriella brought in the mail and laid it on his desk, but then lingered, which was unlike her. Thomas asked her if there was something she needed.

"People are talking," she said.

"About what."

She tried to say nothing more, as if presenting this fact that mouths were wagging would put some kind of process in motion that would take care of whatever it was that people were talking about, but Thomas kept his eyes on her, and finally she blurted out that people were wondering if the guest was here to buy St. Adelelmus. She became tearful. "I don't want you to go," she said.

Thomas smiled; it made perfect sense, and why wouldn't they think this—so often cast off, their livelihoods thrown into peril once again, the most beautiful winery in the region jilted once again. A bad idea to attach your hopes to the fate of a beautiful bride. "No," he said. "I want you to go right out and tell every person you see that our guest was not here to buy the domaine, but to buy our wine. Go tell Mme Murat, if you can, to make sure it really sinks in."

"Oh," she said, trembling a little at that final thought.

Thomas wanted to hug her, but of course that couldn't, and shouldn't, be done. Instead, he thanked her for bringing this right to him, and when she left, he sat for a moment or two more, thinking of her, how in these few months he had known her she was beginning to lose her girlish round cheeks, now seemed to move with a kind of long-legged grace he hadn't noticed before. Thomas knew so little about girls, young women, despite the fact that growing up, one of his two best friends was a girl; he'd married her, which skewed the lessons. Now that all hopes had been fulfilled with the birth of a son named Randall, he hoped for a household of girls, each as pretty as their mother, as *mignonne* as Gabriella.

He turned to the mail, and as he flipped through the pile, he noticed that one letter was postmarked Bordeaux. He'd sent several inquiries to growers there about buying scions, and that's what he figured this letter was about. He put it aside to read later until it came to him—sometimes the path from eye to brain is a long one—that the name Hardy was on the envelope. He reached over and snatched up the letter. It was in a man's hand, and Thomas, still thinking about grapes and grafts, assumed that either through a large coincidence or in the more likely event that she had urged him, Eileen's father was offering to do business with him; not many growers in Bordeaux were. As he was opening the letter, he did not have time to sift through his many shards of emotion, but what he understood was that he was pleased to have this connection to her and was relieved, overjoyed really, not to have done anything to her that a father could object to. And nothing, he hoped, that Beal could not readily forgive; besides, it would be the untruths he had spoken during that fateful conversation on their last day in Paris that would need to be forgiven, and not anything, he believed, that involved Eileen.

From the first line, Thomas knew Eileen's father was not writing about business. "Dear Mr. Bayly," it started. "My daughter Eileen, who I understand you knew for a time in Paris last year, spoke of you and your venture in Languedoc quite often, and I came to understand that you had meant very much to her and perhaps then that she had meant something to you."

Thomas's breath stopped; his hand started to shake. "Thus in great sorrow and grief, and in the hope that I am not intruding into your personal affairs, I write to you that my daughter died this past April 29." The letter went on to describe her brief illness—Russian flu? Pneumonia? Her father didn't say exactly what it was, because it didn't matter what it was—and to say that neither a doctor's round-the-clock care, nor the fondest hopes and prayers of family, nor any appeal to the goodness and fairness of Providence could slow the march to the end. Whatever had passed between Eileen and her father in the past few years, this was a letter wrenched with grief, with despair over losing her; her death was an insult to beauty, her beauty, a life simply stolen for no reason. "Nearly to her final hours she remained lucid," he wrote, "and she fought her illness with a passion, but when it was too much, she let herself go, and I watched her being welcomed into death." Thomas could feel the pause in the letter, the moment it took him to compose himself for his final thoughts. "When parents by their tender care and pains have raised a child to maturity, they expect to reap the joyful gains of their companionship. But then death appears and turns the joyful hopes to Sudden Grief. What thoughts can shield us or give us some relief?"

Thomas trembled as he lowered the letter after reading these last, ancient-sounding lines, an accidental piece of verse. What thoughts indeed. When he picked it up again to read the ending and the signature, he noticed that the ink was a slightly different color, and he realized that just as he had paused in his reading, the letter had sat for a day or several because her father—Alan, his name was: Alan Hardy—thought he might say more. But there was nothing more to say. This unbearably raw outburst to a stranger, a stranger who had, if not broken, perhaps wounded his daughter's heart. Had she told him about Beal, about her coming to Galignani's to look at her? Had she told him about the peach walls of Montreuil, which she had once hoped to show to Thomas, back when she thought he was a nice, somewhat aimless young man looking for a life? Had she admitted to him that this young man went to Languedoc because of what had seemed her contempt for Bordeaux, this place where she had died and was presumably now buried? But of course, was anything she might have said to her father Thomas's business?

He stood up from his desk, sat down to read the letter again, and then left his office. He went out to the terrace and sat at the stone table, where he had written letters to Beal more than a year ago and where he had thought he should write to Eileen, but had not. He pictured her red hair, the sight of it through the bookshelves the last time he saw her, and then he pictured it splayed out on a pillow, dank with her fevered sweat, tied aside with a ribbon by the nurses caring for her; or, much worse, pictured it as a tangle of snakes on the linen, this hair. It seemed to Thomas that it had been a talisman, something that would protect her. Why would God give it to her for such a brief span? As her father had said, what relief was there from this, and what kind of lonely grief for Thomas, lonely because he realized even from the instant he read the first few lines that he could not tell Beal that his friend Eileen had died. How would he even raise the subject? He could tell no one that if he hadn't married Beal, a woman whom he might have wanted to marry was dead. He couldn't bear the thought of this beautiful person closed in her casket, and thus he began to weep, at how unfair it was that her last year or two had been so . . . unsettled: a quarrel with her father, a lonely sojourn in Paris where her hopes had been dashed, and then this move to Bordeaux. It was presumptuous of Thomas, conceited, that he could imagine her happy only when she was with him, having tea, even . . . that one time quite successfully forgotten until this moment, when, upon leaving the tearoom, she had casually taken his arm as they walked under the arcade of the rue de Rivoli and he had held hers tight to his side.

13

On Christmas Day, Xavier Murat reflected that 1894 had been a good year. Why annual plants like tomatoes and string beans would, year after year, produce vegetables of uniform characteristics, yet ancient vines could produce fruit in certain years that was all but unrecognizable . . . well, this was part of the mystery of the vine. Some years, people who liked a warm and fruity beverage were happy; other years favored those who wanted something as thick as ox blood and approaching fifteen percent alcohol—although that didn't mean that when the *pichet* was drawn from the cask, they wouldn't drink whatever was brought to them, good or bad. Whether *gras et vigoureux*, or *flasque et boueux*, they'd drain the glass. No one would remember that 1894 had been a good year or a bad year, except the people who grew the grapes.

So 1894 had been a pretty good harvest, the Aramon as usual heavy with clusters, the Carignan a little more sparse but fine. The little bit of Grenache was a nice surprise; he'd planted it over the objections of the Belgians and was pleased that the new monsieur approved. Approved rather heartily, in fact. Xavier agreed with the monsieur that Syrah should be next, but he wasn't sure about restoring Mourvèdre: too many disappointments in the grafting shed for that. Still. There had been no oidium to speak of; a little dusting of Bordeaux mixture in one corner of the Carignan had been all it took. Good pruning, once again, had limited the damage from the butterflies. As for the wine, Xavier had blended the Grenache and Carignon in two casks, and he liked the result—nice color, good size, a little more fruit. M. Bayly seemed to have opinions and plans in that regard and had even suggested that if blending was indeed in the future, they might hire someone to help them. A university boy from Montpellier, perhaps. Which was just fine with Xavier, who was a man of the soil, a man of the cask and not of the bottle.

The year 1894 had been good for his family. His mother was becoming more and more of an invalid, and more demanding every year. This was true, but what could one do? Besides, Françoise took care of her most of the time. The boys were well launched; the oldest, Bruno, was sweet on a nice girl from the village, and the younger, Antoine, was a little dim-witted, it had to be said, but a hard worker. Xavier and Marceline were aging well enough; at times they drove each other crazy, but neither could imagine any other life, any other partner. And on the domaine there had been no accidents, dismemberments, knife fights that he knew of, conflicts of the blood or heart, significant deaths in any of their usual forms: childbirth, weakness of lungs, wasting away, protracted declines, painful entries into the great beyond.

And it had been a good year, all things considered, with the new owners. It could have been so much worse—had, in the past, been so much worse. Thomas Bayly had arrived with a decent idea or two and was a quick learner; the visit during the summer by that rich American—well, there had been talk about *that*—seemed to have accelerated some of his thinking. There were nice little holdings all around the village to be had for sadly reasonable prices, but if they harvested so much as a single additional grape, they would need a new press. Bottling: a nightmare all its own. Pasteurization! Xavier's mind might begin to spin, and Marceline sniffed loudly, but neither of them would trade this sense of the future for the slow death of the phylloxera years. The young madame was much liked, and her little brown baby was still a source of amusement throughout the district, *le pitchoun* with that perfect chocolate nose and ears. And even that lumpy Jewish artist. This very morning he had stunned every family in St. Adelelmus by presenting them with photographs; he'd been posing people, whole families when he could, dogs and cats, all summer and fall, but no one ever dreamed he would give them copies; the very idea that they had disappeared into his camera was enough for them, but the gift of the photographs brought unspeakable wonder and joy. Xavier looked down at the one Arthur had given him, which he was holding in his hands: He wished Maman had been willing to appear, but that was perhaps asking too much of her, with her arthritis and rheumatism and thin blood.

But for all this, changes were under way; that's what Xavier was thinking about on Christmas Day. He and the monsieur could understand as well as anyone—better than most people in fact—that the wine lake was growing, the price was falling, and the authorities were doing nothing about the *fraudeurs*, and if this kept up, the triumph over phylloxera would be nothing more than a delay on the road to ruin. As soon as the harvest was complete, they hired laborers from the village to pull up almost five hectares of Aramon. This was not a popular decision: Aramon, with its enormous yield, had saved Languedoc after the blight. Everyone agreed on that. So why would anyone exchange a plant that produced so abundantly and reliably with a new one that at best would produce half the fruit and require twice the fuss, the pruning, the dressing. A delegation, led by M. Cabrol, came to Xavier to protest.

"There is no reason to do this," he said. Cabrol was a man of reason; he and Xavier had grown up together, lifelong friends.

"Friends," Xavier said, "M. Bayly and I believe that we must separate our prospects from the rest of Hérault and Aude. They will keep growing Aramon until they drown in its juice. We must look to the future."

They left, grumbling, but there was never any question of a revolt; they only wanted reassurance. By the middle of October they had begun replanting with Terret, an ancient vine that had evolved over the centuries into a fine dark-skinned fruit. And once again, the delegation was back. They were planting all wrong: the rows were too narrow, the space between plants too crowded. "This will not allow each vine to produce a sufficient quantity of fruit," M. Cabrol said, and he was right. These were good workers; grape juice ran in their blood, but times had changed.

"Romieu, my dear friend, we want better fruit, not more fruit. We must crowd the vine, eh? We must make him uncomfortable. Not let him strut his stuff for the ladies." There was a round of laughter; Romieu, true to his name, always had an eye out for the ladies.

"Lower yield, higher quality. This is our owner's plan. Thirty, maybe thirty-five hectoliters," and even as Xavier said that, arousing a chorus of anxieties, he had trouble not wincing. It seemed rather extreme to him. With Aramon, in almost any year, they could expect at least seventy hectoliters per hectare.

The men looked from one to the other; there were five of them. During the harvest there might be fifty or sixty day laborers, some of them *prix-faiteurs* who helped with pruning and cultivating, but these five vignerons were the heart of the domaine, as their fathers had been, as their grandfathers had been. Patrici Sardou, the oldest and often the wisest of them, spoke the real anxiety. "That is all fine," he said. "But how can thirty-five hectoliters support all of us, all our families?"

"Don't worry,'" said Xavier, and he tried to follow his own advice. "Better wine, higher price." He knew that once they started pruning in the new year, the delegation would be back, complaining that they were leaving too few shoots and too few buds per shoot. A sort of madness, perhaps, but as Xavier finished his quiet Christmas Day reflection—the goose was ready to carve, Françoise needed help getting Maman down the stairs—he concluded that M. Bayly—he had insisted that Xavier call him Thomas, but that would take some time—was giving them a plan for a future, and for the first time since the day the vines started dying on St. Adelelmus, he reflected that the year just past had been good and the year to come might be better.

As had been the custom for many centuries, the new wine year began on January 22 with the Feast of St. Vincent. To mark this event, as always, long tables were set up the length of the pressing room; families from the village, merchants, even some of the many traveling artisans of the region—coppersmiths, match sellers—started arriving in the morning. After the blessing of the vines was complete, the men prepared for the beginning of pruning with a groaning table and last year's wine by *la grosse cruche*. M. and Mme Bayly and their brown baby sat at the center, along with M. Arthur, now a great favorite of everybody. The women served them and then retired to the stove—warmer there anyway—to serve the children and have their own dinners, and when the eating was over, the tables were pulled back and everyone gathered for the pageant about the saint and the donkey, which was put on by the children. This year Gabriella Zabala played Saint Vincent—or was it Saint Martin? Xavier could not be sure, but this was tradition at St. Adelelmus, this acting out of the famous story on this day of the year. The saint was always played by a girl because saints, after all, were kind of *efféminé*—but the lead role was the hungry donkey, always played by the domaine's freshest, wisest boy, a child who could be depended on to ham it up. Bartolomieu Pujol, a *bêcheur*, a *gros malin* if there ever was one, did a fine job: he snorted, he butted Gabriella, he rolled his big brown eyes and shook his tail, and by the time he finally took his first fateful nibble of the vine shoots—so the story went, the donkey had demonstrated that a pruned vine grew better fruit—the younger children in the audience were screaming with excitement.

After the explanations given to the previous delegations, and after this reenactment of custom, there was no real voiced complaint about the pruning, which started the next day. If the men believed they were slashing into their own livelihoods, they did not say so. The pruning would go on until early March, and it was challenging but meticulous work; each man had his own style, and Xavier could walk down the aisle and name the man who had pruned each vine. Depending on the weather in the months to come, one style could do better than another, but who knew about the weather? There was little for Xavier to do during this time; once the broad objective had been laid out, supervising another's pruning too closely would simply not be tolerated.

In the beginning of March they sold the last year's vintage to M. Fauberge—the price they received was not encouraging—but not before he and M. Bayly had put up a few dozen bottles of Xavier's Carignan/Grenache blend for their own purposes. Xavier had no real idea of the proportions—he just mixed it roughly half and half—but whatever he had done seemed to live up to Bayly's expectations. M. Fauberge was pleased; his business, like Xavier's, lived by the cask, but his heart was in the bottle. "Fine color," he said, holding a bottle up to the light. It had a little purple—a little eggplant, but redder, more like cherries. Like a pomegranate, M. Fauberge had said, but Xavier thought that was getting a little fussy. "No more than thirteen percent," Bayly added. M. Fauberge took a sip, sloshed it around his mouth, and spat it out. "If I am right," he said, "a year in the bottle will soften it."

"Or replace the Carignan with Syrah," said M. Bayly.

"As on the Rhône."

"And then perhaps, bring some Mourvèdre back, for strength during shipment."

"Ah, M. Thomas," said M. Fauberge, pleased with his apprentice's ambitions, however impractical. "I cannot encourage our poor Mourvèdre. Even the Spanish are giving up on it."

"M. Murat agrees with you," said Thomas with a slight laugh.

Xavier liked Thomas Bayly; there was a reserve about him, and from time to time after they had ended a conversation he would linger, as if there were more to say, which made Xavier feel he had missed something. Perhaps there was a touch of melancholy about him—this was M. Fauberge's argument in his favor—but it actually seemed that during these odd pauses he was simply rethinking. There was nothing—nothing—weak about this man; even Marceline seemed to be relenting in her earlier dim view of him. He took himself seriously, but nothing made him laugh harder and more heartily than his own mistakes, his own foolish misapprehensions. Bayly was a man who did not smile so readily, but when he did, his whole face transformed: a mouth that tended downward reversed direction; eyes twinkled. How could one not enjoy the easy hours when working side by side with such a man?

And then the summer was upon them. June was too hot, too dry. Xavier and Bayly both worried about the new Terret vines—now *this* was an ancient grape Xavier could get completely behind—but they would be driving their roots deep, looking for moisture in the shale, and if they survived, they would be bringing the flavors of the earth into their fruit from the very first *vendanges*. Little Randall, just over a year old, was full of health, and if Marceline was right, Madame was early into her next pregnancy. M. Arthur was in Paris; they missed him and hoped he would be back soon. M. Bayly was still talking about Mourvèdre, but Xavier believed they would have to buy a holding on the opposite slope—he did, in fact, have one in mind—because their terrain was too dry for Mourvèdre. *Pourquoi pas l'Aspiran?* A fine grape not extensively replanted after the blight. Or perhaps, suggested Xavier, Morrastel-Bouschet, a crossing with our own Graciano made by M. Bouschet *fils* just up the coast in Mauguio? Early ripening? Fine color? Oh, said Bayly, far too much Aramon in its lineage, and Xavier had to agree.

When Arthur returned to Paris that July, he did not reenter in triumph, but he could ride in with some success. Within an hour of arriving, he went to Galignani's and then up the avenue de l'Opéra to the new Brentano's, where he saw displayed prominently his book of drawings, *Les vignerons de St. Adelelmus*. He thumbed through the book in both stores and each time was surprised by the strange warmth inherent in these line portraits of people at their trades; he wasn't quite sure what had guided his hand to achieve such a result. As far as money was concerned, this was the first time in almost three years that he had earned anything at all. Three years with no income was scandalous to him but miraculous: it made him feel positively aristocratic, but it also showed how little you needed if you reduced your living expenses to zero. What he had spent money on—his paper, his pencils, and now, one of the reasons for this trip, his photographic equipment—was all part of a deep investment that, improbably, seemed to be paying off. Totally abandoning hope, continuing only because you had no other ideas in your head, recognizing that your youthful self had been a delusional fool: all seemed to be part of a successful artist's career path. That afternoon he went back to the old Café Badequin with Stanley, and because Stanley had once again placed a painting in the Salon, the new crop of students barely acknowledged him. The young aspiring artist: what a motley tangle of fear and desire. As far as Arthur was concerned, this unwillingness to remark on the success of others was as it should be, as it must be: it was the true marker of victory. For little Stanley Dean from Pittsburgh, being invisible and diffident to a fault came naturally; for Arthur, it was an acquired taste, but it had been acquired all the same.

But no one in the cafés or on the promenades or in the Bois was talking about art that summer. They were talking about Jews. Even in the distant world of the Midi, Arthur had picked up word of some of this—that the unfortunate Colonel Dreyfus was a Jew had not led the story in the provinces quite as it had in Paris—but from the moment Arthur stepped off the train, he sensed that things had changed. The newspaper typesetters were simply grinding their *j*'s, their *u*'s, their *i*'s and *f*'s down to little smudges on the page; the passersby could now take in Arthur's heavy Semitic features and all but raise their fists in anger and alarm: *Spy! Traitor! Enemy of the Republic! Next stop, Devil's Island!* Arthur could almost persuade himself that he was overimagining it—this was part of his new maturity, part of his sojourn in the South—but Stanley, naive, unsuspecting Stanley, told him that earlier in the summer the three Jews at the Académie Julien—two Americans and an Austrian—had dropped their studies and gone home. "I almost told you not to come," said Stanley in a whisper.

Arthur felt no need to lower his voice, especially not in English, and especially not to the crowd at the café. "It's just what they've been thinking all along," he said loudly, casting his glance around the other tables. "Always the Jews, eh? Now they have a scapegoat. Now they can say it aloud."

Stanley winced. "You think Dreyfus is innocent?" The *f* in Dreyfus, the *f* in *juif*—the conversations overheard in the cafés that summer were fuzzy, like bees.

"I have no idea," said Arthur. "Does it really matter to anyone but Dreyfus himself whether he is innocent or not?"

"Some people think so. The memorandum was a forgery; it was a trick to find the real spies. The cleaning lady was being paid by the Catholics. Things like that."

"I wouldn't expect to see him back from Guiana anytime soon."

This was all a little worldly for Stanley, and really, so what, thought Arthur. It was always thus. They dropped this, and Arthur was pleased to spend a few moments watching the people, the ladies, passing by. Beal had asked him to tell her what was new in fashion this year, but Arthur didn't know what had been fashionable last year, so he couldn't really help. What he did notice was that the outfits seemed a little slimmer, a little less flouncy, sleevy, busty; in other words, they seemed to be dressing more like Beal herself, more the way she'd dressed two years earlier. Two years!

"Everyone is talking about your drawings," said Stanley.

"Who?" asked Arthur. He couldn't resist.

"Maître Rodolphe, for one. He says they are *captivants*. He means it. When I look at them, I feel I am right there in that cooper's shop. The family scenes are almost too intimate. I had no idea you liked children and dogs so much."

"Thank you," Arthur said, trying not to sound too feverish with pleasure. "I think playing with photography showed me something."

Stanley was not ready to adopt this heresy. "If you say so. But tell me about them." He meant, of course, Thomas and Beal.

Arthur did his best to describe St. Adelelmus, Thomas the vigneron, Beal the *maman*. Stanley listened attentively, but Arthur knew there was little about this life that Stanley would understand, much less find appealing. He had regarded Arthur's provincial dress with horror, which inspired Arthur to play it up. He affected his beret, which attracted attention everywhere he went. Arthur, a man of the garrigue. Imagine!

"What I don't understand," said Stanley, "is how you would be willing to live in a goat shed."

"It sounds primitive, I agree."

"Don't they smell?"

"Stanley, I don't share the place with goats. Calling it a goat shed is kind of a joke. I don't think there have been goats there for centuries."

Stanley considered this for a moment and then asked the question Arthur had been waiting for. "She's happy there?" said Stanley. "Really?"

"Why not? She grew up on a farm."

"They both grew up on a farm. She was just biding her time."

"Where? Here or there?"

"In both places, don't you think?"

This was actually a perceptive thing for Stanley to say, and Arthur told him so. Arthur wanted to say more, but he couldn't think of anything to add. He might have wished he had argued the point differently, but he had to let it stand.

"Tell me something," said Stanley.

"Sure."

"Why did Beal let you do her portrait and not me? I don't really care. Neither of us has turned out to be a portraitist. But I've always wondered."

"Well," said Arthur, "that makes two of us. Never could figure it out."

Arthur was staying in a horrible little hotel not far from his former studio, which was fine for him, though he realized that his life at St. Adelelmus had forever changed his thinking about city life. Light and wind, as Thomas had said once—it is unnatural to live without either. Still, in the darkness and dankness and the back alleys there were several people he wanted to catch up with, some perhaps less presentable than others. He hardly remembered the names of the girls he had once passed time with—no *grandes horizontales* for Arthur, just a glass of absinthe and a quick poke—but he knew where to find them. One of the former models from the Académie came back to his hotel with him, and he was almost repelled now by her scrawny body, her pale skin. Beholding her, he recalled Thomas telling him that if he didn't have syphilis already, it was something he wanted to avoid. When the time came to enter her, he simply backed off; there was nothing here worth risking anything. She was confused but dutifully took care of him by hand; Arthur leaned back to take what pleasure he could, but he encouraged his mind to wander into a healthier and more erotic tableau, substituting the image of Jouselet, the baker's assistant in the village, with whom he had spent several very pleasant hours in her father's hayloft.

Though he did not want to—in the height of the Dreyfus controversy, he now had even more reason to shun the Catholic Church—Arthur had promised Thomas and Beal that he would look in on the old nun, and thus one hot morning in July he announced himself at the gatehouse at the Hôtel Biron. The porter was a broken-down, suspicious little weasel—*Juif!* Arthur saw the cry in his eyes—but what Arthur noticed more was his shabby suit and the general atmosphere of decay on the property. Hedges were untrimmed. The shutters on the gatehouse were peeling, and as he approached the main building, it seemed that this very morning—the slates were lying in a jumble—a small section of the roof had given way.

He was directed to the kitchen door, but he did not take immediate offense to this as he knew that Madame Bernault was now living in that wing. At length one of those terrible nuns appeared and said, in adequate English, that Mother Lucy was in her room and would be willing to see him. She seemed surprised by this. He followed her through the kitchens, through the heat of the stoves and the chill of the ice rooms, and was shown the door to Madame Bernault's room.

She was sitting down, but even so, Arthur could see through the folds of her habit that she had lost weight, that she was doing what his beloved great-grandmother had done, which was to become more and more birdlike, until the day, it seemed, she had simply flown away.

She greeted him warmly. "Mr. Kravitz," she said. "This is very kind of you."

Arthur didn't know quite how to respond. "It's my pleasure," he said.

"Please. Sit down," she said. Her room was spare—her bed, a small dresser, and two stiff chairs—but it was dominated by a large window through which the sun was pouring. The chair was a spindly little thing; Arthur felt like a bear in this place, a bear trying to say and do the right thing.

"Beal was sorry to hear that you had to give up your room in the attic," he said.

"God has taken away my sense of balance," she answered. "Most of the time I feel as if I'm floating. It's not totally unpleasant."

Arthur smiled. Such unquestioning good cheer—where did it come from? None of this was in the Semitic worldview, at least what he knew of it. "But I am sure you're more comfortable here," he said.

"I resisted being moved, but between you and me, this is much better. I can go outside anytime I want without getting one of the lay sisters to help me downstairs." Arthur thought he might mention that the grounds seemed a bit gone to seed, but she jumped to it herself. "Of course, nothing is quite as it was. You know the government is trying to close our schools."

"Maybe I'd heard something about that," he said. "I'm not sure."

"Anytime the French get uncomfortable, they lash out at the religious. It's been that way for a hundred years."

Arthur had not expected to enter into politics. "We live in a time of strife, I think," he said. "I am struck by this here in Paris. The Midi just goes along as it always has."

She cut right to the chase. "Colonel Dreyfus is innocent," she said. "Jews. Catholics. Forces are trying to turn us against each other, but we are all under attack."

"That seems the way of it," he said.

Madame Bernault retreated for a moment into her own thoughts and then came back. "I have heard about your drawings. I am so pleased for you. I want you to know that, Mr. Kravitz. Your success gives me joy."

Arthur was a bit overcome. He thanked her; before he got too excited that his acclaim had traveled into the back halls of a convent, he realized that Thomas or Beal would have told her this news in a letter. But still, these days, this was an easy entry into Arthur's heart. "I have been given a second chance. I am trying to make the best of it, trying to be worthy of it." This struck him as a rather clerical way to put it, but it was how he felt.

"Tell me about our friends. Tell me everything," she said.

Arthur did, followed the rough outlines of his conversation with Stanley. Arthur was getting a little tired of this, and as long as he had come over from the Quarter, he had planned his next stop as a call on the Richards, where he knew he would have to go over it all again, though in that case, he was promised a fine lunch. But he felt the privilege of being the bearer of the news, and he talked for perhaps ten minutes, a long spiel for him. He had brought her a gift of a photograph of Thomas and Beal and Randall, and while he talked, she held it in her tiny hand. A few times she responded to what he said by raising the photograph to her eyes and studying it, as if she were looking for clues, signs to prove or disprove his report. Which she was.

"They look well," she said. "The baby is *mignon*."

"Yes. You'd hardly recognize Thomas. So much has changed for him."

She studied the photograph again. "I never doubted him. He has all his sister's talents, but he's a kinder person. He understands the world better."

"I'm not much for wine, but his ideas seem good."

"Yes," she said. "And . . ."

And Beal, she meant. They both knew the conversation would end with Beal, that whatever their differences, they could recognize in each other one who loved her and worried about her as much as the other. "She had a dip in her mood after the baby was born, but this happens, don't you think?"

"Certainly," said Madame Bernault. "I'm told that happens. A few moments of adjustment must be expected." Her mind appeared to wander a bit. "If you could have seen her that first day, three years ago, when she came off that steamer. So frightened, but so resolute. So young, so beautiful. A child not ready for any of this."

"I have never seen her as a child. Sometimes the things she says seem to come from a much older person. Sort of a spirit trapped in a girl's body." Arthur tried to stop there, but knew he owed her a fuller account. "She gets confused, and sometimes she listens to the wrong person."

"Ah," she said, as if she knew all too well what he meant. He let her reflect on this for a moment. "Is she listening to anyone now? A wrong person?"

"No. I don't think so."

"But—"

"Mother Lucy," he said, realizing that this was the first time he'd ever presumed to, or wanted to, call her by that name, "I would be talking out of turn to say anything more."

"She confides in you, yes?"

"We talk, she and I. I think it helps her. She loves Thomas far too much to speak her fears. But she hasn't confided anything in me lately. Really."

She ignored the unnecessary "really." "I am glad you are there," she said. She stopped, and there was a long pause. She had put the photograph on her dresser, and now she reached for it but decided not to pick it up. "There is nothing we can do but let her find the way. Find her way. I have told her all this."

She was tired, and Arthur took his leave after promising to convey every ounce of best wishes and blessings back to St. Adelelmus. He retraced his steps down the drive to the gatehouse, and this time the porter struck him as nothing other than sad, almost sorry to see a guest, any guest, even a Jew, leave the premises. This whole edifice was crumbling, the institution collapsing in its own gravitational pull, and nothing could stop it. Arthur knew all about gravity, about being pulled down and back, and now—miracle—as he walked out the gate, he could feel himself pulling free, escaping a final demise.

He enjoyed his walk over to the Lion d'Or, recalling with disbelief that he had once, in this neighborhood, stalked Beal, that he had trailed that African who was likewise stalking Beal. Turning a corner, he trod over the precise spot where she had caught him following her. A few weeks earlier he had dragged himself over to the Louvre and into the main gallery, and finally he stood in a similar spot of shame in front of the marble bench where he had blackmailed her into sitting for him. Two American ladies were perched there, and they looked up warily as he lingered.

He could recall no particular outrage he had perpetrated at the hotel, so he entered with a slightly clearer conscience. There they all were, awaiting his arrival, and once again he remarked to himself that being Thomas and Beal's friend had made him more popular, more acceptable than he had ever been in his life and, yes, had seemed to make him a better person. All the Richards were well, and there was one pleasant surprise: joining them was the journalist, Morris Malone, who had unwittingly crashed the goodbye party for Thomas and Beal two years earlier. Oh yes, it was explained, he had begun French lessons with Céleste the day after they left, and unless

Arthur misread what he saw—well, it was crashingly obvious—
Malone was on the way to becoming a member of the family, though
not, alas, with Céleste herself, but with her sister, Oriane. Céleste
watched this realization and gave him a brave, almost defiant smile:
Yes, she was saying, *Oriane was always the prettier of us two.*

The lunch concluded, Arthur went out the door with Malone,
who was now, it seemed, employed by a New York newspaper as a
correspondent.

They walked a few paces. "Say," said Arthur, "you're from Boston, right?"

"Yes."

"Then tell me. You know a store? A store called Goodrum or
something?"

"Goodrum's? Oh yes, but it's not the kind of place where people
like me shop. Very upper-crust. I hate the place, to tell you the
truth." He poked Arthur with his elbow, Irishman to Jew.

"Hmmm," said Arthur. "Do you know the family that runs it?
The Goodrums?"

"No. I don't think I do. I don't know anything about them.
Our paths wouldn't be likely to cross. They probably live in Back
Bay."

Arthur tried to recall the details from the conversation a year
ago. "South Boston, I think."

"No. I grew up in South Boston. Not too many Goodrums"—
he rolled over the name—"in South Boston. It was probably the
South End. I'd advise this family to get out of the South End, if I
was asked."

"Why is that?"

"It's headed down the drainpipe, I'm afraid. I hope you won't
think me prejudiced when I say that the only people moving into
the South End are Negroes. Why do you ask?"

"I met one of the sons last year. He was over here buying wine,
I think. Seemed an interesting sort."

The past year had not been easy on Lawrence Goodrum, on Goodrum & Sons, on the whole Goodrum family. This was hard for

any of them to admit to themselves, much less to one another, but for some time the Pierce brothers had been opening a gap between themselves and the Goodrums, and lately Wyeth's store and the Wood family in Cambridge—once rather insignificant competitors— had been capturing the trade in Harvard Square and to the west. These other establishments provided neither superior products nor superior service. Neither the West End or the South End—the base upon which Goodrum's had been built—showed signs of growth. On the contrary. It was becoming obvious to Lawrence that his family's investments in the South End had been a mistake; the signs of decay were everywhere, starting with the appearance of men walking down Tremont Street in their shirtsleeves or a lady on Shawmut Avenue cussing out a dressmaker so loudly that passersby could hear every vulgar word. Families were moving to Back Bay, selling their houses and all their contents, it seemed, for anything they could get. Behind all this, seeping into the open from the back alleys, echoing hollowly in the voices of customers, was a slight off-odor that had previously been easy enough to ignore or to mask, the one vexation that was an arrow in the Goodrums' hearts. Perhaps they had allowed themselves to overreach. The day of the Negro elite in Boston just might be fading, and the free fall, from their heights, could end in places none of them could bear to imagine.

During all this time, Lawrence Goodrum's obsession—he called it "love," though he knew it was an odd kind of love—with Beal presented itself as his one possible joy. It didn't matter that he had spent no more than twelve hours in her presence. That moment on the grand stairway in the moonlight, Beal laughing at his stupid joke, this was enough for him. And enough for her, unless he was wildly misinterpreting her manner at dinner, which he was sure he wasn't. It didn't matter that she was married; her professed loyalty to her husband simply revealed her as the kind of wife he wanted. None of these other things mattered, and the fact that she lived in France meant that she could appear, as if by magic, not as divorced or separated or any of those labels Lawrence could hardly tolerate. She was, in herself, a world apart, apart from the difficulties of his family's business, apart from the squabbles he seemed to be having on a daily basis with his brother. Over what? Cabbage! That was yesterday's fight: Lawrence dreamed of a future in French wine and Spanish leather and Russian caviar, and Randolph wanted to talk about cabbage! Beal was a princess in a château in France, and if, after the current patch of downturns in business had been overcome, she would have him, they would reenter Boston arm in arm, and when they took a stroll down the mall on Commonwealth Avenue—in his mind, he'd made the move to Back Bay by then—people would lay petals and blossoms at their feet.

What Lawrence realized was that feeling love for another is more necessary to the deprived soul than feeling loved; to do its magic, it was not required that the love be returned. He preserved and treasured those minutes he had spent with her as if they were pockets of air; if his woes suffocated him, the thought of her revived him. Each time he was able to mention her plausibly, the name "Mrs. Bayly" or "my friend Beal Bayly" exploded on his lips, sent jolts of heat through his body. He was a man past thirty years old, but he believed that if he never saw his love again, the joy, the grace she had given him in those few hours would be enough to last him the rest of his life.

That would be fine for the rest of his life, but not for now. He had pledged to Beal—*threatened* would be a better word—that he would see her the next summer, and he intended to make the trip even though his father and brother had concluded that their business could no longer afford his long-standing strategy on French wine and his trips to France. They felt this especially after his fruitless sojourn of the year before, and they knew that this infatuation with a grower's wife was the cause of some of it. Calling it an "infatuation" made his behavior at once more forgivable and more frivolous, and the Goodrum family had time for neither. Orders could be given, but it seemed that orders would not solve the problem. Lawrence's father loved him deeply, and amidst all their troubles, Lawrence's sorrows were at least one thing that could be lessened.

"All right," said Lawrence Goodrum *père* one afternoon in the gray gloom of early March. They were sitting in the office that hung over the main floor of the shop. Through the knee-high windows along one wall, almost every transaction could be monitored; the snow cover outside was thick and icy, clotted with manure. "We will send you this last time, but by year's end we are going to have to reckon whether our customers' interests have changed."

"You mean," said Lawrence, "we'll have to reckon whether our customers are no longer our customers. We'll have to reckon"—he knew it was impertinent of him to keep repeating his father's word—"what it will take to get them back."

"And what is that?"

"It is what it has always been. Quality."

The senior Goodrum had grown up as the son of a man who started out in business as a ragpicker. "Perhaps," he said. "But you will swear one thing to me. You will do nothing improper. You will not compromise your integrity or the honor of this young woman. If she and her husband can help you see your way forward, that is all to the good. We need you here. But if you cause a scandal, I will not see you when you return."

14

Thomas had a letter from Lawrence Goodrum in the spring advising him that he would be making his trip to Europe again this summer and would like to return to St. Adelelmus—"if I could be so bold as to ask for an invitation." This surprised Thomas, as they had agreed the last time that it would be at least two years, and probably more, before he had anything of sufficient quality to export. Goodrum's letter seemed hasty, implying that there was some sort of deadline that had to be met. But the letter also pleased Thomas; he had liked Lawrence well enough despite his airs, thought the feeling was mutual, and would look forward to his visit as something more than a business call. Over the winter he had thought of him more frequently than he would have expected, and he mentioned him several times to Beal, in part as continued apology. Beal was indifferent, maybe even a bit dismissive. She had showered Lawrence with attention that evening, but by the end of the visit last summer she had seemed a little less enthusiastic. *Not like any man I ever knew,* she had said, returning that day from La Fontaine. Thomas thought that was the point: Lawrence was a man of a different sort, a man for the new century perhaps, and in any event Thomas believed that Lawrence could win her over.

Over dinner one night Thomas told her about the letter. "You remember: the man from Boston."

"Yes," she said. "Of course. All the best families."

"He was just trying to get our attention."

"So. What did he say in this letter?"

"He is hoping to come back for a visit this summer. He seems to be inviting himself for several days."

"Why? Why would he want to come back so soon?"

"I don't know, really. Maybe he liked us. Maybe we have a friend in Boston. Do you have a problem with this? Should I tell him not to come?"

"No. Of course not. He's someone you like."

Thomas accepted this, although obviously he had his own reservations. "I'd have thought he'd be someone you liked."

"Let's not get into that again, okay, Thomas? There'd be no real reason for me to like him."

She said she didn't want to get into that again, but she was doing it; as far as Thomas was concerned, he was getting tired of being put in that corner. "Yes there is, and I don't know why you can't acknowledge it. You liked hearing his stories about Boston. You thought he was funny. You like people who talk. Who talk more than me."

She put her hand on his arm, which he took as a peace offering. "There is nothing in this world I like more than just *being* with you."

"Still, maybe this summer will be the time for us to open up a little. Let's let him come."

It was now August—dead, deadly August—and the date of the visit approached. Arthur had only just returned from having been gone all summer, and they all knew that a diversion might well be a good thing before the harvest began. But on the day Lawrence was to arrive on the train from Narbonne, the domaine was in a panic. As the visit approached, the Señora seemed to become more and more agitated, and that morning she turned up missing, and when they did not find her in her usual spots, all of St. Adelelmus hitched up the carts and carriages and went looking for her. Beal went out with Gabriella and her father, but it was M. Cabrol and the cooper, M. Esquivel, who found her on the far side of the village, still heading west quite happily. She was always jolly and amenable when they found her—this walking made her feel good—but she had a deep gash in her leg and her skirt was torn. Gabriella was almost hysterical before they found her, and once the word came back that they were on their way with her, she was desperately assuring everyone that all was well, a sort of misunderstanding. Down to the youngest, newest worker, St. Adelelmus knew what was at stake here, or would be sooner or later: if she got worse, they'd have to do something, and aside from the asylum in Béziers, there wasn't much else anyone could think to do.

When it came time for Thomas to pick Lawrence up in the village, there was not a vehicle or draft animal to be had, so he walked down. He was late when he got to the village, but it took him very little time to spot Lawrence in the small crowd on the market square: a black bowler in this sea of boaters and berets; a stiff collar and sporty jacket, just the sort of thing to set him apart from the rumpled dress of the provinces. He looked distinctly uncomfortable and annoyed as he was knocked aside by a man with a cart. But none of this put Thomas off. In turn, he realized that Lawrence might have difficulty spotting him, as he blended so much into the scenery. "Lawrence," he called out.

Lawrence looked up with relief and walked over to Thomas.

"Mr. Bayly," he said. "I didn't expect that it would be you meeting me."

"It's August," said Thomas. "No one is terribly busy in August."

"'It's August that makes the wine,'" said Lawrence.

"Well, yes. That's what they say."

As Thomas expected, Lawrence attracted some curious stares, this man clearly from somewhere outside the Midi. He had brought a relatively large suitcase with him, and he was looking around for the carriage. Thomas explained the situation at St. Adelelmus, and they arranged to leave Lawrence's case at the hotel.

"We'll send someone down after the dust clears. But we'll have to walk. I hope you don't mind."

"Not at all," said Lawrence, fanning himself with his bowler. "I walked last year with Mr. Kravitz. I gathered he was in Paris. I had hoped to see him on my way through, but apparently I missed him."

Thomas was a little surprised by this, as if Lawrence had inserted himself into St. Adelelmus more than he realized, surprised that Lawrence's contacts in Paris seemed to run so deep. "Actually, he's just back from Zürich, I think. He's having a wonderful success."

They set out past the church square and down the steep streets to the flat where the road to St. Adelelmus branched off. In this wild and heaving land, everything was built on a hilltop or a peak, or even on a slight crest, but the corridors of transport took the lowest and flattest route. So it was on the Eastern Shore, with the original holdings taking what amounted to the heights, but the differences there were subtle: ten feet above the water's edge, twenty maybe—these were the heights. Maybe it was warring tribes that drove the choice to take the high ground in France, but on the Chesapeake it was disease they feared, from which twenty feet did little to protect them.

"I'm pleased you have come," said Thomas. Lawrence was already panting. "I hope you'll have scheduled enough time to visit some of our attractions."

"Yes. This is very kind of you. In the snows of Boston I found myself thinking of St. Adelelmus often, imagining this very moment. It was a long winter."

"I hope business is good. I hope your family is well."

"Oh yes," he said. "Our business continues to thrive."

Thomas politely waited for him to expand—last year he had avidly carried on about his life—but he left it at that. "I wish we had something to sell you, but we've made a start." He planned to open a bottle of Xavier's blend at dinner.

"The last thing I would want is to rush the wine."

"Especially ours, I would guess. Out of the cask, it's a little robust for American taste."

"We feel the American wine market is just waiting to be educated. As you know, Thomas Jefferson was a great oenophile."

Thomas had heard this about Jefferson, but he wasn't sure it meant very much. The fields at this moment, still on the relatively low and flat ground, were planted with wheat and barley; as soon as the rise began, they would be in the vineyards, which went all the way to the summits of the mountains. "Before I came to France, I had never drunk a drop of wine in my life. I didn't even know white wine existed. Champagne, of course, but that was it. Our red is hardly Champagne."

"Your wife said much the same thing last year. A family in the wine business that does not like wine. How amusing."

Thomas wasn't sure that this was *amusant*, and it surprised him a little to hear Lawrence make reference to a private conversation with Beal, but all of it was roughly the truth. And besides, in the few minutes they had been together Lawrence seemed a little uninterested in wine himself. "There will be time for all this business," said Thomas. "We have been looking forward to your visit. My wife is eager to see you."

"I look forward to seeing her," he said, a bit out of breath as they walked.

From the moment Beal left Lawrence Goodrum at La Fontaine the year before—threw him out of the gig, in her memory of the event—she knew that a new obstacle had landed in her path, an obstruction that would try to force her somewhere she did not want to go. The conversation on the ride to La Fontaine had bristled with trouble; Lawrence had lunged at her like a cornered fox. This would never end—people either putting things in her way or taking pieces of her away. This is what she had said to Arthur, and Arthur had been Offender Number One at that time. But no, that wasn't true. That was unfair. Because if she included Arthur, she'd have to include Mother Lucy and then work back to everyone else who wanted her to be this or do that, such as her brother Randall, and then back to crazy old Aunt Zoe, back to everybody except her parents, who were just raising her the best way they knew. Why did it matter to people so much what she did, why did they have so many opinions? Beal had no opinions about how others should behave, what they should do with their lives. One of her best friends in Hampton had left the colonel's house to take up with an oyster tonger, and Beal had offered whatever points of view she thought might be useful, but she didn't have *opinions*. If her thoughts were ignored, she did not press them. How was she to know, anyway?

But—men. Men. Oh, men had been desiring her since she could

remember, and that had never bothered her much, as most of them had no opinions. They didn't care what she thought or how she behaved; they just wanted to get her into the hayloft. The real problem was the men who wanted to remake her before they did this, and the real, real problem was that she couldn't ignore them. That Hampton student, Hiram Whatever, couldn't let a moment pass without critique; so what if she had country manners—but around him she was confused. *But what* should *I have said?* These men had this hold on her, this purchase, this way of attaching to her fears that made them impossible to ignore. How did they do it to her? They could do it because they alone seemed to have answers to the questions that most bedeviled her; if their lessons were demanding and stern, the rewards could be great. What was the right way to say this? she asked herself, poised over her journals, her "writin'," as she thought of it in that dismissive country way. *What you doing all that writin' for, Beal, honey?* She did not need to reprise the story of Diallo Touré—"DT" as she wrote—except to think how much she regretted everything about that affair, how foolish it made her feel in retrospect, how weak it made her seem, how ashamed she was that she had fallen so easily and would remain shackled to that secret for the rest of her life. And yet this man had found something unfinished in her. He'd reached inside her and latched on to a loose end, something that needed or wanted to be tied off, taken care of, gotten over. He yanked on it, and she followed all the way to his bed, because the loose ends were real: ever since she was six years old, everyone had been telling her—everyone but Thomas, that is—that she was silly and flighty and inattentive. Beal knew better than anyone that she was young and ignorant of the world, that *au fond*—these days, French phrases had a way of coming to mind first—she was just a girl from Tuckertown, destined, at best, to live out her life as a domestic or, if one really dreamed high, as some kind of clerk or office assistant. But so what? And so what about Africa and stupid Senegal—she had never, from that first night in the dining salon, had the slightest interest in Africa— and so what about Boston, and so what if she had married a white man? After all, that white man was Thomas, and how could *he* be an issue, no matter *what* he was. Others had tried that attack, beginning with her own brother, and it hadn't made a bit of difference. And so what, finally, about sex? She knew now the pleasure it could give, not just while doing it but simply while thinking about doing it, but at the end of the night with Thomas her body was so completely at rest, so sated, she feared that when morning came, she wouldn't be able to move a foot. If she understood what Léonie intimated from time to time, not every woman felt the same about it.

Beal's mind was afire with questions that winter. She turned twenty-two, asking, Who am I? What have I done so far and why did I do it? She did not mind this turn; it was past due, maybe, and there was an ease even in the stony drafts of St. Adelelmus that encouraged meditation. Confession, even. To herself, anyway. But her thinking did surprise her from time to time; the questions that popped to her mind were usually far more troubling than the answers. Such as, what would have happened to me if I had married Lawrence Goodrum? She spent many hours on this one. How that might have happened, what possible sequence of events were necessary to have made it plausible, who indeed she would have had to be—well, no need to figure out all *that*. This was daydream, after all, speculation, a thought experiment. Maybe that was the way to put it. She'd be nursing Randall or sitting in the kitchen with Gabriella or marketing, and an uninvited voice would break in to these moments and inquire as to how her life would have been different if she were Lawrence Goodrum's wife, living in Boston, Massachusetts. Yes, she did miss those city mornings, the sounds of the city coming to life, that massive machine, the markets, Les Halles, those hundreds of thousands of people. In their own way, each Paris morning was like a rebirth, when everyone took their last minutes of sleep and solitude before the engine began to rumble. In Tuckertown, everyone seemed to wake up shouting at the highest volume, and at St. Adelelmus it was the opposite, where the mornings in summer seemed so still, so silent that when she awoke, she could easily imagine that she was the only person on earth.

On the day Lawrence arrived, Beal saw him and Thomas coming up the hill to the bastide, but she was busy helping Gabriella and her father, who were frantic with relief and alarm, and the

Señora herself, who, utterly refreshed by her outing, was in the best of spirits, eager to get back to her labors. When Beal found Thomas and Lawrence on the terrace, Lawrence had changed into an open-necked shirt and rough, baggy trousers, the clothes of the workingman, and he looked remarkably handsome, much handsomer than Beal remembered, older, pleasantly weathered. "Mr. Goodrum," she said. "You certainly look more comfortable than you did walking up the hill."

He took this with good cheer. He stood up for her arrival and made a slight show of modeling his costume. "I came prepared. I had to find a mean little shop in Montpellier. They couldn't believe I was buying this for myself."

"I'm sorry things are so disorganized."

"I'm sorry to hear about your cook. I remember that you were very fond of her."

"She gets restless," Beal answered, and then considered mentioning Aunt Zoe and the "walkers" back home, but somehow this didn't seem the kind of thing he would understand, or care to hear about.

"I am eager to see what you have been up to," he said to both of them. Thomas had brought out two bottles of Xavier's blend, and in the sun they radiated a ruby light.

"You'll find out more than you want," said Thomas. "M. Murat is set to show you all our new vines. Tomorrow will be a long day." From here, Thomas went on into Terret and Mourvèdre and other cultivars, and Beal thought he was being boring. In fact, Lawrence didn't look all that interested.

"I'm sure Mr. Goodrum doesn't need to hear quite so much about our grapes," she said. She didn't mean to sound so dismissive, but Thomas, cut off in mid-sentence, gave her a querulous look.

"Certainly," said Lawrence. "I look forward to it all." He turned to Beal. "Thomas tells me that you might be persuaded to take me for a picnic in the mountains. Just like New England."

Beal had not heard of this, and she wasn't pleased to have her services offered like this. To have her companionship offered by Thomas. She glanced up at him, and he signaled back an apology, a shrug that said *What else are we going to do with him?* Maybe, thought Beal. "I'll see if Gabriella can come," she said.

"Lovely girl," mused Lawrence.

In the end, Gabriella worried about leaving her mother that day—it seemed the Senora's moods had something to do with the phases of the moon—and Beal could not persuade Arthur to come. "I'm not going to be your chaperone," he said. "If you're concerned, you shouldn't go. Why is that so hard to figure out?"

Beal was stung. "I am not concerned about anything. I am just trying to be hospitable," she said.

"I don't get why Thomas is permitting this."

"Permitting?" she said. "He arranged it."

"Hmmm," said Arthur.

Beal knew what that sound meant—it meant that her portrayal as an obedient little wife left out some relevant details—and she did not want to explore it with Arthur. Tests were being administered, it seemed, if not deliberately by Thomas—Thomas didn't give tests, she had figured out in Paris, he simply gave people the freedom to figure out their own hearts, which was, in itself, the most rigorous kind of test—then Beal was testing herself, and testing Lawrence Goodrum. It had to come to this. She'd spent a year speculating about seeing him again, and maybe, just maybe all this would simply go away; maybe the *proper* would take over from the *unseemly*. He would treat her with indifference, would be slightly irritated to have to amuse the wife when he came to do business with the husband. Maybe he would tell her that he had gotten married over the winter; maybe he would spend the whole time talking boringly and embarrassingly about his family's store and about the best people and that church and that music hall and all those people and places that seemed to mean so much to him. Maybe when they returned from the picnic, she would be free of him, of the idea of him, which was honestly the best part of him anyway.

But that was not to be. The stableman Ibarra was the driver for the day, and he spoke nothing but Basque, and as soon as they mounted the carriage, the lunch basket was secured, and they were a few feet beyond the last fence post, Goodrum turned to her and told her that he had been looking forward all year to seeing her again, and she knew the test was on.

"We weren't quite sure why you came. You must have much

more important business than inspecting vines that won't bear fruit for years."

"I do. It was you. I came to tell you I love you." It was all too clear that this was not a blurted-out indiscretion, but something he had planned for months to say in exactly this naked way.

She considered responding with a startled or perhaps bemused *Moi?* but instead she jumped right to it. "I am a married woman," she stated. "You are a guest in my husband's house. Thomas expects to do business with you. I have a child. If you persist in this, I will tell Ibarra to turn the carriage around." Beal had never spoken to anyone in her life in quite this tone, and she was pleased that it stopped him for the moment.

"Ah," he said. "Perhaps."

"Perhaps what?" she snapped.

"Perhaps I misunderstood." In other words, he was leaving it to her to name the indiscretion, which she would not do for him. When she did not pick up on this, he said, "Don't worry. I'll behave."

Beal was silent, too busy trying to figure this out. There it all was once again. Why this instant onslaught? What had happened in those hours a year ago that could be "misunderstood"? Why, in spite of the breathtaking list of reasons she had just enumerated, did he promise only to "behave"? If she could have simply stopped time for a second or two and asked him to step aside and explain what he had just done, she would have. A plea: *Tell me, because I really want to know. Am I an unfaithful person, so faithless that none of the facts of my life can protect me from anything?*

They reached the fork in the road, with its shrine and its three branches. The year before, she had remarked only on the two choices, the far left down to the village, and the middle to La Fontaine, but this time they were there to take the overgrown far right up the side of the mountain. Ibarra turned around, as if to make a plea for the horse's sake that they not take this road, but Beal beckoned him onward. "La Montagne Noire," said Beal to Lawrence. "*Montanha Negra,* as they say in Occitan. They call it that, but it's really a whole mountain range. The Pic de Nore is the highest point. There are all sorts of stories about it. Tales. Superstitions."

"Is that so?"

She ignored this tepid response and pushed on, describing the fact that all the water for the Canal du Midi came from the mountain, from a vast reservoir on the western slope. "It was built by a mad genius in the seventeenth century. The canal was his idea, connecting the Mediterranean to the Atlantic, feeding it with water from the mountain. He died before it was opened. The whole thing bankrupted his family. One of those ideas that seemed to kill anyone who touched it."

This time Lawrence's response had shifted from mocking her to a sudden stab of reflection. "Yes. It makes one wonder why you try to put anything in the world."

"I'm sorry?" Beal was just trying to fill the air a little—the canal, after all, was one of the technological and economic wonders of France—but she could no longer ignore his bored, and now glum, responses. "Mr. Goodrum. Lawrence. What are you saying? If you're just going to pout, let's go back."

Her tone brought him up. "I'm sorry," he said. "It's hard to run a business. That's what your story about the canal builder says to me. There is always uncertainty, even for those as well established as we. And maybe we aren't as well established as we thought. The key to it is quality, even if others want to relax standards. This is what your husband understands, and I hope we will both be right."

"I'm sure it will be fine," said Beal. In fact, she did believe this: a store like that in Boston? What trouble could there be?

"Let's stop talking about all this. Tell me about yourself. How did a beautiful woman of our race come to be married to an American living on a vineyard in France? I am dying to hear it from you."

"You have heard other versions?"

"Well, yes."

"I'm not sure there's much all that interesting in it. When we were children, we weren't even aware of the differences between us, or we didn't think they mattered, and by the time we'd grown up enough to notice them, we'd fallen in love. Or he had fallen in love with me."

"Not you with him?"

She heard the hungry uptick in his voice and might have wanted to quell it, but this thought, which came out of her mouth before she understood what she was saying, knocked her back. "It didn't quite work that way," she said. "He chose me, and nothing in the world makes me happier, but now I am trying to learn what that means." She avoided his avid look. "My brother Randall would not have liked to hear me say it this way, but that's the way it was." Yes, it was—is—the way it was. He started to speak but she cut him off. "Maybe none of this is easy, but there's nothing more to say and there is nothing in my story that is worth dying about."

They left it there for the moment, as the wagon had reached the end of the road, and Ibarra turned to suggest that whatever frivolous and time-wasting thing they had in mind, it was going to start now. They descended and started clambering on foot up to a crag with flat ground and a good view. Lawrence carried the picnic basket, looking the part: healthy, rugged. That is, until she heard him trying to catch his breath and felt the softness of his palm when he took hers to help her crawl over a boulder. They found a flat spot, and Beal spread out the blanket. She took out the food that had been packed for them, and they ate quietly. She had been too agitated about this day—this "adventure," as Lawrence had said on bidding her good night the evening before—to eat any breakfast, and she was hungry. So it seemed, was he. It amused Beal that he, like her, seemed to avoid the cheese: cheese and wine, France's great accomplishments, and she liked neither. She still shuddered with horror at the gobs of Camembert Mme Vigny tried to smear on everything: meat, bread, chocolate.

"Tell me about this"—he pretended he was looking for the word, but only pretended—"Tuckertown. It sounds very beautiful to me. I see that look you get when you talk about it. You're an exile pining for home."

"Really?" she said. "We were just surviving in Tuckertown."

"You would be surprised how many of us in the North look to the South as our real home." He ignored her look of surprise, then horror. "Georgia, maybe," he mused. "Not Mississippi, not even Virginia. But Georgia. Not that anyone would admit to it, but that yearning for a simpler place is there. It's crazy."

"It *is* crazy," she said. "Do you have any idea what you are saying?"

"Of course I do. But . . ."

"You wouldn't want to trade Tuckertown, much less Georgia, for what you had, I can promise you that."

"Sometimes I wonder," he answered.

"You. A college boy. You'd be pretty out of place in Georgia."

"College," he said, with some bitterness.

Beal didn't know what to do with that tone, so she went on. "My brother went to college, but I never got a chance to talk about it with him. One of my sisters spent a year at the normal school. But I was just a silly girl, and I went to work instead."

Lawrence paused, then continued haltingly. "Yes. I read Latin and Emerson and studied chemistry and was never so cold, so lonely, so miserable, in my life. Every night that I went to sleep in the mean, frigid little room in the only boardinghouse in Maine that would have me, I cursed my father for sending me there. It was as if he thought it would purify me—the weather as much as anything—but in the snow I was coal black. Even if I force my mind to forget those years, my body remembers."

Beal could say nothing about this; instead, she put her hand on his forearm, he clasped it there with his other hand, and they remained joined like this for a few seconds. "I'm sorry," she said finally.

"I would have been happier in Georgia," he answered.

There was a breeze coming from the valley; there was always a breeze from the south in the summer, a dry and cleansing wind off the garrigue, fragrant with the herbal perfumes of this land. "Don't that feel good," she said. "That breeze."

"Feels right special to me," he answered, laying on his version of a southern accent, which was about as convincing as his French.

She smiled; a stupid joke, but she liked it anyway. "In the winter the wind comes from the north," she said. The mistral, they called it in Provence, all the air in a semicircle of southern France being sucked into the Mediterranean, as if it were being pulled out of your lungs. "It's an Occitan word," she said. "It means 'master,' because of the way it howls. They say the winds off the mountains could drive you crazy enough to kill your wife. Some poet said that."

Below them Beal could see Ibarra harnessing the horse, Philippe, such an immense and unquestioning beast, nothing but horsepower; Beal appreciated him but was not interested in him. "I miss the mules," she blurted out. "You'd never guess what personalities they have. Their soft noses. How they love their jokes. They look at you, and their eyes laugh. Did you know that?"

Lawrence knew nothing of mules and therefore said he didn't; they didn't use mules in Boston.

Once Beal started on this, she couldn't stop. "I miss corn. Isn't that crazy? Sweet corn on the cob, your chin and cheeks slippery with butter. I miss eating it that way, not caring about the mess. And you're right," she said, "I miss the sound of Tuckertown, lying in bed on a hot, hot night and hearing the grown-up voices, just barely, from the porches, as if all over Maryland people were speaking simple truths in the darkness. You tell me our people are rising in Boston, but I'll say this: I don't think our people, any people, have ever been wiser, more honest about themselves, than they are on those porches in the South." She gulped back the emotion in her throat. "I miss those women who called me 'child' and drew me into the pillows of their big, soft breasts, comforted me from time to time. And I miss my Mama and Daddy." She turned away so he would not see the tears on her cheeks, and as she packed up the picnic supplies, she quickly dabbed her face with a napkin.

He gave her a minute. "I have left nothing behind that claims a tear. No one would cry over Boston," he said. "And no one would cry over Paris that way either. Maybe you don't really know what you have lost."

She waved away his comment wordlessly, even as it grabbed her by the shoulders: What *had* she lost? What was she trying to forget?

"I'm sorry," he said. "I am a fool. I have been complaining. I see you as living this perfect life."

"Not hardly. I don't know if there is anywhere in the world where I really see myself. Maybe that's stupid to say."

"No. It isn't stupid. It's what I was trying to say just now. That we are both people without a place."

"Last year you told me everything was perfect in Boston."

"Well, maybe the way is not quite as smooth as all that. If we stop rising, we plummet. But we have to be careful how high we get."

"Like Icarus?" she asked.

"Yes," he said, but it was so clear that she had astonished him with this reference that she had to go ahead and tell him how she knew the story.

"He's on a ceiling in the Louvre. Icarus falling. I'm afraid of heights," she said, but then added the final bit of explanation. "I spent most of our winter in Paris at the Louvre."

They were almost back to the carriage, and when she said this, Lawrence took her hand and stopped them in the path. "It was fate that I met you," he said.

"Well," she said, "it may have been fate, but it got the timing wrong. I am married. You must let me live my life."

"I can give you everything. The city. The town. The wilderness. You could do so, so much more."

"Lawrence. Please. You must leave me alone. If it really was love that brought you here, stop trying to make my life impossible."

At dinner Beal let Lawrence carry the show, describing the outing, exclaiming about the savage beauty of the landscape, the wind, how grateful he was to Thomas for lending Beal to him for the day. She let him carry on, and he did in his most charming way—teasing her for her long lecture on the Canal du Midi but praising her for her making such a home in this overlooked region of the world—but she could barely listen. She could barely look at Thomas. This guest putting on such a fine show had just, a few hours earlier, all but asked her to run away with him, to leave Thomas and steal his son, along with a new child that she now firmly suspected was within her. And what had she done? She had said *Please, Lawrence* and *Oh, you're making my life difficult*, and most important was what she had *not* said, to Thomas, which was *This man is wooing me and he must be sent away now*. And the next day, when Lawrence and Thomas went off on a trip he had planned to see the crushers and presses at another domaine, it made Beal sad. Whether or not Thomas figured it out now or later, this was not a friendship he should have anything to do with. Thomas had had so few friends in his life, nothing that came close to the intimacy he shared with Randall when they were boys, but even before

Randall was killed, they had quarreled. Theo Milhaud was Thomas's friend, sort of, but Theo was a moody man, often bristling about something; Beal had spent far more time in his presence than Thomas had, and in the end he was not someone she entirely trusted. Thomas and Arthur were devoted to each other, but they were not friends who had been drawn to each other in a crowd; they had been forced upon each other in ways Thomas did not suspect. They were like brothers, those sorts of wildly dissimilar siblings one encountered from time to time, two men who were as often at odds as they were at peace. In addition, Beal thought of Arthur as *her* brother, Thomas could make no special claim. No, Thomas had only one true friend in the world, and she was it.

Lawrence had never said how long he would be staying with them, and neither Beal nor Thomas asked. He settled in, was often found at the stone table next to the figs, reading or writing letters or simply staring at the view. He took dinner with Thomas and Beal, though after several days he reached a level of comfort and ease and some evenings arranged with the Señora to take his supper in the kitchen. "He likes Gabriella," said Thomas, though they could barely communicate.

Beal wasn't sure how she felt about that. In the course of his visit Lawrence had become a common sight in St. Adelelmus, though it was clear that people were wary of him, even if he was often in the company of their most beloved *étranger*, Arthur. The children teased him, made him say things in French and then howled with laughter. Beal learned from Gabriella that the year before, she had tried to quash the rumor that he was here to buy the place, but it persisted; she learned also that people were confused by his coloring and believed he was Algerian. Gabriella said that because Beal was the only American Negro they had ever met or even seen, they assumed they would all be her color. All this came out amid hesitations, diverted eyes, embarrassed pauses. But none of it mattered very much. Nothing had to be explained to anybody, although Thomas, a man running a business, did wonder about Lawrence's obligations back in Boston. "For an importer on a buying trip," he said during one of their dinners without their guest, "he certainly is taking a lot of time at a stop that has nothing to sell to him."

Beal said yes, it did seem a little odd.

"Has he said anything to you about his plans?"

"I get the impression that their business is having some trouble."

"Me too," said Thomas. "Should I tell him it is time for him to think about moving on?"

"I don't know why. You seem to enjoy having him around."

"So do you." Thomas did not say this without an edge, but his tone stopped short of jealousy. In the days since Lawrence's arrival, Thomas had largely turned him over to her, and though she avoided as much as she could any time alone with him, those stray moments of encounter occurred all the time. He did not repeat any of his professions of love; now there was warmth between them in the place of unrequited desire, which Beal liked. "He's been a good guest," she said. "He tries to be helpful. And he's talking to Arthur about buying some of his work. His photographs, actually."

"Ah. Then someone is doing some business with him."

That was where they left it, and Thomas had turned to other things. At some point in the past few days it was as if a small bell had rung—Beal could hear the sound—something as tiny but clear as the ping of a triangle, an invocation, and a farm that was deep in the summer doldrums suddenly recognized that a harvest would soon be upon them, and the trips to the vines took on new meaning, new questions. Each afternoon shower was looked upon with anxiety, and everyone walked a little straighter, with more purpose. *Les vendanges!*—even the small children felt it. For these two months all eyes, all their parents' eyes, were on the grapes; the children too would put in their hours in the harvest, but around the edges of the days, out of the main line of sight, freedom! Thomas said little about the crop—no farmer ever, ever wanted to be asked about the crop, the season, before it was in the barn—but Beal inferred from M. Murat's few remarks that they all thought it was going to be very good, that the concentrated fruit from the radically pruned vines would win over a doubter or two, that Saint Vincent and Saint Martin and Bacchus and Osiris too were considering being good to them.

Lawrence was in for all of it. Beal thought, actually, that he was being rather silly, tagging along like a toddler, almost pathetically eager to help, doing most of it wrong. Thomas indulged him, but he was spoken to sharply more than once by M. Murat, and one afternoon Beal found him under the figs, holding his beret in his hand. "I assume *idiot* means what it sounds like," he said. "Someone else called me *un pec*. Not nice either, I suspect."

"No. But really, they're just having their fun with you."

"That's not what it sounds like."

Beal sat down; with Thomas deep into the harvest preparations, the two of them were together more than not. "Lawrence, what are you doing here?" she asked.

"You've told me I cannot say what I am doing here." He waited for her to reaffirm that prohibition, a mere nod or an exasperated groan would have done, but she gave no sign. "If you want me to go, come away with me."

"Don't be foolish."

"I am not being foolish," he said.

"Just pack up and leave my husband, my son?"

"Of course you wouldn't leave Randall. He would come with you, to Boston."

"And Thomas?"

"Thomas would not put any obstacle in the way. You know that. He is a strong man, an extraordinary man, but he lacks the will to fight for you. He doesn't believe in the human heart, he doesn't trust it. He expects to be alone in the end."

"How can you say that? He gave up everything for me. What have you ever sacrificed for another?"

Lawrence held his hands out to indicate himself, his body, his rural clothes, his presence. "I should have been on a steamer out of Le Havre two weeks ago. Our business is suffering. My father is furious with me. He says that if I do not come home immediately, he will send my brother after me."

Beal could well believe all that; the poor telegraph boy in the village had worn himself out trotting up the hill to deliver cables to Lawrence. "Why?" she asked. "What is it that makes you do this? Whatever I have said or done to invite it, can it not just be forgotten?"

He reverted to his former position. "You have told me not to say."

"I am asking you now."

He did not answer. He didn't have to; instead, he turned it all on her. "You have chosen a course that requires you to be absolutely certain of your desires. But you don't really know what those desires are."

This hit deep; sometimes she felt as if she were being invented from above, that a unique sun bore down on her wherever she was. But then she also recognized that the most unyielding scrutiny on her was brought by herself, the hazard of all this *writin'*. "And you do?" she asked. "You think you know my desires better than I do?"

"Yes. Otherwise I wouldn't be here."

"I have made mistakes, but I am certain about Thomas and the family we hope to build."

"Then if that is so, I will just say that out of every human being in this entire world, on every continent, there is no one like you. I have already told you this. If you came with me back to Boston, you would be crowned queen. All those proper ladies would simply pale away into nothing around you. You are the next in line to carry us to the levels we deserve to occupy."

"I don't want to be no queen," Beal answered, with the almost hallucinatory feeling that none of this was real, that once again she was being pursued like a prize. "Enough. You must leave. Today. I'll tell Thomas you got urgent news."

"Whatever you command. But I will be back next year, and I will ask the same questions. If your husband will not invite me here, I will take a room in the village."

Thomas was not blind. He had been a little slow, but not blind about that African either, and when he'd discovered that note, it was not surprise that hurt him, but a feeling that the inevitable had happened. He faulted everyone—the way of the whole world—for what had happened, but he did not fault Beal; she was just trying to get by, and he knew it. Nor did he blame her for Lawrence

Goodrum as the man lingered, quietly tried to charm, pressed his suit. Beal's response to him—Thomas could see this—was simply not to respond one way or the other. Lawrence was caught, and if Thomas read him right, even he had begun to recognize that he was merely getting in line and rounding out the cohort of her current admirers. Lawrence might realize that he was acting the fool, but he didn't seem to care. There were a couple of unused huts and sheds on St. Adelelmus. What if Thomas filled the place with suitors, opened the spaces of the bastide for their jousts and brawls?

This was all about love, about finding a person in this world. Thomas could remember the astonishment he felt, at age seventeen, when he began to believe that Beal, at fifteen, would seek out time alone with him because she loved him, that she would take his side in the petty squabbles—and then, increasingly, the deep conflicts— with Randall because she had made a choice between her brother and the boy she loved. At night, in bed at the Retreat, he could recount to himself what had happened with her during the day, fun things, and feel them as a warmth in his blood, a tingling of pos- sibilities, a small whispering voice from deep in the feathers of his pillow. He had never felt anything like it, anything remotely like it, being chosen—winning, he might even say—though back then, there didn't seem to be any others in the race for her. They were just children, yet who would argue that a child could not under- stand that he was being offered a gift. Who would argue that a boy or girl had no ability to confer such a blessing.

After his seventeenth summer, everything began to change. Beal went to work as a maid for the Lloyds, Randall began to turn away from him, and later they were sent to college and Beal to Hampton, and through it all Thomas understood that what Beal had given him that summer could never be taken away, even if, as seemed likely, Beal herself would turn in a different direction and he would slowly succumb to the pressures applied upon him by his sister, Mary. Thomas had not expected Beal to remain true to him over the years, and if it was on the day of his father's funeral that she finally reaffirmed her love, it was on that day that her commit- ment to him was most ready, once and for all, to be forgotten. Aside from her love for her parents, there was nothing at home for her—her mother, more than anyone, argued this point—now that the peaches were gone, now that her father had taken his place once again as a mere farmhand.

Thomas had often wondered what might have happened if his father had died a mere month later. It took no effort at all, not a single fillip of imagination for Thomas to play out a completely different conversation with Beal, a conversation that would end with a handshake, with *You been a right good friend all these years*, or *I surely am sorry about Mr. Wyatt*, or *Well, I gotta be gettin' along before Aunt Zoe comes huntin' me up*. So easily what happened could not have happened. If it had been a rainy day and they couldn't have devised a way to meet; if her parents or his sister had prevailed and left one of them, either of them, sitting at the meeting place alone. Humans are strong, they live whether they want to or not; love is the reed, the weakest of nature. Could all that uncertainty really be washed away by a single yes? Believe me, said Wellington after the Battle of Waterloo, nothing except a battle lost can be half so melancholy as a battle won. This had been one of Thomas's father's favorite sayings, though in his father's life there had been few battles won.

After Lawrence left—it seemed to be a rather abrupt departure, though that required no explanation—Thomas descended deep into the harvest, the pressing and casking, into the first few assays of what they had got, always anticipating the ailments that might, overnight, render the entire year a loss. But at odd hours he thought a good bit of Lawrence Goodrum as a lost soul, a sad man but a good man, and perhaps, as Thomas pondered this years later, he had been too quick to dismiss the threat. Yet he simply could not regard the man as a rival as much as one of the legion of the lost in love.

Late in October, Beal sought him out in the vatting room. "Well," she said, with a small smile on her face, "it's got to be true."

Thomas excused himself from M. Murat. "What has to be true?"

"I'm pregnant. Four months. Something like that."

"Damn," he said, feeling dumb, searching for something better to say. "Four months," he repeated, thinking this put conception somewhere back in July. Not that it mattered, he supposed.

"Aren't you happier than that?" she asked.

"Of course I am." He made a show of being happy, eyes bright, arms raised. "But for a man, it just seems sort of far away. It's going to happen to me, but it isn't yet."

She laughed; she really was happy about this. So much happier, on the surface, than on that late night two years ago.

"You waited five months to tell me the last time," he said.

"I wanted you to know before everyone else figured it out."

He gave her a hug and then drew her away. "You're not afraid? Women don't think of pregnancy with some fear?"

"No. Of course not. Why would you ask that? I think it's unlucky to ask a pregnant lady that."

He apologized with a guileless shrug. "It just seemed that with Randall, you got more and more nervous. Even Arthur noticed it, if you can imagine such a thing."

"Oh," she said. "You try to give birth, then tell me it's nothing to be nervous about."

The wine was now doing its work in the casks, aging in its own private juice; they'd bottle some of it in March, but for now, there was nothing to do but wait. They had pulled up the last of the Aramon, and unless Thomas was kidding himself, the domaine was not sorry to see it go. In September he had purchased the hillside across town that M. Murat had in mind for Mourvèdre; Mourvèdre and Grenache and Syrah, such an obvious blend. He had been trying to figure out why it was so hard to graft. Yes, he was his father's son, but he made no backward glances; he thought only of grapes, dreamed of grapes.

Arthur joined them for Christmas dinner, complaining that his mother would never forgive him if she knew he had marked this awful holiday, and then he complained further when he realized that the roast goose being placed on the table was his favorite from the flock. "There are so many nasty geese," he said. "Why did the Señora take him?"

"I don't think it was a deliberate choice," said Thomas.

"Of course not. She took him because he was friendly and willing to let her draw close. He waddled over, and she grabbed him by the neck. Next stop: the oven. A lesson here."

"Arthur, what's happened to you? You used to be such a fine misanthrope; now even the geese like you. You're a regular Saint Francis around here."

"You mean the guy with the birds and bunnies?"

"Right."

At the end of the meal, in the slanting light of later afternoon, Beal left to attend to Randall, to help in the kitchen. The Señora had resisted this help, this intrusion, from the beginning, but now, after almost three years, she seemed to realize that Beal was never going to stop, that she did this work because she enjoyed it, that the community of women in the kitchen was something she wouldn't be giving up. Often there were more women than just the Señora and Gabriella, wives and daughters from St. Adelelmus taking a moment to themselves, enjoying a small glass of wine with this woman who spoke all the languages of the domaine and none of them. Sometimes there would even be a tiny drop of absinthe in a glass of water.

Thomas and Arthur remained at the table. "Beal and I are so happy for you," said Thomas. "Proud of you, if I can say that."

"If you can say that? Yes, you can say that. You saved my life, so I think you can claim almost anything you want."

Thomas deflected this. "What was I going to do with an old goat shed?"

"What you did has nothing to do with real estate."

They sat companionably for a few minutes. "So," said Thomas. "Is 1896 going to be the year you finish Beal's portrait?"

Arthur smiled; if the portrait was still on his mind, it had nothing to do with a career as a portraitist, as a painter in fact— which Arthur had now abandoned. He wasn't even drawing very much these days, giving his all to photography. That autumn he had bought a pretty good horse and a small depot carriage, with shelves and brackets for his equipment, and now he was off for days at a time. "That portrait was always more about me than about Beal. It was about what I wanted back then. I haven't taken it out of the crate since I got here."

"Or is Beal herself too unfinished?" said Thomas.

"That's not like you, Thomas," Arthur said, the smile gone. "Doing what?"

"Asking a leading question. She seems happy to me. She seems to have made her choices. She's said nothing to me that would make me doubt that."

The noise from the kitchen was cheerful; the bastide, Thomas reflected, was filling up nicely. He'd come to that conclusion in the course of the fall, and though his boyhood and his family's life in Maryland were now happily further and further into the past, he could not help—as if to give one last kick—comparing this bustle to the Retreat, which had become emptier and emptier as the years passed. And now, he reflected sadly, it was just Mary there, sleeping alone in their father's bed.

"Beal's pregnant," he said. "Due sometime in March."

"Yeah," said Arthur. "That's what she said."

"She told you? I should have guessed."

"Yeah," said Arthur again.

Thomas would not ask another leading question. Arthur was like her journals, a source that could not be tapped. In the fading light and now, in the quiet from the kitchen, they sat for a few more minutes. This whole thing, his life, was moving forward, obeying its own laws, and even if those laws were somewhat unknown to him, they represented order and goodwill. For now, it was the best he could hope for.

15

In early May, Madame Bernault took a bad fall in the hallway outside the kitchen at the Hôtel Biron. Suddenly she was flying through space, and as she landed, she marveled at the firmness of the stone meeting her face; God had put us on this earth to learn certain lessons, she thought, and the reality of the firmament was one of them. There was charity in such hard knocks. She heard herself say "Ooompf," and the next thing she knew, the lay sisters and the baker, M. Jolly, were propping her head up on a pillow and debating whether she had broken any bones. Word had been sent for the doctor, and as they all waited, she lay there, surprisingly comfortable, sort of elevated, with a series of restful images passing before her eyes, images of Quebec mostly, of the attic where she and her three brothers slept, but a few of her years here in Paris. Among them an image of tall, awkward, austere Mary Bayly standing at the curtain of her cubicle, expecting praise. Mother Lucy did not think she was dying—it was possible, of course, and no problem if that was so—but what seemed more likely was that she was *en état de choc*. Madame Bernault's conceptions of life and death, and of the rebirth and afterlife, favored what was plain, what was likely, what was small. If a modest and unassuming religious of the Society of the Sacred Heart was to be lifted in order to observe her own passing, then this was fine, but until that was proved, *choc* it was. Still, she knew as she lay there that she was in a very different realm from all the faces around her—somewhere between here and there.

She was barely aware of the time passing, of the doctor arriving, of the sisters carrying her into her room and putting her into her nightgown, and once again, with an almost ecstatic warmth circulating through her body—maybe she was already dead after all!—she felt bathed with kindness from all around her. She basked in their concern. She could not imagine that all these people would do so much for her—little, nondescript Lucy Bernault of Lac Fermat, Quebec. Then she slept—she had no idea how long—and this time when she awoke, the comfort was gone and her entire body felt as if she had been stoned, which wasn't far from the truth; one eye seemed swollen shut, and though her tongue found all her remaining teeth, her jaw felt as if it had been shattered. She knew then that she'd gotten all this attention because she needed it.

"Well, Mother Lucy," said the doctor, who seemed to have appeared instantly, "you had quite a fall."

She tried to agree, but couldn't get her mouth and lips to cooperate.

"It would seem that you have broken no bones. Luckily, the strongest bone took the brunt of the fall."

She was able to raise her eyebrows, or one of them, high enough to indicate that she wondered what bone that was.

"Why, your skull, of course." He said this happily. He was a young man, freshly minted from medical school, but for all his high spirits, he couldn't avoid taking things to a darker place. "It will take a while for you to recover. You will feel very, very sore. I hope it is bearable."

"Yes," she mouthed. Was unbearable an alternative available to her?

He asked her what had happened, and since she could not answer, he told her: she had not tripped on anything; her balance, which had been getting worse, was simply no longer reliable and she could no longer live as she had; honestly, it would be best if she kept to her bed from here on out. "You are so fortunate to be here in the hotel, where you can be looked after. You have earned this care," he said. "I hope you will accept it without complaint."

Which she did, because she had no ability to complain at that

point, no real capacity to reflect on being told that she should remain bedridden until she died. Episodes like this conversation with
the doctor passed in review before her eyes, but they seemed completely unrelated; they floated in time without context. As the days
passed, the pain of her injuries slowly diminished, and with help
she could get herself to the water closet, but she had no desire to
do anything more than that, returning to her bed thankfully. Her
thoughts, her memories, were now her vocation, and she had no
problem with this; one must accept. To do otherwise was to deny
God's grace. She reflected that their Blessed Foundress, Mother
Madeleine Sophie Barat, had spent her last years confined, at least
during the winter months, and that some of her most beautiful letters came out of this period. The illnesses and fevers of winter had
been God's way to slow her down, which was good because the end
had come swiftly. Her last words had been rather prosaic: "My head.
My head," she said on that morning in May 1865, falling face-first
onto the breakfast table.

Mother Lucy had no way to keep track of the days, and she
rarely asked. One of the priests would come in to celebrate the
Eucharist from time to time, and she figured those times were
Sundays, but she had no way and no need to keep track of how
many Sundays had added up. She had never been much of an intel-
lectual, but she recalled what Saint Augustine had said about the
nature of time: "If no one asks me, I know what it is." Any of these
man-made ways of keeping track of time began to seem completely
pointless, which amused her when she thought of her lifetime of
adhering meticulously to the canonical hours and the daily schedules in the various *pensionnats* where she had taught. These schedules carved something human out of time, and she had served as a
foot soldier in that good fight but was now willing to surrender.
The hours rushed in like the hordes at the gates, pell-mell, un-
marked, unchallenged. Death was the only clock that seemed
relevant now.

Madame Bernault would not have been surprised to learn that
the young doctor had announced that her end was drawing near
and that word should go out to her many friends that the time to
say goodbye was upon them. But she was surprised when people
began to appear, made manifest, it seemed, out of her memories

and dreams. They would come in and talk for a bit, mostly about years passed, and Mother Lucy knew that most of these visitors were in the flesh, but she also assumed that some of them were not. One day, about ten of the girls she had taught in Louisiana arrived, all in their frocks, none of them aged a bit, which was not possible. They sang her a little folk tune that she realized she herself had taught them, probably illegally. Her father paid a nice visit. She had last seen him more than sixty years ago, a kind if taciturn man, of a sort of which she'd known many. She was certain that this one was her father, as he was missing three fingers from his left hand. He asked her how it had all gone for her, and she answered that it had gone quite well, that she had risen far, much higher than could have been expected. This hurt his feelings about the humble circumstances he had provided for his family, and she spent the rest of his visit praising his goodness, his constancy, his intentions.

So Mother Lucy was not surprised one day to see Beal enter the room. It was a warm day, perhaps the first day hot enough to be called summer. She was not surprised, or she would not have been if there weren't two Beals entering the room side by side; this was a new wrinkle for her, as if, in her condition, she could now see the soul's shadow. One or the other, or both, must be an apparition. Of course, when she looked more closely, focusing her eyes, she realized that the other Beal was actually a different person, a younger, lighter-skinned version of Beal, a very beautiful girl.

"Mother Lucy," said Beal. "How are you?" She had come to her bedside and taken her hand.

The mental effort required to make sense of this dual apparition had sharpened Mother Lucy's awareness of the moment, and she was conscious of her own responses, that she was speaking out loud. "I am very well, my dear," she said. "I am so happy to see you. I have thought about you so often."

"Did M. Richard tell you I was coming?"

Now that Beal mentioned it, perhaps he had. Or perhaps not. Perhaps he had forgotten. Or perhaps he had asked Céleste—she visited often, of this Mother Lucy was certain—and she had forgotten. There were simply too many permutations, and Mother Lucy's brain no longer worked quickly enough to give any sort of response. Beal waited for a few seconds, then turned to indicate the girl with her. "This is Gabriella Zabala," she said. "I have told you about her in my letters."

The girl came forward, took her hand, and said how pleased she was to meet her after all Mme Bayly had said about her.

Mother Lucy was now quite in the moment, remembering well that this was the daughter of the couple who helped them in the Midi, that she had become Beal's almost constant companion. Her accent and dialect made her hard to understand, but Mother Lucy was raised speaking québécois, had come to maturity among the Creoles of Louisiana, and had long ago acquired the ability to focus not on the blossoms of language, but on the roots.

"Of course," she said. She reached up a hand to Gabriella's face, proving to herself once and for all that this was not a mirage. The face was warm; the girl leaned into her hand like a cat.

"Gabriella has come with me to help with the children. We have taken an apartment on the rue Cler for the summer in order to be with you."

The mention of the rue Cler threw Mother Lucy's grasp of time out the window once again; after all, a place could be anywhere in time. What children? Those two little girls, what are their names? She decided she would have to take all this in slowly, and indeed, when she next looked up, Beal was gone and in her place was a charmless novice. Perhaps, after all, Beal's visit had been one of those otherworldly ones, but this was a part of her life she was determined to keep straight to the very last breath, and she asked her sitter whether she had had guests earlier in the afternoon.

"Yes, Mother Lucy," she said.

"Two young women? There were two of them?"

"Yes, Mother Lucy. A Negress and an Occitane."

Oh, what joy. To see Beal again before she died. She hadn't even prayed for such a thing; faith is the assurance of things not seen, she knew that, but still, it seemed wrong to pray for anything in this life that you don't believe can ever come to pass.

Beal had never for a moment doubted that someday she would have to return to Paris, to finish with it one way or the other. Eons ago Diallo Touré had predicted that she and the City of Paris would be in a duel to the death—and since then she had read *Père Goriot*, horrified when she got to the end to find the words he had quoted to her: *À nous deux maintenant*. As in almost everything else, he had not been entirely wrong. So here she was. From the instant she and Thomas heard from the Richards that Mother Lucy had fallen and would probably not live much longer, they had agreed that she and the children would go to Paris and stay as long as it took for Lucy to recover, or depart; Thomas would join them when and if he could. Gabriella's going with them seemed obvious; introducing that beautiful girl to this beautiful city had been such a sweet thought, but Beal herself rejected it as soon as it came to her: she knew that Gabriella would never leave her mother. A rare visit from Gabriella's father, Señor Zabala, had made the difference. He was a wiry and slightly bruised man; if he weren't married to the Señora, he would have been invisible on the domaine. Beal was surprised when he sent his wife to her study to announce him, and he entered holding his cap and told her that there were no riches he ever could have hoped for, no blessing he could have imagined equal to his daughter being lifted to Paris, and if that happened, he could die tomorrow a happy man. For Beal, this was not Gabriella's father speaking this way about a daughter; it was her own mother, Una, begging her to seek a new life.

The apartment on the rue Cler that Thomas had taken for them was much smaller, much more modest than the generous spaces of the avenue Bosquet, but there was a nursery for the children and a small room for Gabriella with a window on the inner courtyard. Beal's bedroom opened right on top of the bustle of market days, which other tenants might have objected to, but Beal did not. There was no Mme Vigny this time, just the two young women and the two babies, and when it was hot, they would cook their fish or make their soup and then eat as a family at a little table by the window in Beal's room, watching as the spindly shadow of the Eiffel Tower marched down the street, their own perfect way to mark the hours.

Years later, Thomas treasured this image of them. Beal and Gabriella—he imagined them as a couple, though not as lovers. In her letters to Thomas, Beal scolded herself for spoiling the girl, buying her things at the Bon Marché, sending her off in the morning to wander as she herself had done, and then impatiently waiting for her to return with stories of wonder. As Beal had described in her journals, he imagined their sleeping arrangements in those brutal nights—a hot summer, one of the hottest in memory—as Randall and little Céleste fussed and had to be taken from one bed to another, Beal and Gabriella passing in the night in a swoosh of nightgowns, and by morning they'd all be in Beal's bed, not because all these hot bodies nose-to-toes made it more comfortable, but because their intimacy made discomfort more bearable.

Nearly every day, one of them, one or the other, went to visit Mother Lucy, and after a few weeks she seemed to have stabilized, to have become more lucid, at least when she wasn't tired.

"I have no gift for words, as you do, as Mary Bayly does," she said one day in the midst of a discussion of chestnut blossoms. "I was very simply educated."

By now, Beal was used to these sudden swings in Mother Lucy's conversations. "As was I. If you could call what schooling I had an education of any kind. But you can't be taught wisdom."

"Well yes. That is perhaps the point. But here is what I know: Before God, we can always speak from the deepest reaches of our souls."

Beal did not know quite where Mother Lucy was going. She said she supposed what she said was true.

"These past few weeks I have been trying to recall my prayers, my meditations before God. To remind myself what God, in His mercy, spoke through my body. This is something those who do not live a life of faith and devotion do not understand about prayer. They think we are just asking for favors."

Beal allowed that she felt *her* prayers were so often unworthy, were just about silly things. Mother Lucy said that when she reflected on this prayer life, by far the most important topic over the past four years had been Beal herself.

"Me? Mother Lucy, why me? What could you have said about me? You have bothered yourself too much about me. There are so many people, so many other young girls who need the light of your care."

Mother Lucy answered as if Beal had not spoken. "Some of it

might be painful for you to hear, if such a thing could ever happen, but that is the nature of grace."

Beal could imagine what recollections and perceptions Mother Lucy might be talking about. The painful ones, the hours of her agitated meditations when she saw Beal wavering in her marriage. And at this very moment Mother Lucy could know nothing about Lawrence Goodrum, who had arrived in Paris earlier that week. He'd written Thomas, begging an invitation to St. Adelelmus, as he had threatened to do the previous summer, and Thomas had replied that he was welcome, but that Beal was in Paris attending the death of a friend, a nun. Beal did not know why Thomas did this; perhaps it was simply his way of putting Lawrence off, as there was nothing in the letter about wine. Or perhaps it was his way of belittling Lawrence, treating him as a child. Or, more likely, it was simply a way of putting the challenge where it belonged. There it was in his first letter to her, dropped in as a complete afterthought, something that hardly deserved any notice at all: "Lawrence has written that he would like to visit. I told him that you and the children were in Paris caring for Mother Lucy. I haven't heard anything about his plans."

It had been sometime about the first of June that the concierge gave Beal a card and a short note from Lawrence. *À nous deux maintenant.* The note was quite correct, respectably addressing a wife accompanied by children and servants, separated from her husband while a friend—a nun, yet!—breathed her last. He had proposed that the next time she and Gabriella took the children to play at the Champ de Mars—she did not ask at that time how Lawrence knew this was something they did almost daily—they might meet for a lemonade. For his return address Lawrence had supplied not his hotel or other accommodation but a post office branch somewhere by the Panthéon, which seemed a little odd to Beal, but perhaps even safer. The last thing she ever wanted to know, for the rest of her life, was the address of the lodging of any man who was not her husband.

A day after he left his note at the rue Cler, Lawrence received her reply. Yes, she said, as he apparently had determined, when the weather was not too hot, they liked to walk at the Champ de Mars, to take an ice or lemonade at a little stand opposite the École Militaire, and she would look for him the next fine day. Lawrence had already seen them, from a spot behind one of the elms. What a vision! Beal looked perhaps a tiny bit heavier after her last pregnancy, but she still moved with grace—not catlike, really; more like a fox in a pasture. She would forever be a creature of the fields. The girl Gabriella had grown up as well, or maybe it was seeing her in this splendid park, so far from her life in Languedoc, that made her appear more mature, more worldly. When he first saw them, they were dusting and comforting Randall after he'd fallen on the pebbles. Together, with the two little children, they seemed a family almost too perfect to disturb. But onward.

He had spent the morning composing his approach, considering his affect—be plain, he kept saying to himself, be yourself—his words, practicing a facial expression somewhere between warmth and irony, but as it was, they approached from a direction he didn't expect, and they saw him first from behind. On hearing his name, he spun around practically in Beal's face. "Mr. Goodrum," she said, "here as promised."

It was not exactly the kind of greeting he'd hoped for, so proper, so chilly. He could do nothing but respond in kind. "Mrs. Bayly," he said, thinking he might follow through with the playacting, but—be plain, be yourself—he did not restrain himself. "Beal," he said, hoping the tremors he felt in his throat were not audible. He took her hand. She looked alarmed; it must be because of the girl, he thought, and let it go.

"You look very well," she said. "You look at home here in the city."

Something like this was what Lawrence was prepared to say—that she was even more beautiful here than at St. Adelelmus—so the best he could do was "You, too." Even as these meaningless bits were escaping his lips he was asking himself, You waited a year and crossed the Atlantic to say *this*?

She looked at him expectantly, as if he would do better, but when all he could do was smile blankly, she turned to reintroduce him to Gabriella. And then everything he had planned to say to

Beal came rushing out to the girl. "How wonderful it is to see you and how marvelous you look. So far from St. Adelelmus, and as pretty as ever. I would recognize you anywhere." Since he said all this in English, Gabriella understood very little of it, but she gave him a small, not totally friendly, perhaps even ironic curtsy when he had finished.

"Come. Let's have an ice at those tables," Beal said, pointing to the spot where he'd seen them before. When they reached their iron table and sat, he could think of nothing innocent to say; maybe the girl had picked up some English over the winter. The baby was asleep in the pram, but fortunately, the little boy began to tug at Beal's arm. Beal appealed to Gabriella, and off they went to chase pigeons. Lawrence saw the girl shrug a little, absolve herself as she walked away.

He turned to Beal. "You can't imagine the joy it gives me to see you. Here. In Paris. The city of light, the city of monuments. It seems like fate."

"That's what they used to call Baltimore."

"What?" Lawrence wasn't sure he heard right.

"The monumental city. That's Baltimore."

"Oh, Beal, for God's sake. Don't do this to me. Aren't you surprised to see me?"

"Thomas told me that he told you we were here," she said. "I don't know why he did that."

"And you're not glad he did, for whatever reason?"

"I don't know. It's nice to see you, Lawrence. I meant it when I said you looked well. Very handsome. Once again in France on your business?"

This wasn't exactly right. This time he was officially off the books, against his father's wishes. But in the end all he cared about was seeing her; he would travel thousands of miles just to post a few new images in his scrapbook of memory. He would travel like a penitent, book himself in steerage, and stay at some shabby lodging. He would pay for this without a cent of support from Goodrum & Sons. With each indignity, each fallen rung, he would further plight his love; he would stand before her a man without pretensions, without baggage of any kind. Just himself. He would invent his own path and, in so doing, become free, responsible, without excuse. That was his plan, and so far he had followed it; the boardinghouse he was staying in was indescribable.

"No," he answered. "This time I have come only to see you."

She let out a small puff of exasperation, but it was small enough for him to ignore; perhaps she was just doing it for show.

"You and the girl look very happy together. I'm sure you don't notice it, but your ménage gets looks from everyone who passes."

"We are having fun. How could we not be?"

"I thought you were here because this nun was dying," he said.

"We thought Mother Lucy was going to be slipping away, but actually she's getting stronger. I think Gabriella is offering her one more project, her last student. It makes me weep."

"But happily?"

"Yes. Of course. The things she says. The way she sees her life. She's my conscience, and she is with me all the time, showing me a good path."

"Which you don't always take?" Lawrence pushed himself to say this. It was stupidly forward, but this might be his single chance, and he had resolved that he would not go away wishing he had said more.

Again she ignored his subtext. "Mother Lucy is not rigid. She understands that people sometimes need to wander."

They sat for a minute. Beal jiggled Céleste's pram. It was a hot day, and all the women and girls were perched around the edges of the park, adjusting their parasols, fanning themselves idly. Across from them, the sentries in their boxes in front of the École looked like they were wilting. The parade ground in the middle shimmered like the Sahara, but the boys were all in the shimmer, playing tag, chasing, running.

"Boys," said Lawrence.

Beal laughed. "I spent all my childhood around boys. Were you this kind of boy, or were you more"—she hesitated—"shy?" In fact, Lawrence was more than shy as a child; even as his younger brother Randolph headed out into the fray, Lawrence hung back. But he saw no reason to apologize for himself as a child; Randolph, he thought, had become a dumb brute. As he reflected, Gabriella and the boy came back. The waiter brought them their ices, and Beal fussed a little with Randall's hat before she put a spoonful into his mouth. "*Mmmm. C'est bon,*" he said.

"He speaks no English?" Lawrence asked. Beal and the girl shared a look, and the girl smiled obscurely, a wordless exchange full of confidences and shared experience; Lawrence couldn't compete with that, he knew.

"*Gustatzen zaizu?*" said Gabriella to Randall.

"*Ona da,*" he said, laughing.

Lawrence assumed that this crazy language—whatever it was— was part of a joke between them, and he let it go. The children finished their *goûter*, what he knew they called a snack, and the girl took Randall back off to play at the edge of a fountain. He watched them go, and he could see the quais along the river and the buildings of the Right Bank through the spread palm of the Eiffel Tower. He was struck, even in this white heat, with how lovely it was, this moment. "I meant what I was saying. This city is the only city on earth that is your equal."

"Not Boston?" She smiled.

Lawrence took a start. He couldn't tell if she was teasing him or playing the coquette. But the mention of Boston, with all its stresses and uncertainties, dampened his mood. "Oh," he said.

"All is not well in Boston? That seemed to be what you were saying last year."

"No," he said. "Our prospects have never been brighter." He could tell that she didn't believe him, but she understood that he simply wanted to move on. He asked her about St. Adelelmus and the weather so far, about how Thomas and M. Murat saw things this year. She answered as well as she could. "But you'll see for yourself, maybe. I think Thomas may still be interested in working with you. That may be why he told you I was here."

Lawrence could stand this no longer, and the idea of going back to St. Adelelmus, where Thomas was master and where, Lawrence had every reason to believe, he would soon be leaving a brilliant mark . . . well, the idea of all that finished him.

He took her hand. "Beal. You know why I am here. You know what you mean to me. You know how I feel."

She did not try to remove her hand. "Yes, Lawrence. I do."

"I am not here to compromise you," he said.

"I understand that. I think."

"Then?" he said. He knew this was unconscionable, to thrust this question back at her, to make her define everything about where they were. In business, he had learned to manipulate suppliers to make the first offer, and he was doing that here. He was pleased, after a moment's reflection, that she didn't fall for it. She withdrew her hand and put it in her lap.

"Then what?" she said.

"Will you let me court you? For these few days. Here in this magical city. May I press my case?"

"Even if you have no chance?"

"Well, that's why you court someone. Because you have to win against long odds."

"I suppose," she said. She glanced toward the fountain where the children were playing.

Lawrence had never seen her look more Parisian, more desirable, more unassailable. "No one has ever courted you properly, the way you deserve," he said.

"That's what someone else once said to me."

"The same man who you said had shown you the ropes here in Paris?" Lawrence asked this innocently—there had seemed to be something there when she let this drop last year, but he made little of it at the time.

She snapped at him, a surprising snarl from her, something he had not seen before. "Lots of people 'showed me the ropes,' as you say."

Lawrence knew now that he had an opening; she had been wooed, it seemed, if not courted, and by someone other than her husband. He waited for her to compose herself. "Well?" he said.

She was still a little angered, and she responded forcefully, as if rising to a challenge. "Yes. You may. For these few days. In this magical city." She had finished by mocking one of his phrases again, but he had the answer he had come three thousand miles hoping to get.

Beal was not going to overthink any of this. The fact was, she was getting a little tired of this cramped domestic scene, the visits to

Mother Lucy, the walks on the Champ. Even Gabriella, sent off to find herself, was having more fun than she was. Gabriella had found the quarter where some Basques lived, and there was maybe a boy she liked; Beal had spied them meeting up on the Pont de l'Alma. Charming, lovely, and, with Céleste in her pram as cover, innocent. Maybe Beal was getting tired of innocence; Paris was supposed to be decadent, wasn't it, but actually it seemed strangely ordinary to her. Bread is bread wherever you eat it, so maybe bread itself is the problem. When she left Paris, it had seemed as if something had been ripped out of her body, but here now, she felt larger than the city and thus could not imagine what had been taken from her; it had seemed so tangible, this missing thing, but it was nowhere to be found. The Richards were as hardworking and good-hearted as she remembered, but for them, everything, every thought revolved around their hotel. In her first week she paid a call on the avenue Bosquet, and the girls Gilberte and Monique were no longer friends, had no interest in Beal. One of the mothers—whichever mother it was—was just a snob, the sort of person who would last two minutes in the Midi. It took moving there for Beal to see this, which struck her as disappointing. Who was I, back then? she found herself wondering. Do I really want to know?

So the next day, as Beal was dressing for luncheon with Lawrence in the Bois de Boulogne, she couldn't help feeling a small sparkle of pleasure. And why not, when there was no danger? The problem was Gabriella, as Beal had known it would be. They were talking in Beal's room, and she was looking out the window onto the rue Cler for Lawrence to arrive in a cab. Their argument was almost sisterly. "I have not complained when you have gone off for the day. Many days," said Beal.

"Madame knows that it is not my place to comment on how she behaves."

"Mr. Goodrum is a friend. There is nothing improper in my having lunch with him."

Gabriella gave her a pouty, disapproving look.

"Don't be impatient with me. You're acting jealous."

"That is not possible," said Gabriella in an almost haughty tone. "A servant does not feel such things about her mistress."

All this was especially irritating, or hurtful, to Beal, because over the years she had told Gabriella much—perhaps too much—of her life as a maid for the Lloyds at Blaketon, and then in Hampton, and about how she was supposed to behave and what she was supposed to notice and what she was supposed to ignore, and none of this, all these petit bourgeois airs, was how they lived in Languedoc. Neither Beal nor anyone else considered Gabriella a servant; there was work to be done in the house, a job, or jobs, and she did them.

She appealed for understanding. "Untxi," she said, using the pet name, Rabbit, that the girl's parents used. "Please."

The name helped, and Gabriella relented. "Oh, Beal. Don't go out with that man. I don't trust him. What are you doing this for?"

Each of these words caused Beal a slight jolt, but at that moment she heard the ringing of the cab's bell below, and she did not want to let Lawrence announce himself to the concierge. Putting on her hat and gloves, she took Gabriella in her arms, kissed her, and kissed the children on the way out.

Lawrence had arranged a picnic on the banks of the lower lake in the Bois; he seemed to have scouted out a place that was secluded enough for privacy but open enough to the paths and lanes to reassure her. Beal recognized this calculation as soon as she saw the spot. She waited while Lawrence spread the blanket, and after they settled, they sat for a minute enjoying the vista of the lake and the massive cedars, chestnuts, and lindens on the rise above the opposite bank. Families and young lovers paddled by.

"I was thinking of renting a boat, but I remembered that you don't like the water."

It was true; she recalled that she had said something like that to him. "I don't know how to swim."

"At college I had to pass a swimming course in order to graduate. The tests were held in a pond next to campus, and they waited until late October, when the water was as cold as it could get before it started to freeze. The cold was part of the test. And of course, we swam naked."

What a thought, all these naked boys in the freezing air. "Rich people, white people," Beal said, "they have to invent hardships to overcome. Wasn't so for us."

"No. But you have lived a charmed life. It seems that way to me. Your parents spoiled you?"

His last comment was raised to a question, but Beal turned her head sharply to face him; this was going a few steps too far, and her first impulse was to demand how he claimed to have any knowledge of her parents. But then she figured out where all this came from. "Oh, I get it," she said, relaxing back on her elbows a bit. "Arthur's theory about me. He has enough of them to fill a book."

"And he has written some of it down? Part of a study?" Lawrence was reacting to all this in a lighthearted tone, banter about serious things.

Beal was silent long enough for Lawrence's bemused expression to fade, but at that moment she was thinking about her own writing, and now there was this thought: "Arthur's portrait is like a book of theories about me."

"And you have never seen it."

"That's right. It's not from a part of my life I really want to remember." As she was saying this, all the confusion of those few months rushed back in a jumble, a collage of unwelcome visions: Arthur's studio, stripping naked in front of him, Touré, Les Halles, the Louvre. For a second she wondered how she had survived any of it. These, then, were the missing things. Why wasn't it past time to admit that she did not want them back? "I mean, it was from a difficult time, but I made it through."

"I think that's what Arthur meant to say."

"Well, what else did he say? About me. What confidences did he break?"

"None," said Lawrence. This time he was the one to straighten, to deflect the moment by opening the picnic basket and spreading out the food. Bread, ham, mustard, fruit, a sugar cake. Beal was relieved that he didn't bring along all those French foods that she would never really learn to appreciate: cheese, paté, cold fish in mayonnaise.

"None," she repeated, and then added the word he'd left space for but hadn't said. "But?"

"No *but*. Just that you and he do share confidences. Keeping secrets means you have secrets. I envy him. He loves you, but he doesn't want you. He's the luckiest man alive. He is a free man in your presence."

"I don't want anyone to be anything but free in my presence."

"That isn't something you have any control over."

"But not something I have to accept."

He handed her a deviled egg on a napkin. "Good?" he asked.

"Yes." As she was finishing the last of her egg, an especially charming young couple emerged from the bushes right above them, and the young woman glanced at Beal first in apology, glanced at Lawrence, and then looked back to her with a wink of solidarity. With Thomas, this was the kind of thing that never happened: that second look was always perplexed, at best.

"Is there really no girl for you in Boston? Someone to make you forget about me?"

"I am under great pressure in Boston. I would have to marry a queen. Like you."

"Please, Lawrence. Not this again. I am trying to live my life."

"I know," he said glumly. "I know you are."

"Can't we just drop this? Goodrum and Sons and St. Adelelmus. We're not in Boston and we're not in Azay-sur-Cesse. Can't we just be gay? This is so beautiful. If you're going to court me, I'd like it to be a gay courtship. Not something tragic. No opera, please. I would like just to be gay for a few days."

The next day, she took him to the Louvre. Although he hadn't planned it this way, she was showing him the stations on her way that winter, the paintings that had seemed to speak to her, to comfort her during those times. They lingered, because they could not help it, in front of the gigantic *The Raft of the Medusa*, and she laughed when he said, "Look at that African in the back. He's the one person in this whole scene who does not deserve what is happening to him."

She told him the story of the sinking of the French frigate *Medusa* off the coast of Mauritania, 150 men left drifting on a makeshift raft. "No one went to look for them, and only fifteen were alive when they were rescued—by accident. The colored man was named

Jean Charles. I don't know why he was on the ship in the first place, but he's the one who is actually looking for a way out."

They toured the various galleries that had been home to her in those months, and she surprised herself by how much she knew, how much she had to say about so many of the paintings. The Dutch—what fun it was to see again their little scenes of the home, of lives lived fully, without want. She didn't try to impress Lawrence—that was the last thing she wanted to do—but by the end he was both bored and amazed by the depth of her knowledge. "Three months before you sat here, you were a housemaid in Virginia. Can that really be right? There wasn't some gap in there that I know nothing about?"

She laughed. "No college. No swimming tests. Just my winter"—she waved her hand around at the Titians in front of them—"here."

"Doesn't that strike you as kind of amazing? I mean unbelievable, literally. Kind of hard to believe?"

"You're telling me I am lying? That Thomas and I have made up the story of our lives to deceive someone?"

"Of course not. But there was another man in there. Wasn't there. That sort of gap, in your story."

"There was a man who haunted me and tried to hurt me, and if you want to talk any more about that, I will refuse to ever see you again."

She had stopped him, but he did not want to let it go. "Well," he said, "you have been made over. I guess we leave it at that."

"That's the specialty of Paris," she said.

As they came out of the Louvre, he suggested that they wander over to Les Halles, perhaps find a nice café. Was he toying with her? Could Arthur have possibly told him anything about this? She stopped walking and stared into his eyes, but the truth was, she saw no knowledge, no subterfuge. "You know," he said, "the market?"

"I know Les Halles," she said, "but it is time I got back to Gabriella and the children." Which it was; Gabriella had not relented in the least, and Beal bought her way back in by telling her that she was being silly and that Lawrence would soon be leaving for his buying trip. She loved Thomas and her children, she said, and she loved Gabriella. Who could doubt this? Gabriella pointed out that Mother Lucy seemed to have stabilized. She was worried about her own mother, she was homesick, and she hoped they would soon be going back to Languedoc. "Of course we are," said Beal. "Don't you think I am homesick too?"

But two days later Lawrence was taking her out to the theater, and dinner afterward, and a few days after that, an afternoon at Montparnasse and then a long day trip to Versailles. These were all the sights any tourist would see, but on her first sojourn here, Beal had seen few of them. She and Thomas had not been tourists; their stay had been all business, if also all love. These outings occupied the gray area in between, and she realized that people made trips like this not so much to see the sights as to have an excuse to spend time in one another's company.

And then—would there be the other kind of time in his company? Lawrence had been mysterious about where he was staying in Paris, and that suited Beal, but would he offer a country inn on their return from Versailles? Pop off the train in Sèvres maybe, everything all arranged. Beal didn't want to think of it, but she did think of it because that's what courtship was supposed to lead to. Because that was the test, it seemed, of everything between a man and a woman, as stupid as it sounded when said like that. Beal was a farm girl; there was no domesticated species she hadn't seen copulating. Lawrence was being proper, but he was as sneaky as a rooster. Would he pounce? It was easy for her to imagine the whole thing, the awkwardness, the undressing, the touching—easy for her to imagine because she had done it before. She could even imagine that it would be fun, that she would like it. She assumed that Lawrence thought of it every day, but it was one subject he never even hinted at. Then, in the train back from Versailles, she had an extraordinary revelation: He had never had sex, not even with a prostitute. Lawrence had indeed been a shy boy, and he was, for all his show, a shy man who didn't know the first thing about how to make it happen. So if it were to be, Beal knew it would happen only if she took the lead, which was the best possible situation.

To keep from having to think of this, they talked. Talking was all that she needed from Lawrence. They talked and talked and talked; such a change from Thomas. She had grown up in Tuckertown with storytellers but had never known anyone like Lawrence, someone who talked as he did with such ease, who could talk about anything, and about nothing. It felt good to Beal to *say* things, to *converse*. But sometimes, riding in a cab or sitting in a café, she found herself a little tired, wishing for the ease of silence. She had delayed their return to St. Adelelmus once again, but all this bright chitchat, all this gaiety—well, once she recognized that he would never be able to back her into a corner, that she couldn't escape except through a bed somewhere, the chatter lost its thrill. It was becoming tiresome. Lawrence seemed too eager to please; she guessed that was what he thought courtship should be, but for her, the whole thing was a spectacle, all those professions of love. Paris was just a backdrop; for all she actually went into the buildings on street after street, they could be stage fronts. Who were the players here, the ones this city had been created for? Perhaps not Beal, though for a few tiny instants in the past—say, January of their first year—she believed it could be for her. But not now. The more this went on, the more it became an unreal city for her, a city of ants, or dreams; she began to wonder what she was doing here when St. Adelelmus beckoned, when Gabriella and the children were caught in the froth of her indecision, and now, of her boredom. Things were becoming clear to her, thoughts became objects that she could observe, tuck away or bring forth. Lawrence was not one of those objects; he was mist, or foam. She felt as a physical sensation pieces of herself rearranging, like a ship's cargo that had become unlashed in a rough sea.

After three weeks of this, one afternoon Beal and Lawrence were walking along the Champs-Élysées. She did not want to admit it to herself, but all along she had been steering them toward safe territory for her, these Right Bank haunts where she and Thomas had never gone, where none of the artists she knew would ever visit. Far too expensive, for one thing, though Lawrence seemed pleased to let Goodrum & Sons give her the kind of luxe she'd asked for. They ended up at the bottom of the avenue in a café called Le Rond Point, and Beal surprised herself by asking for a glass of Champagne. He ordered a bottle. She found the first sparkling glass surprisingly refreshing and asked the waiter for a second. That morning she had promised Gabriella that this would be the last time she saw Lawrence. Why not have fun, why not be dangerous? Why not, especially because he had pressed his case, had made his last wagers and had fallen short. For the first time, she asked herself exactly what it was that had attracted her to him. The wine was helping her see things clearly; maybe wine had a use after all.

"Sometimes I used to think I married a man who is too serious for me," she said. "I was just a girl who loved to laugh. The only times I wasn't laughing when I grew up was when I was with Thomas. I had to change my face when I saw him. But maybe that was good."

Lawrence seized on the opening, as she assumed he would. "I don't care about whether the man you married is too serious. I just care that the man you married isn't me."

This response struck her as stupid and dull; ardor is a tune with one note. She was getting tired of this, and the bubbles had loosened her manners. "Oh? Tell me. What would my life be as Mrs. Lawrence Goodrum?"

"You're teasing me."

"No. Really." She leaned forward to prop her elbows on the table and tip her chin into her hands. There was a painting of a woman doing this that she had always liked. Was it Toulouse-Lautrec? Manet? A girl at a bar.

"I have already told you. I have already proposed to you."

"But you have not proposed that we sleep together."

He recoiled, but was able to stammer out that sleeping together would be a joy too complete to be imagined.

"I have thought about it, you know. I have thought about you and me together. Over the winter, when the winds near blew us off our feet, I found myself wondering what I would be doing at that very second if I was married to you. Would I be having ladies, white ladies, to tea? Would I be at the dressmaker's? Would your sister and I be walking in Black Bay?"

He corrected her: "Back Bay."

"Oh, wherever. Now you're being a pill."

"Beal. Please."

"When we met you, it was Boston this and Boston that."

Even as she was spouting away like this, Beal realized that she was causing Lawrence pain. She didn't know why, but in some awful way it gave her pleasure. This snippy, mean little girl thing; the pleasure it gave her in the pit of her stomach was all sexual. This was the only sex she would have with Lawrence. She'd seen the Parisian girls practically make their suitors crawl on all fours, and the men did it willingly. At the Bon Marché, back then, she'd see the sick, almost terrified look on the men's faces as their lovers amassed their purchases, and Beal knew, as not all people would, that the women were sucking every centime out of the man's purse. She realized now that this terror and abuse was part of the dance, that when the girl finally allowed him into her bed, he would attack her, stab into her just to get back, and she would be sore for days; the kind of girl who played this game would want this rough treatment at the end. Yes, the man would take what he'd paid for and then some, and just to make sure she had understood everything, Beal lingered on this image, the lovemaking, and she could feel the warmth of it in her own body.

"Ask me to sleep with you," she said.

"So you can refuse? So you can destroy me?"

"I'd like another glass of Champagne," she said.

"You have had enough. You're not used to it. You're drunk. I'll get you a cab."

"So tell me. Why don't I know where you are staying? Why do I have to send my letters to the poste?" It seemed with every word she was scoring more points, making him wince.

"It's just more convenient."

"Show me."

"There is nothing more that I would like. But not now. Not with you being like this."

"Like how?"

"Like unworthy of yourself. Like worthy neither of me nor of your husband."

Beal couldn't believe she had earned quite *that*, a two-pronged assault, shaming her on both sides. Wasn't she just being a little playful? Wasn't this how one flirted? She was too wobbly to be angry but sober enough to be hurt. "Why are you so mad at me?"

"Because you have no idea what it has cost me to spend this time with you."

"I never asked you here. I told you not to expect anything from me."

"Don't be a child. You have encouraged my affections since the first time you drove me to La Fontaine. The mistake I made was to believe you wanted them. That you weren't just playing the coquette."

Beal wanted to defend herself, but useful words did not come, and besides, she could see fury in Lawrence's eyes.

"All this talk of 'my husband.' All this 'I'll tell Ibarra to turn the carriage around.'" For a second she was frightened of him. "You think you're innocent, but there is nothing the least bit innocent about your innocence." Beal's head swam with that, as much of the meaning as she could parse; each attack seemed unfair yet strangely illuminating. "I'd hate to think that I have wasted years of my life, that I have longed almost to die, that the greatest love I have ever known has been for a woman who . . ."

Beal's brain was flooded, flooded with wine, with all this hard truth being poured into the middle of a harmless little pastime. "Who what?" she asked blankly.

"I don't know. You tell me, if you want. What kind of woman have you been to me?"

She tried to answer, but it was impossible, and soon they were in a cab, her cheek rattling against the window. Lawrence walked her up to the apartment, and as soon as Gabriella saw her, she recognized that she was drunk. Words were spoken between Lawrence and Gabriella, but Beal could not concentrate enough to make out what they were saying, in what language, with what intent. It was still only late afternoon, but Gabriella put her to bed. She awoke in the middle of the night with a headache, miserable, mortified. She sat at her window and waited for the predawn arrival of the merchants, those kind and simple people who had befriended her when she couldn't say a word of their language, when she was innocent of almost every offense she had now committed. It was the Champagne. Why was Thomas in the business of making this sort of thing happen to people who were otherwise decent and thoughtful? Was this what St. Adelelmus was wreaking on the world? But that line only went so far. It wasn't Champagne, she understood, that made cruelty into pleasure. That made her unworthy. Maybe it was the city, Paris itself, that made her behave like this. She nodded off for a time, and when she awoke again, the greengrocers and fishmongers and butchers had begun to set out, as they did day after day after day, their wares in colorful array; imagine if they knew what Beal had been up to, the cruelty of her favors. The fault did not lie in Paris, but it was time to go home. Mother Lucy was beginning to suspect something; there could be no secrets from her. Beal was risking all, beginning with Gabriella's love. And Thomas; it had been almost three months since she'd seen him, since she had heard his voice, felt the intimacy of his body.

But she could not simply leave it with Lawrence like this. She couldn't have him in the world thinking she was unworthy. In the morning she sent him a note of apology—what could she say?—by pneumatic post, asking if he would agree to meet, and if he did not come, she would take that as the answer that she most probably deserved. She would tell him that the whole terrible episode was her fault, that yes, she had lied to him, a little, when she said he had no chance with her. Because he did have some sort of chance. She didn't mind a bit being courted, and when, finally, she figured out what she was doing, she lashed out. Yes, she was unworthy. She would tell him that he had given her the gift of his affection, his belief in her, and she was unworthy of it. She proposed dinner, a final dinner in her mind, and a few hours later the response came that he would call on her at the rue Cler at six o'clock. About dinner the reply said nothing.

It was a rainy day, a day with a touch of fall to it. They were into August, which meant the summer was done; the Paris idyll was over. She would be leaving with no regrets. Whatever Paris had ever meant to her, whatever it could do for her, it was done. She had outgrown it; Diallo Touré was right again. The rest of Paris was left to the greengrocers, to the grisettes and the clerks, to the artists, to the families and aristocrats. Beal was none of these.

She had told Gabriella that she would be going out that evening, that this was the end of it, that there was nothing to fear. She begged Gabriella to believe in her, to trust her this time. Gabriella said that she could have no opinion on it. Beal must do whatever she thought was correct. What they had, earlier in the summer, was now gone, and Beal grieved for that almost as much as anything else. Those hot July days, those nights with Gabriella beside her in bed, smelling her hair, a hand on her hip. Why couldn't that have lasted; why did she risk it? Randall was becoming a little boy; Céleste was sitting up, almost getting ready to walk at a ridiculously early age. Beal was ready to return. She wished with all her heart that she had not agreed to the evening ahead, that she could send a note to Lawrence with her regrets.

Around four in the afternoon she heard the heavy clang of the knocker, and soon the muffled sounds of the concierge talking to a man, and for a moment she feared that it was Lawrence, that she had gotten the time wrong. But it was not Lawrence. When she opened the door, it was Arthur Kravitz who appeared.

"Hello, Beal," he said. He bowed, as if this were theater, as if he were waiting for the audience's murmurs of surprise to die down. At this point there was almost no one in the world whom she needed more than Arthur, and no one in the world she wanted less to see. He stood in the doorway like death, a dark, heavy figure, a spirit here to extract some sort of retribution. If Mother Lucy was her conscience, guilty or not, Arthur Kravitz was the one who carried out the sentence. "Are you going to let me in?" he asked.

"Of course. I'm just surprised."

"Figures," he said. He walked in, nodded at Gabriella, who returned his look, revealing no surprise at all. Randall ran over to him and grabbed him by the knees; Céleste pounded her little feet in the air in delight. "Hello, House Rats," he said to the children. Randall howled with pleasure. Beal shushed Randall, and Gabriella—again, this seemed rehearsed—was already preparing to take the children out for a walk. These preparations left Arthur standing just barely in the door, giving Beal time to rearrange her thoughts, to restore the dress she had planned to wear for the evening to the armoire. But once they were gone, she invited Arthur to sit at the table in the kitchen.

She got right to it. "Has Thomas sent you?"

Arthur sat heavily in Gabriella's spindly little chair. He looked wrong there, in this refuge for women and children, a bear, *un ours dans le salon.*

"Not really. Should he have?"

"Not really."

Arthur smiled. "Not really" was a world he understood very well. "You look lovely," he said. "More beautiful than ever. And Gabriella. A young woman now. The two of you together must have driven the Parisians mad."

"You've already seen her, right?"

"Of course. I dropped by yesterday, but you were"—he paused—"out. I have been here for a couple of days."

"Your work?"

"Yes. The photographs. We're preparing an edition."

"I'm happy for you. I'm so proud of you. Are you moving back up here now that you have the means?"

"No. My means are in the Midi. As long as you will permit me to live in your unused goat shed, you have me. This is just my market."

"I'm glad. And painting? Is that over for you? Will you ever finish my portrait?"

"You mean my masterpiece?" He laughed.

"In other words, you'll let me see it."

"Of course. The mystery is over. But you'll have to go back to St. Adelelmus to do so."

"I am going back, Arthur. I am going home to my husband and my life."

For a few moments they waited each other out, which she knew reflected no particular reluctance on Arthur's part to get to the point, but an opportunity for her to open the discussion.

Arthur shrugged. "Lawrence will not be expecting to see you this evening," he said. "Lawrence believes you asked to see him only to be kind. He asked me to say goodbye."

"Goodbye," she repeated, as if delivering the message to herself. "He's not going to St. Adelelmus? Visiting vineyards?"

Arthur looked at her with impatience and a small amount of disbelief. "You think that's what was going on?"

"Well, no. Not exactly. Not here in Paris, anyway."

"Beal, business is not booming for the Goodrums. They've closed their new store in whatever fancy place it was. This is what I hear from Morris Malone. The fact is, the North has caved in to what was always the true American way. Malone said that the real Boston Brahmins are reclaiming their territory, and the Irish and Italians and Jews are grabbing up what's left over."

"How sad," said Beal, a rather lame answer, but maybe she'd never really trusted everything Lawrence said, much as she'd wanted to. "Morris Malone? You've been busy."

"We're two peas in the pod. The Irishman and the Jew."

Beal ignored this line. "Still, the Goodrums must have some family money from their business. Lawrence has been playing the part since he came here."

"What do you mean, his family money? He's been taking you to cafés on the Right Bank, but he's living in a boardinghouse no respectable art student would be willing to enter. Somewhere well beyond the Panthéon. Took me an hour to find it. Maison Vauquer, it's called. The place smells like a sickbed."

Beal tried to sound shocked, or sympathetic—or something.

"You didn't suspect this?"

"Well, yes. I guess I did. But not so bad as all that."

"When I told him I was here to end this, his whole body slumped in relief. I gave him money to pay for his passage home. When I was leaving, he hit me up for a few more francs to buy his train ticket to Le Havre. He spent his last cent on you."

"You mean I took him for every cent he had?"

"No. I don't. The guy's completely gone. He kept saying that I would never understand how cheaply you could buy him happiness. I kind of understood what he meant. You couldn't have stopped him if you'd tried."

"I could have tried. Harder."

"If you say so. I didn't say you were blameless."

In fact, Beal could say nothing. The sun's evening rays were beginning to move across the table. The cafés on the rue Cler were beginning to fill, the voices of the young. Beal no longer felt that she was one of them; yet another part of her youth that had fallen into the gap.

"He made it clear to me that nothing happened between you, as hard as he tried. That you'd told him from the beginning that he had no chance with you. He made you seem unassailably honorable. Pure, really."

"Well, we know that isn't true."

Arthur ignored this. "He said he thought you liked him well enough, and I said you did. After Thomas and Gabriella."

"I have been so mean to both of them. To Gabriella, trying to talk sense to me. I can't believe I could hurt her like that."

"She's strong. Don't worry. She's fine."

"And Thomas?" she asked.

"I was wondering when we were going to get to him."

"Does he think I have been unfaithful to him with Lawrence?"

"I don't think that's the way his brain works. I don't think he trades in suspicions, in conjecture. He'll think you have been unfaithful to him if and when he knows you have been."

"I haven't been. You'll tell him that?"

"If he asks. Sure. I wouldn't be surprised if Lawrence writes to say it himself. And if he does, Thomas will believe him. I would. But really, wouldn't it be best if you told him yourself?"

"I will as soon as we get home."

"No need to wait for that. You can tell him yourself. Tomorrow. Here. He's on his way."

16

When Thomas left St. Adelelmus on the first of August, he was not sure he would end up in Paris. He'd fixed it in his mind that he would go when Mother Lucy died, or when Beal summoned him to attend her last days, yet every letter from Beal indicated that Mother Lucy was growing stronger and stronger, a woman of perhaps seventy-five who had no intention of dying anytime soon; Beal assured him that there was no reason to rush to Paris, that she would be returning any day now, just a few things to pack up. But the "any day" had turned into weeks.

From the moment she and Gabriella and the children left, almost immediately after he helped get them settled on the train, Thomas had been running nonstop. Beginning with the Greeks, people had been making wine in Languedoc for almost three thousand years, but that summer Thomas acted as if the future, a window to do something, could be counted in weeks. There were new holdings to buy, a few hectares here, a few there, all arranged around the compass, as if to take on any cultivar, any season, any storm, any drought and still have something to harvest. There were new vines to see that sent him scurrying back to his library to research. There were growers to spend the day with, dreaming and despairing in equal measure. He didn't have time to travel in a gentlemanly carriage, but instead clattered through the villages on horseback like a cuirassier, minus helmet and breastplate. He picked his way home even in the new moon; one night he got lost and slept in a field. What St. Adelelmus became in the years to come, the reach of its ambitions, the prominence it achieved dated not to the day Thomas bought it in 1893, certainly not to a winter of research at Galignani's library, but to that summer of madness. The farmer's life is about waiting and hoping; Thomas, that summer, resolved to do neither.

Waiting had worked, with Beal, in the past, but this was different. He responded to Lawrence's letter with a flourish of resolve: *Let him try*, he thought, but it wasn't as if he were sure of the outcome.

Arthur thought he was being a fool. "Don't you have to put up a fight? Just for show anyway? Isn't that what women want?"

"No," said Thomas. "This is something Beal has to do alone. You know that as well as I do. I have made a choice about how I want to live. You have made a choice. It's her turn, even if it is late in the day."

"She made a choice when she married you. Isn't that what 'I do' means?"

"No," said Thomas again, this time a little more sharply than he intended. "The way things were on the Retreat then, there was no choice. This was never as simple as boy and girl."

"Maybe you're wrong. Looks pretty 'boy and girl' to me."

Thomas spent his daylight hours single-mindedly, maniacally engaged, but he couldn't do much about the loss of heart deep in the nights in the bastide. The bed never stopped feeling empty; the dawns never stopped feeling grim. St. Adelelmus, the whole domaine, was bereft without her and the children, and without Gabriella; maybe it was nothing but the master's vanity to believe that all the families in the domaine cared a bit about what went on in the castle, but even Arthur felt it. He was getting ready to head off himself. In the beginning of July the Señora's husband had come to Thomas with the admission that he did not feel he could keep her safe too much longer, that sooner or later she would wander so far that no one could find her, that she would fall into a chasm in the mountains, be attacked by wolves or bitten by a viper. From that moment on, even as Thomas tried to ponder the next step for the Señora, he realized that she and Beal were a sort of pair; it seemed tragically likely that the Señora would never find what she was looking for. And Beal? Time would tell. These thoughts spun out into long fibers of speculation, and none of it was fun. At his worst and weakest moments that summer, Thomas could believe that even as the vineyards and winery of St. Adelelmus were marching forward, the stone-cold bastide was cursed. That was what his father had said the morning Randall's body was found in the mule barn at the Retreat: *We are cursed*, he had said into the devastation of that day. *This farm is punished for what it did to the Negro.*

But Thomas didn't entirely believe that about the Retreat, and he didn't believe it at all about St. Adelelmus, and he didn't believe his worst fears about Beal. The subject here was love. What he believed about love was what he had figured out in his first lonely year in Philadelphia at the University of Pennsylvania, that true love is forbidden love, that there is no place in life or literature for a love that faces no barriers. Theirs had faced more than its share because it was a truer love, because it survived and prevailed over greater obstacles. But the time of testing wasn't over, maybe would never be over, and he knew that not just because of what Beal had been through, but also because of what he learned with Eileen Hardy. Maybe the mistake people make about true love, in life and literature, is to think it must be the only love, that the heart can swell for only one. There had been no scandal with Eileen, nothing the priest would have to hear about if that was something Thomas did; but the warmth in his heart and his attentions during those confusing months in Paris, the refuge she offered, the opportunity to be invisible at her side, something in the world other than the notorious Thomas and Beal—he had surrendered to all that for those hours and weeks at the reading room, he had allowed Beal, in those minutes, to be completely supplanted, and that was the most unfaithful thing he had ever done, or would ever do, in his entire life.

He did not commit the same crime that summer in the Midi—surrender to daydreams, pretend to different lives, to different loves—but more and more during these hours he felt that Eileen was with him. For the first time in his life he felt as if he had a confidant, a *confidante*, and more and more he addressed his thoughts to her and occasionally had the terrible feeling that he had spoken some of it aloud. No one around him would understand what he was saying, but still, they'd know that his solitude was getting to him. Imagine what they would have thought if they knew that half of his babbling was her imagined responses, her telling him he was right to keep busy and to trust the hours. She told him that what she saw in Beal's pale eyes in that one instant three years ago was enough for the ages, that wise but ferocious look. And so it was in the course of such reflections that he decided to do what he had wanted to do for the last year and a half, which was to stand on her grave, thank her for her care, and bid her goodbye. It was almost August and Beal was delaying her return yet again; there was no reason not to do it now.

It was a fine day, bright but cool, when he arrived in Bordeaux. He had two hours to make the short walk across the river to the Gare de l'État, where he would catch the branch line to Libourne, next to the region of Fronsac. Over the months, he had learned a good deal about Alan Hardy, and about Bordeaux, which was five or ten years behind Languedoc in the cycle of blight and replanting. Still, no one seemed to be suffering, losing all as they had done in Languedoc. Some of these tiny holdings in Médoc, Pomerol, and Margaux were among the most valuable acreage in the world, and if it had taken a hundred years for a solution to be found for phylloxera, these holdings would not have lost a bit of esteem and value. As long as there was one bottle of wine being produced in Bordeaux each year, that bottle would float miraculously above the ocean flowing out of Languedoc. None of the châteaux were falling down. Money continued to flow in from Paris, from England and Ireland; for every relatively underfunded parvenu such as Thomas Bayly buying a mountainside like St. Adelelmus, there were ten Rothschilds buying ten tiny domaines like Lafite.

Alan Hardy and Thomas had exchanged several letters since Thomas's first quick response of condolence. In that, in his shock, he had stepped closer to the truth than he wanted, but he had spoken out of love, which had been a comfort to her father. Thomas had said that her reconciliation with her father must be counted as a real mercy, and Hardy had taken no offense that Thomas made oblique reference to the reason for their quarrel. From there the correspondence had moved more into business, and Thomas learned that the once-fine little region of Fronsac had been decimated by the blight more than almost any other in Bordeaux, that Alan Hardy was starting over from scratch. Far from being in a position to sell Thomas some cuttings, Hardy saw the much younger, much-less-wealthy Thomas as the veteran, a survivor and a mentor.

Thomas did not have difficulty picking him out in the crowd at the station in the thriving town of Libourne. There was no stunning red hair, but he was short—as Eileen had been—and florid, and otherwise cheerful, unmistakably an Irishman among the darker *bordelais*. He pumped Thomas's hand. "Welcome to Bordeaux," he said. "I am delighted to meet you at last."

Thomas answered that he felt the same way and thanked him for agreeing to welcome him on such short notice.

"Not at all," said Hardy. "Nothing much doing in August. As they say . . ." He didn't bother to complete the sentence.

Thomas laughed; in one minute he felt an affinity for this man—a good soul, if not an entirely spotless one. Thomas had no idea what sort of household he would be visiting, and he was not surprised to be introduced, upon arrival, to Genevieve de Bose, the cause of all the trouble those years ago. She was trim and gracious, but muted, not the type to go looking for a scandal; if they had made one, it was a quiet scandal, and now this couple seemed content to live with little connection to outsiders.

"Eileen's friend," said Hardy to Genevieve.

"Of course." She turned to Thomas. "You can't imagine what this means to Alan, to have you here. We hope you will spend a few days with us."

Thomas thanked her and said he would look forward to seeing the domaine, learning a bit more about the region. He didn't know exactly how to add that he looked forward to seeing Eileen's grave, and the question was not forced on him; that was the reason for his visit, they all understood, but it did not have to be the focus of it.

"Splendid," said Hardy.

The small, comfortable house was a mere hut compared with the châteaux of the left bank of the Gironde, the wineries of the Médoc and Margaux—modest even compared with the larger establishments next door in Saint-Émilion and Pomerol—but it sat on a nice rise, with a view over the copses of oaks and the vineyards to the Dordogne River. The entire holding, Thomas had learned from Hardy, was little more than ten hectares, about a fifth the size of St. Adelelmus, but the small size seemed to fit this gentle land. From where they sat on the terrace Thomas could discern four or five distinct properties, a neighborly way to farm compared with everything he had known, the vast stretches along the river shore at the Retreat, the battalions of vineyards marching up the side of the Black Mountain at St. Adelelmus. Everything was lush and inviting; water was not a problem here. But whatever the differences, Thomas felt the same sort of comfort he felt at home, a lack of pretension, an honest simplicity; the grapes did this, made this feel the way it did no matter where they grew.

"I admit," he said, "that I had certain misconceptions about Bordeaux." He beckoned to the view, in itself so blameless and unassuming, so carefully kept that it provided its own answers to Thomas's "misconceptions."

"That has been clear in your letters," said Hardy with good cheer. "Eileen herself had a quite negative view."

"Yes," said Thomas, trying to evade. "I think she said something like that."

Hardy laughed guilelessly. There were few subtexts with this man; most of him was on the table. "She said she told you to have nothing to do with Bordeaux."

"Well," said Thomas, "it's true. She was the reason I ended up in Languedoc. But she was right. It's a life I'm used to."

"Perhaps that's my point," concluded Hardy. "Really, we are all just farmers. Even at Château Latour they are all just farmers at heart."

Genevieve stood up. "Any time Alan mentions farming, I know we are in for it. I'll leave you farmers to talk about grapes." She left, and they talked, the beginning of a conversation that would last many years, but at dinner it was Genevieve who asked Thomas to tell them about Eileen and that winter in Paris.

Thomas told them everything he could remember. It seemed that each detail, each tiny gesture brought joy to her father. There was no need to prevaricate; whatever misdeeds he had committed, either to Beal or to Eileen, were well understood and long since forgiven in this house, a house that had its own history. He told them about standing in terror in front of the bookshelves that morning, when everything seemed pretty impossible, and then, over his shoulder, the gentle Irish whisper, *Are you all right, Monsieur?* He described their teas hunched at the tiny tables of the tearoom; he didn't have to tell them that their knees touched. He described the meeting they'd had after he came back from Languedoc, how strong she had been, how honest in the face of his untruths. "Oh, now," said Genevieve. He told them that he had misunderstood her boss, M. Vaucluse, who seemed unpleasant and dyspeptic but was really being fiercely protective. As the conversation progressed, Thomas found that he could not tell the story without talking a little about Beal too, and about her winter in Paris and the move to Languedoc and the difficulties in all that. "She's in Paris now," he said.

"From what you have said, it sounded as if she were away," said Alan.

"An elderly friend of ours was very ill, but it seems she has recovered."

"Well then," said Genevieve, "it's right that she is there," but Thomas heard in that affirmation an acknowledgment of all the uncertainties he might have been expressing. They sat in silence for a minute or two, but it was a sort of familial silence: plenty to say, to talk about, but taking a rest. This must be what it's like to have parents, thought Thomas; they're concerned, but they won't probe. This must be what it's like to visit a place you call home.

But in all the pleasure of recalling Eileen, deep into the evening around this friendly table, they could not avoid the fact that after she left Paris, she came to Bordeaux without gladness. She had lived with her father and Genevieve for almost two years after this, and it had not been a happy time for her. They tried to divert her, introduced her to the few women they knew who were roughly her age, tried to interest her in a trip to America. There were men, in Paris before she left and here in Bordeaux, who tried to woo her, but she turned them away. If she had been looking for a husband, she would have gone back to Dublin. Instead, she chose to close herself off here, in a place she did not like all that much. She often took the train into the city to go to the library, to read and also to write, but she was secretive about it.

"We think she was writing about a young woman in Paris," said Genevieve. "It's a novel, we think."

"We would be happy for you to look at the pages she left, if you would like," said Alan.

"I can't imagine I would be the best reader," said Thomas.

"Perhaps not," said Hardy. "But any character based on you would be given a sympathetic treatment."

"I think I'd be more afraid to see what she made of herself, if that's what fiction writers do."

"Yes," said Alan. "She was secretive." He said that even as a small child, she'd have nightmares, and her mother or he would go to her, but she would refuse to tell them what she had seen. It seemed that these fears were private for her, that what scared her, even at six years old, was not something she could share. Her fears turned inward. "We Irish are good at that," said Alan. He paused and then took a turn. "The home her mother and I made would not have helped."

Genevieve put her hand on his arm to quiet him. "You did your best," she said. "So did Maeve." She turned to Thomas, for the first time took him into her gaze. "What I think you need to understand is that Eileen was a girl of some sorrow."

Thomas could not react, a stranger in the middle of this excruciatingly private conversation. But he did not feel out of place, for almost everything they said made him realize that he had understood her better than he realized at the time. He said that he had seen a little of this, the underlying shadow on her smiles, but at other times she could be so gay, so quick with wit; she sparkled the way a real girl of sorrows could not.

"She was that way around you," said Genevieve. "You gave her moments of happiness. That is why Alan wrote to you."

"I assume Alan wrote to many of her friends," said Thomas. He glanced at Alan for affirmation, but Mme de Bose had the floor now.

"No," she answered. "He did not. We recognize that you were married during the time you knew Eileen. We have heard of your quite remarkable wife. People in Bordeaux know your story more, I think, than you realize. But you should understand that for us, for Alan, you will forever be a son-in-law he never had."

The room they had put Thomas in was on the third floor, under the eaves. It was not a room for a guest, more like a room for the youngest boy in the family, but it was the right place for him. On the way up, Genevieve had shown him Eileen's room, the room where she died, all her books still in piles, sprigs of dried flowers and lavender woven into the mirror frame, and when they backed out, Genevieve closed the door behind them gently.

Thomas bid her good night with a handshake and crawled quickly into bed. He lay awake with the echo of what Genevieve had said, and he realized that he could do that, be a son of some sort to Alan Hardy. He lay on his back, the covers to his chin, in a remarkable, maybe even narcotic comfort. The minutes, the hours ticked by on the grandfather clock at the bottom of the stairs; he felt as if he were ten years old again, but a different boy in a different house, with different parents down the hall. He said it plainly to himself: This is something I have been looking for all my life, this is a missing piece, this is air that fills a void.

He would tell Beal all about this trip, every detail. He would start with the first letter from Alan, and he would tell her not in the form of confession of a further wrong he had committed, but as an acknowledgment of a blessing he had received. Of a great light he had been shown, and this light, Thomas believed, would illuminate the path ahead for both of them. He would tell her that he had loved Eileen, and that this love only magnified the love he felt for Beal, for the lives they were living. He would bring her to Bordeaux to introduce her to Alan and Genevieve, and for them she would come to stand a tiny bit for their dear departed daughter. As they grew older, as their children became adults, they would bring them for visits, and these young men and women could show Alan what might have been if Eileen had survived.

Thomas awoke early, came down to the kitchen for coffee, and asked the cook for directions to the town, a mile or so away. He set off before Alan or Genevieve appeared—it seemed that they were staying out of the way for him—and his first stop was the post office, where he sent a telegram to Arthur, who had gotten to Paris a week or so earlier. His next stop was the churchyard, the cemetery next to the ancient *presbytère*, and there he found the simple stone among the more elaborate monuments, crypts, pieces of statuary. It was a lonely sight, this single grave amid the plots teeming with departed families, but it was peaceful and private, and there was room beside it. *Secretive* was perhaps the word, yet Thomas did not feel that she had ever withheld from him. There was no one else in the cemetery, so Thomas sat down at her feet and told her, half out loud, that he had loved her in a very pure way and would remain a member of her family, would be loyal to her father and to Genevieve. He could not imagine a more comforting thing to say to a person who had died young. And then he told her all about Beal, about the obstacles they had faced, which he realized now were not so exceptional, which had nothing to do with race or with cities and farms, but were what one would expect of two people so young and so inexperienced trying to set out in life together. He felt that Eileen would agree, that she would further argue that recognizing this was the first step toward a mature marriage, and that she would tell him it was time he was on his way.

When he got back to the Hardys', he found Alan sitting alone on the terrace. Thomas told him about visiting the grave. "I had thought," he said, "that I would do it with you, but I guess I needed to be alone with her."

"Yes," said Alan. "That is what we reckoned you'd want to do."

Thomas described his visit, sitting on the pebbles of the path, talking to her.

"She loved that church. She asked to be buried there."

"There seems some room for you by her side."

Alan nodded with a cheerful smile.

"I have been waiting for my wife this summer," said Thomas. "She has decisions to make, I think."

"Then I would think you have done the right thing. To stand back a bit."

"We did so much in the wrong order, in the wrong sequence. I believed this time would right things. My friend Arthur Kravitz says I'm nuts."

"Ah, *les vignerons*," said Alan. Thomas nodded, and Alan reflected for a moment. "If that's the way you think of it, this waiting would have required considerable fortitude, but everything you have said makes it sound as if it will work out in the end."

"I've sent a telegram to Paris. It is time I went. It is time I brought my family home."

"I would think so," said Alan. "We'll put you on the train back to Bordeaux tonight and you can catch the early mail express tomorrow. You'll be in the Quai d'Orsay by midafternoon."

"That's what made sense to me," said Thomas, and they sat in this restful silence.

Alan, for all his cheer, was a man who did not fill the air with unnecessary talk—a man like Thomas himself, a man, perhaps it might be said, of sunshine and shadow, like his daughter. Above them, a single white stork, perhaps getting a jump on the flock for the trip to Africa, or perhaps lost, glided majestically in the thermals. "I can't tell you how much this visit has meant to me," said Thomas. "I wish I could stay longer."

"You were very kind to come." Alan patted Thomas on the knee. "We'll have plenty of opportunities in the future to see more of you. But now your only responsibility is to your family."

Beal woke up late the next morning to the sound of Gabriella packing their trunks. Beal had hardly slept. The night before, she had made soup, their last pistou on the rue Cler, and they played with the children until they were ready for bed. They were all happy; even little Céleste seemed to understand that they were going home. After the children were asleep, they sat together at the kitchen table; the light in the apartment was yellow with a very full moon. Beal apologized to Gabriella for what she had been doing these weeks, a sort of *folie*, but now it was over.

"You do not have to say that to me," said Gabriella.

"I need to say it until I am sure you believe me," Beal said, but it was unnecessary. She asked Gabriella if this had been fun for her, being in this great city, and she answered that she was grateful for everything, she would never forget a moment of it, but she missed her home and was glad they were going back.

At about nine a boy arrived with a telegram from Thomas. He was on a train and would be arriving at the rue Cler around three. Arthur had told her that Thomas was in Bordeaux and that he was taking the express, and she supposed she could figure which train it was and go meet him at the station, but standing in a crowd, waving when he appeared—she had done that before, and this time it seemed too public. The words one said on a railway platform were meaningless anyway: *Did you have a nice trip? I have a cab waiting.* Whatever the right words were, they weren't that. Beal decided that she would wait for him here, in this little home; she'd send Gabriella and the children out for one last ice on the Champ de Mars, which they would like. And besides, from the vague way Thomas had written about his plans, it seemed that this is what he wanted too.

It was a strange experience, she thought, to feel that a whole part of one's life could end as if it were a chapter in a novel, that one could turn the page and move on to the next adventure. Arthur had concluded it in just a few lines—Lawrence says goodbye, gave him money for the train. It wouldn't take more than a paragraph in her journals to be done with Lawrence. Maybe even done with her youth, which now, as wife, mother of two, she was ready to shed. Packing her clothes, she lingered with each item: Where did this come from? Who was I then? In the next room Gabriella was singing a tune quietly to Randall, a children's song he loved. "I met my beloved on Monday . . . I met my beloved on Tuesday—*Ai rescontrat ma mia diluns / Que se n'anava vendre de fum. / Luns fum, tòu! / Entòrna-te ma mia, entòrna-te que plòu.*" The sound of those words was like an aromatic puff of smoke from home for Gabriella, but also for Beal; she remembered that the person she always heard singing in Occitan was Mme Esquivel, in the washhouse at night, and that memory brought the rest of St. Adelelmus into her eyes, the little winding road past all the dwellings of the families, a place that suddenly seemed irreplaceable to her. She had always thought of the domaine as Thomas's new Retreat, but she had never realized that this tiny familial village was her new Tuckertown; the memories could be as sweet if she allowed them. Leaving it meant that she had twice forsaken her real home.

Beal did not know what to expect from Thomas. That he had telegraphed Arthur before he contacted her meant something, though exactly what she didn't know: Was it a symbol of the distance between them, or was it a kindness? She didn't know why he was in Bordeaux, and though there could be many business reasons, she suspected that there was more to it. If it were just business, he would have told her he was going. She couldn't imagine him in this Paris apartment, where, in three months, an entire life had been lived that did not include him; he'd be too big for this space. Without a doubt he would hit his head on the door frame of her room. She knew he would be hungry, wouldn't have eaten a bite all day because he didn't like to eat on trains, and she would need to drop down to the markets for some cheese and sausage. Perhaps even, of all things, some wine to wash it down.

She didn't know what Thomas would do, what he had in mind, but she knew her own mind perfectly. She would tell him everything she could imagine about Lawrence Goodrum, and she knew that the more she said, the less important it would seem. Because there had been nothing to it. She would tell him that she was ready to go back to St. Adelelmus, this unlikely refuge, and that now, more than ever before, more than the moment when she agreed to marry him, more than when she stepped on the gangplank to *La Touraine*, when she stepped on the train to Languedoc—she would be admitting much here, much doubt—her heart and mind felt joined, that she was whole. She could not fight the rising tide of joy she felt. So many mercies, and all the more magical because they were undeserved. Undeserved, but she would not dwell on that. She was astonished by what had happened to her. By her life.

At lunchtime she went down to the street to buy the snacks for Thomas. Paris was now in its August lull, resting for another year. September, that greatest of months, would soon be upon them, and if July fairy tales were now being replaced by the realities of fall, that was good. How astonishing! Life itself is a hymn to life! She walked up to the river, and it felt good. She and Thomas had walked here so many times, along the Quai d'Orsay from the Pont de l'Alma to the Pont des Invalides. The first time was in November; they'd been in France for a week, married for three weeks. That was not a lifetime ago, it was a point in her past that was simply irretrievable. She had dozens and dozens of memories from times before— growing up at the Retreat, working in Hampton—that were so fresh in her mind that she could hear the voices, as if these people were standing next to her; those times would always be with her. But those first weeks and months with Thomas? No. She could recall a few outings with the little girls, maybe. Diallo Touré, alas. But nothing distinct and sharp about herself and Thomas, just the sensation of having passed time together, having endured. This made every bit of sense to her. She had been only slightly in the world during those months, too terrified about the next hour to spend any effort recording the last hour. Even now, thinking of this peculiar state of mind, she involuntarily turned to look behind herself, as if something would be sneaking up on her. She had been nothing then; she had wafted through the events like smoke. But now she felt she could grasp her life by the shoulders, give it a vigorous shake, and it would fall into line.

When she got back to the apartment, Gabriella had already left with the children. Beal tried to read a little, but instead she sat by her window and watched the traffic. Perhaps she dozed off a bit, and then she heard Thomas talking to the concierge, heard his heavy-booted footsteps on the stairs and a slight knock before he opened the door. They looked at each other down the short corridor, and for a moment that's all they could do.

"Hey Beal," he said. For years this was how they had greeted each other. *Hey Beal, want to go to the river shore and collect shells? Hey Beal, want to go see the litter of piglets? Hey Beal, want to come sit with me on the bench? Hey Beal, want to go home?*

She nodded. "Hey Thomas," she answered.

17

Many years later—after they had come home from Paris and restarted their marriage as adults, and they and their children began in earnest the life's work that St. Adelelmus became for all of them; after the crisis of the wine lake that almost destroyed them, and the winemakers' revolt of 1907, which made Thomas locally famous; after the Great War and the beginning of the Great Depression, after all that—Thomas and Beal received a visit from Edward Mason, the man upon whom his sister, Mary, had settled the Retreat before she died, in 1920. When Thomas and Beal escaped, in 1892, Thomas had renounced his rights to the place and never for one second looked back, and thus, as Mary was approaching her early death from cancer, she had bequeathed it to this Edward Mason. Their mother, Ophelia, who for many years had had nothing to do with the place or with either her son or her daughter, had died a decade earlier. Edward Mason was, as well as Mary could determine, in the direct line of descent from the immigrant Richard Mason, who'd arrived there in 1658. Over the years, Thomas had gotten several letters from Mason, the first one a gracious and humble letter of condolence; he seemed to be offering Thomas a chance to reverse Mary's act. Just to make everything clear, Thomas replied that he supported all of Mary's efforts to settle the place on a Mason heir, and he hoped Mr. Mason would find a good use for it.

The next two or three letters remained reasonable and deferential. Mason had apparently bought some kind of manufacturing concern in England; the letters adopted a sort of bonhomie, a fellowship, businessman to businessman, suggesting that they might share insights as to the challenges of building a business on foreign soil. Thomas was noncommittal. Over time, the letters—with various return addresses in England—continued, perhaps one every other year, and their tone became a little more aggrieved, as if Thomas and Beal wouldn't understand his difficulties; he was out in the modern world and they had retreated to a sort of fairyland. Mason appeared to have some wildly idealized vision of them, and he felt Thomas owed him something in return. Thomas and Beal discussed this. As far as they could figure, this odd affect had nothing to do with the Retreat. Beal's sister Ruthie tended to send them a semiannual roundup of news of the Retreat, of Tuckertown, of births and deaths and the general level of hope and despair, and it seemed that from one year to the next, nothing was heard from, or about, the man who now owned the farm. To Thomas it seemed that this increasingly needy man wanted some kind of sympathy or support that Thomas, and Thomas uniquely, could provide; he opened Mason's letters with increasing dread.

The letter announcing that Mason, his wife, Edith, and their two young sons would be available to pay a call arrived in the spring of 1934. "He says he'd like to get a lay of the land," said Thomas. "It sounds as if he's planning to buy us out."

"Oh," said Beal. "*Ne sois pas si critique.*" Somewhere along the line, maybe soon after they returned, they had started speaking to each other mostly in French, and then exclusively, except when they were quarreling. Without discussing it, they agreed that speaking in the language of international diplomacy, a language full of deference and indirection, reaffirmed their choices, their love, their hopes for the future; breaking into English for an argument signaled that the stakes of reverting, as always, were high.

Thomas continued. "*Il croit que . . .*" He went on to describe Mason's view that they had much to discuss. "*Pour l'amour du ciel,*" he exclaimed.

Again Beal encouraged him to give the man a chance. "Mr.

French and Daddy both said he meant well." Just before Mary died, Mason had spent a memorable day on the Retreat, mostly with the farm manager and his wife, coincidentally named French. Over the years, Thomas had gotten the unwelcome impression that they spent most of the day discussing himself and Beal.

Once Thomas had written back saying that he and Beal would be delighted to welcome them at the bastide for as long as they liked, Mason turned over the finalization of the details to his wife, and in turn it was Beal who responded, and by the time the Masons arrived in mid-June—they would be staying only for the day—the two wives had formed a warm connection. It was "St. Adelelmus weather," as Thomas thought of it, a light breeze fragrant with blossoms and sea air, the sunlight still yellow and soft. On days like this, even forty years later, he was still almost embarrassed to be showing off such a home to strangers. Just as Edith had promised, at about ten o'clock they heard the car chugging up the hill. From the sound of the gears crunching and the engine racing, it was clear that Mason was not an experienced driver, but these were not easy roads. The car, a massive, expensive Delahaye, roared into view, and when it stopped, it continued to rumble while the driver flayed around at the controls. By then Thomas and Beal were standing at their front door.

When the engine finally died, Mason got out, stretched, and glanced back at the car as at some sort of adversary, a piece of junk unworthy of him. He was a big man; Thomas had had this impression from the letters, yet he seemed very young, over his head with this car, with all of life. Thomas expected this, but he was not prepared for the red hair, and it gave him a chill, this Mason hair, his mother's hair. One of the themes of Thomas's life.

Mason finished his pantomime with the car and turned his attention to the farm and the view; he made everyone wait while he went through a complete audit of the mountain and the vines, all of which he pronounced exquisite. "Beggars belief," he said.

Thomas said he was pleased that they could finally visit, after all these years of correspondence. He hoped they'd had a good trip so far.

"Splendid," said Mason. "Superb." They'd come down from

Bordeaux. From Médoc, actually. A friend, Lord Belsen, owned a château there. This was his car. A terrible brute, the car, not Lord Belsen. Ha-ha. They'd spent the night at Carcassonne. Had Thomas and Beal been there? The Hôtel du Midi. It had seen better days. But this, St. Adelelmus, was lovely.

Thomas was worn out already. "Thank you," he said. "We have worked quite hard." As he looked around, it was notable to him—this was not the first time he made such an observation—that from where they stood, one could see virtually no structure, no amenity, hardly even a cart or wheelbarrow that hadn't been there the day he bought the place. The changes were within, in the caves they had built underground, in the roots of the vines deep into the chalk and schist, and in the bones of the domaine, where they mattered. His sister, at the Retreat, had basically razed the farm after Thomas and Beal left and built a whole new enterprise, a sanitary dairy. Which, if Thomas understood right, had proved to be only a slightly better bet than the peaches. If Mason ever took that place in his hands, they would be very full.

The wife and children were getting out of the car now, brushing out wrinkles, taking in the view. Beal had told him that she liked Edith, Edith the letter writer; she was an unusual-looking woman, dark and secretive, with sharp eyes and cheekbones and a slender frame that would be called lanky if she weren't just barely five feet tall. There were two children, an unhappy and vaguely untrustworthy-looking adolescent and another boy, a timorous lad of six or so.

Thomas welcomed her, and she thanked him in return. "Edward has been so looking forward to meeting you. A cousin?" she said, finishing with a slight question.

"Of some sort," said Thomas. He watched Beal lead Edward and the older boy into the bastide. The younger boy stayed plastered to his mother's side.

"I have so enjoyed writing to Mrs. Bayly."

"Oh, Edith," said Thomas, "if I may. It's Beal."

"Yes. Beal. The legend." She gave this last a nice ironic twist, meaning she understood the reasons that Beal—the negotiator, the deal maker—was known and admired in wine country, even in

Bordeaux, as was Thomas of course, but she thought the idea of a legend was silly.

"Beal said she enjoyed your letters. I hope they continue."

"She's such a beautiful writer. I can't express half of what's on my mind. But she seems able to say things for me."

"That's very sweet of you to say."

"I've been a little lonely," she volunteered, but not as a dark truth, something she would say with lowered voice, but as a statement of fact.

"Beal knows all about loneliness. And homesickness. Believe me."

"Yes," said Edith with the kind of suppressed smile and secret strength in her eyes that showed she would keep any confidence. "She said something like that."

From inside came the sounds of a tour in progress, and Thomas could easily have suggested they catch up, but he was drawn to this fragile but resolute person; everything that had happened to her seemed obvious to Thomas—unhappy marriage, lonely exile. These were fates he and Beal had avoided, but not without struggle. When they entered the hall, he could hear Beal and Mason trudging up the stairs after inspecting the basement. Thomas didn't know why she was doing that—he didn't want Mason prowling around the very foundations of his life—but Edith volunteered that Edward loved old houses. "We have lived in several old properties in England," she said, not that happily.

Thomas surprised himself by jumping to the one topic he had hoped to avoid. "Have you seen the Retreat? Have you been there?"

She said she had not, but that lately it had been on her husband's mind. "He describes it as quite grand," she said. "From his one visit."

"The Mansion House is big. But I would never call it grand, even with whatever my sister did to it after I left."

"So you have never been back? Even before your sister died?"

"No. We haven't."

She seemed to be reflecting on all this deeply, and finally she let it all out in a surprisingly definitive manner. "I've gotten the impression that what you have done here and where you came from are all connected. That you did not come to France to turn your back on the Retreat, but to fulfill it. That's why you have had such a success." Thomas made some sounds of demurral and was trying to process the surprise he felt when she continued. "I am sorry to speak so forwardly, as if I presume to know you. But I have thought of you a good bit over the years."

"Not at all," he said. "Someone said something like that to me many years ago." He stopped it at that, but she knew there was more to it.

"Someone you cared about?"

"Yes, cared about a great deal. A friend who died, but her parents became very important to us, to our family here in France." They stood side by side, sharing what he had said, understanding that within this little tale there were turns and twists that didn't need to be explained; it was all long gone, dust sprinkled onto the earth.

She broke the moment. "But never back to Maryland. Not to visit Beal's family? Might you have arranged to do that safely? You're French citizens now, isn't that so?"

"Yes. Before they threw me in jail in 1907, they had to let me become a citizen."

She laughed. Thomas continued to be charmed. "Jail?" she said. "Not really?"

"No. I never actually went to jail, but after they arrested Marcelin Albert, someone had to talk to Clémenceau. An American wouldn't do, so they made me French." This was all pouring out carelessly; he was hardly thinking of what he was saying, his mind still back on the moment of starting out, when Eileen Hardy had said *How about grapes?*

"I'm sorry?"

He snapped back. "I'm being extremely impolite. To us, all these events have a rather biblical importance, but there's no reason you should know about any of it. In the wine world it was the second Revolution, the only difference is that everyone saw it coming. A big mess back then. But enough of this. Let me show you around."

"That would be lovely."

By now Beal and Mason seemed to have exited through the

door onto the terrace, and Thomas was pleased to wander through the house with the young wife. He showed her his office, and when they turned to leave the room, she saw the portrait on the wall, behind the door.

"Why, that's Beal," she said.

"Yes. I hang it here because she doesn't like to look at it. Our friend Arthur Kravitz did it, our first winter in Paris."

Edith studied it for a minute or two; she had narrow eyes, and she squinted at it as if following the path of each brushstroke. "She looks quite annoyed, doesn't she."

"Yes."

"It's not very good. Her hand is wrong." She held her own hand up to her shoulder and showed that it couldn't quite twist the way Arthur had painted it. She had spoken the truth but was about to apologize when Thomas laughed.

"Good for you," he said. "Arthur would agree. That was back when he thought art could uncover truths; now he thinks truth makes art. That's why he makes photographs."

"I've read his book," she said. "*The Goat . . . Barn*, was it? I liked it."

"*The Goat Palace*," corrected Thomas. "A long-running joke. For years he was grateful to us for giving him a place to work. Then he woke up one morning and realized we had him in a goat shed."

"Not really."

"Well, not exactly. Anyway, he hasn't lived there for more than thirty years, but the building is still his. Some of his old equipment is still set up there. People come by to look at it."

In all of five minutes Thomas had fallen for Edith Mason, this surprisingly tough little doll, not that much older than their youngest, Marie, who was twenty-five. He wondered about this blustery, impatient, and probably doomed man she was married to; why would a sharp woman like this, all edges, marry such a doughy person? He reminded Thomas of their daughter Marie's new beau, who was a law student in Montpellier and seemed just as mismatched.

"So," she said. "St. Adelelmus. What ghastly torture awaited him at the end?"

"Actually," said Thomas, "as far as I can tell, he died comfortably in his sleep at a ripe old age. He was canonized for being a very sweet guy."

"Well," said Edith. "I think that's probably worth sainthood." She laughed grimly.

They were turning to go, but he wanted to give her one last thing, a gift he was sure she would understand. "She was angry, actually," he said. "Beal. In the portrait. Up until that point she'd never been allowed to be herself. Arthur caught her at the time when she was just figuring that out."

They joined Edward and Beal at the stone table under the chestnut tree. One of the two sisters who now worked for them in the house brought tea, and lemonade for the children. The older boy was nowhere to be found, had peeled off the tour, bored by his father's questions and comments, eager to run. As seemed often to be the case, Edith went off to retrieve him.

"Well, Mr. Bayly," said Mason in her absence, "I am impressed, sir." He seemed not all that comfortable sitting with Beal.

Thomas had no impulse to propose that they use first names. "It has suited us. Forty years ago a very wise man told me that running a vineyard was a calling for an entire family. Many times I might have given up without Beal and our children." He said this in part because Mason obviously had no idea what he had in his own young wife; indeed, the idea that one's wife is one's partner flew a mile over his head.

Many times during that summer when Beal was in Paris, while Thomas raced around Languedoc in order to avoid simply waiting for a sign of some sort, he had asked himself, What am I doing this for? Who am I doing it for? He asked those questions not because he didn't know the answers, but to remind himself that he was blessed to *have* answers. And then he brought her home. They returned, riding together with the children and Gabriella up the last climb to St. Adelelmus, and he had never seen such joy and relief and gratitude on Beal's face; she consecrated each rock and rill, each structure and person as she passed. He knew then that as painful as it had been for him, he had done right to let her go, to really release her, and that now she was ready. For the first time, her commitment seemed equal to—no, greater than—his. Maybe that's the only way to see love from another, to trust it: when it is greater than your own. Maybe when love is only equal to yours, it hides, it gets eclipsed. Perhaps she had finally caught up to her vows enough to understand these vows not as promises, but as dreams, dreams that could become hard fact only if one were willing to make them so. Yes, their time at St. Adelelmus really dated from that day, the day when Beal said, in so many words, *I do.*

The return from Paris had not turned out so well for Gabriella. That morning, the Señora had alternately flown from one end of the bastide to the other, getting things ready, and had sat at the table in the kitchen, weeping. Then, when the carriage pulled up and Gabriella ran to greet her, she seemed stunned, confused, unable to speak. It soon became clear that she didn't immediately recognize her own daughter, and from that point on she began the steep decline that ended with her in the hospital at Béziers. It was her size, her strength that was the problem: a normally jolly person, when she needed to move, she could overpower her husband, her daughter, the Sisters of Saint Theresa who tried to take her in. Thirty years after she was taken away, people still shook their heads in sorrow over her.

Thomas looked over at Beal as this journey made its passage in his mind. A little bit of gray hair, a little heavier. Sixty-two years old and not a wrinkle to be seen, not a blot, the face of an angel. His skin: God, what a mottled wreck! Nothing that day would have suggested that in only a year he would be sitting here alone in this cherished spot, and she would be dead.

"We have been blessed by our children," said Beal. "We have been lucky. I won't even try to warn you who will be at lunch with us. Your boys will be right at home with our mob."

Mason didn't have anything to say on the subject of children.

"It's too bad our friend Arthur isn't here," said Thomas. "The boys would like him."

"Oh, yes. Arthur Kravitz. Marvelous. 'The eye of the Midi.'"

Yes, some critic had called Arthur that, though it was presented as an irony that an American Jew had the eye of the South of France. Still, Thomas was pleased that Mason had heard this. "Arthur came to France trying to escape a life in Newark, New Jersey, and found everything he loved about Newark, its people, here in the provinces."

Mason was not interested in Arthur Kravitz. The conversation lagged. Maybe there was nothing more to the visit than this; maybe Thomas had been arrogant to think there might be. "Ah," Mason said as Edith and the two boys returned. "Here they are."

In fact, the group had been gathering for lunch. Randall and Justine. Céleste and her husband, Etienne Milhaud, over from La Fontaine for this midsummer luncheon. Marie, thankfully without her man. Their younger son, Wyatt, was in Bordeaux. Gabriella was visiting from Béziers with her granddaughters, Thérèse and Camille, two pretty girls in matching billowy blue muslin dresses. A smattering of children, most of them Thomas and Beal's grandchildren, but some unidentified. They had all wandered in and plopped down here and there on the semicircular wall that bounded the terrace, on the green bench, or seated at the stone table. Maybe it was all these children and grandchildren—these days Thomas's mind sometimes skipped a generation or two, and he couldn't tell who was whose—but the scene seemed to hark back to a painting or a snapshot he'd once seen—he couldn't remember where—of a nineteenth-century family reunion, Beal in the center, Thomas behind her, his long legs crossed, gazing across the valley; Gabriella seated primly at the small round table in front of them; and all around them the children, the men in stiff collars and bowlers and top hats, and the women with their great skirts and high necks and full sleeves and ample shawls. Thomas wished Arthur were there to take a photograph, but it might not have been necessary, as the image continued to haunt and comfort him until his last days.

They repaired to the dining room, with the French doors thrown open. Additional chairs and utensils were brought in, large books placed in seats to elevate the littlest ones. Thomas sat Edith and the younger boy beside him at the head of the table, putting Mason beside Beal at the foot. Bowls of pasta were brought for the children. Most of the family had been warned that as good hosts, they who had any English should probably try to speak it, but this lasted only a moment or two in the center of the table, and it interested Thomas to see that the older Mason boy, Sebastian, seated in the gaggle of young people, seemed to be doing just fine as the languages flew right and left. An interesting boy, thought Thomas, a most promising youth.

Before he carved the ducks, Thomas stood to welcome the guests, telling all assembled that these Mason visitors were now owners of the family estate in Maryland where Thomas and Beal had grown up, and it did not surprise him that as he sat down, Mason rose to respond. He asked, not unwinningly, for silence from "the peanut gallery." He was very gracious, congratulated one and all, took a sip of wine, and then held it up as a totem of all they had accomplished. This "splendid luncheon" in this "magnificent estate," this family, all these friends—he said that he and Edith, though they were well established in England, missed this part of life and that perhaps one day a meal very much like this might take place in the dining room at the Retreat.

Thomas found this a little overblown, but for the most part he appreciated the sentiments; the little hint at the end was charming. For a second he tried to imagine such an event, under the scowl of the notorious portrait of Cousin Oswald that hung over the fireplace in the dining room; it was a nice idea, a warm gathering in that chilly place. Thomas did not, had never wished the Retreat ill. He looked over at Edith with a sort of pleased, sated feeling on his mind, but he found that she was clutching her napkin, that she looked stricken. For a moment Thomas feared that she had a piece of duck lodged in her throat. "Are you all right?" he asked, leaning forward.

She waved him off. "I'm sorry," she said.

"What your husband said? The Retreat? Is this possibly a plan?"

She took a sip of wine and shook her head. "He hasn't said anything about it before," she said finally.

"Ah," said Thomas.

"Exactly," she said.

The general chatter, din even, of the table allowed Thomas to turn to her, and he marveled that in these few minutes he had become so comfortable with her, and so concerned, that he pursued this. "I've been wondering why he has seemed so intent on coming here, on meeting me. Do you think that's it? Does he want to talk to me about the Retreat?"

"You would be surprised at how much you have been on his mind. How much he has measured himself against you, even though you'd never met. It has everything to do with that farm, as if you are siblings. You're the older brother who has succeeded."

"And he is not having the successes he hopes for in England?"

"No." This required no more elaboration.

"I'm sorry. We had some pretty dark days here, I will tell you that."

"I know. Your wife said a little about it. But that just makes my husband even more jealous."

Thomas reached for her hand and gave her a small squeeze. "*Courage*," he said, in the French manner. "He strikes me as a man with a good heart. You have these two fine boys. I think things will work out for you. If you did go back to the Retreat, you might find that it will be a good turn for you. For the boys especially: two thousand acres to get lost in."

After lunch Thomas took Edward on the obligatory walk through the caves, the pressing rooms, the vatting rooms, the bottling rooms, and then up to the vineyards; he'd taken visitors on this walk a thousand times but never really tired of it. At the crest of the hill above the farm, one could look north and see the Pic de Nore. These mountains had sheltered him and his family for forty years, from the worst of the winter winds, from some of the confusions of this young century, and perhaps they would now have to shelter them from another European storm. Languedoc, this broad plain bounded by the Massif Central and the Pyrenees: it had provided a refuge for its own people and language for eons, but now? Who knew what would survive.

"Beautiful," said Edward Mason. "You have been very lucky."

"Yes," said Thomas. He believed to the core that luck had everything to do with it: from the first day when he realized that this *girl* who hung around him and Randall was actually a person he could love, he and Beal had needed nothing but luck, and they had gotten it. Had they ever. The Catholic women in his life—his mother, his sister, Mother Lucy, all now long departed—would have preferred to call it grace, and he did not resist the notion of a sacred blessing on a humble enterprise.

But what Thomas thought of as luck was not what Mason was implying. "Unfortunately, I am in a business where luck isn't enough," he said.

"Ah," said Thomas. Something to do with manufacturing, he had gathered over the years; he had no interest in learning any more than that. He heard what Mason was saying, and it mattered to him not at all. It did not matter what anyone—especially this most tangential and transitory figure in his life—thought of his own private journey. Thomas could look out at the landscape below them and see the stations on the way, from the plains to the peaks, and that is what mattered. Mason could call him lucky, if he wanted. "Perhaps we should return," he said. "You'll want to get to Montpellier before dark."

His refusal to take up the charge of undeserved success seemed to have irritated Mason even more, but he moved on to the real topic. "This Mason's Retreat," he said with a belittling sneer. "What's it good for?"

"I don't know," said Thomas. "People have been trying to figure that out for centuries."

"Seems a better go could have been made if someone had the imagination."

This was insupportable, to say this about Mary after what she had done—given her life to that goddamned place! Given her life to their father as the peaches failed and he lost heart, given it to the land with her dairy, her campaign to give safe milk to the babies of Baltimore. But now her efforts to make that farm rise above itself, to outlast the stain of its slaveholding, had fallen back into the underbrush, left to rust by the side of the road like a lost farm implement. As far as he and Beal could tell from Ruthie's letters, the farm was lazily bumbling along, feeding maybe ten families. Maybe that was its highest and best use. Thomas almost rose in defense of all that sacrifice and work—he doubted that Mason had even come close in either respect—but then he settled back. The dead bury their dead, he reminded himself. "Well," said Thomas, "perhaps you should make the go yourself." He wished it weren't true, but what he said had some elements of a curse.

"I think I just may," Mason said, then repeated himself in order to underline it as a threat. "I just may do that."

"Your wife? She—"

"Women aren't equipped to be expatriates. They're too attached to their families."

This did not answer his question, but who cared? There seemed nothing but spleen here, so Thomas ended the conversation by setting off on the path back to the bastide. When they returned, Edith and the younger boy were sitting with Beal beside the figs, and the older boy was sitting in the back seat of the car. The goodbyes were brief. Mason, clearly a person whose manners were finer than his impulses—really, manners were invented for people like him—rebounded from the ill temper of the walk and pumped Thomas's hand with a cousinly affection: *just talking man-to-man, no hard feelings.* Edith got into the car, avoiding Thomas's eyes except for the briefest glance but locking on to Beal like a lover gazing back at the platform from a departing train, and after some grinding and shuddering, the Delahaye started up and off they went.

"*Ouf,*" said Thomas.

"*Je la plains,*" said Beal, and with that expression of pity they parted to finish the chores of the day, not taking up the topic again until after dinner, as they were readying for bed.

"It was about the Retreat," said Thomas. "I think he's busted, and he's heading back there whether she knows it or not."

"We talked about that when you were showing him around. I think she'd be relieved, really."

"To be returning to America?"

"Yes. Her family is in Chicago, but that would get her closer. Besides, one needs a place to call home, and she doesn't have it."

Thomas climbed into bed and waited while Beal made her final preparations. This room, these things in it, the window looking out over the terrace, this bed: for a few moments he thought back to the other bedrooms they had shared, beginning with their wedding night in the Lion d'Or in Paris. Time has a way of making life seem so compressed, of collapsing thousands of miles into the dimensions of a single room, the distance between the armoire and the bedpost, and isn't that the mercy of it?

When Beal joined him, he said, "Mason says he thinks women are not suited to be expatriates."

"And?"

"What do you think?"

"For certain women I think he's right."

"For you?"

"Forty years, and you're still asking me that question?"

Thomas was nodding off, and when he came to enough to pick up the conversation and say no, he wasn't still asking that question, it was the middle of the night, a nightingale outside was telling the darkness the story of his life, and Beal was asleep.

Acknowledgments

I have drawn material from many sources for this book, but several of them proved invaluable to me as I began to envision my story. For the Paris sections, David McCullough's *The Greater Journey* and Adam Gopnik's *Americans in Paris: A Literary Anthology* were especially useful. Michael B. Miller's *The Bon Marché: Bourgeois Culture and the Department Store, 1869–1920*, and Phil Kilroy's *The Society of the Sacred Heart in Nineteenth-Century France, 1800–1865*, gave me details about these two remarkable institutions.

I have accumulated several bookshelves on French wines and the history of viniculture in France. Most useful to me were George Ordish's *The Great Wine Blight* and Leo A. Loubère's *The Red and the White: The History of Wine in France and Italy in the Nineteenth Century*. For a more granular sense of the Languedoc region during this period, I was inspired by Gaston Baissette's classic novel *Ces grappes de ma vigne*. I also referred constantly to *La vie quotidienne des paysans du Languedoc au XIXᵉ siècle* by Daniel Fabre and Jacques Lacroix. Finally, of many books about the Canal du Midi, the best one I know of is the most recent, Chandra Mukerji's *Impossible Engineering: Technology and Territoriality on the Canal du Midi*.

By a happy coincidence I have come to know the paintings of the early impressionist Frédéric Bazille, whose father, Gaston Bazille, was, as I say in the book, one of the heroes of the fight against phylloxera. Frédéric was killed at age twenty-eight in the Franco-Prussian War, but he left behind a few wonderful paintings of his beloved landscape around Montpellier. On the occasion of a traveling show of his works in 2016–2017, Flammarion produced a gorgeous catalogue, *Frédéric Bazille (1841–1870) and the Birth of Impressionism*, edited by Michel Hilaire, Kimberly Jones, and Paul Perrin. I have looked at those paintings countless times for inspiration about that life and that landscape.

The story of Lawrence Goodrum and the fictional Goodrum's grocery store is based somewhat on material from two studies of the American black elite: *The Other Brahmins: Boston's Black Upper Class, 1750–1950*, by Adelaide M. Cromwell and *The Original Black Elite: Daniel Murray and the Story of a Forgotten Era* by Elizabeth Dowling Taylor.

A years-long project of this kind doesn't get written without the support and encouragement of family and friends. First among them is my wife, Caroline Preston, fellow novelist and best friend, and our sons and our daughter-in-law Fraley, and our first grandchild, John Preston Tilghman. I thank my colleagues at the University of Virginia and our friends in Charlottesville, and I thank my brothers and sisters-in-law and their families, and our neighbors in Centreville, Maryland. Finally, I thank my splendid agent, Henry Dunow, and my longtime editor, Jonathan Galassi, for everything they have done—and it has been a lot—to keep the story of Mason's Retreat alive.